RUN
AWAY
ON THE
HEAVENLY
EXPRESS

A NOVEL

BY STEPHEN SPICEHANDLER

ZENO

NEW YORK

The author would like to thank the following, whose various contributions have led to the realization of this book in its current form: Martine Bellen, Fritzie Brown, Janine Cataldo, Stephanie Dickinson, Roni Eldridge, Debbie Elkan, Judy Elkan, Marion Farrier, Hugh Ferrer, Joe Hessert, Andrew Kaufman, Rochelle Kraut, Jessie Kunhardt, Neal Kathleen May, Lynne Nugent, Joanne Siskin, Rosalind Palermo Stevenson and the late Elaine Schwager.

The section "To Calvary" was published previously by *The Iowa Review* in slightly different form.

The selection on page 184 is from *Ev'ry Time We Say Goodbye*, words and music by Cole Porter.

Cover photos by Susan Cataldo
Cover design by the author

Library of Congress Control Number: 2013913221
Zeno, New York, NY

In Memory of Susan

* * *

For Kris

* * *

With gratitude to 'zie

I

To Calvary

This toy train Bronx, this serenity in miniature stretching out to all the bridges over the Long Island Sound, this small town Americana miraculously placed in America's most notorious urban borough, this is the view that is spread across Room 1014's glass panorama facing east. I can see the tiny 6 train rumbling and screeching above the tree levels, above the small brick homes, and I can see the ladybug cars vrooming up and down the Hutch and I-95 (and I can envy them all), but all I can hear are the intercoms and IV beeps of the Gynecological Oncology wing at Albert Einstein Medical Center, the brisk voices of the medical staff going about their business and the hushed tones of the ailing and their loved ones.

I am beside my "baby," the roller-coaster love of my life, the Genghis Khan of beauty, now bald and fat and drugged up the kazoo, attached like a medical experiment to machines and tubes, big enough to float but sinking in gray slumber instead. My China doll by way of Marco Polo is fading from me, what with losing the function of one organ then the other (chemo be damned), and her brazen silk personality is more like faded flannel now, still lovely to have in your arms, but worn and needing to be tucked in of a night.

I am struck by the mercilessness with which she has been stricken. Her skull's nakedness speaks of atrocity, the white skin through the occasional black stubble of her need to be protected. Help me, she had cried over the phone, the first time her hair fell out three years ago, after taking a shower. Her sobs were the visceral reaction to the blow she knew was coming. A year and a half later, when her reprieve had been withdrawn and her body was once again a battlefield of poisons, the tears were a gentle echo of the first time. This third submission to the toxic cure was more matter-of-fact. She started pulling her roots out as soon as she saw the stray clump; it was just another part of grooming. Help me, she had asked sweetly, and how could I refuse, who had been spared such ravages. She had told me it would be simple, easy pulling, and it was. There was no resistance at all. Longer lengths of hair than had been visible slowly slid out of her skull and, like rabbits out of a hat, I was baffled by the logistics of it all. Baffled and a little nauseated: my conception of the human condition was shaken and I did not want her to see that in my eyes.

Now I watch her unobserved. She is white and massive from fluid build-up, her delicate skin transparent with patches of green and pink and the yellow of medical swabs. She is struggling in another world, her lips pursed, her eyelids flickering; she is diminished and far away, no matter how large, how close. I wait patiently for the chance to catch her pitch-black eyes shining out at me the way they have for almost twenty-two years, envoys of brio to beckon through the fog.

And then slowly, her consciousness rising in glimmers, she floats to the surface. Her eyes are half-open, they do not shine, but she is here with me and we are together.

"You're back," she whispers, then closes her eyes once more. Then, almost as an after-thought, she returns to me. "Where have you been all this time?"

I tell her about the traffic on I-95, about the parking space at the farthest end of the hospital's lot, but those are not answers to her concerns.

"You've been gone for days!" she accuses. *Why did you abandon me,* I hear. *You've left me at the mercy of strangers when it's you I need.*

Of course I've only been gone overnight. I've been running home each night to our bed and preparing each morning for the new day, husbanding my resources, taking my small comforts so that I can be tireless and as generous to her as I can when we're together. But that is not Jane's understanding.

"We didn't know where you were. I thought you'd left me."

I will never leave her. I open her small closed palm and hold it in my grasp. "I just went home for the night. You knew that. And I'm back. I'll be here all day." I'm glad she's awake and I can stroke the side of her face, be in contact. "Marcie knew where I was."

"No," says Jane, softer under my touch, "she didn't know." And then she purrs noiselessly, her eyes slit and relaxed, letting my fingers soothe her. She can be soothed by Marcie and Jackie and Sandi, by my crew of our friends and volunteers, but I am the rock in her life and she is the ocean in mine. We have become each other's world, even when apart, but Jane's experience of things has become chaotic while mine has maintained its steady downward flow. I arrange, I take care, I coordinate. She struggles, she grasps.

Her eyes are warm and direct. "You were bad," she teases. We've graduated to flirtation, which gives us both a rush. "I have so much to tell you," she says, even though I saw her twelve hours ago. "I have so much . . . strange things . . ." and then she lets loose her grasp, she submerges right below the surface, a wave bathing her in a momentary drug-like repose. I have her, I lose her, I have her, I lose her. I am patient. I am here to be by her side as she rises and falls above and below the ocean's surface. It is my form of meditation. She still has her smile *so glad to see ya* and her hand is still in mine. *I'll be with you in a minute.* Take your time, I'm thinking. Take what you need. I'm here so she can wake or sleep peacefully. I wipe out all other stimuli so that I can be her photographic receptor, second by second: every hair follicle, every skin cell, every pretty breath, every silence fleeing her slightly parted lips is recorded.

And then, like that, her eyes are open and they light up the room. They can darken the room, too, I know, if they want to.

But she has taken only a short commercial interruption and is ready to resume her joy at my being here.

"You look tired, baby," she says, gently pulling me to sit by her side. "I worry about you. Who's taking care of you?"

"You are," I reply. "I know your tricks. Somehow you are taking care of me from your hospital bed. Aren't you?"

She smiles. "I'm not telling. You're not getting enough sleep." She brushes hair way from my forehead. "As soon as we get home, I'm going to take care of you."

"We'll take care of each other."

But that's not what she wants to hear. I've bankrupted her momentary fantasy that she no longer needs being taken care of. She looks aggrieved.

"When are we going home, Ed? Are you taking me home today?"

A long catheter tube arises from bandages on the right side of her back and slithers its way to the left side of the hospital bed where it is tied to the white railing near her feet. The catheter bag is one-third full and imperceptibly keeps filling. A second tumor has strangled her one remaining ureter after her first tumor put a vise around her stomach. Any eating and eliminating is now through plastic, but we are waiting for the surgeons to install a shunt so that Jane will no longer need this twentieth-century tail.

So no, not today. She won't be coming home today. I reacquaint her with the tubing, holding it up for her inspection so we can laugh about her lapse of memory and distract ourselves from her anxiety over when—and how—this latest hurdle will be resolved. She holds the clear plastic in her hand to assure herself of its physicality, and then she tucks it neatly along the edge of the bed, the better to keep her territory orderly and under control, to smooth out the corners of her emotional turmoil.

"I don't want to be here anymore," she says. "Dr. Koenig isn't talking to me. I don't know what's going on, but something is. Why won't he talk to me? We need to talk about what's happening to me. Maybe you can make him come here."

"He's out sick, honey. Remember?"

"No he's not. I see him all the time. He's avoiding me. Go look in the conference room. Maybe you can find him. Tell him I need to speak to him now."

I'm encouraged that she's pumping out orders like a busy general in charge. I like that she still feels in command of things. She sits looking out over her imaginary kingdom and I, her courtier, her adjutant, inform her of conditions in the field.

"Dr. Koenig even had to cancel surgery. I told you yesterday. He's probably not back yet. As soon as he's back, we'll talk."

"He's avoiding me."

"No. He's not. I promise. I wouldn't lie to you."

Jane takes my hand. Our palms kiss and nestle. Her gaze quietly touches my face.

"There are so many things," she tells me. "So many things to tell you. Strange things."

I wait expectantly. I want to know what is on her mind. Her experiences are not the ones I can share. Cancer is not like living through the sixties, or like being there for your child when he's in crisis, or commiserating over broken dreams or rejoicing over those attained. It pulls her away from me; it takes her somewhere I can't go. From now on, I can only follow like an attendant, waiting to be filled in: pain, no pain, hunger, no hunger, nausea, no nausea, and on and on until we reach the point that we did two weeks before when it was breath, no breath . . . *Ed, I can't breathe* . . . The culmination of three years on this journey. I can follow her gurney from the emergency room to the operating room to her room on the oncology wing, but we are not going together. We are only side by side. This is happening to her; it is only occurring to me.

"I think I want to sit by the window," Jane says softly, raising her left hand in my direction. We start the complicated operation necessary to maneuver. The bed's motor propels her to a sitting position, the side railing makes way for her dismount, together we shift her weight so that she sits over the edge of the bed. I hold her bloated calves in my hand as I stretch the hospital slippers over her abused feet; I pull the heavy aquamarine leather chairs over to the bay window and then untangle and gather her train of plastic tubing as I escort her to our impoverished loveseat. This is how you scoop up someone in your arms when they are losing the battle with their bodies: with attention to detail and plenty of patience.

From within our antiseptic cave, we stare in wonder at the view outside. Everything moves, breathes, whistles by with purpose, and watching it is ours. Jane has not been outside now for almost two weeks, and when she was last outside, the exciting tumult of breeze and light and movement was intoxicating and exhausting; she loved it and it frightened her; it took her breath away. She wants to join it, be a part of the tumult: that is her nature. We hold each other's hand; the hospital is our Ferris wheel, and we let the most mundane of boroughs exhilarate us in its vastness. As the wheel keeps turning, our eyes rest on the building in the foreground of our view. Right across the street, shielded by a large crucifix on its forehead, sits Calvary Hospital, a five-story brick structure which spreads out in two perpendicular wings. Inside it, we know, are the terminally ill, finally succumbing quietly to cancer. It looms below us; it is an anchor in a teeming sea.

"The strangest things go on at Calvary." Jane leans in for protection, she leans in to confide, she wants to convey her excitement. She's witnessed revelation. "In the middle of the night, rows of black limousines line up at the entrance. They put these coffins in them when no one can see. Then they drive away. It's spooky."

"In hearses?" I falter.

"Yes, people die there all the time. They have to get rid of the bodies. They don't want people to be upset so they do it when no one would see."

"Are you sure it's not a dream?" I stroke the back of her hand.

"It wasn't just me! Marcie saw it, too! You'll see, tonight.

Every night."

"Jane —"

She pulls back. Her demeanor is icy, sober and acute. "I'm not kidding." She will not be patronized. She will patronize me instead. "How do you *think* an intensive care facility deals with the bodies?"

Why would I ever have thought about this before? I look across at Calvary, all middle-American in the light of the late afternoon, and try to see it as it would appear lit by streetlights, ferrying the dead, practically Venetian. Where do they go? How is the business of death handled in a hospice? You don't think about the unthinkable. Would they wrap the bodies like loaves of bread to be commercially delivered to the funeral franchises? Or would this be the beginning of their respectful, tradition-bound, pious journey to the burial ground? *Forgive me, Jane, for I know not what is done, I know not what you've seen.*

"It must be upsetting for you to see all this!"

Jane comes back towards my shoulder, as if in relief.

"No, it's not! Really! It's just so interesting! I never knew!"

"And I never thought about it."

"And then, one by one, the hearses drive away. Over to that parking lot where they unload the bodies at the crematorium."

Jane's in my arms. Babble behind us. Quiet before us. Calvary's crucifix has a pinhole glare. I don't know what she's talking about.

"Crematorium?"

"Yes, the crematorium. That big building over there." She's pointing at the bakery for the London Biscuits factory across from Calvary's parking lot, a large yellow industrial cathedral.

"All through the night you can watch the smoke coming out as they burn the bodies."

"Jane, that's a bakery. They bake in the middle of the night. 'London Biscuits' . . . ? 'Melba Toast' . . . ?"

"I know what they're doing there! If it was just a bakery, why would they bring the bodies there? At night it becomes a crematorium! *You* didn't see it. Me and Marcie did. Ask Marcie. Why don't you believe me?"

The thing is, I had believed her. I have always believed her. One more chapter in the epic story of Jane's ability to make reality bend to her will, and bring along everyone with her by the intensity of her belief and her passionate persuasion. And one more time I have been her first disciple. I have never felt lied to. It's just that Jane had always been certain, where most of us are not. And for her certainty not to be isolating, she needs to bring us all along. In this sense she has always been a missionary. If she was a "visionary," people could dismiss her as off-kilter, an aberration, mentally ill. Both her father and son have spent time in the wards of state psychiatric hospitals. Which is why she feels it so important people believe in her. Crazy is the loneliest of words. But to know the truth is to be admired and connected, and it is especially important that she remains connected to me, because to be cut loose from that bond is to be without love. We must remain on the same wave-length and therefore, for her sake, I must believe.

"I'm just baffled, is all. You have to at least admit that what you're describing . . ."

"I know," she says comfortingly. "I was surprised by it, too. But when you think about it, it all makes sense. It even seems obvious in retrospect."

Our minds are heading in different directions. The familiar touch of her delicate hand in the grasp of my large one, its coolness, its softness, its physical contact, makes it easier to feel united while, in truth, we're on the first legs of separate journeys. She may or may not be thinking that, but this is what is becoming obvious to me.

"I wish I was near you when you saw all this," I say softly in her ear. "It could've upset you. Maybe we'll see it tonight."

"We will. It happens every night. It happens very late, though. That's the point." She rubs her fingertips along the back of my hand, investigating, soothing, pleasuring. "Sometimes late at night," she intones dreamily, "there's this bright blue flame rising from the roof of Calvary. And, one by one, these jet airplanes swoop down towards the blue light as if they're going to crash. But they don't! Just in the nick of time they fly up and away. Just like that. It takes your breath away. I hope you get to see that tonight. It's so beautiful. Marcie said she's never seen anything like it."

I kiss the chubby cheek of the poet who has re-created this scene for me. Her flesh is manna and her vision is precious to me. I feed her a "wow."

"How do they manage that?" I say.

Jane doesn't know because it's something akin to an everyday miracle. There's no good explanation at her fingertips. But she is a witness to it, and this gives her conviction. She is a true believer. Together we will see.

We sit in our mezzanine seats above the Bronx orchestra, the semi-urban symphony led by an invisible baton.

"Do you remember our first date?" Jane sings the question lightly, like a country air.

"The top of the World Trade Center, sitting in the clouds, zero visibility. I remember."

"No, that wasn't a date."

"What was it?"

"I don't know. It wasn't a date. We were just hanging out. I mean Mostly Mozart. We stood on the balcony during intermission looking out over those gold sculptures that hung from the sky."

"If Titans wore earrings . . ." I quip.

"Drop earrings. Titans wouldn't wear drop earrings," she laughs. "You took my hand as if it wasn't the first time and we looked out at all that colossal gold jewelry, surrounded by everyone. It made me horny."

"Then we kissed for hours after the concert, in front of the fountain at Columbus Circle. . . ."

"Guys yelled cat calls at us from passing cars!" she exclaims, long forgotten pink flooding her face.

"We just laughed and ignored them anyway. What was that restaurant, where we got falafels . . . ? And you told me your life story."

"Amy's," she says without a second's hesitation.

"Whatever happened to Amy's?"

"It's gone."

"I wonder what happened to Esther Benson," I continue to free associate.

"I *loved* Esther Benson," Jane says. "*Linda Goodman's Love Signs*. That's what she was recording. You were a very good teacher. I remember when you reached out in front of me to operate the tape machine and we almost touched. Linda Goodman said we were a perfect match."

"You blushed when I told you my sign!"

"I remember we fucked in Studio C!"

"That was later."

"Maria Rubini called us 'lovebirds.'"

"Maria Rubini! I haven't thought of her in years!"

"I miss Talking Books. We worked there over . . . eighteen years ago!"

"It seems like yesterday," I say, smiling.

"It seems like such a long time ago to me," says Jane with a sigh.

The cars continue in the distance, back and forth, creating rivulets of dull color that massage our vision. We are grateful for the daylight that reflects the outside world back to us with its incessant busyness and for the cloudiness that keeps out the glare. We sit and contemplate; we nuzzle softly and wait patiently for the jets and the hearses.

Without even the slightest rustle, Alma's sweet, nasal soprano makes her presence known.

"Hello, Mr. and Mrs. Cantore." Erring on the side of convention, Alma and the others who work here assume that Cantore is Jane's married name. I imagine myself as a "Mr. Cantore" and enjoy the charade.

Alma fingers Jane's IV pump, probing and jostling the milky lunch.

"You can stay where you are. I'm OK. Mrs. Cantore was worried about you, weren't you, Jane?"

"He was very bad," she replies, still leaning the top of her head against my cheek. "He must have been out with his girlfriend, because he wasn't with me."

"Get outta here!" I slowly drawl in Bowery Boys sophistication. That gets a laugh out of everyone.

"Oh no, Mrs. Cantore, you're his girlfriend," corrects Alma. "He doesn't have time for another girlfriend. That's because he's a good husband."

"Well," I continue the routine, "at least someone appreciates me around here."

"My husband has a floozy." Jane plays with the concept dreamily, still nestled against me. It almost sounds like she likes the idea.

"Mrs. Cantore, how are you doing with pain?" asks Alma.

"I'm OK right now, "Jane says.

Alma takes Jane's wrist and holds it delicately between her thumb and finger.

"Your pulse is good. Soon you can have another Atavan if you want. In another hour or so. Let me take your temperature."

Jane opens her mouth obediently. She puts herself totally, without resistance, into Alma's hands. Alma and Marsha and Claudette and Paz are all her mothers. The doctors she sometimes argues with, even fights, but the oncology nurses wrap their cooing voices and warm eyes around her like a hug, even just to announce:

"Ninety-eight. Very good."

And Jane makes them into her family. She allows herself to talk to them in her girlish voice, soft and high-pitched, playful and vulnerable, sometimes hearty and sometimes needing to be soothed. And in the same even, unrushed flow, they pay attention to the details, listen to her plaints, and encourage. They are her *reliable* mothers.

We are sitting by the shore of Room 1014, the pale blue light of late afternoon saturating the room like the surf that fans over a slapping shoreline. The Bronx day is coming in for a rest while we are set for all the hours ahead of us together; we are a lifeguard on watch. What are we on watch for? The room's curtains flutter where we have left the corner window pane pushed open so that the breeze can lighten the room's stuffy load, and the confined hospital air can escape. Most of the hospital patients prefer the windows closed to protect them from the drafts, but I understand Jane's phobias of confinement and have always indulged her embrace of outside air, a holdover from a childhood when she and her older sister were locked in captivity by their father. We will remain vigilant over our Bronx "front porch," like country folk on swinging sofas, letting the night come easy.

And so we indulge in memories of prior sunsets by each other's side. The elevated views of the Bronx's eastern tree-lined roads become the Catskills ascending in the distance from the renovated one-room schoolhouse where we holiday each summer. The wooden screen door squeaks and clatters behind me. Jane has been industriously sketching with charcoal pencils, sitting on a beach chair removed from our car's trunk. I sit down on the stoop facing her. I try not to break her concentration on the garden plants growing along the side of the house which endlessly inspire her. The sun escapes in lazy strokes from the forest around us, intermittently giving the red schoolhouse a fiery glow. I unfold and rustle the Oneonta paper that I carried out of the kitchen, and then we both stop what we are doing to look up the driveway hill and watch a cluster of black cows make their way home, the occasional moo like a Hank Williams song. "I wish Ellen and Karl would sell this place to us," Jane says for the twentieth time in twenty-years. "We could fix it up and come on weekends . . ." and then she goes on in detailed dreams of what she'd like to do to it. A car comes careening down the steep hill that passes the schoolhouse and with a roar of teenage voices it whooshes away into silence. They're going to town tonight.

The whole piazza at San Marco falls into a blue shadow, glimmery with golden highlights. The setting sun sneaks around the piazza to reflect off Byzantine embellishments and café windows; ballet corps of pigeons fritter the light into broken pieces. We are sitting at an elegant white iron table under a café umbrella, resting after having spent the day traversing Venice's bridges, meandering through her museums, admiring the human form as represented through the centuries in Italianate colors. Our less ideal forms, qualified by time and gravity and, in Jane's case, her fight with disease (and in my case, as a witness to that fight), nevertheless feel like those of honeymooners. We are dancing along the abyss of cancer, though we are not dancing; we are sitting with our chicken and asparagus sandwiches, our sparkling water, listening to the neighboring bands compete by way of Cole Porter or Henry Mancini tunes. A chorus of birds land on the extended arms of a tourist bearing popcorn, the cacophony of wings reaching a boisterous crescendo. Jane doesn't approve. They're disgusting animals. They carry disease. "People are so stupid," she says. But I find it hard to criticize a circus. And besides, so many beautiful creatures carry disease; they cannot be unappreciated because death waits beneath their pageantry. I would not give them up, I'm thinking.

We are setting up our balcony for a summer evening dinner. We play U-2 loudly so that the music will escape through the screened sliding doors. *"Last time we met it was a low-lit room / We were as close together as bride and groom / We ate the food, we drank the wine / Everybody having a good time / Except you / You were talking about the end of the world."* We eat the food, we drink the wine, we sit amidst Jane's makeshift garden and watch the lights flicker on and off from the apartments across the middle-income development's canyonway. Jane has painted the balcony floor a swimming pool blue and soon everything is that color, the city's pollution and the sunset uniting for one moment into a psychedelic splendor before it fades. "This is a good wine," I say as I sip. Her cousin Bobby gave us the wine, her cousin Donna the pasta bowls we are using. Underscoring the fatalistic rock and roll is the persistent *kerplunk kerplunk* from the teenage boys playing basketball six floors below us and across the way. We savor the pasta sauce along with the night; we are scraping our bowls when Jane jumps up and stamps her feet by the corner of the balcony. "Get away!" she shouts. She bends over the large spider plant in the corner. "Those fucking squirrels!" she says.

And now it's a navy blue of a New York City night. We are younger selves strolling through New York City's neighborhood dedicated to San Marco. We cross St. Mark's Place in lockstep, our bodies fitted side by side, walking as one body connected at the hip, comfortably, sexily, arms around each other's waist. Jane has a beautiful soprano voice that she usually saved for her son's benefit only, but he's at home now, too old for a baby-sitter, and she breaks her pattern of musical shyness by singing her favorite Boz Skaggs song. I join her for the chorus: *"Love me tomorrow / Forget your sorrow / Love me tomorrrrr-row,"* as we pass East Village landmarks: The Orchidia Restaurant, the St. Mark's Cinema, the Orpheum Theatre, the funky jewelry stores shooting up between the decades-old mom-and-pop establishments, the Ukrainian butcher shop and the Polish coffee shop happily neighboring Moshe's bakery. We glide right through the other East Village nighttime players as we claim the sidewalk for ourselves. We move onto "Imagine;" we sing softly for own pleasure and the thrill of how surprisingly good we sound together.

The sunset is fading, the streetlights have mysteriously gone on when we weren't looking, and the Bronx puts on its shadowy subterranean colors. I hear the rustle of an overcoat behind us and notice Beverly has arrived. She is a motherly black woman, impeccable in dress and manner, who, when she is not reading her bible, dotes on her charge as much as her charge will allow.

"Oh, I won't bother you both," she says. "You can ignore me if you want. I'll be out in the hall, Jane dear."

"Oh, hi, Beverly," sings Jane. "Is it that late already?" Beverly is the only attendant I've found who Jane has totally trusted. Sometimes Beverly is a little too hands-on for Jane and her independent ways, but Jane loves having someone doting she can depend on and she allows Beverly control, if at times reluctantly. Mostly Beverly uses her power gingerly, using a soft touch to get Jane to do what Beverly thinks is best.

"How are we this evening?" asks Beverly. "Last night Mrs. Cantore was a bit agitated. She asked for you all the time. You wanted to be home with your husband, didn't you, Mrs. Cantore?"

"Yes, I did," Jane said, looking longingly in my direction. "I wanted you to take me home."

"Was it a tough night?" I ask Beverly.

"Oh, we were fine. We had a fine night together. Sometimes we needed more Atavan, didn't we? The nighttime, you know. She gets nervous and all. But it wasn't too bad. We talked and she tells me all about herself and I talk about myself, don't I, Mrs. Cantore? She's such a sympathetic listener. And we watched a little television, but not too much. She slept most of the time. I think we were fine."

"I wanted to go home," Jane said, not having moved her glance from my face. She wanted to be home with her twenty-six plants which I've had to manage not to kill; with her sketch pads and her pastels; with her canary, Calvin, to take care of and talk to and fuss over; with her floor-to-ceiling shelves of poetry books, many of them by friends; and with me. The apartment is filled with familiars to keep Jane company. And if she can watch *Rosie O'Donnell* and *Regis and Kathy* in the hospital, they are even better at home where the sounds of the neighborhood can fly up to our sixth-floor apartment and she can watch the people off to market, the kids playing at recess time at the parochial school, watch the same parking garage attendants she's had in her view for the last three years, all of them neighbors. She has always been a lover of neighborhoods, and she doesn't have that out the window at

Einstein. There the only community is that of doctors and interns and nurses and orderlies, all of whom she has gotten to know and many of them like, but none of whom she wants to be around. Because this isn't home.

"Well, I'm going to go change into my comfortable clothes and then I'll sit outside so you two lovebirds can have more time together," says Beverly and she leaves us to the evening light.

"Don't you want me to come home?" Jane asks, forlornly.

"Of course I do! I can't wait for you to come back to me, you know that. But right now you're not ready. When they take out the catheter . . ."

"I don't know if I can believe you."

I'm too tired to be able to think of how best to react, how best to get her mind off of this track. I emit a sigh, and say "I don't know what to tell you. If you don't know if you can believe me . . ." All I can do is shrug my shoulders. There is this space between us which we both wait for the other to cross. *Show me I can trust you. Show me you have faith in me.* We remain connected by the warm sensual touch of our hands, but we are separated by our mutual grievances.

"Hey, is it OK to come in?" a hushed male voice breaks the silence.

"It's Ray," I say and let go of her hand to stand up and welcome Jane's brother.

He is not alone. He has brought his daughter, Chryssie, with him. She is in her mid-thirties, just a few years older than Luke, Jane's son from a short-lived marriage when she was a teenage runaway. This is only the third time Chryssie has seen her aunt since she was around five years old, the first two times being within the last few days at the hospital. Chryssie had always reminded Ray of Jane, especially because of her thick-headed, rebellious nature, and over the years he had unintentionally created a deep bond between Chryssie and her aunt by often calling his daughter by her aunt's name when mad at her, and then telling Jane about it when we had last seen him. That was twenty years ago when Jane told him of our plans to get married. Chryssie has Jane's coloring, her high cheekbones and black eyes, and has even of late developed a weight problem like both her father and aunt. No matter how different their style, her presence at Jane's bedside was uncanny at first. Jane had taken Chryssie's face between her hands and said in amazement that it was like looking into the face of her own daughter. Since then Chryssie has tried to accompany her father as often as possible, to try to cement the bond which had only had a spiritual foundation prior to this hospital bedside relationship. She is now Jane's lady-in-waiting.

"How are you, Janie? How you feeling today?" asks Ray. "You feeling any better?" He looks like Richard Gere with an extra fifty pounds and he seductively, Richard Gere-like, commiserates with his baby sister. It suddenly strikes me that when her cousins, or anyone else, would mention how attractive they thought Richard Gere was, Jane would contemptuously call him a ferret-face. But all the Cantores in the room are strikingly attractive, and definitely look related. "Isn't my brother handsome?!" Jane had gushed when he had first come back into her life merely days ago.

"I'm sad. I want to go home."

"But you feeling OK?" Ray persisted.

"I'm tired. I feel a little pain. I'm ready for my Atavan soon."

"Should I get a nurse?" worries Chryssie.

"No, Paz will bring it soon. Help me back into bed." All three of us, like too many cooks, tangle and untangle the wires, move chairs back and forth and offer her hands to help her back into bed.

"I want to go home," Jane says when settled into the pillows. "No one will allow me to go home. They want to keep me here."

"As soon as they can take out the catheter, we'll hear what Dr. Koenig has to say," I reply.

"You see," she says quietly to her brother. "He doesn't love me anymore. He doesn't want me home. He's tired of me."

"Janie, of course Ed wants you home. He's crazy about you.

Anyone can see that."

"You'll be home sooner than you know," adds Chryssie "You'll see."

"They have rules here. They don't allow anyone to leave! It's all red tape. They just move you from room to room. And I don't know *what* happens to some people. They just disappear! Ed doesn't believe me, but it's true. Ray, can I stay with you if Ed doesn't want me?"

Over thirty years ago, Jane had gone to Ray to ask him to let her live with him and not her crazy sister. He told her instead that a foster home would be the best thing for her, and that was when she ran away. He has to be aware of the parallels in this question, as he tries to steer away from answering her.

"Ed wants you, believe me."

"Honey, I love you. Please, it's just a matter of a few days."

"You promise?"

"Absolutely." What's the purpose right now in worrying about the fine details? Just give her a definite answer, that's what she needs.

Jane pushes the button on the side of the bed for the nurse's station.

"Can I help you?" blares the speaker above the bed.

"Yes, nurse. I need my pain medication."

"OK, we'll be right over, Mrs. Cantore."

Jane's face looks haunted. She pulls me to her side.

"Egg"—she uses the nickname she has invented for me—"why are my father and sister here?"

She asks me in her soft sleepy voice, yet not so soft that Ray and Chryssie can't hear.

"What do you mean, doll?" I ask her.

"Didn't you see them? Go look. They're in the room across the hall. What are they doing here?"

Ray looks sucker-punched. Chryssie blinks her eyes in confusion, looking from her father to me.

"Jane." I stroke the back of her hand. "Don't worry about

your father and sister. They died a long time ago, remember?"

She looks like she's trying to battle the heavy weight of her eyelids by trying to focus on her thoughts.

"Then what are they doing here? Isn't that strange?"

"I think you're hallucinating. I think it's the medication, sweetheart. Ray and Chryssie are here, Beverly's outside the room, I'm here . . . no one else. Your father and sister aren't here. They can't bother you."

"I could've sworn . . ." she says as she slowly slides off into a narcotic sleep.

"What did she say?" whispers Ray, who knows full well what she said. He didn't mean to bring anyone besides Chryssie, but apparently he's brought invisible company, and he's not happy about it. If he could've killed his father himself, perhaps he would have, now only to find that even so, his father might one day be staring down at him on his deathbed. Now in his Cantore eyes, he's afraid he's brought his father's and sister's eyes with him, and he looks like he would like to tear them from his sockets.

When Paz arrives with a small plastic bag to attach to the IV pole, Jane looks like the medication has started kicking in before it even enters her bloodstream; just the anticipation of it eases her. She is certain of Paz's love and tenderness and competence; it is something the rest of us still must prove. She lets the grayness soothe her, lets herself feel the attention of all those who are there for her—Paz flicking plastic tubing with her finger, Beverly sitting just outside the door in silent conversation with Jesus, Chryssie with her head atilt sympathetically and her long dark curls cascading over her right shoulder, Ray stolidly claiming his ground, and me drinking her up with my guilt-ridden eyes as if it would be unforgivable to let her out of my sight for a second—and momentarily she allows herself to feel mothered: she closes her eyes.

I can't keep up with her fantasies, her deliriums. I don't know where her drugged mind wanders. I don't have a growth that keeps my stomach in a tight vise or a stint somewhere under my back; don't know what it feels like to be invaded by technology or disease. I don't know what it's like to have memories of the Bronx in the 50s: I wasn't there to see her between her older brother's arms as he rode her on his bike or to see her with baby Chryssie in *her* arms when she was fourteen and wanting something desperately to love that would singularly love her back. I don't know if there is room for me or Luke or the ten years or so of make-shift East Village family living in her consciousness when she submerges as she does now. I just know how blank we feel as we witness her dip silently into her vast reservoir for a little R&R.

"Maybe she'll sleep a little," says Paz, studying Jane before she lightly steps about her business and out the door. We three stand around as if contemplating a gravestone marker before we catch ourselves and step back to acknowledge each other with our eyes.

Ray comes around to put his arm around me. "How you holding up?" he asks me softly.

"I'm OK. Always tired, but OK. She's better in the early part of the day, and then it gets a little hairy as the sun goes down."

"She was really great on Sunday, when my mother was here . . . and the cousins," says Chryssie. "Looking at pictures. . . . My mother was so glad to see her." Jane had told Chryssie *not* to bring her mother, but Chryssie brought her anyway, deciding it was time for a reconciliation. Suddenly, thirty years of resentment seemed irrelevant and picayune. "We were so young and foolish!" cried Tina when they hugged. "We didn't know what we were doing!" And Jane beamed in the presence of everyone's love. In that moment, in a hospital many years after she first needed it, Jane finally was able to feel the love and care of her whole family—at least of the family that survived—which included her ex-sister-in-law.

Ray looks uncomfortable. "Yeah, she was good on Sunday. Except for—"

"Well, that was a mistake, Dad."

"I shouldn't'a done it. I thought it would make things better. I don't know . . ."

When Ray had received a copy of Jane's book of poems from

her cousin Donna, he read it hungrily, looking for references to the family drama. Before most people arrived at the hospital that Sunday, Ray had asked Jane if the poem that included a line saying "I can hear you call my name in the street" was a reference to the time he had gone through the East Village looking for her when she had run away from home.

"Did you know I was out there looking for you every day, going up and down the streets calling your name? Did you hear me?" he had asked.

"The poem's not about you," she said tersely.

"Oh," he had said disappointedly. "I mean, you know I always loved you, don't you? I never didn't love you."

And in one move, with all the power in her body, Jane sat up in the bed, huge with fury.

"You didn't give a shit about me!"

And Ray quickly retreated, Chryssie aghast at the side of the bed at how her father had clumsily tipped over the entire fucking apple cart, deciding that this was the time to bring up years of primally painful memories: when Jane was on morphine, mustering her energy to stay alive and well.

"I'm sorry, Janie," Ray said, his face all red. "Forget it. I didn't mean to upset you."

Jane sank back into the bed and covered her face with her hands.

"You waited too long for this conversation . . ." she mumbled.

"I know, I'm sorry. Please forgive me."

And she appeared to. The room went back to tentative small talk, Chryssie stroked Jane's hand, little by little places were found for affectionate jokes, and Ray joined in. But he has been berating himself over his contretemps ever since.

"You know, back then, when all this happened . . ." he begins. I motion him to step outside of the room with me, outside of Jane's possible hearing. Chryssie, who had never been filled in on anything about her father's family life—other than that it was too painful for him to talk about—looks torn between hearing what she can that would explain her father to her and taking the time to spend as much time with her newfound aunt as possible by watching over Jane while she sleeps. She starts to follow us but then slowly makes her way back to the chairs I had moved to the window, turns one around and sits by Jane's side.

"I was just a kid myself, then," he goes on in a low voice. "Eighteen when I got married to get away from my father. And when Jane was fifteen I was still in my early twenties. I couldn't take care of someone like her. She was trouble. She was hanging out with the wrong crowd, smoking cigarettes. And my sister Ginny was nuts. So I understood why Jane couldn't stand living with her and Uncle Al anymore. But I didn't know how to take care of her. None of us did. No one had ever taken care of us! We were too screwed up, I admit that. So I thought a foster home would be the best thing for her, people who could give her a real family and straighten her out. That's what I was thinking."

I look over towards Jane; she looks wintry white, as if she's slowly being covered in snow, her mouth slightly ajar, deeply overcome by sleep. This is her chance to hear Ray's story and her chance to answer it, to rebut his benevolence with the indifference and hostility she remembered, the anger of the brother who was just plain tired of dealing with her and her needs, who resented someone as needy as she then was, loving him, depending on him, hoping he was her salvation, the way he once had been, using his fists against their father. I realize she would have answered him the way she already had. She would have told that to anyone in her family who tried to bring up the past. No, if she wanted a family now, it had to be without looking back, without absolving them, without blaming them either. She needed their help now and this was their chance, and Ray's, to finally look after the baby. And I know that is why he is here. So I don't say anything. I just listen.

And now we are both listening as words bubble up from Jane's depths, little moans of words evaporating into the room's cozy atmosphere. Her eyes flutter, struggling to open; she is grasping for contact. Chryssie bends over her, as if to scoop up her wishes, and Jane turns her head to her, her neck a long bow of yearning.

"I can't understand you, Aunt Janie," says Chryssie. "What can I do for you?"

Her words sound like a child's whimper.

"Where do you have to go?" is Chryssie's reply.

Tired of this communication, Jane wails my name. She's ready for the shorthand approach. Chryssie falls by the wayside of her consciousness and she makes a direct cry to me.

"Help me! Ed!"

I rush over to the side of the bed opposite Chryssie and ask her to tell me what is ailing her.

"I need . . . I need my bathrobe! Quick, please!" Her hands clap my arm to hasten me.

"Are we going somewhere?" I ask her as I bring her red flannel robe to her.

"Yes!" she cries with an urgency that is almost joyous, but not quite. "We're going home!"

"Jane —"

"We're going home!" She is stern and insistent. "We're going home." She whispers in a loud breath of words. "You've got to get me out of here. You don't know what goes on!" Then she turns to Chryssie and asks sweetly, "Do you see my slippers there, sweetheart?" as if she's forgotten her name.

"Jane!" I try to focus her by grabbing her shoulders and riveting her with my eyes, trying to reach way down into her where she can hear me. I point out the handiwork attaching her back to all the plastic engineering, but she shushes me with these words: "It's not safe here. People disappear. No one's allowed to go home! They don't tell me what they've done with them. Please, Ed, please, please, take me home, I know you don't want me to disappear! Where would you find me? Imagine how you'd feel!"

Before I can reply to her heartfelt plea, assuming I could even find the words, Beverly comes into the room to see what is going on.

"Are we going for a walk, Mrs. Cantore? That's a nice idea."

"Yes, a walk! A walk!" cries Jane, throwing her legs over the side of the bed. If I don't help her, she will muster the energy to do everything herself.

"OK, let's go for a walk," I say, signaling to Ray and Chryssie my facial equivalent of a shrug. I motion them towards the IV pole on the other side of the bed so as to wrap her wiring around one of its arms and to unplug the pump's wire from the wall socket. But Jane is already on her way.

"Jane!" I cry, to prevent her pulling wires straight out of her body. "Watch it!"

"Now!" is her reply. "We've got to go now!" and she's off, Beverly receding out of the way, Chryssie and Ray doing a Keystone Kops routine with the pole and wires, and me running to catch up with her, her catheter (which I hurriedly unwrapped from a bed railing) in my hands. I hand it over to our IV team to attach to the rest of their equipment as I hustle out the door.

Soon we are making a calamitous procession along the corridors of Ten South, her highness in red flannel trimmed with blue posies, I anxiously by her side holding her arm tightly, her brother and niece running with her train of wires, and Beverly following from a distance, watching over us.

"Which way is the exit?" asks Jane urgently.

"Jane, we can't leave the building. Turn around! Turn around and look at all the equipment that is following you."

But she doesn't look. Her eyes are on alert for an escape hatch, an exit door, an elevator, a hidden tunnel, a great escape. She will not bend her will for those who just cannot understand, who do not know, who have not experienced. She will take care of herself if she must, and her brain is working feverishly, devising a plan of delivery.

"Which way?!" she repeats. "You know where it is—let's go!" She is pulling me forward, having found a strength that surpasses mine.

"Well, we can take a walk in that direction, but we can't leave for another few days. And then you'll come home."

"Good! Now show me!" And we scurry along.

"Hello, Mrs. Cantore," says one of the nurses as we approach the Ten South reception desk. "On a walk with your family, are we?"

"Yes, Anita!" Jane says in a loud, clear voice, her eyes never swerving from her focus for a second. "We're going for a walk!"

"That's nice."

"Bye, Anita!" she says, her expression unchanged throughout the conversation.

"Here, we go in here," she says, attempting to drag me into a semi-private patient's room, one she had been in in one of her many stays at the hospital over the last three years. The two new patients are invisible, opaque in sleep and the room's pitch black darkness. But I am fully aware that the room is occupied, if she is not, and I try to prevent her entry.

"Where are you going?" I ask with a laugh, as if this is merely a silly mistake.

"This is the way, let me in," she whispers, not looking at me.

"No, Jane, there are patients sleeping. . . ."

"I know, I know! But there's an exit in there. We have to hurry. We won't make any noise."

"No, honey, you're mistaken." I still have her by the arm. She struggles to slip it free, casually, but forcefully.

"Don't tell *me*! This was *my* room, not yours. And I say there's an exit door in there."

"No, Janie, there are people . . ." says Ray.

". . . sleeping!" continues Chryssie.

"Jane, dear," says Beverly from behind, "I have a good idea. Why don't we go back to our room —"

"No," she says urgently, "there's a way out through there! *Please!*"

"I'll show you where the exit is," I tell her. "It's not here. It's further down the hall. This-a-way . . ." gesturing away from the room.

"Are you OK, Mrs. Cantore?" asks Anita, who by now has noticed a hint of a problem.

Jane looks thunderstruck. She steps back and turns directly towards me.

"Oh my God! Oh my God!" she repeats, turning gray in horror. She holds her hands in front of her as if to keep me away. "You're one of them! You're one of them! I thought — I thought you were on my side. You're working with them!"

"I'm not working with anybody! You're going to wake these patients!" I am urging her with the most intense, hissy whisper I can imagine.

And then, with the strength of her fury, Jane walks right up to me and fills the doorway with her presence so that she seems to tower over my six foot four inch frame.

"*Get out of my way!*" she bellows, no longer the invalid but the bully. She looks determined to walk right through me if she has to. As if throwing myself in her path, I stand up as tall as I can and refuse to budge. I don't know what to expect.

"No," I calmly tell her.

By now the nurses have realized, at the very least by her outcry, that something is up and they start to scurry around the reception desk. Jane looks at me as if I have betrayed her. She exhales fumes of defeat and frustration.

"I don't believe you!" she says in contempt, and turns towards the direction we came from.

The posse starts up in pursuit. Except for me. For one second, and one second only, I exhale, cleansing my lungs, as if in one breath I can be clean of this painful, absurd experience, and, unsoiled, look Jane straight in the eye again. I take a new deep breath and move on now.

Jane's energy has not relented; she urges her wakened, weighted body forward, catapulting it back towards her room as if going back to bed was the exit she had in mind. Beverly is relieved at the prospect and compliments Jane on her good sense, when

Jane, oblivious to Beverly, continues past her door toward the corner rooms on the wing. Everyone is sure she's failed to recognize her room, and they shout out her mistake to her, but it's not a mistake. She is heading directly to the last room on the corridor, a room she's never been in before, and, consequently, one she seems sure leads the way to a new beginning. Ray and Chryssie shout out as Jane heads into its bright light. We tumble into it with her, Alma following, expecting to see her overwhelming the patient assigned to it.

But we are overwhelmed instead. The room is spanking clean and empty, the bed has been rolled away from the wall and lifted high, lightened of any load, stripped of all hospital linen. It is a monument to a previous departure, of a patient who has succeeded in escaping from the hospital before Jane could manage to, or, in converse, evidence of one who has been "disappeared." The room's blankness is startling. Startling to Jane is that there is no exit in the corner of the room through which she can flee, nor which would explain to her the means of egress or of sequestration of its previous tenant.

"Where's the exit?" she demands, as if someone's pulled a fast one on her.

"This is just another patient's room," I begin to explain. "There is no exit —"

"I'm not talking to you!" is her response. "I don't know what they did with the exit." She's pacing back and forth, just one step in either direction, forming tight circles of flight leading her back to where she stands, a trapped animal. "Chryssie, can you help me?"

"What, Aunt Janie?"

"Pick up that phone and call a car service. We can meet them in the lobby. We do that all the time. A car service can take us. I'll pay you back, don't worry."

Chryssie looks back and forth from Jane to the rest of us, unsure of what to do. Jane wastes no time and scurries forcefully over to the phone, picks up the receiver and dials "0." She stares intently into space, and keeps pushing the "0" key.

"No one's picking up!"

"Jane, they unplug the phone service when a patient leaves," I try to calm her.

"Operator! Operator!"

Alma matter-of-factly walks up to Jane. "Mrs. Cantore, why don't you just stay in this room for a while. There's no one in this room tonight, so if you want to sit here for a while instead of in your room that's OK."

Jane looks over to Alma as if she's getting some much needed relief.

"Thank you, Alma. That's fine."

Alma leaves the premises, having informed me that she will check to see if Jane can now be given more medication. The rest of us are all gathered around Jane, waiting for new instructions for the game for which only she knows the rules.

"Maybe I should call Suzanne," Jane thinks out loud. "I know. I should call Suzanne! She'll help me. Why didn't I think of that?"

Chryssie and Beverly look confused. Suzanne's name had not come up before, to their knowledge. Who is this savior?

"Suzanne—she's the woman who was here the other day, wasn't she?" asks Ray. "Who I spoke to. Her therapist, right? Suzanne's your therapist, Janie?"

"Yes, yes. I know she'll come and get me. She's always there for me whenever there's an emergency. I need to call her."

This is going nowhere. "Jane, it's Sunday. Suzanne's not in her office."

Jane turns to me contemptuously. "She checks her messages," she says simply, not bothering to add "you jerk," as that goes without saying.

"I've got to get this phone to work!" She pounds the receiver with her finger repeatedly, trying to force it into submission.

"Now, Jane," says Beverly, "you don't want to break the phone. Why can't this wait till tomorrow? Your friend Suzanne will be there tomorrow, and there's nothing going on tonight that can't be dealt with tomorrow. What do you say?"

"Tomorrow will be too late! This is the time for me to get out of here. The hospital will be busier on a Monday, that's why I have to get out tonight. If Ed won't help me, then Suzanne can. I won't let you keep me locked up here," she addresses to me. "Suzanne won't allow it either."

I walk over to where Ray and Chryssie stand and grab the IV pole with one hand, the translucent tubing that heads out to Jane on the other.

"Jane, look at this! Look at it! You're all connected to wires. Look at it."

"You have a bad attitude!" she exclaims. "You can make things happen if you want to enough. You just don't want to. I'm going back to my room. I can call Suzanne from there." She is panting heavily in excitement, as if she's getting out of breath.

With tremendous relief, everyone encourages her relocation. A great hubbub starts up, an arrangement of bodies and medical equipment, people shuffling out of each other's way, Jane with her hands in the air like a toddler signaling to be picked up as she tries to direct her entourage.

"We're going into the other room! Hurry! The other room!" As Ray and Chryssie struggle with the wires, Jane turns to me, forgetting my role as her nemesis to mutter, "My father and sister always gum up the works!" And then to everyone: "We've got to hurry!" Ray takes a moment to be appalled by what he's over-heard, and Chryssie uses it to sum up her understanding of what is going on, before they can put it behind them and keep up with the wagon train.

Jane is waiting for me when I get into the room, impatient and in turmoil, penned in a cage, anxious to get out.

"I need to know if you will call Suzanne for me. I don't re-member her number."

"OK. I will call her. Try to calm down."

And then everything stops as Jane pulls back her arm and zings me with a fast, hard slap across my face with all the power she can muster . . . which is plenty. She's a dynamo of power fighting for her life.

I am startled. I can feel a sting where her fingernail traveled across my cheek, her slap being both powerful and a little clumsy.

I want to be her savior, but instead . . .

No matter my shock, or the depths of my anguish, I know I have more to do and do not take the time to nurse my outrage and despair. There is an audible intake of breaths from those around me, perhaps someone calls her name, I don't know. I grab her hand forcefully and stare her in the face sternly.

"You can't hit me!" I say with emphasis.

"Don't you condescend to me!" she cries in fury.

By now I've grabbed both arms to steady her by force and focus her attention on me.

"You cannot hit me! You can't hit!" I am outraged but manage to transcend the outrage so as to get through to her. "I will help you, but you must calm down. The nurses will tie you down if you act like this and I . . . don't . . . want them to! OK? Please . . ."

"But why aren't you helping me? I need Suzanne! Call her, call her."

"I'll call her, but just —"

"Call her now!"

Beverly puts her arms around her and engages her in conversation, I don't know what about, probably about how everything will work itself out, how Suzanne will save her. I dial Suzanne's office number, the last three digits the reverse of the first three digits, easy to remember.

The phone rings once . . . twice . . . three times . . . four. The machine hasn't picked up. Fifth ring . . . sixth . . . *What's going on?* I'm thinking. *Why now?!*

I've no brain cells left. I look at Ray, perplexed.

"The machine's not picking up!" I tell him so Jane can't hear.

None of us want to see Jane explode again. We want to see her at ease, once again with faith she's taken care of. Ray looks at me as if he had never imagined I was a numbskull before.

"Lie!" he whispers, excitedly. It never occurred to me that to take charge could mean taking charge of the facts.

"Oh. Hi, Suzanne," I start my monologue, imitating the monotone customary for addressing an answering machine. "This is Ed Zucker . . ."

"Is she there?" perks up Jane, expectantly.

I motion with my hand for her to wait. The phone is still ringing. I continue to address the gods of night who seem light years away from us on this particularly dark and scattered night. They do not pick up their calls.

"I'm calling for Jane from the hospital . . ." I begin when Jane, energized with determination, gets up to grab the phone.

"Let me talk to her!"

"Wait! I'm talking!"—to the sound of Suzanne's phone ringing. I'm in the middle of my act here and am about to be exposed as a fraud. "Hold on a minute!"

Jane grabs the receiver but I hold onto it as if fighting for *my* life. I am determined to save *something* tonight, even if it is the mere illusion that I am helping her to escape her fate.

"Let *me* speak to her!" Jane pleads fiercely, begging with her eyes widescreen. "Please. *Hello Suzanne!*"

Our heads almost butt as we form a passionate ménage à trois with the telephone receiver, she devoting her attentions to the mouthpiece and I to the earpiece, while the phone continues to purr imperviously, "nobody home, nobody home."

"Suzanne! It's Jane! I'm calling because I need your help!"

The jig should be up by now, but instead Jane seem oblivious to the ringing tone.

"It's really important that you call me as soon as you receive this message!"

And now it seems as if she's oblivious to the phone itself, as she floats back a step or two while continuing to leave the message.

"If you could please call me at Albert Einstein in the Bronx, I would greatly appreciate it! My number is 718-624-1014. 718-624-1014."

By the time she has come to the end of her message ("I hope to hear from you soon. Thank you!") she is several feet away, bathed in her own inner spotlight, her voice at a friendly melodious sing-song. Jane has made her connection and she is at peace.

I hang up the receiver in awe of her transformation. She is an angel now, blessing us all with the power of her beaming light.

She looks off and up to the side as if communing with the future.

"Suzanne will help us," she says, encouragingly. "You'll see. Everything will be alright."

I'm not quite sure what's happened. I feel the wind has been knocked out of me, but perhaps for the good. We all stand christened by a storm and peaceful in its dewy aftermath.

"Yes, everything will be alright, Jane dear," says Beverly, extending her hand in aid, expecting and hoping to escort her charge to bed.

"Yeah, she's a good therapist, right?" Ray chips in awkwardly. "So she'll give you the help you need. She'll take care of things."

"That's wonderful!" encourages Chryssie, trying to be of help. We're all so excited that Jane is no longer in the mighty grip of panic that we want to shower her with praise.

I still feel a bit cast from Jane's inner circle, having played the role of archfiend in her perception of things. But Jane's perception has made a one hundred eighty degree turn and she walks her joy over to me as if we've both won a prize.

"Everything will be alright, Egg! Don't worry," she says, as if I had been the patient and she the provider of moral support. "Oh, look at your face! You're bleeding!" She holds my face in the grip of her right hand as she studies the scratch that she left on my cheek. "Beverly, can you reach a tissue for me? Oh, poor baby, you're hurt. Relax; I'm going to take care of it." And with her pinky in air, she delicately and precisely touches the tissue to my cheek, dabbing it carefully. "That's better," she says. Her face is so close to mine; her eyes gently wash my right cheek with loving concern. I take hold of her ministering hand so as to show my thanks for her care.

"I'm OK," I assure her. "Thank you."

"I'm almost finished," she replies, doggedly cleaning me up. "That's better." She doesn't mention her physical assault; she merely takes care of her loving business.

Once I am completely doctored by the patient, the patient— her job all done—confesses to exhaustion coming on. But she's not ready for bed.

"Come to the windows," Jane says to me. "Keep me company by the windows for a little while."

As if they are a backstage crew, everyone bustles around, moving poles and wires and furniture to their rightful places on cue. I hold Jane's hand aloft so as to prevent entanglement with wires, and then escort her, minuet-like, to our improvised love seat.

"I think I'm too tired for any more company," Jane announces both with a tone of apology and declaration. In either case, it's the exit line Ray and Chryssie have been waiting for, wiped out themselves by the evening's furor; now they can leave with a sense that the drama is coming to a close. Chryssie wraps her arms around Jane's shoulders from behind the chair, giving her a farewell blessing; Ray is next in line and pats her shoulder while giving her a brother's kiss on the cheek. They turn to me simultaneously and I'm struck by the look in both their eyes. This evening they've shared an experience with me after a lifetime of us never having had any shared experiences. This evening has secured a friendship between us. We've gone on an expedition, been there and come back. This is how you know someone, their eyes say.

"Get some rest," is what their lips say.

"I'll see ya tomorrow," says Ray and he gives me a hug. I stand surprised. Chryssie pecks my cheek and tilts her head in sympathy.

"Good night, Ed," she says. "Good night, Aunt Janie!"

"Good night," Jane replies, her fatigue reducing her voice to a loud whisper.

"Oh my, what an evening," sums up Beverly. "Well, darling, I'm going to sit right outside, reading the Good Book in case you two need me." And that's exactly what she does.

I seat myself next to my lover of twenty-two years and put her hand in mine. Twenty-two years ago we sat across a small table from each other eating falafels, Mozart and Schubert still echoing in our consciousness. Twenty-two years ago Jane opened herself up to me, overwhelming me with her life's tale of family brutality, teenage recklessness and over-the-top misfortune: negligent families, a depraved father, a psychotic sister, opportunistic strangers, a baby boy cursed with severe handicaps, and an unloving young husband who expressed himself with his fists. Tales of the Bronx in the fifties, of Yonkers during the generation gap, and the East Village at the height of its psychedelic infamy. Tales of a girl who saw her mother die of cancer when she was only nine and too young to understand how someone could love you so little as to leave you so unprotected so young. I listened to these tales in amazement and awe. I thought I could learn a lot from someone who had been through so much, and yet was seemingly filled with a greater capacity for joy than I, in my comparatively sheltered life, could ever imagine.

Only many years after, in fact the year before Jane was diagnosed, did I discover that I had missed the entire point of these stories.

"I was giving you fair warning," Jane told me one night in an Outback Steakhouse in Vestal, New York, a night during which we were unceremoniously and mutually tearing our marriage apart. "I was giving you a chance to get away! Don't you get it?"

"What are you talking about?!"

"So that if you were going to leave me, it would be before I fell in love with you!"

If that was her intention, she had totally failed: I had gotten the wrong message. Far from noticing the damaged woman she was trying to reveal, I had only noticed the miracle she was instead.

And now, so many difficult and lovely years later, she still worries that I will abandon her, but it is, in fact, she who is leaving me. So, tonight, we are sitting side by side on the tenth floor of Albert Einstein Medical Center, facing a Bronx that is slowly turning out its lights. In the distance, moonlight glimmers over the Sound, and contrasting rows of headlights pierce the darkness. "I love you, baby," I say as I turn to kiss her forehead, which lies on my shoulder. "I love you, too," she replies. The day has been numbing, but after we've had a chance to let it slide from our consciousness, the night begins to seem magical and new and dangerous at the same time. Calvary Hospital sits down below us in the foreground of our view, and soon, like a stage show that is about to start, I'll see it lit up with fanfare by the lights of approaching jets, lights that will spotlight a beautiful cold blue flame. It will sit on the center of Calvary's roof, beckoning, beckoning, and we'll gasp with the pleasure of shared love when the jets, so close to their pale blue immolation, veer just in time, straight up to the heavens.

II

Run Away on the Heavenly Express

The train wrenched itself free of the tracks and, with a heavy metallic shift beneath her, Jane felt the train start to lift, slowly releasing itself from the pull of gravity. Jane held her breath, hoping to keep the train aloft as it floated over the now-shrinking brown buildings of the Bronx. She turned to her mother who sat next to her, her inky black hair and eyes mirroring Jane's with a liquid exaggeration. "I hope these angels know what they're doing," Jane said urgently, watching the approaching white wisps in the cerulean blue outside the train window, vertigo pulling at her guts.

Jane awoke, putting an abrupt halt to the ascent. She had landed facing the delicate crevice created by the back of a still-sleeping companion and a thin mattress, the woman's mussed head of hair sprawling towards her. The woman breathed slowly, her face buried in the ether of darkness. Jane lay still, lost in the forest of the woman's hair. She usually woke up alone and at home. But now she was neither. She could hear the distant sound of traffic. It was the moan of the city. She was in the city, sleeping in the city. And then it was clear. Not lost in a forest. Lost in life. With Annette. In a flophouse on St. Mark's Place in New York's East Village.

For a while, she didn't move so as to avoid waking Annette with the twang of the cheap box springs. Finally, she slipped out of bed and made her way to the desk where she had left her bag. She scrounged around in it, searched for the half of a joint that she had left, and after finding it and an almost toothless book of matches in the corner of the bag, lit it with a tight inhale. What could tomorrow hold in store for her, she wondered, waiting for the pot's fuzzy, insulating sensation to wallpaper her brain. The possibilities were almost vertigo-inducing on this pre-dawn morning.

It was February 1968, and the year had made its inauspicious debut at St. Vincent's Hospital in Tuckahoe, with Jane walking her older sister, Virginia, back and forth outside the emergency room. That night Virginia's stomach had been pumped for the sixth time in four years.

"Ginny, this is ridiculous," Jane had said.

"It is ridiculous!" Virginia had replied, and then, unable to go on, having succumbed to a slippery descent into helpless wrenching laughter, she threw her arms around her taller, younger sister as if the end of the world looked hilarious from here. She looked straight into her sister's surprised, bemused, brown-eyed gaze and howled with an exhausted bray, a farcical love call if ever there was one, trapping Jane in their familiar sisterhood while lassoing her into her own freefall of delirious laughter. This was becoming a really bad joke, and though there was little in truth for the sisters to laugh at, these concerted inept efforts to wipe herself off the face of the earth had entered the realm of a painful slapstick.

Soon, the harsh hospital lights brought out the weariness in Virginia's demeanor, and with tears streaming down over the tightening rictus of her smile, each wrenching contraction of her frame resembled grief as much as a kind of jaundiced abandon. At moments like these, Jane could remember her love for her sister again, from the years before she had practically come to own Jane and treat her like the Raggedy Ann she'd desecrated as a furious, ruined little girl. They were again the two sisters united by the same nightmarish adventure that was their family.

"Come on, Ginny, you've got to keep walking!"

"I'm walking! I'm walking!" but the laughter would force her to throw herself on Jane almost the way she had on their mother's coffin when they tried to lower it into the ground, and Jane would try, weakened by paroxysms of machine-gun-like yelps, to get Virginia back on course on her own two feet.

But those shared moments, which had vaguely resembled love, were history by the time Virginia returned home to Jane and Uncle Al, who they'd been living with for the last four years. It was as if nothing had been stripped away, as if all the pretending and game-playing had not for one night been made totally irrelevant, as if there had not been that primal undertow of sisterly connection. Virginia was back in old form, manipulating Uncle Al with her feminine helplessness and raging at her younger sister ceaselessly.

This time things were really coming to a head. Just weeks earlier, Virginia had been caught stealing cutlery from the Alexander's Department Store she worked at after they transferred her to kitchenware from the cosmetics department, where she believed her beauty was put to best use, and she found herself without a job and a paycheck. And on another front, her generally manic behavior had come to terrify her fiancé, Pete, who tried to drive cross-country to get away from her after he broke off their engagement, only to be arrested after she called the Selective Service Bureau to accuse him of being a draft dodger. Her feelings were so charged and violent that they'd led her back to the emergency room and now, home again, with nothing but more of the same to look forward to, her focus easily fell on her more independent, somewhat wayward, smarter baby sister, whose new diet pill regimen threatened Virginia's one area of confidence. "I know you're the smart one," she'd once confided to Jane, "but I'm the pretty one," and it felt important to her that it stay that way.

One night within two weeks of Virginia's emergency room visit, the fury that Virginia had that night directed at herself was now aimed at Jane. Poor Uncle Al, the eternal bachelor once helplessly besotted with his brother's wife, now regularly moved by his older niece's ragged beauty, tentatively put his hand around her shoulder to calm her down, unconsciously replicating in a passive way a position that Jane had often seen her father in with respect to Virginia, and it made her sick. Virginia—petite, blond, furious—continued to hurtle raving insults at the imposing dark glares of her smoldering sister, and the living room rumbled with implosive atomic energy until Jane could no longer keep herself bridled and burst with a force that resulted in magazines splattering against walls and ashtrays flying in both directions. She wished her sister's next suicide attempt huge success and that her uncle go screw himself for good measure, and having burnt all possible bridges, she grabbed her coat from the hall closet and slammed the door behind her, setting off for her brother Ray's place up Bronx River Road. It was cold and dark outside, and her footsteps smacked the Yonkers pavement with little stabs of echo.

This is over, she had said to herself. *This is over. It's really over.* Ray *had* to take her in. He *had* to.

Jane, standing alone in the dark in the small hotel room on St. Mark's Place, now took another toke of her joint. She experienced her family as an avalanche falling all around her, and Ray, unbelievably, as the one who would finally bury her in the cold. She proceeded to wipe Virginia and Uncle Al and then Ray off the face of the earth with each inhale, which had the added fillip of preventing her from re-visiting that final, painful scene with her brother.

The effusion of marijuana smoke, like water on the drenched pages of a notebook, finally ran the details of Jane's last two days into an indecipherable stream. Only the present was real: this shadowed closet over St. Mark's Place, surrounded by the pulse of the nighttime city outside its drawn window shades, the sound of other comrades-in-spirit scraping along in the dark, the sight of Annette's three dimensions sprawled across the bed, the music of Jane's own vibrant heartbeat. All she could see was an endless *now* stretching out into the night-lit darkness like some kind of an awful tease.

* * *

Only two and a half years earlier, Jane had felt desperate enough to make her way to the office of Father Marco, the priest at the parochial school that she attended, to ask him to help her find another home. He'd seemed surprised, almost disheartened, that one of Blessed Virgin's students, and a dedicated one at that, would actually believe that the church could be an actual, as versus spiritual, refuge from the trials of the material world. Few of the students he had contact with were quite that naive.

"Now, Jane, you're starting what year now?" he asked her, his hands folded on his belly.

"Eighth grade," she replied softly, her heartbeat seeming louder to her than her strangled voice.

"You know, many young people feel their parents—in your case, your uncle and sister—don't care at all about them. It can be hard to believe sometimes, when parents are strict, that they can also have their children's interests at heart. You know that, don't you?"

As he watched tears start to roll down her cheeks from her downcast eyes, he grasped at how to respond and he thought to offer her his pocket handkerchief.

"Here. It's clean."

"My family doesn't have my interests at heart, Father," she said after wiping her tears with the corner of the still-folded white cloth. "That's why I'm here. I don't know where else to go."

Jane waited for the Father to offer a solution more in keeping with the Home in *The Bells of St. Mary's* or something, but she was afraid to volunteer her thoughts in case it betrayed her immaturity. Her teachers, the nuns, she thought, showed more of an interest in her than her sister did, as witch-like as she'd become once she no longer had Daddy to terrorize her. She thought nuns could be her family, like older, saner, loving sisters.

"Do you pray, Jane?"

"Yes," she said. She sometimes did. Not on her knees, but sometimes silently, while lying in bed under the covers, or when camped on the toilet seat or when watching her sister bemoan her life while crying on Uncle Al's massive shoulders. *Please, Jesus, take me away. Lift me out of here. Save me from my sister's hell. Bring her up to heaven where she can't hurt anyone anymore and where you could heal her. Make my brother and Tina let me live with them.*

"Well, then" the Father continued," pray for Jesus to give me guidance while I take the next few days to figure out how I can best help you. Now go home and try to stay out of your sister's hair and remember to concentrate on your studies and we'll talk in a few days."

As Jane gathered up her strapped-up textbooks, she said, "I could live in an orphanage," as quietly as if she was making him an illicit offer.

Father Marco looked surprised, as if he hadn't heard properly.

"Well, you go home now," he said, as if scattering wild puppies, "and I'll come up with something. I promise."

Jane walked through a kind of purgatory for the next couple of days, afraid to hope and equally afraid to despair. She concentrated on her textbook descriptions of the French Revolution, on Huckleberry Finn scampering on and around the Mississippi River, on commutative equations, but all of them seemed to mirror the sense of emotional suspension she was experiencing. Where would her life lead her?

By the time Saturday rolled around, she assumed that Father Marco had forgotten about her. She snuck out of the house early enough to avoid bumping into Virginia, who could be found around the apartment thumbing movie magazines at any time of the day or night, made it over to the small neighborhood corner mart to buy a Drake's cake for breakfast and then made her way to Mark Twain Junior High to hang out at the basketball court. She took a lesser part in the raucous goings-on than usual, content to mostly act like an embittered grown-up who smoked Marlboros and saw through the childish cares of her peers, until Frank Willis, a ninth grader, made yet another unnecessary verbal swipe at her body size, making all her girlfriends giggle before shouting at him to cut it out, and she decided to take a walk to Central

Avenue.

"Where ya going?" asked Rosemary, running after her. Rosemary lived in the same building. "Don't take it personal!"

"I don't care about him," Jane said contemptuously. "Anyway, I've got better things to do!" when, in reality, she only had things not to do, places and people to avoid. After Rosemary shrugged and walked away, Jane slowly strolled through the neighborhood, cigarette hand bent back at the wrist delicately down near her haunches to hide it should she need to. The day was empty so she had time enough to get as far as the movie theatre where *Love With the Proper Stranger* was on a double bill with *This Property is Condemned*. Both titles spoke to her in some inchoate way, and she fished out the dollar and a quarter from her jacket pocket the way she'd lit her cigarette earlier, as if submitting to unwanted attentions, and that afternoon she allowed herself the darkness of the movie house and the envy of Natalie Wood's beautiful predicaments.

When she arrived back at the apartment, which looked vividly flat and banal after living in the world of the movies, her sister and uncle were sitting at the kitchen table. They stared at her blankly, as if they'd been expecting a stranger to arrive and the stranger was her. Rather than penetrate the familiar air of conspiracy that enveloped them, Jane just headed to her bedroom. Within minutes, Virginia and Uncle Al materialized at her door like unwanted apparitions.

"We had a visitor today," Virginia said. "Do you know who it was?"

At first Jane seemed unresponsive before her expression turned quizzical.

"It was the priest from your school, this Father . . ."

"Marco," said Uncle Al.

". . . Marco," Virginia repeated.

Jane felt the blood drop from her face to the floor.

"He said you wanted to run away, that we were mistreating you or ignoring you, I don't remember."

"He said 'neglect,'" Uncle Al interjected.

"I've never been so embarrassed," Virginia continued.

"Jane, your sister felt humiliated."

"I can't believe you'd do that to me," she went on. "I'm your family! Father Marco said 'Family is everything.' Everything, Jane. We belong to each other. I need you. You know what I've been through. If you can't be part of my team, my family, we'll both have nothing."

Jane knew her sister meant that, among other things, as a threat.

"And don't I pay for all your expenses?" asked Uncle Al. "Here I'm doing you girls a good deed and now . . . You know I try the best I can."

"You know when I yell," Virginia added, "that I don't mean anything by it. I just can't help it."

What Jane did know was that Father Marco had now as good as locked her up in the loony bin and thrown away the key. Although, for the next few weeks, her sister and uncle acted conspicuously caring, she knew that before long, Virginia's rage at the world would get the better of her and being at home would again be hell on Earth. So Jane did the best she could to just stay away, and over time found a life somewhat more convivial, not in the church, no, she'd never go there again, but in the unsupervised homes of new school friends, listening to music, smoking cigarettes and generally being as precocious as the uncharted changes of the sixties allowed.

The thick black eyeliner around Annette's eyes would've informed you of the dark vision behind them. Compared to Jane and Marie, her buddies, she was the most nihilistic of the bunch. If Jane was the one most filled with restless energy, and Marie the most open to suggestion, Annette was the corner of the triangle most grounded in a comfortable, sardonic passivity.

"I hate this place," she had said more than once, referring to their home town, her long, heavy curls seeming to pull her head back and to the side lethargically, as the girls would sit cross-legged around an ash-tray in her bedroom, sending smoke signals to no one in particular.

"Yes!" Marie might typically reply, jumping in sitting position—her long blonde hair jumping with her—it not much mattering whether Annette was referring to the bedroom, the row house her parents owned, or the whole of Yonkers. Marie's antic energy would elicit a laugh from Jane, perhaps while taking a toke of the communal joint, causing her to cover her mouth and blush while in the throes of a pot-induced giddiness.

"Let's run away to the East Village or someplace," Annette would drone sarcastically in her husky voice, "stalk Bob Dylan"—the thought of which entertained her friends enormously—"rob the Azuma on Eighth Street, beg for change . . . *that* would be exciting!" Then she might lie on her back and let the jangly percussion of *Their Satanic Majesty's Request* soothe her working class-suburban anomie.

Neither Jane nor Marie ever took this suggestion seriously. They all felt that their current lives were a bad fit, but bad fit or not, these were the lives they had. Annette's home life felt suffocating to her, Jane's was borderline psychotic, and Marie's sterile, but that said, the bottom line still remained that there was always something to find in the fridge. Their thinking of getting away from all this preceded their yet having the legs to do it.

If Annette's family life was killing her, her wit curdling with each passing day, Jane's, on the other hand, was honing her; she was bursting to find outlets for her frustrations, and high school had begun to supply them to her. If her family—and her friends' families—thought of her as unadulterated trouble and bother, her teachers were encouraging and inspiring her—and her new diet-pill regimen had given her a different kind of attention than usual from her peers.

That said, at the end of the day there was still always Virginia, whose own life had been dead-ended years ago, to make sure—

with or without trying—that nothing good would come easily to her fifteen-year-old baby sister either.

This time Jane had had enough. After running out on her sister and her uncle only weeks after her sister's suicide attempt, she'd deposited herself at her brother's door like a rain-drenched Christmas delivery.

A delivery he wasn't accepting.

As far back as Jane could recall, her belovedly handsome, supercool big brother with the perfect pompadour of shiny black hair, was always trying to extricate himself from the reach of his family, and for good reason. Closeness usually brought him within proximity of his father's fists. He and his father had been fighting so long, he would always say he couldn't remember if there had ever been an initiating incident to set it off. His father seemed to resent him at first sight, which was on his release from the sweaty, hellish Burmese front where both rowdy, drunken GIs and scorching enemy bombing runs had vied for the chance to inflict him with bodily harm. Ray'd cried, buried in his mother's embrace, at his father's brusque, impatient parental overtures, and Mario, seeing the look in Betty's eyes, treated Ray as his competition from then on. Even at dinnertime, Ray had to sit with his plate on the windowsill, watching not to get burned by the radiator or his father's tirades. Betty's pleading for calm and Virginia's terrified screams would make Jane numb as she sat between all the warring camps, Daddy on one side and Mom on the other with Virginia and Ray further from the center of the storm.

And now, once again, Jane felt she was being sacrificed to the God of Crazy while her big-shouldered brother still couldn't get far enough away from any of them.

"I can't deal with you right now!" was Ray's response to her arrival, agitated that Uncle Al wasn't handling this. "I got my own problems! I got a marriage to save!"

"I'll stay out of your hair, I promise!" Jane had said.

"It's not *that!*" Ray floundered in agitation.

"I'll baby-sit for you!"

"Yeah. Right. You know Tina wouldn't allow it," he replied, resting his fists on his hips. "And you know why? Because she thinks you'd be a bad influence. And you probably would. You need real parents is what you need. Someone to put you on the right track."

"Like *Virginia!?* Like *Uncle Al!?*" she cried in disbelief.

"No. I'm saying like – *parents!* A mother and a father with good values and stuff."

"I *had* parents!"

"Yeah, one's dead and the other shoulda stayed locked up. I'm talking foster parents here."

"You're throwing me away?!"

"A father! A mother! *A family!*"

"What about Aunt Connie and Uncle Vito?! Or Aunt Mae and –?"

"They don't give a damn about us. They never lifted a finger – forget about it. I'm not kidding, Jane. Stay here, but then I gotta call some organization and find out about foster care. That's what you need."

"*I can't believe you!*" Jane cried. "Tina won't come back! You're just *kidding* yourself! *She's* a fucking *bitch*, but you'd do *anything* for her and *nothing* for me! Fuck family! If *you* won't help me, why should some fucking strangers?"

"Watch your mouth!" Ray blustered.

Fury made Jane huge, more huge even than her muscle-bound brother. Her eyes narrowed to pinholes and her cheeks were a rolling mass of clouds.

"You can go to hell!" she erupted and she stormed into her niece's vacated pink-frosted-cupcake-of-a-room and slammed the door.

"I'm not going to a foster home," she said calmly the next day. She had gone to school without books, sat through classes as if she was struggling unsuccessfully with her period, and now sat in front of her lunch tray carrying an apple juice and two Devil Dogs. She, Annette and Marie sat conspiratorially, elbows on the table, their long hair screening them off from notice as they spoke to each other in loud whispers. "I've got to get out of here before some social worker or someone gets ahold of me."

"What are you going to do?" Marie asked in a tone pitched between pity and awe.

And that's when she hatched her plan, right in that moment; there was no more reason to put it off. She was going to jump down that rabbit hole and take her chances on the East Village, no more dilly-dallying on the Yonkers-bound local, she was going to fly on that heavenly express straight to Wonderland where she'd be embraced by a community of scraggly runaways, impassioned politicos and transcendent visionaries far from the sludge-like existence that Virginia and Ray and Uncle Al inhabited.

"I'll go to the city. No one would find me there." She looked away from them. "Maybe no one will even look. Maybe they'll be glad." And then a devilish glint found its way to her eye, as she turned to the girls and said, "Well, *I'll* be glad. I hate them."

The anger they all bore toward their families was now stoked by Jane's, and Jane's bravery in the face of catastrophe made them all partisans. Over the years, the three had been intensely bonded by both adolescence and their habitual pot soirees into what felt like a kind of secret society, the world outside becoming irrelevant, far away and inane, their families dropping off the edge of the earth. And that's what happened now.

"Fuck," Annette said. She was sprawled across the cafeteria table, her cheek supported by the heel of her palm. "I'm going with you."

There was something radical about the moves Jane was making, and Annette coveted the radical position in the group. If Jane *had* to leave home, Annette would *choose* to.

"Let's just fucking do it," she said. "Finally."

"Are you serious?" Jane was incredulous.

"I've been talking about this forever," Annette replied. "If I don't do this now, it might never happen." She was ready to strike a match and watch her Yonkers life slowly burn up from the edges.

"Holy shit," Marie said softly. She sensed a current of exhilarating anxiety running across the table, kind of like the anticipated consummation of a dangerous romance. It was painful to be so close to it and not be part of it.

"When do we leave?" she asked, leaning further over the table as if she was crawling between her friends.

Jane felt blanketed on all sides, her loneliness assuaged. She felt grateful. *Family is a lie*, she thought to herself. *Friends are the only thing that matters.* And now her best friends were willing to jettison their families, putting them all on equal footing. Either everyone should have family or no one should.

"Tomorrow," Jane answered, her heart pumping with adrenaline. She took each of her friends' hands and held them tightly in her grip.

She wanted to say something about how she was feeling, about how she never felt alive until this moment, about how intense her love was for them. And then the bell for sixth period rang. For a couple of minutes, they remained in their seats, holding hands across the cafeteria table, not wanting to break their self-imposed spell.

Jane wouldn't miss Yonkers anymore than she had missed New Rochelle after she and her sister had been taken from their father's care four years ago. She happily bid goodbye to Bronx River Road and Frank Sinatra records, to her sister's True Confessions magazines, to Uncle Al's boxer shorts drying over the shower curtain. She would leave no notes for anyone, no hints where to look or what had happened. Her sister would have one less person to scream at or lie about, one less person wrapped around her little finger, one less person's soul to pull down with her on her downward spiral. And Ray would not have to take her in or, more likely, as he threatened, find a foster home for her. She no longer needed anything that her family had left to give, which was only melodrama anyway. When she left she took mostly essentials with her: a few changes of clothes, a toothbrush, her diet pills, reading material and her bankbook—and then she closed the prison door behind her.

The next day, keeping their eyes out for truant officers, the girls boarded the bus headed to the Woodlawn Cemetery in the Bronx. Woodlawn, they knew, was where they could pick up the IRT, which would zap them into the heart of the city. At the Bronx terminal, they boarded the rusty brown train with its rattan seats and sat near the train doors. Soon they zoomed over Jerome Avenue with a racket until, after around a half an hour, they suddenly plummeted into the underground darkness of Manhattan. The train filled up with men in fedoras and women in pumps and dispersed many of them throughout midtown. They noticed a young man wearing glasses with black plastic frames, his scraggly hair reaching almost to his shoulders, and followed him off the train at Union Square. They walked across the subway platform and waited for another train, already imagining themselves Greenwich Village girls with their hoop earrings, fringed bags, and long scarves variously wrapped around their necks or covering their bare heads.

They followed their scraggly White Rabbit onto a local and off at the next stop which took them to Astor Place. He didn't notice his retinue and unwittingly led them across the plaza through a chaos of streets and avenues. The March wind whipped their long hair and scarves in all directions, propelling these new immigrants to the Lower East Side onward.

Scraggly White Rabbit disappeared into a large old building of heavy brown stone right off the square, where a lot of other young people congregated. The words "Cooper Union" were embossed in the stone above the entrance. The girls looked at these Cooper Union students enviously. In their eyes, they had purpose, money and sophistication in a distinctly New York City way. The girls felt a bit like pretenders.

"Somebody here's bound to have a living room we could

crash," said Annette. "Don't you think?"

Jane took out a cigarette box from her bag and shook it so that some Marlboros extended from the pack.

"You want?"

They all took one and Jane lit a match to them all, lighting hers last. Then she walked over, with Marie and Annette trailing her, to some girls at the building's entrance and interrupted their conversation.

"Excuse me," she began. "Do any of you know a place we could crash for a night or two? We just arrived in New York and we need a place to stay."

The students looked at them quizzically, like they weren't sure how Jane's world had collided with theirs. They tried to adjust to its reality by asking where they were from.

"Westchester," said Marie.

"Yonkers," said Jane. "I need to find a place to stay or I'm going to be put in a foster home." She took a drag from her cigarette. "My parents are dead," she said softly, knowing it to be a half-truth "and my brother and sister don't want me, so they were going to give me away." She brushed back her hair with her cigarette hand, momentarily averting her eyes. "We won't be a bother to anyone. Oh yeah, these are my best friends."

"We're looking after her," said Marie.

"Families suck," agreed Annette, before taking a drag of her Marlboro.

The group of students looked heartsick for Jane, their eyebrows arched to demonstrate pity. They couldn't help, they said, but they wished the girls well.

They went from group to group with their story until finally one young guy with pronounced stubble said they could spend a night in his place, but he had class to go to.

"No problem!" Jane said enthusiastically.

They agreed to meet him in a couple of hours in front of the statue of Peter Cooper at the small Cooper Union Park.

They decided to get lunch and found themselves across from

the hotel at the gateway to St. Mark's Place. They walked east on the street towards Second Avenue, passing the blue-painted building that housed The Electric Circus, where young people could be seen navigating the outdoor catwalks and fire escapes like hippie trapeze artists. At the end of the block, a raffish group was sitting behind upended floppy hats, trying to stay warm while begging for change. The newness of the scene was exciting to Jane and she longed to join it.

On Second Avenue, next door to an old theatre that was showing a revival of "La Strada," was a counter place. They plopped down on stools and fed their ravenousness hamburgers and fries, each girl quiet with her unquiet thoughts.

"I think my father's having an affair," Marie announced at one point.

"Holy shit," said Annette.

"Yeah," Marie continued. "There's something going on. A lot of 'not talking.' And he's away a lot . . . Mom eating by herself. I don't know. There's a lot of 'not talking.'"

For a moment, 'not talking' prevailed in the diner as well.

"That would be an improvement in my house," Annette finally responded.

"There's a lot of things flying through the air in mine," Jane said, trying to suppress a smile.

They all laughed, released from a slender knot of indefinable tension that was developing. They quieted down, and first Marie, and then the others, started giggling, the ribbon of ludicrous imagery continuing to unravel in their minds.

Marie couldn't keep the edge of a smile from showing as she tried to get serious. She fluttered her hands in front of her as she tried to find expression for her thoughts.

"I guess what I'm trying to say is, now that I'm thinking about it . . ." She pressed her lips together to pinch away the smile, took a few breaths through her nose and then dived back in. "I don't think this is a good time for me to be doing this. I mean, I think my mother might need me right now." Then she turned to Jane and said quickly and softly, "Don't hate me."

Jane did hate her—for having a choice. And then it no longer mattered. This was going to happen with or without Marie.

"We'll be OK," Jane said.

"I wish you could stay with me in Yonkers," Marie said. "But my parents would never allow it."

"Your parents think I'm a bad influence."

They all giggled. They were all bad influences on each other like the closest of friends.

"I can't go back," said Jane.

"I know. I know. I feel terrible. But you're going to be OK now that you have a place to stay. You'll meet more people, and who knows, right?"

"I'm still with you," said Annette. "It'll be cool. We'll get to do all kinds of shit."

Marie made it back to the subway, hoping to arrive home as if it had been a normal school day, while Jane and Annette made their way back to Cooper Union Park. It was a little before the appointed time, so they took out two more cigarettes to warm up with, pushing back stray hairs left by the breeze on their faces. It was getting cold and they looked forward to seeing their benefactor at any minute. They stood in the plaza while clusters of students slowly melted away. When it was fifteen minutes past the allotted meeting time, Jane knew she had been abandoned yet again.

"Goddamn it!" she said while stamping out her latest cigarette. "Why would he be so mean?"

"He probably forgot," Annette suggested. "Let's wait a little longer."

"We gotta find a place to stay *tonight!*"

They decided to take up the unspoken invitation of the panhandlers. They tentatively joined the community of the hip and hungry, standing just a bit off from them, making their case more plaintively than did their affectless, slightly older compatriots. Just not plaintively enough to catch the attention of policemen. Ultimately, though, there wasn't anyone on that chilly March night willing to take on two teenage girls, Jane's pleas working no better than they had with her brother, and so the girls found themselves surrendering to the grungy lure of the seedy St. Mark's Hotel, which was happy to welcome them no questions asked. The only requirement: cash.

After two nights of flophouse living, vigilantly watching the doorknobs to their room each night, listening to all the voices of vagrants and con artists and strung-out prostitutes traversing the hallways, Annette was beginning to feel strung out herself. She started to yearn for her safe bedroom on Bronx River Road. This freedom had burdens of its own: daytime spent fruitlessly trying to hustle for a simpatico place to crash, nighttime spent confined behind ratty curtains in a room hardly big enough for *one* person, trying to get some sleep. Jane seemed unaffected by the depressing environment, as if she didn't notice that the world was full of oblivious strangers and dangerous curves. She spoke to everyone as if this was her neighborhood, too, as if she had always lived on the Lower East Side, as if her repeated sob story and request for help was a commonplace here and even gave her credentials of a kind. At night, when Annette tried not to feel that everything was collapsing, Jane would be reading from "Howl" or Lawrence Ferlinghetti or the East Village Other.

It was Friday morning. Today their plan was to hang out in front of the Fillmore East where the Doors were scheduled to play their eerie psychedelic rock at the much-hyped new venue. That, they thought, should bring a good crowd of people hospitable to runaways, willing to absorb them into their midst.

"Jane, I want to call home," Annette finally said, twisting a string of long hair with her finger. She was looking at her Fred Braun "shitkickers" that she always wore, not in Jane's direction, her voice hoarse with a forlorn sound.

"I should let them know I'm OK. I don't want to torture

them anymore."

After a pensive moment, Jane said "You can't tell them where you are."

"Of course not," Annette said sadly.

"Because your parents would rat on me, man."

"Yeah, I know," Annette said. She stared blankly ahead of her. "I just don't want them to worry."

Jane didn't say anything; she just stared at Annette as if she was studying her, watching her moves for clues about their future. Finally Annette let go the twisted strand of hair, nodded her head twice in self-encouragement and got off the bed to get her bag.

"I'll go find a phone."

"I'll come with you!"

They wrapped themselves in their winter uniforms and headed outside. It was a sunny winter's day, cold and mercilessly bright. The world moved around them vividly and purposefully without drama. The drama would hover only over the telephone booth on the noisy corner at the Bowery, across from the hotel.

Jane watched Annette through the closed glass doors of the booth. She thought having butterflies in her stomach was retarded, so she turned away and leaned her back against the glass, her head bent back as if soaking up the winter rays. Annette listened to the dial tone with her head down, her tresses veiling her face. Suddenly she looked up.

"Ma —?!"

Jane closed her eyes. Annette sounded underwater to her.

"Yeah, ma, it's me."

Jane let the word "ma" float away above her. She hadn't said that word herself in more than six years. *Ma.*

"Calm down. I'm alright, ma."

Jane opened her eyes and felt around for her pack of cigarettes. *Fuck mothers*, she thought. An image of her mother, pale and puffy, lying on the hospital bed, indifferent to her children gathered around her, passed like cigarette smoke before her eyes up towards the streetlights.

"I'm sorry. I know. I know. I'm with Jane."

There was a pause on Annette's side of the conversation.

Jane watched a Puerto Rican mother bustling her two kids across St. Mark's. "Hold my hands! *Mis manos! Mis manos!*" the mother was shouting.

"Just don't worry about me," Jane heard Annette say softly.

Jane lost track of the conversation when Annette's voice lowered in volume to a muffled drone. The sound was as comforting as a mattress. Jane didn't miss *her* family and she felt exhilarated by the tailspin she hoped they were in.

She heard the receiver fall into its cradle, and she was surprised to hear her heart pounding. Annette suddenly appeared before her and wrapped her arms around Jane's neck.

"I've got to go," she whispered. "Come home with me. I'll get my parents to take you in until we figure something out."

"I don't want to live with your parents," Jane said, passively letting herself be hugged. "I'm free of parents and family and I'm never going back."

"I know. I know," Annette replied, disappointed in herself. "Look, I'll come back on the weekend and bring you stuff! Whatever you need! You just have to let me know where you are and we'll meet. I'll come every weekend! Things'll be so different by the time I see you again. Oh, and by the way," she added quietly, "your brother and sister are looking for you. They called my mom."

"And the fucking police, I bet. If they can't *stand* me so much, why won't they just leave me *alone*?! All this just to give me away!"

Jane's face had grown big and puffy with anger, her eyes pulverized into cold black dots. Annette watched nervously.

"I won't tell anyone where you are. I promise," she said.

Jane slumped in moody resignation. The two friends then went back up to their room to pick up their things, each to head in different directions.

* * *

It was a couple of hours after sunset and Second Avenue was busy with the dirty light of vehicular traffic. Ideally Jane would have found a place before dark, but she wasn't thinking about that now. She was buzzed on the anticipation of being part of the scene in front of the Fillmore East; she was drawn to the crowd of ticket holders to that night's Doors concert, oblivious to anything but the floodlights at the theatre's entrance and the silhouettes of the crowd starting to gather before it. The east coast version of the Fillmore was brand new, and the venue was as much of a star as Jim Morrison was.

A block-long line had formed extending from the front door—a conglomeration of peacoats, scarves and bare, unruly heads. Jane viewed everyone from the curb with a mixture of excitement and dismay. She walked along the edge of the line, looking left and right distractedly, trying to gain equilibrium, trying to feel connected.

"Do you have a light?" she quickly turned to a young man halfway down the line, extending her Marlboro between her fingers in the direction of his. He and his friends didn't look that much older than she was and initiating a conversation with them felt easy.

"Do you guys live around here?" she asked after she lit her cigarette with his.

"Naah. Brooklyn."

"Bensonhurst."

"Oh," Jane said, disappointed. She turned as if she could scout an East Village denizen at a glance, but then slowly turned back to her new acquaintances.

"I kind of need to find a place to stay," she said as if thinking out loud "or I'll be in a lot of trouble."

The guys didn't have a response, so she took a drag on her cigarette to kill a minute's worth of time. Her companions subtly appraised her tall, weighted, Mediterranean beauty and made eye contact with each other.

"Why don't you guys live here, so you could offer me a place to stay? That would be neat," she laughed. "I don't know Brook-lyn."

"You going to see the Doors?" asked the curly-haired kid who had given her a light.

"Maybe," she smiled, and tapped some ashes to the sidewalk. "Someone probably has an extra ticket. You can get in if you know the right people. I bet the ticket takers live around here and know of a place to stay." But she continued to huddle where she was, trying to be part of the agglomerating crowd.

Jane jabbered for a while, amusing as well as intimidating her middle class audience of high school boys who would be taking the B train home to their parents after Jim Morrison sang his last pagan note of self-apotheosis. When the doors to the Fillmore were opened and the line began its sludge-like flow towards the entrance, Jane was part of it, volunteering to be pulled along by its centrifugal force, letting it give her momentary direction.

"Tickets," said the orange-sneakered ushers at the door. "Tickets." The crowd shuffled by, Jane glued to the boys from Bensonhurst. "Tickets please."

"What songs do you think they'll perform?" Jane was saying to Curly as they approached the door. "*Light My Fire*, of course. And *When the Music's Over* —"

"Tickets."

"Have you heard *The Unknown Soldier* yet? They've been play-ing it on 'N-E-W. It's their latest."

"You can't get in without a ticket."

Curly's group moved ahead, spreading towards the lobby.

"I'm with them! Hey!" she yelled ahead, "I'll catch up with you! Hold on," she said to the ticket taker, "can I move over here so I can look for my ticket?" she said pointing towards the door.

"Over here," was the reply, and she was hustled gently toward the curb. "Tickets."

"I can't find it!" she said, rustling through her shoulder bag. "My friends will be worried about me!"

Jane watched from the curb as the world of ticket holders

calmly disappeared behind the mammoth door. Hundreds of people with homes to go back to, some even in the East Village. She knew she'd let her attention stray from the job at hand, distracted by the chance of being at one with an electric moment, of being synchronized with all the other good angels in the good fight.

Jane wandered the streets around the Fillmore, deciding to revisit the scene in an hour or two, when she could try to catch up with Curly, or better yet, find someone older from nearby who would take her in. The narrow vestibules of the surrounding tenements were brightly lit and Jane entered one of them to keep warm. There were many Eastern European names on the letter boxes, unfriendly to casual pronunciation. She found the inside door wasn't locked and she entered the tired old building's stuccoed hallway. Near the rear she could see some stairs. Perhaps no one would mind if she sat on them for a while. She stationed herself along the wall, leaving room for people to pass, her shoulder bag resting on her lap. Then she took out her copy of "Coney Island of the Mind" to keep herself busy.

"Hello?" she heard in a deep phlegmy voice. She awoke to the sight of stem-like legs in tight blue jeans. Her forehead hurt from having used the stuccoed walls as a pillow.

"I'm sorry." She druggily started to shift her position, then she looked up and her heart jumped a beat. A giraffe with an Afro and facial features that looked unfinished was leaning over her. He looked like a young man with an old man's face, hawkish, sunken and pale.

"Are you OK?" he asked.

Jane was groggy, trying to regain some sort of mental balance and to find a past, present and future that would be the right fit.

"Oh, what time is it?!" She tried to get to her feet. "I've got to find a place for the night. I'm sorry," she repeated.

The man looked at Jane. Her long black hair was matted on

one side; she looked long-limbed and womanly in shape yet almost waif-like in expression. He thought he detected someone struggling mightily against gravity's pull. Kids like her had almost come to define the neighborhood recently.

"You a runaway? You need to eat something? I probably have something in my refrigerator."

All of his misshapenness looked friendly to Jane, a man who couldn't afford pretensions. *I'm hungry*, she thought to herself. She noticed the wire of tiny colored beads around his long neck. *I'm so tired.* His black high-top sneakers made her think of circus clowns. It made her feel safe.

She said, "OK. Thanks," as she pulled herself to her feet. Her steps echoed the creak of his as they went up the stairs.

He stopped and turned to her. "I'm Louis Paglia," he said and extended his hand.

"Jane," she said with an appreciative smile. "I'm Jane. Jane Cantore," and they shook hands.

"Cool," he said. "A *paisan*. Welcome to my humble village." He elicited a laugh from her and then continued his traipse to the uppermost floor of the building.

Upon entering his apartment, Louis flicked on the kitchen light. The apartment was unlike any apartment Jane had known in Yonkers: a series of small boxes all in a row, no doors between them. The kitchen light spilled into the adjacent room where she could see furniture that looked taken from the street. The distant rooms were shadowed. At the edge of the pool of light, Jane could make out the bottom of a curtain covering a doorway.

Louis took out cold slices of pizza from the refrigerator to warm up in the oven. Then he took her coat and left it somewhere in the darkness. She was going to be his dinner guest. She could hear him plop an LP onto a phonograph turntable, and as the harmonica shot out over the sound of guitar and dulcimer, Louis re-entered the room.

From out of his shirt pocket Louis produced a tiny manila envelope and some E-Z Rider rolling papers.

"Do you want some?" he asked as he sat next to Jane at his bare kitchen table.

Jane giggled. "Sure." She *really* wanted some, hoping the pot would make her feel relaxed, and help to turn her fight against gloom into some kind of rejuvenation. The music was sounding like an Indian raga now, pushing up under a piercing vocal duet, spreading its adrenaline into the kitchen.

The pot stoked their appetites and their conversation. The pizza was gloriously messy and Louis was funny, his ancient clown face italicizing his offbeat humor.

"What are you running away from, besides everything?" he asked wryly, exhaling a pungent waft of smoke.

"I have no place to live," said Jane as Louis handed her the joint. She inhaled the harshness and held it in her lungs. "My family fell apart," she said hoarsely on the exhale. "My mother died and my father . . ." Jane paused, trying to catch the words from the ambient smoke, finally deciding to go with: ". . . well, he disappeared. We don't know where he is. I ended up with my uncle and my older sister. And she's crazy. I mean *really*. She's *mental*. She controls everyone, especially my uncle. And she screams at me all the time. They don't give a damn about me. I couldn't take it anymore and so I went to live with my brother. He told me I had to either go back to my sister's or go to a foster home. His wife hates me," she added in explanation. Jane tried out a smile but it didn't work. "So I figured, 'Fuck them.'"

Louis' face looked blank. His rhythm was off, a couple of moments behind.

"Your father disappeared? Wow."

"All I know is no more lunatics to tell me what to do."

"No strings," said Louis. "Like Pinocchio."

Jane was glad Louis gave her an excuse to laugh.

"I used to love that movie!" she enthused.

"Hey, it changed *my* life." And then, in response to her blank stare, he half-sang "*'An actor's life for me!'*"

"You're an actor?! Really?"

He nodded. "I just came from rehearsals at La Mama."

Jane never heard of La Mama, but it sounded very exotic. This was the kind of company she wanted to keep: actors, artists, musicians, poets. People who could touch you without leaving a bruise.

"We're working on a piece called *Pig!*" Louis slowly continued. "It's about the Establishment. A little like the Living Theatre, you know."

Jane decided to let it seem like she did.

In the background, the eerie folk duet urged her to let typhoons lift her wings and rile her raven hair. It's preciousness made Jane giggle, Louis mistaking it for his own *bon mots*, when in fact the pot was giving everything around her equal claim to her attention, a carousel of distractions, all fascinating. She would intermittently clue back into their conversation, and Louis' echo chamber voice would become one of those distractions, sometimes separating itself in her mind from his words, words like "Grotowski," "absurd," "New Jersey." When the raucous music ended, a rush of silence cradled Louis' voice.

". . . stay the night. You can have my bed. I'll do the sleeping bag for tonight. . . ."

"Oh wow," she found herself saying, feeling disconnected from her own voice. ". . . That's so cool. . . . You don't mind . . .?"

The chairs roughly scraped the floor as they pulled away from the table. Louis then led her toward the front of the apartment still in darkness, flicked on a table lamp and pulled aside the curtain to reveal a small Spartan bedroom. When he turned to her, Jane noticed that the shadows under his eyes had crept further down his face.

"Well, goodnight, Jane Cantore. I'm going to slip into my cocoon and you slip into yours."

Jane brushed a lock of her raven hair behind her ear and nodded her head. She felt inadequate for some reason. All she could say was "OK" and then she threw Louis a smile. They stood awkwardly for a second and then Jane said goodnight and closed the curtain behind her.

She threw her bag alongside the bed and sat on its edge for a while. She looked out the window where the lampposts revealed a helter-skelter of sleepy tenements. It was quieter than the St. Mark's Hotel, with only the occasional breeze of car traffic and the echoing footsteps and subliminal voices of stray nighttime wanderers. From behind the curtains she heard the unzipping of the sleeping bag and then the sound of it being wrestled to submission.

Jane wrapped her arms around her waist to pull her maroon turtleneck up over her head. When relieved from its hold, she folded it neatly away in her bag and sat in her bra on the bed's edge holding her elbows. Then with a swift dive she pulled out a sweatshirt from her bag and threw it on over her head, quickly escaped from her bra and pulled the sweatshirt down. She left on her jeans but unbuttoned and unzipped them, left on her socks and got under the covers.

To the right of the small table lamp was a lavender, soft-covered book. "*The Theatre and its Double* by Antonin Artaud" it said. Jane flipped it open to discover photos of Artaud who looked like an emaciated, drug-addicted Svengali to her. And sometimes like a Romantic poet. She found him attractive and scary. She turned the book over. "We cannot go on prostituting the idea of the theater," the back cover quoted Artaud, "the only value of which is in its excruciating magical relation to reality and danger." She looked at the photos again. One with his eyes closed made her think of her Uncle Vito. She turned out the light.

She was dreaming of the Bronx, of walking through the cemetery where her mother was buried and finding none of the miles of gravestones had her mother's name on them, when she realized someone was in the room. He was sitting on the edge of the bed. It reminded her of her father standing outside the bedroom doorway when she and Virginia were tucked in for the night, how he would stand there staring into the darkness, looking at them for minutes at a time. *Mommy, daddy's scaring me!* she'd cry. Or Daddy leading Virginia into his bedroom each night after Mommy had died. The person on the bed moved closer. Jane felt a shadow envelop her.

"Do you want to fuck?" he asked softly when she opened her eyes.

It was Louis' voice.

She didn't answer at first. Was this expected? she wondered. Will he kick me out if I don't want to?

"I'm sleepy . . ." she mumbled.

"Let's fuck," he whispered. His head was near her pillow now, blocking out the street lights. She slid suddenly away from him.

"I'm . . ." She froze. She didn't attempt to finish the sentence, preferring this suspended moment of silence.

"What?" Louis finally said, jolting her from her sleepy spiral down.

"I'm . . ." she whispered on the faintest of breaths, "a virgin."

"Are you afraid?"

She nodded her head, and then realized he might not be able to see that.

"Uh huh."

"I can be gentle," he pleaded softly.

And then, in a plaintive whisper, she said "Do we have to?"

She heard him sigh.

Then it was quiet for a long time. She could see the outline of his long body and the pale light on his white jockey shorts. Finally she saw him stand up and slowly disappear from sight.

The room had a grayish blue cast when she awoke. All was illuminated; every item in the room now had outlines: the engraved wood on the side of the bed stand, the Gauguin poster, the chest of drawers painted black. Jane sat up in bed expectantly. The apartment sounded clean of any activity. She wondered if

Louis was up yet. She imagined him meditating cross-legged on his sleeping bag, still in his jockey shorts. She waited for her new life to approach her, or at least part the curtains. When it didn't, she approached *it*.

The apartment was free of shadows – light and airy. Louis' sleeping bag was nowhere to be found and the same went for Louis himself. Jane felt a little disappointed. It would be fun to wake up to Louis' outrageous companionship, have breakfast together like old friends. Instead, she had to settle for the company of a note on the kitchen table with two keys laid on it.

Jane, it said, *I have to work on Saturdays. Take what you want from the fridge. After you lock the doors when leaving, please place the keys under the doormat. Thanks. L.*

Jane walked to the refrigerator in a trance and opened it. It was mostly empty but here and there were a few edible items. She took a pita bread from its opened wrapper and then found a plastic container with a brownish spread in it, smelling of garlic. She walked it over to the kitchen table, and using a butter knife she found in Louis' silverware drawer, spread the messy concoction on the bread. After she had licked her fingers clean, she walked into the next room where she found a number 2 pencil on Louis' desk. She pulled the kitchen chair under her and then, in a very neat handwriting, wrote a few words on the bottom of Louis' note, bracing herself over the page like a schoolgirl.

Dear Louis, she wrote. *Thank you so much for your hospitality.* Then she drew a peace sign and added *and love*, signing it *from your friend, Jane.*

P.S., she added. *I hope I didn't hurt your feelings.* Then she decorated the page with a viny flower.

She emerged from the dark hallway of Louis' building into the clear light of a brisk March Saturday morning. She walked down Louis' street relishing the new day of her adventure. She felt her first day without her friends had been a success: she had made a connection with a stranger without bringing catastrophe upon herself. This validated her theory that her life would be better as a runaway than at home with her sister, that sanity was a lot more abundant outside of her family home.

She walked east, enthused with the idea of finding Allen Ginsberg. She'd look out for people who she could imagine as part of his crowd and follow them or maybe ask them if they knew where he lived. She bet she could count on him to take her under his wings or at the very least take interest in her plight. Last night with Louis had been a kind of warm-up for this: for getting along with anyone she came in contact with.

It also taught her that she might be considered desirable. Years ago, way before she had found over-the-counter diet pills, her father had told her that she would never find a husband, so the two of them would have to live together forever, taking care of each other. And until now, she had believed him: she was unlovable. But today she knew that, at the very least, someone could want to *make* love to her, and it made her feel rich to think about it.

She eventually found herself back on St. Mark's Place, after having found many people who looked like they would know Allen Ginsberg. Someone told her he lived on East 10th Street, but pacing back and forth along 10th had not borne fruit. On St. Mark's there was, as usual, a lot of activity. Across the street from her, around the corner from the Gem Spa soda fountain on Second Avenue, an older blonde teenage boy sat on the low stoop of one of the buildings, a big floppy hat upended on the ground in front of him, set up for spare change. From the distance, his bony figure reminded her of the Kinks' Ray Davies, her favorite musical performer after Bob Dylan. The boy seemed indifferent to the passersby, huddled in a long threadbare coat and scarf, with a cigarette dangling from his long thin fingers and his lank hair falling diagonally over his face, curtaining him from the neighborhood traffic.

Jane watched him from across the street for around fifteen minutes before she built up the nerve to approach him.

"Hi," she said. "Is it OK if I share the stoop with you?" He looked up at her and watched her impassively. "I've been walking around all morning, looking for this friend of mine," she said, embellishing the facts.

He nodded his head as if granting her permission to curtsy, then looked away as she sat down.

Jane opened her carrying bag and went scrounging through its contents. After a few minutes of that, she stopped, frustrated in her search, and sat with the bag on her lap.

"You don't have an extra cigarette by any chance?" she finally asked her companion.

He lifted his cigarette hand as a visual aid, saying laconically, "I merely have this one."

"Oh," she said, wondering if he was British.

"Oh, wait. Here's one," she said, pouncing upon a slightly bent, lint-covered runaway that had fled its box of Marlboros to hide in a fold at the bottom of her bag. "Could I get a light?" she asked as she labored to re-shape it with her fingers.

She took his extended cigarette and assiduously mated it to her own until its orange tip crackled.

"Thanks," she said upon returning it. She hugged her knees and then turned fully towards him.

"I'm Jane."

He didn't respond. Then he looked out at her from behind his veil of hair. Jane thought his eyes showed a whisper of interest.

"What's your name?" she continued.

"Tony," he replied. He covered his face with his hand, fingers outstretched, so as to take a drag of his cigarette. A passerby dropped a quarter in his hat and Tony responded with a flick of his hand in thanks. Jane thought, *I wonder if that guy thought we were together.*

And for now, that thought made it so. She basked in the confidence it gave her and tossed her hair back like a trapeze artist waiting for the bar to swing in her direction. Everything was focused on the moment, calmly, clearly with exactness. The future spread wide open before her, like Cinerama; the late winter day like spring.

"What a beautiful day, man!" she said. Tony looked at her, then quickly cast his eyes down, bearing an invisible expression on his face. Jane's heart went out to him. He sat, she thought, like the burden of angel wings lay heavily on his shoulders.

Jane looked around her. All that was visible was the sunshine, the innate optimism of pedestrian activity, the flowering youthfulness of the neighborhood, the promising jingle-jangle of days to come. She knew in her heart that, although love is all you need, in the interim she could get by with a little help from an endless horizon of new friends she would make.

She took a drag from her cigarette, closed her eyes and leaned her head back. Warm, persistent sunlight tried to worm its way into the darkness under her lids and kinescopes of all manner of demented, furious and bloody angels flickered, threatening to materialize. But she blew them away with a stream of smoke that slowly kissed the white sky above St. Mark's Place. And then she waited—hungrily, languorously— to be kissed back.

III

Long Ride Home

We needed to get to Einstein as soon as possible. I was weak, feverish and I couldn't catch my breath. My body was too big for me, it was suffocating me. I wasn't eating food anymore, but I continued to expand. Dr. Koenig had explained that the cancer cells were sending false signals to my normal ones, leading them to believe that I was dehydrating. In response, they turned their spigots on and never turned them off. My body was flooding itself.

Ed got the car while I sat on the bench in our building's foyer. I looked through the glass doors for the smudge of blue ink to drive up into view. I was a big fish in a giant fish bowl. I was drowning.

The car glided into view and Ed popped out. He strode purposefully down the path to the entrance of the building and met me halfway, grabbing me by the elbow to lend support. He put his other arm around my back as if he could shovel me out. I'm not steady on my feet, I go slowly as quickly as I can. I am afraid. The world is smothering me.

I can barely sit in my precious, baby-new Passat. I cannot bare to be strapped in. My expensive gift to myself is now swallowing me. I can't breathe. I sit forward in the passenger's seat, bracing one hand against the top of the windshield, trying to drink the air from the view before me. Ed tries to keep the drive fast and smooth so I don't get killed. I exhale little pats of breath. I don't say Ed's name the way I want to: I want him to help me, but he already is, there is nothing to say. I won't distract him so he will get us there as quickly as this bubble with car smells possibly can.

Ed finally pulls up the long driveway to Einstein's emergency room; it feels as long as the driveway for Xanadu in *Citizen Kane* that curves endlessly up to the mansion, passing giraffes and zebras along the way. I am the celebrity that gets out to visit Mr. Kane. No camera lights to greet me, just God's, His bulbs flashing like crazy. I sit in the waiting room, high on my ass like a queen in exile, while Ed runs to move the car to a parking spot. I am big, I take up room, trying not to breathe too hard. I stare blankly. I don't see anything but the flash of those lightbulbs all around me and then they call my name and Ed is back and he leads me to the emergency room, where the nurses draw curtains around me and nurse me with tubes of cool air.

I agreed with Ed that the best place for me, considering the circumstances, was Calvary Hospital, just across the way from Einstein. I had watched it from my hospital window every day and so, after he convinced me it was the way to go, it felt in hindsight like it had been inevitable. Ed told me about the discussions with Dr. Koenig, who had disappeared on me for some reason I don't understand, and how I had been delirious and physically out of control most of the time, and that I was still strong enough to create havoc without meaning to. I was surprised. I still don't remember this. It makes me laugh to think of how much mischief I must have caused, how it must have firmed up my reputation for trouble, but it saddened and embarrassed me, too. I don't like the idea of being loony bin material. And I hate to cause Ed problems. I've learned the hard way that home is where Ed is, and Ed looks like he's in a state of disrepair. Have I robbed him of his color, his *joie de vivre*, his health? I want Ed to be happy, with me in his arms, the two of us entwined. I want him to feel he *could* take care of me and that he *did*. I want to die in the middle of a love story, holding hands with Ed, like Rex Harrison and Gene Tierney in *The*

Ghost and Mrs. Muir, and one day, after he's lived a long, pleasant life, he meets me in heaven. But I don't want to be what kills him, and he's looking terrible. So we agreed that my coming home would not work, and in a few days I would cross Eastchester Avenue and drive up to the building with the large golden crucifix over its front door.

And then the day arrives. It feels so momentous. I imagine myself starting anew in a stately sunny room, finally given succor to by Catholic mothers and sisters in sweeping, embracing floor-length habits. They'll dote, they'll smile, they'll touch my forehead with the backs of their hands. They'll pray for me. This will be where all the orphans and runaways go, not at the start of their tragedies, but at the end . . . who would've thought? . . . when cancer would bring us home to the blandishments of soft-spoken Ingrids and delicate Audreys of the Bronx.

I'm moved ceremoniously into a wheelchair. An attendant navigates me to the elevator and then down in it, Ed alongside carrying my odds and ends. We are as quiet as items on an assembly line, and as numb. I sit wide-eyed, not knowing what to be nervous about, there could be so much to choose from, but everything is orderly, part of the routine of transfer from hospital to cancer care, part of a process, and a process is something that keeps on going—a life of a sort—so that I could not really see anything resembling an ending. This would be just another stay, was all I could imagine, with tubes of oxygen and nurses in hallways and food menus and meds for pain and a day with no night and night with no day, just sleeping and waking. I can do that.

I'm elevated into the ambulance, methodically strapped in place. We drive across the street and, with business-like fuss, I'm dislodged from the Good Humor truck and wheeled into the Cancer Hotel, modern and corporate and clean. *I will die in a dorm room*, I realize when they wheel me to my bed, and I'm overcome with a sense of dread. I hunger for cool air for my brain, for the room to have breath to lend me. The hospital décor—sterile as gauze—has no breath to give, only a tiny golden statue of a crucified Jesus hanging on the wall, and a large overhead television set. This is wrong.

I want my home back. I want my windows with their north-eastern light bluing the living room, sprinkling my spider plant with little showers of sun. I want color: upholstery color, art color, tree color. I want space to breathe in the vistas from our balcony. I want the spray of children's voices in the nearby schoolyards. I want domain. I have none of it here. I try to be patient. I'm confused, the weeks have gone like a whirl—I can't recall them through the pain and then the drugs to smother the pain, but this can't be right. I am alert, I can think and, through the doorway, I can see other patients, sicker than I am, frailer, older. I'm in a way station for the dying, a quiet, gentle one, but it's not home, and I'm not ready to die. *I might have months yet! Months!*

I make the best of it. Every morning, my brother Ray sits by my side, dependable in a way no family member has ever been before. He tells me I'm in a good place and Ed will always make sure I'm well taken care of. Then we reminisce, always about the unimportant things, the important ones being so thorny, so hurt-ful, too potentially divisive. We both tread delicately to avoid any tear in the fabric of our new relationship. Then Ed comes in around lunch time and my two men attend to me for a while before Ray leaves. And then I'm with Ed until the evening. With Ed, I feel home but not home, like we're in the wrong movie, and I tell him so. He looks pained and confused, and then, on the second day, he tells me he agrees with me. The night before he had seen the old woman across the hall, lying emaciated, her mouth open like a black butterfly net trying futilely to catch some air. This was no place for Jane to spend the remaining months of her life, he'd thought. I'm jubilant. I know for sure that, after all these years, a lifetime of both love and discord, of an ecstatic struggle to survive as a couple in the late twentieth century, my husband loves me. I'll always have his long, long arms around wide, wide me. I can count on sitting comfortably in the passenger seat, chauffeured by my driver, my husband, my love. I'll have the time to tell him whatever I needed to. I'll be in our home. We'll be together. We'll get a hospital bed and put it in the living room, so I can look over my sixth floor universe, my own personal Manhattan skyline. When I awake from my opium sleep, I will hear the raindrops on the window or the brassy avian chorus of a morning, the heavy silken chimes on the balcony. I'll be where I need to be.

During the days, while Ed has been making all the arrangements, I've been experiencing a strange—perhaps inappropriate—optimism, like in my heart now I know that I can handle what lies ahead. I can handle my body's struggle, I can handle this demise. I have a burst of renewed energy, and one day, Ed and my friend Marcie take me down in the wheelchair to a party that Calvary has in a room near their courtyard garden. Ed wheels me past the sky-lit garden into a club room with many tables. The room is filled with patients and their families. Hospital workers bring little ice cream Dixie cups to each table and I dare to let the cream touch my mouth. In the center of the room, a middle-aged man sings Italian folksongs, the kind my grandfather sang back in the Bronx over forty years ago. Patients around me swoon with nostalgia or because they are comforted by his beautiful tenor. I, too, am comforted. I can tell my face is beaming. Marcie looks sweetly at me, and Ed, poor Ed, tries to surreptitiously wipe tears from the corner of his eyes. I close my eyes and let the notes take me. Soon enough I forget that I'm not the one who's singing them.

I allow my mind to wander two days ahead, when Ed will pick me up in my beautiful blue Passat. I'll be regally wheeled over to Calvary's front doors, which will glide open and deposit me in front of my little automotive jewel, my expensive plaything. Ed'll leave the driver's seat and walk around to help me in, like a father tucking his daughter into a luxurious, comfortable bed on wheels. And then, as we traverse the highways of the Bronx, I'll treat my handsome husband in my beautiful blue Passat to my own childlike serenade.

> I'm go-ing home . . .
> I'm go-ing home . . .
> I'm go-ing home . . .

Our old '53 Dodge, the big, gray, comfy cloud, low to the ground with the weight of family, keeps coming back for me. A vision driving right up from the past, it stares at me with its windshield eyes over its fat friendly cheeks, waiting for me to hop into the back seat so we can get going and split this sepulchral joint.

"Janie, don't make us wait any longer," my mother shouts from the open window of the passenger seat, the fingers of both her hands splayed like little Chinese fans against the door exterior.

We're going for a ride! We're going for a ride! I sing to myself. I want to scurry out the front door with my little chubby legs. I can't get there soon enough.

The car is big and round and womblike, and I, of course, am so small that I experience it as a kind of play room on wheels. There are no seat belts; I can stand up on the seat to look out the back window and lean my whole body into the rear alcove if my older brother and sister give me enough room. Sometimes all three of us will stare out, watching the Bronx drive away from us on our way, say, to James Baird State Park, where we'll picnic with the rest of the family, or to Villa Barbieri for a week or two in the Catskills.

Some mothers might call out "Janie, no standing on the seat!" but my mother is a master at benign neglect; if you fell on your rear end, you'd learn from the experience. Later on—when I won't forgive her for dying way before we can take care of ourselves—I'll look back at this kind of thing and think it meant she didn't care if I died in a horrible accident or not, it's one more example that proves she was a terrible, terrible mother. But I think now that she was just too overwhelmed with all of the family's problems, and actually thought that of the whole trouble-some crew, I was the one she had to worry about least, that I was the one most resilient and most likely to survive life's many bounces. That, and that she wasn't perfect.

I was probably first brought home from the hospital in the Dodge, but, naturally, I don't remember that. But I do remember that, for a while, I was the one privileged to sit on Mommy's lap in the front seat if Daddy was driving. When I get too big for that, sitting in the back seat with Ray and Virginia will feel like banish-ment from favored status, which I'll never have again or at least that's how it seems. I spend so much time trying to get Mom's attention, but all it does is boomerang on me. The clearer I make it that I need her, the more annoyed she is. She likes it best when I walk in, tell her what interesting thing I've done and then go on to my own devices. She has enough on her hands keeping Daddy and Ray from fighting and dealing with Virginia's screaming fits and grand mal seizures.

In the Dodge things are calmer. For one thing, Daddy is far away from Ray and Virginia, up front in the driver's seat, with Ray sitting in the back seat at the furthest remove from him. The back of the front seat serves as some kind of Maginot line, and we can drive somewhere in peace and quiet. *I'm* not very quiet. Just like now, I babble away about everything that interests me, re-peating pieces of information I learn from watching Grandpa—who lives downstairs from us—putter around his workroom in the garage, or reciting numbers in Italian he's taught me, or telling Mom that I need a pony to play with really badly. Some-times they'd have the radio on with William B. Williams and the Make Believe Ballroom, but in the summertime, peace is assured by listening to the Yankee game. Occasionally, Daddy and Ray will even cheer at the same time before they'll catch themselves, remember how much they hate each other and go back to their tense, sulky stand-off.

Other times, we sit quietly as Mom and Dad talk in Italian. That means they're discussing something serious, and Daddy's saying something you shouldn't say in front of children; later I will realize it was probably along the lines of a firm conviction of his that Uncle Frankie's daughter is giving her brothers blow jobs, but at the time, I just wonder if they're discussing putting us all in orphanages: Ray and Virginia for Daddy's sake, and me— maybe—for Mom's?

The best car trips are when Mom takes the three of us to Villa Barbieri without Daddy, who joins us only on the weekend. Everything is carefree, light as a feather, Mom sounding so affectionate that even *I* can't do anything wrong in her eyes. That's when driving in our fat, gray cloud feels the most like heaven. We arrive at the bungalow colony, greeted by all our aunts and cousins away from the uncles for a few days, and we run around the pool and eat hamburgers off the grill with macaroni and Coca Cola, and play cowboys and Indians around the driveways and gardens, hiding behind Uncle Vito and Aunt Connie's big black Cadillac, Frankie and Marie's maroon DeSoto, and our powder puff Dodge, as if they were the Badlands of South Dakota. I'm really fond of shooting cousin Bobby because he revels in his death scenes, falling to the grass in fine expressions of tortured ecstasy, which makes me laugh, and he does that often because I'm the baby of all the cousins and he likes to make "the baby" laugh.

The Olds, uninvited, stealthily pulls up before me, as if it devoured the Dodge whole. Certainly, it could have. It was a big, dark green shark of a car, its rear fins stretching to eternity, its snoot stretching out equally far in the other direction. It was like Daddy's weapon. Especially on the highway, as he barreled past all other vehicles on the road, flaunting his power and, I suppose, his impatience. One good thing was that we could each maintain an even greater distance from each other in its sprawling interior. I could spread out my drawings that came with my Venus Paradise colored pencils if I wanted to. I liked having things to occupy myself with at all times around the family. That way I could avoid hearing what sounded like the tearing of an electric saw that ran beneath us like a current.

The car was so spacious that I could curl up in the rear window space and take a nap. Sometimes, rather than get a baby sitter, Mom and Dad would take me along with just the two of them to the Whitestone Drive-In where they would see the movies that weren't family films while I slept in the window. Then I might wake up in the middle of these turgid black and white movies and see all these adults in meaningless anguish, crying and hitting each other, smashing glasses, driving convertibles at night into trees, running down corridors in straitjackets, and these images became indelibly tied in my mind with my parents, being the rare times I would catch sight of them when they thought they were all alone. It captured something about what I understood in those days as the really unhappy way that grownups were tied to each other.

Daddy loved the Olds; it had size and prestige, and was shiny like a Sinatra LP.

"Janie, you want me to teach you to drive?" he asked me the first summer we took it to Villa Barbieri. I was seven years old then.

"Yes, Daddy!" I had squealed, unable to contain my excitement. It was just the two of us, and he had taken me with him to pick up some groceries in Ellenville and we'd just returned. There was a flattened field which served as a parking lot in the bungalow colony where guests could park their cars. It was pretty empty that weekend, and he invited me to sit on his lap and grasp the big white steering wheel with both hands. He would accelerate the car slowly and tell me to steer, holding me tightly in place with his big hands anchoring me by my hips. It would take some heavy lifting for me to turn the wheel in those pre-power steering days, but there was no turning really necessary anyway, I just shifted the stiff thin wheel side to side in quick little shimmies. Eventually, I noticed that Daddy's fingers were squeezing me near the bottom of my panty line and when I shifted in his lap, I felt a part of him poking me, like some kind of puppet, which struck me as kind of funny at first except for the fact that he was hurting me holding me so tight.

"Daddy!" I complained, squirming around in his embrace.

He said he was sorry, but he didn't relax his grip, and I sat there kind of blank, holding onto the wheel without moving it. Daddy breathed deeply like he was sleeping but he was very much awake and I was confused and so I started to cry, and then I realized Daddy had been rocking me ever so slightly, because now it stopped, and his hands relaxed on my lap. It was really, really quiet, like the sound of the kitchen after the refrigerator hum goes to sleep.

"What are you crying about?" he pleaded softly. "Stop that! I let you drive, so why are you so cranky? Wasn't I nice to you? Wasn't I?"

And he was, he had been very nice, it's just that the car was the stinky green color of poison, the color of those bottles in the medicine cabinet that you weren't allowed to touch, the ones with dark, foul liquids inside them.

"I want candy," I said mournfully.

Years later, when Virginia and I lived in New Rochelle with Daddy after cancer took Mom and Ray had married Tina, the big green Oldsmobile kept guard over us like a dragon parked in front of the house. Daddy had very strict rules about us leaving the house after school and on weekends. Because he wanted to terrorize Virginia into staying at home so she couldn't make out with her boyfriend, he would come home on his break from whatever construction site he worked on and lock us in. I was too afraid to try to escape, but not Virginia. Sometimes she climbed out of the bedroom window and I would plead for her not to go, because I knew Daddy would hold *me* responsible for allowing *her*—four years older than me—to get away, but I had no control over her at all. In fact, she sometimes would convince me to join her, and I wouldn't enjoy myself for a second, knowing the beating that awaited us when we got home. But I couldn't seem to help myself. I think I didn't want to be home alone when Daddy returned.

One Saturday morning when he had left early for one of his weekend shifts, I woke up to hear Virginia screaming in hysterics. Her voice sounded far away, and it took me awhile to realize she was not in the house. I ran outside in my nightgown and she was standing out on the lawn, shrieking her fucking head off, and I could hear the sounds of windows opening along the block as people wanted to see what the fuss was all about. She was looking at the big, green, shiny behemoth parked where it usually was. It looked like Daddy was just sitting there—not moving—in the driver's seat, even though Virginia was carrying on like a banshee. It was almost scarier that Daddy hadn't come out to smack her across the face for waking the neighborhood, and just sat like a lump as if he was sleeping in the front seat. And suddenly I realized Daddy was all shadow, strangely indistinct, and I gasped when I saw it wasn't Daddy at all. He had tied and folded pillows and blankets and wrapped his jacket around it so that from a distance it suggested he was sitting in the fortress car, watching over us. If Virginia hadn't left the house, we might have presumed it was him all day until he'd gotten home later that afternoon, dropped off by a co-worker. I pleaded with Virginia to come back inside, and she eventually moderated her cries to a whimper, and we left "Daddy" to sleep in his murderous, psycho car.

And now here comes Uncle Al's black Buick. Maybe it was a year or two older than Daddy's, because it was a little rounder, less aggressive, kind of like Uncle Al. Things felt a lot safer after we were placed with Uncle Al, but for the four years I lived with him and Virginia, it never felt like a home to me; I was "visiting" for four years in the home he made with Virginia. Now that she didn't have Daddy to fear, Virginia dominated the household. She was as much of a holy terror in her way as Daddy had been, but instead of it being physical, it was vocal. She screamed, she whined, she pouted, she cooed. It had more of an effect on Uncle Al than it did on me, but even I couldn't resist her all the time. It was just like when she escaped Daddy's house and got me to follow. That kind of seduction happened in Yonkers, too, but as her behavior went further and further over the top it had less and less of the desired effect on me, until she got so out of control that I just had to get away.

When Uncle Al drove, the Buick felt like a big fat barge float-ing down the Bronx River Parkway; it was heavy and steady, even stately, and it even had these little portholes on the side of the hood as part of its insignia. But when Virginia was old enough to drive, it was like an outsized motorboat skipping along the top of the waves. She drove furiously, which I was used to because Daddy drove the same way, but that doesn't mean it didn't feel dangerous. It's just that danger had been ever-present so I had learned to make myself numb to it. Only the thrill of the speed was left, and when Virginia—eighteen years old, hair teased and dyed blonde in the sharp style of the early sixties, eyes lined in black— zoomed us along, it felt crazy (like her), but crazy and *cool*, and so I, at fourteen, was cool, too—at least for those mo-ments in the car. What was even cooler was her speeding along the parkway and getting her grand mal seizures. As she would start to elevate out of consciousness, her foot would lift off the gas pedal and the car would slow to a coast, sliding off the road onto the shoulder. I'd be screaming and trying to steer the wheel with one hand from the passenger seat. She would be able to sense it coming on beforehand enough to know she had to pull over, but she was never in full control, and somehow, she managed not to kill us both, though luck and traffic and where we were on the highway had something to do with that. Then we would just sit and wait for her to get back her focus; the cars would whoosh on by and I would sit blank and helpless. The worst would always be before the car had come to a stop: if I struggled with her to try to prevent her from swallowing her tongue—a trick I had been performing with pencils since I was around five—I could've contributed to an accident, so passive was the only way for me to go there.

My life was still in the hands of mental cases and I did the best I could to spend as much time with my real family—my friends— as I could. Raised by "crazies" of varying kinds as we were, we were all compatibly fucked up in our different ways and had been self-medicating since we were thirteen. In their company, my sister, my uncle, my brother, the Buick, all of Yonkers, could seem like anachronisms.

Until they actually were. Anachronisms. When they no longer had any bearing on my everyday life. Via buses and trains taking me to the East Village, I zoomed into this unnervingly exhilarating freedom, bypassing any transitions to independence and adult- hood, determined to unlock—and bolt from—all doors that closed me in. I was alive and young and stupidly fearless, and so, so happy to find myself lost in the delirium of my new neighbor- hood, at one with the big city, desired—even romanticized—by men, and there was no reason not to give in to whatever beck- oned. The only cure for captivity was a furious hedonism. No one could tell me what to do! *No one!*

Certainly not Tony. Somewhere, if I searched hard in my cat- alogue of memories, I could probably find a week or two of feeling in love with him. I had landed myself a pretty, older boy, something that would have seemed impossible in my high school universe. The quiet, discerning hipster I found on a St. Marks street corner, who seemed to tolerate me well enough in bed to invite me to share his squatter's space, turned into this supercili- ous control freak when he wasn't having psychotic episodes on LSD seeing Jesus in every corner of the abandoned tenement on East 11th and Avenue A, through the broken floor slats or scurry- ing with the rats—Jesus night sweats would keep me up all night which I quickly tired of. And then, the next day, the juice having washed through him, he walked distantly among us, blessing the world with the aloofness Jesus must have shown him. I tired of him and he tired of me, enough so that if he aroused me at night, I'd wake up furious in the morning, feeling like confronting his opaque iciness with some good old-fashioned plate throwing, which I only came close to once—after he'd spent the previous evening at a party courting a new prospective disciple while sitting right next to me—but before I got to the point of reaching for a breakable, he just walked out and never came back, leaving his make-shift apartment completely in my hands.

Although now free of yet one more jerk, I soon realized three new things that had the potential to compromise my newfound liberation. One was the news passed along the grapevine that someone had bought the building we had squatted in, meaning the days in my free apartment were numbered. The second was that, in the meantime, I didn't feel a hundred percent safe in the abandoned structure, even if everyone else squatting there knew me. And finally, I hadn't had my period in over two months.

I still felt so empowered by having no one to answer to that all of these risk factors merely seemed part of the grand open-ended adventure to me. Being homeless, vulnerable and pregnant was a step up from being locked up, bruised, screamed at and neglected by the people who were supposed to take care of me. Not having to answer to anyone made up for all these complications.

There had been this frisky, puppyish guy who had attached himself to our crowd of free-floating misfits named Barry who would hover around me whenever he could, and now that I was unattached, I found his attentions easy and welcome. I took him home the next night after Tony left and, appreciating his playfulness relative to Tony's withholding charisma, allowed him to make plans that included me in his future. Right now, any direction seemed as good as any other, my universe being the blank page that it was.

* * *

I had hoped, when I'd accompanied Barry by bus back to his mother's home in Woodstock, that I was leaving New York City for a secure roof over my head, at least for a while. He was willing to give living with his mother another chance if she'd take us both in as a couple, and he seemed sure that in her regret at throwing him out of the house for his pot-smoking, she would be willing to do so. Although Woodstock had already begun to develop some of its now-fabled notoriety, it was still mostly a poor rural town like most of the Catskills, and Barry's mother, being a hard-scrabble townie, ended up assenting only grudgingly to a situation she clearly disapproved of. There was one condition: that I sleep in Barry's brother's former room and not with Barry.

Each morning we'd watch from the kitchen table as Mrs. Bullock prepared for her job driving around local roads delivering mail, knowing that we had a full day ahead of us to smoke our joints, listen to records, and indulge ourselves in the way teenagers can even in meager surroundings like the Bullock home. Since all of Barry's friends were still in school, we spent most of our time together until the late afternoon, whatever personality quirks of the other that irritated us usually smoothed over by the hermetic bonding induced by secretly getting stoned and then getting into Barry's brother's bed together.

Mrs. Bullock seemed to look at me the way my best friends' parents had in Yonkers, as if I was the only reason their children were straying from the path of virtue. On the contrary, we had all connected because we were all compelled in the same direction to begin with, the only difference being that I had no parents to plead with me to reform my degenerate ways. In any case, there was no love lost between Mrs. Bullock and me, and that only worsened after Barry and I'd lost track of the time one afternoon, hungrily chasing connection behind his brother's bedroom door only to find an ashen Mrs. Bullock standing in the hallway when we were through.

The next day, when Barry's mother said she no longer wanted me around the house, Barry got into another fight with her. When it was over, Mrs. Bullock was without her son again. This time, instead of finding his way down to New York, where we'd both connected as East Village runaways, he led me around to the junk-ridden field behind his mother's house where his older brother kept his decrepit Chevy Nova, and, since his brother was off in Vietnam, no one prevented him—even though he was still only sixteen—from driving me out of Woodstock into its surrounding woods.

The woods had grown a community of old Chevys and the like, inhabited by disenfranchised young dropouts. Each of us was parked a respectable distance from the other for privacy, but close enough to gather in different cars in which to smoke dope. At that early point, Barry was still infatuated with me, not minding that I was in my early stages of pregnancy by Tony. My life, as ramshackle, you could say, as my upbringing had been, contributed to my ability to acclimate myself to the ramshackleness of living in a community of old run-down cars. They were cheap relics from the early part of the decade or older, with worn—sometimes patched—upholstery and a casual litter of effects throughout. I didn't carry very much, but I had accumulated a few changes of clothes over the months in the East Village and now I kept them in Barry's trunk, changing my clothes in the early morning hours, using the Nova as my dressing screen. There was a fierce, treacherous stream not too far away to wash up in—it was very cold in May, I remember—and it was a good place for me to hang out and read when I wanted to get away from Barry. It was also a good place to meet the other discards, mostly young, rural guys with nervous airs they tried to cover up with stonedness. I got along swimmingly with all of them, the pot and acid keeping me laughing obligingly, and, as Barry and I started drifting apart, he re-assessed our relationship, I suppose, and left me stranded in an upstate forest with Mike, Davey and Gunther.

Mike and the gang lived in a freaky two-tone: a white and orange Chevy, a model, they said, that had been discontinued after one year. Everything about its design seemed wrong, as if it's designer had misjudged the direction that the decade was heading in: it seemed to want to continue the bloatedness of the fifties. The stale, heavy breath of pot and cigarette smoke tried to cover the old car smell and the dank mixture of what I guess would've been B.O. and beer. When the rain or evening darkness drew us indoors, we'd sprawl inside the vehicle, some of us leaning on the windows with our legs casually interlacing, and we'd listen to music on a portable radio around as big as a paperback book, not using the car radio so as to save the battery as much as possible.

The living conditions now being more crowded (and even shabbier) than in Barry's car, we sometimes slept on blankets on the ground, like kids in a nursery taking a nap, all huddled together back to front. In this particular nursery, though, this childlike intimacy led to arousal, and pretty early on I happily acquiesced to furtive nighttime advances by Mike, while Davey and Gunther either slept or pretended to.

Mike was the car's driver as well as the group's nominal leader. The car being his gave him a certain amount of power. If Davey or Gunther wanted to do some kind of transaction in town (which could range from scoring or selling drugs, to stealing junk food and reading material), Mike had to be in the mood. Davey, the slightly slyer personality of the gang, seemed to be in charge of the dealing and, consequently, the keeper of our stash of grass, pills and tabs of assorted chemical composition. Gunther was the most eccentric: reedy, bookish and terribly amused by whatever internal dialogue he was unable to share easily. He had a funny habit of nodding his head, as if he was marking the rhythm to an inaudible song. If there was any reason to not feel totally comfortable with these guys, I was too stoned to notice.

We were all gloriously damaged, and happily trapped in the eternal present, with no future imaginable. The others in the group, being older—and maler—than me, all had the draft and Vietnam hanging over their heads. Mike and Davey were overdue to pay the draft board a visit, but dared their draft notice to find their address in the woods. Gunther was still seventeen. All of them were determined, should they ever have to report, to be tripping their brains out at their physical rather than be fodder for the military industrial complex. We were part of the growing army of the disaffected—in our particular cases we were also the products of working class domestic battlefields, the offspring of the dead, the jailed, the alcoholic and the psychotic. We never talked about this exactly, at least not all together; our usual mode was energized party laughter and urgent revelatory insights, the celebration of the cosmos and the absurdities of civilization's detritus. If someone were to ramble into our area of the woods some night, we would sound like the vocal equivalents of twigs popping in a campfire, youthful bursts of exclamation points.

The Chevy was my home, and the guys my roommates, for about two or three months. The dusty gray dashboard décor, the car mats littered with Coke cans, Miller cans and old newspapers, the lazy guttural sound of guys on all sides of me, the boniness of male bodies, the running current of the radios' high treble rock and roll, these were the textures of spring 1968 for me. When my belly started getting bigger with Luke, though, we all started getting nervous; no one wanted to handle that. So one rainy May day, we all took the engine-groaning ride to town so that I could get the bus back to the city and the Catholic Home for Unwed Mothers, where we presumed this future mother could get a little mothering of her own for a change. I really loved the way my belly felt, so ripe with baby, and I wanted a baby badly. I had so much more than just sex to give away and babies are beautiful things. I'd been godmother to Ray's little baby girl, and she was such a burst of pink, detailed tininess, with little fuzzy black hair and a voice that spoke directly from the source—her heart? God?—whatever that well of pure feeling comes from—and I was really happy to be having one of my own. Still, I felt sad leaving the guys—*my* guys—because as stupid as they could be some-times, it was a stupidity I was OK with. It wasn't just tripping in the woods and the way the pokey sunshine sometimes danced to Jimi Hendrix; it wasn't just the attention I was getting from their happy-as-a-puppy boners—for after a while I had fun with Davey as well; it was the sense of eternal freedom which would now be restricted by the concrete realities of life in the city and having to go through the initial loneliness of starting friendships from scratch. And perhaps, as well, that I knew the center could not hold.

"Stay stoned, guys!" I said cheerfully to them when I was ready to get out of the car.

"Peace!" said Davey, very casually, like we had just had a friendly conversation in a bus station instead of three months up close and personal. They all looked like mere acquaintances and perhaps I wasn't very significant to them after all or they to me: they were just the respite I needed at that time and place and no more. Mike had his hands on the wheel and through the windshield he flicked three fingers of one hand in an abbreviated goodbye. When the car turned around, I saw Gunther, staring out the back window in my direction, disappear into the shadows of the escaping Chevy.

The black-robed nuns at the Home were both brusque and compassionate in queer but equal doses, hard for me to fathom, yet gratifying for their reliability. We girls in their care found it funny to think of ourselves as soon-to-be mothers; it felt like a biological mistake, as if somehow we were graced with a deformity. We spent as much time in slippers and robes and haircurlers as suburban housewives, and when we were too tired or teary over our situations, we would bond in our giddy satire of older, weary pregnant women. Hanging over all the care and discipline and security of the Home was the reality of what waited for us after we'd delivered our bloody angels to the soliciting hands of obstetricians: the outside world, indifferent and/or hostile to babes with babes in their arms. Or the sense of loss for those who planned on surrendering their offspring for adoption.

The nuns had often encouraged me to consider that, seeing

little in the way of positive prospects for my situation, but I wanted that baby more than anything. As unlovable as I felt, I hungered for the unconditional love of a drooling love machine, someone who I could mother the way I never had been, as if I could sew up that tear in the universe.

The initiation into motherhood that I went through entailed more physical suffering than I was prepared for. For twenty-four hours my baby resisted the fate that awaited him, and my body responded in a kind of panic as if it didn't expect to survive: I was engulfed in hives as I was convulsed by a litany of merciless contractions that tried to wring the life out of me. Finally, a high bleating ripped the air as if born from my very own screams, and it was over, I was breathless, I was wet and sticky, I was alive and so was something else, something separate yet a part of me, now a baby boy. My Luke.

I was so in love with a wailing, hungry-eyed miniature of muscle and spittle and delicately-folding flesh, my sleepy baby for his sleepy mama, and it was a while before I was strong enough to emerge from the cradle-like surrender to his and my physical needs. But eventually I had to stand on my feet and take steps into the sober, functioning world that Luke was birthed into, that world outside the sanctuary I had landed in.

I didn't have the option to stay on indefinitely at the Home as, say, an assistant to the nuns, helping them greet and mentor the incoming tide of new mothers that followed behind me, as I probably would've loved. The nuns entreated me to allow them to contact my so-called family, that being the option they always preferred. I was tired, I needed rest and four walls, and so, when Virginia, who was now living alone in her own small house, offered me use of her back apartment, I put on my instinctual blinders and succumbed: I said yes.

She doted over me to the extent I could tolerate and especially over Luke. Every evening, home from her secretarial job working for a Yonkers accountant, she stopped by to wrangle Luke from my arms, implying how much more he seemed to enjoy being cooed by her than by his mother. Having spent all day with Luke, I had no insecurities about his preferences in caregivers. My days had been spent in the bliss of attending to his every need with great enthusiasm and lathering him with affection. In the late afternoon, friends home from high school would drop by to ooh and ahh over him, not to mention pass a joint around behind a drawn shade for the sake of mom and her friends. As happy and contented as I was, some of that had to have come from the herbal self-medication I'd been providing myself for years, the only way I knew how to keep my head above water and my existential rage miles below the surface. My small two-room apartment would be filled with both merry trilling voices and rushing whispers of endearments as we took turns feeding him from his bottle, all in the aromatic haze of pot. Until Virginia would come by, by which time Annette and Rosemary and Marie (who, to my shock, would OD on heroin within the year—a substance I never would have tried and didn't think she would've) and whoever else they brought along were long gone and I had to put up with Virginia's proprietary demonstrations of mothering.

One evening, squeezing a sleeping Luke in tightly-folded arms, she looked at me maternally and said: "I've been thinking.

"You know what we should do? I'm thinking that if I officially adopted Luke, you could go on to finish high school and, not being burdened with a little baby, you could do whatever you wanted with the rest of your life. You're too young to have to be worrying about a little baby, Janie. I could see you still want to have fun with your friends. You want to meet boys who will treat you right and who one day will want their own children. You know, men aren't that interested in girls with babies. You have a promising future, if you think about it, and really, Janie, do you really think you're even mature enough to be a mother? I'm not so sure. . ."

"Well, I am! I'm a great mother," I replied, and said to her simply and directly so that she could understand my meaning while extending my arms to relieve her of him, "I don't know about those other things but I do know this: He's mine."

"Oh Janie, of course he is. But I could be so good with him," she insisted, folding him closer to her chest. "Look at him," she touched her fingers to his drooling lips, "look how happy he is! And I can't do the things you can do. But I could do this. And you know, I didn't have to take you back when the Sister called me." Her tone had changed. "I could've rented this place out and increased my income. But I saw what a wonderful opportunity this could be for both of us, to make amends, to start off in the right direction. And really, Janie, if you think about it, I'd be the better mother for him. I'm not a kid like you are. And besides, you have so many talents you could utilize in life: you're smart, Janie, you draw good, people like you. If you got your act together you could move to the city, except this time the right way, without frightening everyone to death and having to live on the street. You could be a high-paid secretary in New York, maybe in advertising or something."

She was making me sick and very, very upset.

"I don't want to be a secretary," I said. "I want to take care of Luke. And I don't like this. I don't know what you're doing but please give Luke back to me. Now."

I wanted her to leave.

"Well, don't be upset. I'm trying to be helpful, like a sister should. And it's for your own good. Listen to yourself. That's not a very mature attitude," she said. She tried to ignore my presence as I hovered over her, but eventually my shadow penetrated her thick skull and she nervously handed Luke over to me.

"OK, be that way. See, I'm leaving now. Out of your hair. We'll talk tomorrow, OK?" She stared at Luke from over near the doorway which she was reluctant to vacate. "Bye bye, Lukie! Aunt Ginny will see you tomorrow!" She stared at me like the lost waif she always was, the one I always needed to take care of because it was always made clear by everyone in the family that she was the most needy and vulnerable of all us Cantore babies. If someone could only give her the love she deserved, if only people could understand all she had to offer and what it's like to have been through what she's been through, they would do anything she wanted of them.

But that was not for me. When she finally left the apartment, I locked the door behind her as if that by itself could keep her out of my life. The scraping footfall of her high heels against the pavement as she circled the front of the house and the awkward clapping of her ascent of the porch was an aural spider's web wrapping itself around Luke and me. Luke's head nestled against my shoulder and I let him be the narcotic for the troubling night.

And here's where my father's violence becomes the final fist in my face and I am triply broken. His mauling of my girlhood, the impact of his occasional blows, and now his total destruction of my sister's ability to love or be loved.

It takes me a while the next day to understand why there is a woman with two policemen outside my door. Incongruously, the woman looks a bit like an antiwar protester, young, long-hair parted down the middle, a sympathetic intelligence emanating from her eyes. What is she doing with these pigs? In those days, these two groups would seldom have been working together. It was hard to absorb and I didn't absorb it . . . until I saw my sister standing in the driveway several feet behind them, not at work as she should be. And then the woman's words start to make sense and I begin to understand that she's a social worker accompanying these cops on a drug bust where there's an infant involved.

My sister will walk into the room as the police rifle through my drawers where I know my two rolled joints are and I will stumble backwards towards Luke's crib. *Why?* I am shouting, *why would you do this?* I am shaking as I try to keep Virginia away from Luke who now starts to wail. She's jabbering nervously about my not being fit to raise a child, how my drug habit causes me to neglect him, *see how skinny he is* and the social worker can clearly see that he's not and she's looking confused and as the cops separate my sister and me and I start to sob, the woman asks if she could see Luke closer and I fall to the floor releasing great gulfs of annihilating tears and my sister is jabbering, jabbering to the woman that Lukie will be in her good hands now and how she's tried to steer me from my dissolute ways and the cops are now talking to me, the two joints in their hands that will rob me of— that will tear me from—my baby, and they get nervous as I start to slap the air around me, *no no please go away, I need my baby*, and there are handcuffs and the social worker tells my sister that the baby looks healthy and my sister cries *It's because of me, because of me, I make sure he's OK, she's too irresponsible, look at her, she's a marijuana addict,* and the social worker nods her head and says the baby must be taken for a full examination upon which time a family court judge will determine the baby's placement. And now it's my sister's turn to cry.

"But I love him! I did it for his sake!"

And then the pinching handcuffs and the stuffy police car and the asthmatic wailing create their own whirling vortex and I just let go and spiral down it.

I live under the world now in a soft-lit cavern of square flat planes, a sterile yet plush hideaway. It is in Scarsdale, a wealthy suburb, and I am playing with two little girls, my sweet blonde sisters who are not my sisters, they are my charges. I have been given away by the courts and have found myself in that foster home I had so dreaded, with the tacit understanding that I will take care of the house and children of my foster mother in ex- change for not living in a reform school. Somewhere on the other side of Westchester County is my no-doubt confused baby, prob- ably in some state of dislocation: he's lost his mother's voice, her smell, the touch he's known from birth, and struggling to adapt to aliens, probably affectionate new parents who have been deemed to deserve him. My new charges play enthusiastically with their pretend mother, their real one reserving her most profound love for the more worldly occupations of her Manhattan work-a-day world. I wade in the shallow pool of their affections, always aware of their non-Lukeness.

This existence—for it is nothing more than that, not being able to bear to think of what brought me here and having lost the will to imagine where there is yet to go—is punctuated by the surprisingly pleasant visits of my social worker, the same woman who wouldn't leave my son with Virginia, and for that I always appreciated her. She tries to do the impossible, but patiently: to convince me that I can hope for things for myself. Eventually. At some point. She notices my interaction with the girls, she mistakes my docility for something other than depression, and she acknowledges the injustice of the system that has deemed me unfit to raise my own child just for smoking pot—I suspect she'd tried a toke or two for herself at some point by then—even though he was lovingly cared for and nourished.

But she pushes at the universe, intent on showing me that change can be effected. She suggests that I become the legal ward of my brother. She suggests that he can give consent to my marrying the baby's father. She suggests the father might even be willing, even anxious, to raise and support his own child. She even suggests she can find him for me. And when she manages to effect all these things, my baby in my hands, Tony and me married, I in an ankle-length Mexican dress I found in an inexpensive East Village shop, Tony with a long thin silk scarf tied around his neck in Midnight Cowboy drag, it's as if it still isn't happening. Because I no longer dare believe in love, in possibility, in grace, in God or in any of His subtly camouflaged angels. I only believe in pain.

The pain of living without love from now on. The pain of trading one prison for another. The pain of living under duress in the Staten Island home of Tony's disapproving family until he can find himself a job. And after he finally gets one and we find our tenement flat, the actual pain that overwhelms my lower back each afternoon after spending the morning with my baby, when I collapse on our bed, unable to rise from my rack of torture. I thought I'd hit bottom self-lobotomized in Scarsdale, but now I lay pinioned to the bottom of some cold dank well where I can hear my baby cry out for me a few feet away while I don't dare move a muscle to reach him. With local Stuyvesant clinic doctors unable to pinpoint the cause for my physical distress, that was my afternoon for almost two months as I futilely waited for this episode to pass on its own.

It did pass. But not on its own. In loft spaces filled with young men and women in their underwear, thrashing their way back to infancy on thick gym mats, shaking and pounding and screaming to the coaxing of young, determined therapists, and I contributed to this orchestra with primal notes of rage reaching octaves that were frightening, raw and naked and released like a river. I laid waste to all, I devastated every Cantore and I cried over them as well. And my pain eased. Some people left those loft spaces weaker than when they'd arrived, regressively addled, the walls of their personalities leveled without any structure to replace it. But not me. I came from brutal stock. I could handle it. I am a stockade.

Strange that I can feel like that. Sturdy and vulnerable, back and forth all in the same person. Not so sturdy now. But as I began to feel stronger and healthier, my emotional life rebounded. I was more myself, which wasn't always what Tony would've wanted. I suppose he didn't want me at all, but he gave it a try because now he had a son. The idea had its romance for him. That said, he was always the fairly passive father; the human world always seemed to interest him a bit less than the world of the abstract. That was not my métier. I inhabit the planet with physicality and voice, with pleasure and pain. He doesn't inhabit it with any vitality. He's lighter on his feet, traipsing around in the recessed alleyways of his brain, tripping off on concepts and words and highly evolved fantasy worlds. I joined a group of local parents who were creating a day care group, and when Tony showed up he preferred to sit quietly with Luke than converse with the adults. He used to creep out Marcie, the one among us who we all eventually chose as day care director. She was impassioned and determined to put an order into the chaotic structure created by the majority of us East Village parents, comprised largely of artists and free-thinkers, but she stopped even trying to proselytize with Tony. She thought he seemed to always be thinking of something else as he pretended to be focused, as if his thoughts were light years behind his face. There were occasional individuals he could *grok* and they would nod with quiet intensity over some esoteric trivia like the films of Ed Wood or the curdled ravings of Brother Theodore or the latest Isaac Asimov book, but all these relationships had the aura of conspiracy. He couldn't bother to engender a sense of trust.

Basically, he was doing what he felt he had to; he had little desire to do more. If I needed him to take Luke out for a while, he tended to lose track of him because Luke couldn't be found between the covers of a book. Twice we had to call the cops to help us find Luke and each time I would've relished having Tony's head on a platter. I felt like I had two disabled kids to handle with no one to help and this tension ate away at our relationship.

The death knell was probably Luke's diagnosis. At two, my baby stopped talking. And he started screaming and throwing things in frustration, as if his thoughts were also light years behind his big brown eyes and they couldn't be heard all the way here. It was all my fault was all Tony had to say, I was a lousy mother and had damaged his son. To make matters worse, doctors had their own theory which was that Luke had traits of autism which implied in those days that his mother was cold and cerebral like some over-educated Park Avenue matron (or even one from Scarsdale). At Bellevue nursery, even the receptionists would glare at me with contempt as if I was a child abuser. And even though Tony knew that I wasn't capable of having those qualities ascribed to me, he started treating me as if their theories were valid, as if his sense of self depended on it.

By the time Luke was five, our hatred for each other was palpable. Luke was talking again after two years of wordlessness, but he was clearly developing differently than his friends at the day care center, leaving us exhausted and anxious for his future. And Tony's angry sputterings were usually so ineffectual that my vehement replies finally led him to top my argument with his bony fists. Big mistake! He spent most of that night gathering his clothes and his precious LPs off the street where they'd been scattered after flying from our tenement windows.

And now here I am. Never thought another man would ever marry me. Never thought any man could love me. Though I knew by now that many men could want to have sex with me. I had been taught early on that I was unlovable and my experience with Tony only served to corroborate that. My father used to say that he would always have Janie to live with, the implication being that I was too fat to even be desirable. And happily, I succeeded in becoming undesirable to him or I might have ended up following Virginia's path to life fulfillment. I was a damaged woman with an unruly child. What guy could possibly want someone like that in their right mind? I guess I have to thank my angels for eventually finding me one who was in the other kind.

IV

His Femme Fatale

It had been a dank February day, back in 1980. It was the first winter he had spent with Jane and her eleven-year-old autistic son, Luke, and he had very quickly taken to the lifestyle of East 7th Street in an era when low earners and artistic adventurers lived side by side with Ukrainian and Polish working families. Ed had just finished his frigid walk home from his job near Union Square, through blocks of tenements and brownstones and the night-lit avenues of mom-and-pop stores rubbernecking with the flourishing punk scene, a walk he had come to relish, and he was surprised by the enigmatic statement—"My sister finally did it"— that Jane greeted him with after he'd made his way up two flights to their tenement apartment and opened the apartment door.

She signaled him into the front room outside of Luke's earshot where they could discuss her sister freely. As Luke hyperactively whispered ray gun noises and space explosions up in his bunk bed, Ed joined Jane in the brightly-painted yellow room facing the street.

Jane sat in the red-lacquered wicker chair, its base peeled of its color by Zsa Zsa and Tessie, who purred nonchalantly, sprawled at her feet.

"She finally succeeded in killing herself," Jane said. Her eyes calmly studied Ed for a reaction, almost as if he was the subject for a laboratory test or for a photograph she needed to light properly. She herself was showing no emotion at all.

Ed went over and put Jane's hands between his and sat on the floor beside her chair. He wasn't quite sure how to respond; this seemed like the thing to do.

"Are you OK?" he asked.

"Of course," was her sober response. Jane had already shown Ed the card her sister, Virginia, had sent her shortly before she and Ed had become an item. Inside the flowered Hallmark was a photograph of a thin woman in her thirties with dyed blonde hair in a mild bouffant. It was a picture she had posed for for her business enterprise—a child modeling agency, of all things. In a slightly stilted, delicate hand she had written a note. *Dear Janie, It's been a long, long time and I wonder how you've been. I am fine and I now have a business of my own. I am sending you my business card so you can see that I am really getting my act together. I think about you and Lucas all the time and hope you have forgiven me by now. This is a recent picture. Hope you like it. Love, Ginny.*

"I'm fine," Jane continued. "I'm going to take a day off tomorrow. My brother called to tell me about it, and I'm going to meet him in Yonkers at the train station and then we're going to bury her. He took care of all the details," she said, shrugging her shoulders. Her glance checked in with Ed, and then it wandered away. "Thank God my sister died, or I'd never have heard from my brother again, either."

Ed just listened. He'd never met her brother or sister, but he'd heard enough of the stories to understand what elicited this bitterness. He watched Jane staring at him as if by gauging his reaction she could somehow gauge her own.

"Do you want me with you tomorrow?" he asked.

"Why?" she replied, quizzically, as if it was a strange thing to ask.

"You know, in case . . . in case you feel you need . . . emotional support or something!"

"I'm fine," she said, her expressive brown eyes expressing nothing, except perhaps, Ed thought, the slightest suggestion of amusement. "I've actually been wishing for this for a long time. And now, it feels—I don't know—" she pursed her lips, "—

anticlimactic. Anyway, this isn't the time for you to meet my brother. Tomorrow is about my brother, my sister and me," she said with finality. "I want to keep it that way."

There was a pause as Ed noticed that his desire to help now, somehow, felt like subservience.

"Whatever," he replied.

Ed came home the next day unsure of what kind of mood he'd find Jane in. He was surprised when, on his arrival, she turned around from the kitchen sink, where she was washing some dishes, to actually greet him glowingly.

"I'm so glad to see you," she said, throwing her arms around his neck, the dishcloth still in hand.

He embraced her, encircling her waist and pulling her towards him.

"You're in fine feather!" he said, his face nuzzling her behind the ears.

She smiled.

"It was a good day. Kind of." She gently pulled away to walk back to the sink and deposit the damp towel along the side of the bathtub which abutted it, a kitchen layout that was common in New York's shabby walk-ups dating from the end of the previous century. "I had fun with my brother! I didn't expect that!" She sat at the end of the kitchen table. She played with a pack of cigarettes that she'd removed from its resting place in the glass bowl on the table's center. "He was making all these jokes and we kept *laughing!* End of the world humor? I don't know. It was strange, but it felt good to be with him. I mean, it was almost like Virginia had died years ago. I guess she had, as far as we were concerned." She flipped a cigarette from the pack and rolled it between her fingers thoughtlessly. "He didn't hate me today. Maybe because I told him about you. Maybe he figured I was *your* problem now. Another burden off his shoulders."

Ed sat opposite her at the table. He didn't know what to make of a remark like that and decided he'd rather not know. She counted on that.

"What'd you guys have to do?"

"Not a lot, actually. She'd been living in a motel off the Bronx River Parkway, so there were just her belongings to collect."

"A motel!"

"Yeah. A fitting ending, I guess, to her fucked-over life. A seedy hotel where she could entertain a string of boyfriends. No one could ever take her for too long. Apparently, some of her boyfriends were *black*, Ray said. That surprised me. Not the image I had of my sister or anyone in my family. People are more complicated than you expect. Even the complicated ones like her.

"Anyway, then he took me back to his apartment. And it turns out he's really into photography, just like me"—Jane often talked about having a darkroom of her own in which she could sequester herself, pulling images from the ether like an alchemist, finding them a home on paper—"and he takes all these pictures of flowers. Like Sierra Club pictures with special lenses and everything. My brother! This big macho construction worker taking pictures of flowers! I was impressed! I liked him today!" Then her beaming face darkened and a smirk rose to the surface. "But I bet I never hear from him again. I think he's glad to get rid of me. He probably feels the same way about me as we both did about Virginia." Jane noticed that Ed looked kind of shocked. "*You* know," Jane explained. "Like we're both—I don't know—*quicksand* for him. We were all quicksand for each other, I guess. All the Cantores. But I didn't feel that way today! I felt *good*, standing there with him, just the two of us at the bottom of this hill by her grave, which was actually just a few feet from the highway behind some bushes." She took a breath to remember the pathetic setting. "I felt good because we were alive and she wasn't," she added. "And she could never take anyone away from me again," and here her voice found its gun-metal hardness.

At this point, Luke came out of his room to ask about dinner; he was getting hungry. Jane walked over to him and surprised him by enveloping him in a big hug, leaning her head against his, as if she didn't want to ever let him go. He wrapped his spindly arms around her head and patted her back. He didn't seem to notice anything unusual about her burst of sentimental affection. He probably thought she was upset because maybe Ed was going to do the cooking that night. That would've been enough to upset *him*.

In Jane's version of events, her father must have raped her mother when she was conceived. It was the only way to explain her mother's behavior towards her. Everyone else had referred to her mother as a saint, but Jane hadn't experienced her that way.

"I remember when she was sick in the hospital, sometime before she died, I gave her this get-well-card. She never kept it out for display or anything; she immediately had it put in a drawer. She hated me."

Ed's mother, in contrast, would have fetishized the slightest thing he'd done and, in her humble-pie way, managed to extol it far and wide.

"Maybe," Ed said, "she couldn't deal with the sadness of leaving you behind. Do you think? Maybe she did love you. Maybe she just couldn't cope is all it was."

"She hated me. I was an overweight little girl and she would give me *adult* portions at dinner and second helpings! What kind of mother does that? She would give me money to get candy at the corner store just to get me out of her hair. Like I needed candy! I would never do that to my daughter!

"She used to do all these things for strangers. One time when I was in the car with her, she pulled over to stop these teenage boys from beating up a girl and took the girl home with us. She was so nice to her and she calmed her down and everything and I was so jealous. What did I have to do to get noticed?

"At the cemetery, after my mother died, everyone was crying. Wailing! The whole Italian thing. Everyone was trying to calm down my sister. And I just stood there. I was nine years old and my mother had just died. And I didn't feel a thing. I told my brother that I didn't care that she was dead and he was really angry with me."

Jane reached for her pack of Vantage Lights on the kitchen table and shook out a cigarette. She used the moment to light it with her dark green BIC and compose her thoughts.

"I know my father was crazy, but at least he loved me. It's too bad that, of the two of them, it was the one who frightened me who loved me most. Even when he stopped . . . you know . . ."—she twirled her cigarette hand forward, letting it stand in for the unspeakable—"he still always treated me like I was his favorite.

"I was so young when they took him away I feel like I don't really know what he was all about. Everything I know about him is colored by what my brother's told me. My father might've been the only person who ever loved me and I don't know him at all."

Jane had never pursued this line of thought in the years before Ed had became a part of her life. She was still too young, too angry, too burdened with making ends meet and taking care of Luke to think of anything other than the moment and how to inhabit it, and so she did. Her life was filled with turnstile men, with loyal friends, and with all their children, until poetry came along and, in front of a notebook with ruled paper, the past seeped into the present in manageable leaks. With the glimmerings of a family life—even here in this renovated tenement apartment in the midst of a ramshackle bohemia—she could slow down enough to wonder if her long-repressed hunger for loving parents of her own was perhaps attainable after all. As far as she knew, she still had a father somewhere on the surface of this planet and now she felt settled enough to think maybe she could start risking the attempt to get more of what she hungered for.

One evening before Ed got home, Jane dialed Information for the Bronx and found out Uncle Vito's telephone number. Uncle Vito was surprised to hear from her. "Jane! Jane!" he kept rasping in his deep-fried voice. "Madonn'! Little Janie! How are you sweetheart?" and sweetly asked after her health and her child.

Jane liked Uncle Vito and Aunt Connie and she was happy, even relieved, to tell him that she was doing just fine.

"And your son, I forget his name. . ."

"He's fine, Uncle Vito. Thanks for asking. He's eleven now, growing tall."

She asked about Aunt Connie, and Uncle Vito—without skipping a beat—told her how Connie had died in her sleep three years before.

"She didn't have no pain. That's what we all want, isn't it? And she had a good life. It's not like when your poor mother left us so young,—*madonn'!*—that was so terrible. It was heartbreaking. And Connie would say 'I wonder how Janie is doing' every once in a while. 'I hope she's OK, wherever she is.'"

When her mother had died, there had sounded inside Jane a deep melancholy chord not felt before and which young Jane found herself unable to tolerate. Now Jane felt a light restrumming of that chord. Just for a moment. Ray had told her that none of the family cared about them, but it seemed like he was wrong. Could he be wrong about her father as well?

Then she asked Vito if he knew how she could reach him.

The next day, she took out some pale blue writing paper from her box of stationery and wrote to him.

March 17, 1981

Dear Dad,

I spoke to Uncle Vito last night and he gave me your address in South Dakota. I live in New York City. I'm all grown up—not the little girl you last saw—with a boyfriend and a young son, and I'm trying to come to terms with all that happened to our family. I try to piece things together, but I was so young, and I was so confused, that I thought maybe I could grasp things better now and try to find out who you really are, or who you've become. And maybe understand myself a little better.

Does that make any sense? I don't know. I'm a little nervous about doing this—no, make that very nervous—but I do remember a mixture of things, some very nice, and I need to find out what's what. Whose daughter was I? Who is my father really?

If you don't want to bring up painful memories, I will understand if you don't reply. Here's my telephone number if you do.

She signed the letter, *Your daughter, Jane (the baby)*.

She slipped the letter into a pale blue envelope, licked a stamp, placed it neatly in its corner and walked downstairs to the mailbox as if on automatic pilot, afraid that if she thought of what she was doing she might come to her senses. Then she went across the street to the Kiev Restaurant, sat at the counter and ordered a piece of seven layer cake.

The day Mario Cantore called his daughter was a day of great excitement. He was alive, sweet-voiced, emotional, and clearly as nervous as Jane had been. It was nearly twenty years since any of his kids had spoken with him. It was a Sunday and Ed was home, and he listened to Jane laughing excitedly as she spoke in bursts on the phone.

When Mario put his wife, Irene, on the phone, Jane thought she had a crinkly Midwestern sound that seemed incongruous attached to someone connected to her father.

"Oh, your father and I met in a bar in Sioux City so many years ago now. He's been a wonderful stepfather to my boys—Tommy's in the Marines and Charlie in the Army."

"Janie's a poet!" Mario, still on the line, interjected. "My daughter! Isn't that something? And her boyfriend's an actor!"

"Oh my!" Irene exclaimed. "An actor in the family! And your father *loves* the movies! He makes me see just about all the pictures that come to Sioux City!"

Jane's face was flushed with rosy pleasure. This was what family was supposed to be like, but never had been. Daddy sounded normal, like anybody's Daddy, and now somehow maybe she could reconfigure him in her mind. Maybe it was Irene that had made all the difference.

"Your father always says his baby Janie was his favorite child, and how much he loved your mother."

"Your mother was a saint," Mario added. "I still have her picture in my dresser drawer."

Jane felt like her mental circuits were in overload and she couldn't find an adequate verbal response. She struggled to find any word, but her brain was like a crowded polka floor with everybody's jumping in circles leaving her breathless. The silence, however, sounded like awkwardness, infecting the whole conversation, and the conversation petered out. They agreed to talk again next week.

Ed went over to Jane. She was almost trembling, vibrating like a tuning fork, ringing the room with a bell-like confusion.

"It was *OK!*" she said with relief, not looking at Ed, but off to the distance, out past the kitchen windows where sheets were clothespinned across the alley.

Later that week, Jane received a small package from Sioux City. In it was a cassette accompanied by a letter from her father.

Dear Janie,

I thought you'd like to hear this. I like to do this in my spare time.

From Dad

The cassette was a collection of accordion renditions of old standards like "Stardust" and "Laura" and "Que Será, Será." Jane heard a snippet and then turned it off. She didn't want to listen to the whole thing. Mario used to entertain all the kids of the extended Cantore family with his piano-playing down in the basement. The cassette sounded like someone alone in the basement playing to himself, and the accordion's wheeze gave the songs an aberrant sound. Still, the corniness of it all made Jane squeeze out a smile.

Mario continued to call, making the attempt to construct a more solid relationship with his Janie. One weekend, Jane sat listening to Ed talking to her father when he'd called and Ed had picked up. It sounded like they were having a warm conversation and the incongruity of the turn of events tickled her like a little white feather against the inside of her belly.

Ed then handed her the phone and sat in the living room chair at the far end of the room. He wasn't paying attention to Jane's words, just to the music of her bell-like voice ringing in a new dawn. It took a while before the song, he realized, was starting to lose its melodic banter and dissonant tones were creeping in.

"Dad, that's not true," Jane was saying. Ed turned in Jane's direction. "Please don't say that. . . . I don't care!" she continued. "I was *there*, Daddy! I was *there!*" This was not going right. "I need you to stop!" Jane stood up from her seat around the kitchen table. "I can't talk about this anymore! *Listen to me!* . . . Dad, please if you can't stop . . ."

Ed walked across the apartment over to where Jane stood by the red wall phone.

"I've got to get off the phone, Dad. I'm sorry. This has been a mistake. . . . Please . . . No, you're not 'just saying!' There is no 'just saying!' It's twenty years later and you're still 'just saying' this. I can't listen to this anymore. I'm going to hang up. And please, you've got to promise me you won't call me again. . . . I've got to go!" and she practically threw the receiver onto the phone's base. Her hands rushed to cover her mouth as she burst into tears.

"What have I done?! What have I *done?!*"

Ed grabbed her and tried to pull her to him.

"What happened?!" he whispered urgently.

"He *is* crazy!" she sobbed. "He's *is* still crazy." Ed could feel her tears dampen his shirt. His hand lay flat on her back as she trembled. "I thought . . . I thought . . . he was so different last week." After she blew her nose into a tissue Ed gave her, her face was pink and glistening, her breath shallow. "*What was I thinking?* He couldn't stop talking about Virginia, saying this *garbage* over and over. He kept saying it wasn't his fault, it was all Virginia's, he called her a *slut* . . ." She shook her head as if to say this couldn't be, this *shouldn't* be. "*He was still obsessing over her.*" Jane took deep breaths to try to calm herself before she continued. "He said she was giving *blow jobs* to boys and it *grossed me out* to hear him talk like that. And then it all came, like, flooding back to me, the way he used to talk . . . ! And this woman . . . this woman allowed him to raise her *kids?*" she said in disgust. "I wonder what he must've done to *them?* She said he met her in a bar—maybe she's an alcoholic or something! How else could she marry him?"

She buried her head in Ed's chest. "Oh, why did I do this? *Why?*"

Ed didn't know why. He just kept stroking her almost coal black hair flat across the curve of her head.

"I'm frightened," she said. "I gave him my address! I'm so *stupid!* What if he tries to find me? This is why I always kept my phone number under Tony's name even after I kicked him out. How could I do this?"

It would be almost three years, at least one year after she and Ed decided on a whim to get married, before Jane would feel safe again. In the meantime, she prepared for the possibility of his finding her as she always had when she'd felt threatened. When no one was around to watch, she went to the medicine cabinet in their tiny W.C. and stared at the bottles of pills she'd hoarded over the years as in some kind of ritual, and then went into the kitchen where she lit a joint and walked toward the refrigerator, intent on turning her body into a fortress of cake.

Eight months earlier, in the late spring of '79, Ed had been thrilled by the effect he seemed to have on Jane when they'd work together in the recording studio, he showing her how to use the equipment and introducing her to the actors reading books for the blind. He'd had to reach in front of her to set the tape and handle the controls, and their physical proximity to each other made his skin tingle. Jane was excited by her promotion, by Ed's confidence and by the camaraderie of the actors, and she laughed easily and playfully beside him, as if they'd been a long-standing team. He found himself seduced by her joyously expressive brown eyes, by her blushing pink cheeks. For the prior six months, Ed had hardly paid attention to her. She'd originally started working there through her friend Jeannie, who had been one of a slew of poets who congregated at the sprawling, rustic, arts-centric St. Mark's Church and who were supporting their creative efforts by working at the studio. She'd worked next to Jeannie for those months in the small room in the far corner of the third floor hallway, her long black hair head-banded by large headphones that she used in order to proof the taped tracks of the actors. Once, Ed noticed a studio colleague hitting on Jane fairly aggressively to her apparent enjoyment and that prompted Ed to keep a distance; his less aggressive manner could hardly compete went his thinking. And now, suddenly, he was in her company one-on-one, not by his own doing, but rather by administrative fiat.

He'd only been her trainer for a week, but they'd become so comfortable in each other's presence so quickly that it seemed like they'd actually spent a month together. Within as early as a week of working and lunching together he found out she already had a guy in her life—not surprising—and *that*, perversely, emboldened Ed to be *more* flirtatious. What did he have to lose? He noticed that his out-of-character boldness was just the *right* character for his new, beautiful and curvy colleague. There was electricity in her laugh when he cavalierly suggested via some idiomatic mangling that just maybe she could handle more than one egg in her basket.

Ed soon realized that he was one of many guys in the department who were pursuing her. Her mirth, her enthusiasm, her full figure in loose man-tailored shirts, her easy blush, all were found inviting and unintimidating and at the union meeting they had at Town Hall, Adam had already suggested they spend a night together, and the more circumspect Ralph had asked if she was available to go on a date the coming Saturday. Ed had done neither, but apparently his feelings were obvious to her.

"I'm fat, you know," she said at one point some time after he had plopped himself into the aisle seat next to her and they had picked up on their flirtatious banter. He didn't know what she was talking about. She had said it as if she couldn't believe he could be seriously interested in her. Considering all the hormonal attention she was getting from so many directions, he didn't quite understand the relevance of her statement.

"You are?" was his reply. He tried to put his thoughts together. Fat sounded unattractive, but that didn't begin to describe her.

"I thought you were just . . . big-boned!" he offered, shrugging his shoulders.

"I'm trying to find someone to go to the top of the World Trade Center with!" Jane had announced to Ed one day. "It's supposed to be beautiful this weekend. You should be able to see for miles. Have you been on the roof? It's fun!"

Ed never had. He was scheduled to be down in Tribeca that Saturday, not too far from the trade center, for a Movement for Actors workshop organized by people he'd met at an experimental theatre festival that spring. And so after cavorting around a loft-space wrapping himself over and around the bodies of other playful twenty-somethings, he met Jane on Chambers Street and they walked past the sun-blanched, deserted office buildings down to the looming silver towers.

Although bright and warm on street level, there was zero visibility on the roof: the top of the Trade Center sat in a cold, fuzzy cloud. When the mist would clear, they could see glimpses of distant city summer life below them. They sat and talked the afternoon away, transported away from the rest of humanity by their very own cloud, two pinpricks communing a hundred stories above the city. When they descended from their lofty heights, they followed the labyrinthine path to the nearest subway. Normally, Ed's train would be the one Brooklyn-bound, but he knew that Jane was heading up to the East Village. There was an awkwardness at the station entrance. Ed was having a hard time ascertaining whether Jane's feelings towards him were romantic or platonic. Could she want him to come home with her while she was still seeing this other guy? He decided that was too presumptuous on his part.

"OK, well, I guess this is where we part," he said. "I had a great time."

"Me too," Jane replied, and then Ed did a loping shuffle as he tried to nonchalantly walk away.

"Bye," Jane said after him, confused as to why he wasn't grabbing his opportunity. She wasn't used to men with such compunctions.

When they saw each other at work the next Monday, they felt like they had consummated a relationship that they hadn't. Their friendship had moved to the next level and when Jane invited Ed to her coming poetry reading, he felt like he was being anointed, like this time he *had* been asked up to her apartment.

The reading was on a Thursday night at Club 57 on St. Mark's Place. Ed spent some time beforehand thinking which of his pay-no-attention-to-me casual clothes would cast the best light on him. After making his decision, he made his way across the river to the City. The evening seemed to have a shine to it, and St. Mark's was extra vivid, scattered neon smearing the edges of the night's shadow. Ed found the club and entered the establishment with what resembled a mild dose of stage fright, heralded by the sting of an anticipated coronation.

The small hall was filled with large round tables. There were many people already there, some sitting on stage, and there was the friendly clatter of beer mugs and yawping voices. Jane sat at a busy table, lit with her own natural spotlight. She was wearing a red silk Chinese jacket and long earrings and she was responding with an aria of laughter to the boisterous words of her nearest table companion, a burly, balding, blond extrovert. Ed went over to let Jane know he had arrived.

"Oh, thanks so much for coming!" she said, waving away her cigarette smoke with her hand. "Everybody, this is my friend Ed from work."

"Hey, Ed!" came back at him severally.

"Hi, Ed!" waved Jeannie in frantic gesture, ensconced at Jane's side for encouragement.

"There are seats at that table," Jane said, pointing to the next and furthest back table in the joint. "Everybody's there."

"Everybody" being everybody else from work: Tracy, who had been at the job since Ed had started over a year and a half ago; Ralph; Adam; and Peggy. Ed sat down next to Tracy, a good friend with whom he'd bonded fairly early on the job, and smiled, trying not to register surprise or disappointment. He tried to acclimate himself to just being part of the crowd.

The first reader was introduced, a portly poet with a tone both slightly sardonic and prematurely avuncular. It was apparent that most people in the hall knew each other, and there was a strong sense of the reading as a quiet conversation among friends. Ed was not one of them, but the first poet's colloquial odes to New Jersey were diverting enough.

There was a beer break, and Ed's table gingerly indulged in shop talk until the reading's host called the room to order by clearing his throat at the mike.

"Our second of three readers will be Jane Cantore. Jane Cantore is a single mother who has been living in the East Village for over ten years, since she was a teenager. She has taken several workshops at the Poetry Project and was one of the stars of this year's workshop readings. Her poems speak directly from the heart, with candor and the joyous juice of her writing voice. Please welcome . . ."

And with whoops and cheers from all around, Jane rose laughing from her table, taking a stack of papers, a beer—and that joyous juice—to the podium.

"Thanks, guys," she said after settling her papers on the reading stand. "I heard that, Dave!" she addressed to a Falstaffian presence sitting on the side of the stage. "You're making me blush. Stop that! Go home to Lynn," which elicited a roar of approval from Dave and then some jovial heckling from Jane's burly friend at her table.

Then she said in an even, uninflected tone, "Remember My Name," and, with concision and rhythm, her verses flowed with an easy adrenaline, charging the atmosphere. Her poems snapped in Ed's ear with the spark of a Beatles song and he started to feel an aural elation. Some of her poems met with shocks of applause, and there remained the back and forth of raucous conversation. Ed fell in love with her talent, and, when the reading was over, he felt a bittersweet pang of jealousy as Jane returned to her table to a big smack on the lips between the outstretched hands of her blond companion. Later that night, Ed left with Tracy instead of Jane (as he had originally expected), and they trod the streets of the Village quietly discussing the evening before they waved goodbye at Fifth Avenue. He got on the D train heading to Park Slope feeling fully the evening's correction.

And then, a week later, their relationship seemed to be in drive again. Ed was proofing a recording of a novel when Jane and Jeannie fell clumsily into the room, as if they had been pushing each other.

"Do you want to go to a Mostly Mozart concert this weekend?" Jane asked abruptly, announcing her presence. "I have an extra ticket."

"Sure," Ed replied, after a second to ask himself *"Huh?"*

"OK. Great!" They made arrangements to meet before Jane and Jeannie giggled their way out of the room.

And that Saturday, to the sprightly meter of Mozart and the darker tones of Schubert's "Death of a Maiden," the romance was finally sanctioned. They stood, during the intermission, overlooking the vast lobby from the balcony railing, and encouraged by the golden, aristocratic glitter of Avery Fisher Hall and the hushed roar of the chattering crowds, Ed grabbed Jane's hand, cementing his intent, and she moved in for the close-up, beaming and lovely and happy.

Afterwards, at a nearby newly-opened falafel franchise, they sat across from each other at a white plastic table and talked. And talked. And talked some more. And Ed left the discussion with a large open wound where Jane's traumatic life story had lodged itself, and Jane came away listened to, naked, but wrapped in the furry warmth of Ed's patient, penetrating gaze.

They walked hand-in-hand from the falafel place down to Columbus Circle. They stood in the plaza, facing Columbus gloriously staking claim to the Indies, the surrounding fountain enhanced by the splashing lights of approaching vehicles. The cars circled like a Roman carousel of traffic, with occasional hoots of derision alternating with cheers as they passed the tall, thin, curly-haired guy locked in embrace with his sexy, curvy gal. They hungrily snacked on each other's lips and tongues, their bodies finally rewarded with envelopment. They were in the thrall of the eternal now of the kiss.

"Come home with me," Ed said. Jane reached up and pulled his head down to her mouth.

They made their way south where they climbed the two flights of stairs to his small Brooklyn apartment. He delicately unburdened her of her shoulder bag after they drank a bit more from each other's lips, and then they slowly disrobed, one item of clothing after another, folding them neatly on a nearby chair until—naked—they lay on Ed's bed, approaching each other gingerly. He first kissed her mouth and then reached to touch her breast; her hand lightly brushed his thigh. He languidly moved his lips down her neck until she cupped his head in her hand like it was a baby. He met her breasts with his mouth and then rose up to silence a moan with a deep kiss. While he hovered over her, she gently pulled his hips down to her body—and suddenly he was grabbed by a fit of self-consciousness.

In short time, Jane flew out of bed. She threw on her clothes almost violently and strode noisily to his tiny kitchenette. Suckerpunched, Ed couldn't focus on anything but his breath, in and out, in and out, as if to cleanse himself of his humiliation. He could hear Jane pacing about, striking a match, walking some more.

And then, suddenly, he heard a huge metallic crash accompanied by the cry of "Shit!"—her song of frustration and fury. Ed sat up in bed and saw one of the bridge chairs usually placed at his age-worn dining table now lying across the room near the opposite wall, the battered victim of a mauling. It was nearing 1 A.M. and Jane was slugging them over the fence in his studio apartment.

Ed just stared at her, wide-eyed, for a few minutes.

"What are you doing?"

She didn't reply. He could see her breathing heavily, her chest rising and falling in waves.

Ed was no longer thinking about his own inadequacy. Jane's had taken center stage. *She's crazy*, he thought. Sitting on a chair she'd spared, she exuded a sense of indomitable power, fueled by a murderous rage she now struggled to control. She looked away from him as he studied her, trying to gauge the situation.

Her emotional release and his accusatory gaze slowly served to quell the atmosphere. Then Ed abruptly turned away from her, went back to bed and lay facing the wall, essentially closing the door on her. She could do whatever-the-hell she wanted as far as he was concerned.

He awoke in the semi-darkness of the Brooklyn night to sense Jane lying next to him. She was a hazy, indeterminate silhouette, her curves folding heavily into shadow

"I'm sorry," she said softly, plaintively. He listened to the light brush of her breathing. He would never have believed that the night would have ended with *him* in the position to forgive *her*.

He felt comfort in the close weight of her, as if he could feel where her body touched the mattress. He let his arm rest on hers and after a short while he moved closer. It felt good to give her solace. It felt nicer to forgive her than to scorn her. It felt more masculine.

"I'm sorry, too."

She moved into the curve of his body and he lightly wrapped his arm around her. They slept that way until midmorning when they woke, still entangled, and their bodies slowly slid into a love knot.

* * *

Jane and Ed were now together as often as possible. In between recording sessions they managed to find spare moments in which to touch, to flirt, to make coded eye contact, to tease, to even unzip and quickly consummate, each adventure increasing the temptation to eliminate all those parts of their lives that kept them from that sweet nexus where their bodies met.

Jane's being a single mother meant that that would never be as possible as they might like, but she hoped that she could minimize the obstacle that parenting could be to a passionate love affair. Until now, when Jane brought guys home, she'd kept their interaction with Luke to a minimum. If any of her sleep-over guests was still around when a bedraggled Luke, suddenly teleported down from his bunk bed, appeared moseying around the kitchen, the visitor would be introduced as one of mom's friends if she thought Luke might end up bumping into them again, or otherwise not introduced at all. She didn't, after all, expect to see most of them a second time, and it would be almost five years before she could imagine having another man regularly in her life after her love-free, five-year marriage to Tony finally came to its roughhouse end. And except for that "sort-of" boyfriend, none of the other possible contenders for a relationship with Jane had quite panned out. Until, hopefully, now?

Jane knew, it was time for her to work on merging the intimate and the familial compartments of her life in a coherent way. A week after Luke was home from his Special Ed camp, she pulled Ed into the exit stairway near Studio E, threw her arms around his neck and gave him a kiss.

"Listen, Jeannie invited Luke and me to her parents' summer house on Fire Island this weekend. Why don't you come? You could meet Luke!"

Her eyes were bright and hopeful.

Ed smiled nervously, taking a moment to register this pending transition in their relationship.

"Sure! OK. Yeah, I guess that would be good. I mean, that's OK with Luke, you think?"

"I'll talk to him. He loves Jeannie—she's his favorite babysitter—so even if he's a little uncomfortable at first, he'll have a good time."

Ed smiled meekly.

"I'm getting in-between him and his mother . . ."

"I hope at least sometimes," she said.

They made plans to leave Friday evening after work. When Ed wrapped up his last recording of the day, he went downstairs to Studio F where he could see Luke sitting behind the glass enclosure, talking into the microphone while Jane pretended to be recording. Luke was then an elfin ten-year-old with his dark hair in a pixie cut flapping forward over his forehead. When he looked at Ed, it was always through the corner of his eyes, as if he wasn't sure whether he should look or not.

"Hey, what have we here?" Ed cried. "A new actor?"

Luke pinioned his arms tightly between his legs, and moved around nervously in his chair.

"Luke, this is Ed!" Jane said. "Come and say hello."

Luke slowly walked out of the studio, but instead of approaching Ed, he sidled up next to Jane, looking down towards her body so Ed could only see his profile.

"Hi Luke, it's nice to meet you. Jane tells me great things about you."

Luke's eyes showed he was listening, but he couldn't look at Ed. He looked like he would smile if he could stand the attention he was receiving.

That was pretty much how things stayed for most of the weekend, with Luke trying to avoid Ed's gaze, intermittently appearing like he was paying attention when not preoccupied with the likes of shovels and buckets and coloring books which he would color in with large unsteady scribbles. The only time he clearly responded to Ed was the day Ed pretended to be drowning under the breaking waves, inciting Luke to jump up and down on the shore with glee. Ed prolonged the burlesque for as long as he could, that being the closest they came to a conversation that weekend.

Around a month later, one Sunday night when Ed was at Jane's for his usual weekend visit and was getting ready to leave for Brooklyn, Jane pulled Ed close and held his hands in a warm, tight grip.

"Don't go," she pleaded softly.

"I've got to," he replied. "Work tomorrow. I need my stuff. You know."

Jane exhaled as if in resignation.

"I hate when you go home. I want you to stay here." And then she said with uncontained excitement, "Move in with us!"

"What!" Ed was taken aback by the unexpected suggestion.

"Move in with us! Don't you want to? *Don't you want to?*" Jane was huddling against Ed's chest, her neck bent back as she tried to lure him with the playful entreaty of her eyes. Her siren song was flattering and sexy. He was being asked to surrender his separateness and give her his all and there was something erotic about the abandonment of boundaries. It was like pulling the rope ladder up behind you: you were now committed to the venture; *you were in deep.* Yet Ed had been in relationships with unhappy endings before, and was hesitant.

"What about Luke?" he dodged. "How would he feel? It's his home, too."

"OK," Jane said accepting his challenge, "let's ask him."

She and Ed walked down two flights of stairs to the front stoop where Luke was sitting. From behind him they could see his skinny body in restless agitation, his head bobbing up and down as if he was in a heavy conversation with Obi-Wan Kenobi. They sat next to him on the stoop, Jane sitting between him and Ed.

"Luke," Jane said, "Ed and I want to ask you something."

Luke stared at Jane expectantly and snuck a sidelong glance at Ed when his name was mentioned.

"I asked Ed if he wanted to move in with us. And Ed said he would like to, but he thought we should talk to you about it first. What do you think, Luke? Would you like him to live with us? Do you think Ed should move in?"

Luke still seemed shy and wary of Ed, so Ed was really surprised when Luke said, "Yeah," with a vigorous nod of his head as if he really meant it. They all laughed in relief, in celebration, in bafflement at the sudden change of events. And Luke laughed at the delight he had aroused in the grownups, though it would be another ten years before he would give Ed any other endorsement.

The three of them gathered themselves together and marched happily up the creaky tenement stairs, their very first steps embarking on their reckless adventure.

"You know, just because I asked you to live with me doesn't mean that we own each other," Jane explained gently one night as the two of them lay on her bunk bed. Considering Jane had asked him to move in with Luke and her, Ed found this kind of maneuver of hers disorienting. It was sometimes almost as if she found any comfort in their domesticity anxiety-producing, something that she needed to set ajar before it either suffocated her or was suddenly taken away.

"OK," he said cautiously. "I don't own you. You don't own me. Nobody owns anyone here."

They stared at the ceiling.

Jane turned on her side to face Ed. "You're a one-woman sort of guy," she reasoned sweetly. She laid her hand lightly on his sternum. "I'm just not like that."

"I don't *have* to be," Ed said, letting his diaphragm raise her hand up and down.

"Yes you do," Jane said with what sounded like a teasing smile in the bunk bed darkness.

"If you want to sleep around, then you've got to agree that I can, too, if I want. Otherwise: no deal."

"You wouldn't do that." Jane rolled in Ed's direction, sleepily, cozily.

"I guess you'll have to take that chance," he said. He stretched out his right arm so she could rest her head against his chest.

Ed knew that when Jane spent time at the poetry readings at the St. Mark's Church she was part of a crowd that included that blond guy who had kissed her at her reading—her one-time "sort-of" boyfriend, Steve—and certainly, when Jane took as provocative a stance as she just had, he thought, she had one of her poet cohorts in mind.

And yet, to Ed's surprise, within a month of his moving in with Jane, this Steve had moved in with Tracy, of all people, after Jane had more-or-less "set them up." This, Ed had thought, had the earmarks of love on the rebound. Could it be that Steve, this great, high-spirited poet that Jane admired, who had seemed the life of the party at Jane's reading, had not wanted his relationship with Jane to end? That she had broken *his* heart? And this, irrespective of the fact that, as Jane had intimated, Steve was some kind of a stud?

Ed had found this realization empowering and it helped him right now in accepting Jane's dare, just as it had helped him to parry the outrageous invective which was Steve's social modus operandi when Ed first met him.

"What are you, some kind of a homo?" Steve had exclaimed on the day Ed and Jane helped him move his belongings to Tracy's duplex studio apartment. He was referring to Ed's sky-blue-and-yellow running sneakers. "You've got to really like it up the ass to wear those things!"

Steve was carrying on as if he was entertaining the crowd, oblivious to the fact that he was getting no particular reaction from those assembled. Ed, meanwhile, experienced Steve as he had experienced Brooklyn rounds of pinochle in his teens: scenes of raucous intimidation.

"I've never had it up the ass, so I wouldn't know," Ed replied, deciding not to even attempt to compete in the rank-out game. "But I'll let you know as soon as I find out."

Steve gave a crooked, Popeye smile. Ed had succeeded in giving the impression that he could handle the insult, which, in turn would make such insults a waste of time.

Over time, the two got used to each other, and the couples continued to socialize. Steve was a major raconteur and included Ed in the circle of people he could regale with his endless supply of tall tales, ones that often ended with him "giving that guy one he'll never forget": a wicked barb, a balled-up fist, or a word to the right people. Ed realized that he had to take Steve with a grain of salt, and he let Steve become part of the fabric of his East Village life, one dense with the motley of creative and original personalities. At times, Ed and Tracy, the two non-poets, would attend the regular poetry readings at the St. Mark's Church where Jane and Steve could usually be found in the back of the parish hall with their usual crowd, drinking beers and laughing as Steve jovially (and not so jovially) heckled readers. But typically, Ed and Tracy were content to leave those nights on the poetry scene to the two poets, both of whom were grateful for this license to nurture their unspoken bond without consequences.

One weekend, a few years later, it had become Jane's turn to host the monthly collating party for the hand-stapled magazine *Polyphemus*, and a dozen or so poets and artists each showed up with fifty copies of their one-page contribution and casually strolled around the kitchen table she and Ed had moved to the center of their renovated apartment for the occasion, each adding one page at a time to the issue they held in their hands before each copy attracted its share of staples. On this occasion, Ed had joined the party, no artistic contribution deemed necessary.

Steve was one of the regular members of *Polyphemus*, and with a beer in hand, he could usually be found regaling the group with his colorful free-associating. He did more kibitzing than actual collating, truth be told, but his poems were usually so cracklingly alive that people were happy to indulge him. They all chatted, gossiped, admired each other's work and generally teased each other.

They usually did that endearingly, but this time Steve's jibes managed to veer off in the direction of actual insults, something he was always in danger of doing. Propelled by both shocked laughter and his own hyperbolic instincts, Steve started savaging one of the contributing poets.

"Reading your poems is like reading *Women's Wear Daily!*" He was laughing and talking at high volume: he was on a roll. "Come on! Joel, how long you been a moron? Didn't anyone ever teach you anything? You know, you're not Frank O'Hara just because you're a funny cocksucker!"

Very few people were laughing any longer, and those who did were laughing at least partly from embarrassment. Joel, himself, gave a high-pitched little chuckle and tried to deflect Steve's remark by adlibbing "Well, no one ever called me *funny* before," but the rancid tone of Steve's remarks made the joke fall as flat as a stale vaudeville routine in a near-empty house. Ed, meanwhile, was stunned at how no one else responded to Steve, at how passive they all became, as if waiting for Steve to just run out of steam.

After the last copy of *Polyphemus* was laid on the pile, people took bundles of copies and some started to make their farewells, but Ed felt like he had witnessed a mugging and had then hidden behind closed blinds. Steve had moved into the kitchen, continuing to pontificate jovially on a different topic, and Jane and a few others were guffawing appreciatively.

Ed slowly walked into the kitchen.

"You know, Steve," he said in a slightly hushed voice when the moment seemed right, "I wish you hadn't done that."

"Excuse me?" said Steve, looking up from the kitchen chair. The room faded to a polite silence.

"Joel is a guest in our house. You shouldn't have insulted him like that."

Joel was sitting at the other end of the open space that made up the main part of Ed and Jane's apartment. Everyone who hadn't left yet just watched.

"Maybe I better go," said Steve, surprisingly gently.

"You don't have to go," Ed said in as friendly a tone as he could muster. "I'm just saying you can't do that."

"No," Steve said. He was sitting near the door. He stood up slowly, said "I do have to go," and then slid out.

"He didn't have to leave." Ed turned to Jane, concerned that she might be disappointed at Steve's departure.

"He's embarrassed," Jane said softly.

Jane was surprised by Ed's taking such action, but she didn't protest. She felt unsettled, like two of her worlds had just collided. For the last year or so, she had been trying to end her own problematic behaviors. She had become part of the zeitgeist's embrace of twelve-step programs and was no longer drugging or overeating. It was hard for her, and Ed's tendency toward the straight and narrow was comforting in a way she never would have acknowledged needing before she met him. But she *understood* Steve, his violent wit, his hedonistic rage, his attraction to the edge—all of which she struggled to control in herself. She wondered, sometimes, how long her charade could go on. She loved Ed, but she didn't think she could live in his black-and-white orderly world. The stability of it seemed masculine, almost protective, and that appealed to her. But it could be suffocating as well. And it could be dulling. And she needed that *zing*.

In spite of their ups and downs, in spite of the lonely, discordant moments that occasionally passed between them, Jane and Ed had a powerful rapport. Their moods did not always coincide—Jane might glare out at the world in the morning and Ed might experience sociability fatigue at night—but they always went back to the well of their interpersonal connection: the intoxication of mutual attraction, their genuine amusement at each other's foibles, their respect for each other's judgment and intellect. All their temperamental differences were usually buffered by communication, and when that failed, by longing for each other, which seldom did.

"Do you like the name Alessandro? If we had a boy, that would be a great name!" This was a game they liked to play, wedding their futures to each other with imaginary children of their own.

"What's wrong with good old Alex? Alessandro Zucker seems a bit much, don't you think?"

"No it doesn't! Alessandro! It's beautiful!"

"Well, we can't have kids, anyway, right? Which is just as well since we make so little money and we've got Luke on our plate, after all."

"No. We probably can't. I'm pretty sure that infection I once had took care of that," Jane said ruefully.

"It would be nice having a baby with you," Ed said, petting her silky cheek. "But it would be more than we could handle, really. If it were a girl, I think we should call it Sylvie."

They each had different ways of dealing with the anxiety of intimacy. For Ed, that might mean an emotional withdrawal that would infuriate Jane. For Jane that might mean trying to throw a monkey wrench into the works. In their early days of courtship, Jane had put Ed through tests of various sorts, like the time she told him what her friends visiting from England had said on meeting him.

"Penny and Joe really liked you. They said you seem like a really nice guy." Then, without the hint of a pause, she'd added, "They said I would probably destroy you."

Ed hadn't known how to respond.

"These are your *friends?*"

Jane didn't reply. She stared at him, studying him unsmilingly.

He'd felt strangely insulted by the remark's inference. It implied, he thought, that they saw him as fragile, naïve, a man of little complexity, ill-equipped, a friendly, smiling man lacking deep reserves. A man whose interior life was all smooth surfaces, a shiny pleasant bowling ball. They didn't guess that in Jane he saw a reflection of his own better-hid jagged edges and a chance to own them; in her tempests he would find his own sea legs while in his steadfastness she might find safe harbor.

Over time, however, Jane continued to infer that she could be his undoing.

"You don't know everything about me," she said lazily over the kitchen table one day during their third year together.

This surprised Ed. What more could she tell him about her hard-grapple history that hadn't shocked him already?

"I don't?"

"I have secrets," she said quietly, not looking in his direction.

"Well, *I* don't!" was his plaintive reply. And it was true. She knew all his transgressions, like his teenage suicide attempt, even his short liaison with a man. He believed his not having secrets was his strength.

"I know you don't." And that was all she said.

He took a moment to reflect.

"Well, I guess you're entitled to secrets," he conceded. And then he went back to browsing through his *New Yorker*. He refused to indulge in his sense of grievance.

This kind of behavior frustrated Jane. Here she was, telling him there was a part of her he didn't know, and he refused to take the bait, implying it was OK not to know her, not to own her completely, and she experienced it as a rejection. She never would've *told* him her secrets, but it was important to her that this should drive him to distraction.

Over the years, Luke's long, twittery limbs grew longer, his elfin dark eyes attained a sultry quality, and his more solid frame gave him a manly presence. At the same time, his developmental problems increased his isolation, as childhood friends grew away to be socialized adults, a trick he hadn't mastered. His hyper-enthusiastic recital of Star Trek fantasies and presidential minutiae alternated with a late-adolescent surliness that was a real challenge to Jane's and Ed's parenting skills. Jane realized she needed to make a commitment to getting him the kind of professional help that she and Ed had not been able to financially provide, so, following Ed's example of a few years earlier, she quit the low-paying job that she had had since meeting Ed, bid a fond adieu to the eccentrics of the theatre world with whom she'd interacted there, and—even though it meant engaging with people who had no compunctions whatsoever about acting as inappropriately as Luke might—she went to work in the offices of corporate law firms for the higher pay. She decided she could put up with crazies (after a lifetime of experience) to help Luke get a psychiatrist.

Luke loved Dr. Mariassi, the psychiatrist Jane and Ed found, and he "trusted her implicitly," a phrase he enjoyed using. But no amount of counseling could convince him to accept his disability; any way he looked at it, being "special" was a curse. He hungered for connection but he had none of the skills necessary for it. His attempts to socialize usually pushed his fellow classmates in his Special Ed high school away from him, and by nineteen, still in school, he developed a perverse attraction to the people in their neighborhood who used to frighten him when he was younger: the homeless, who were now concentrated in the tent city in Tompkins Square Park. He sensed he could finally belong to a community of people—the community of those who couldn't function in communities—where he'd be both in the midst of company and left alone at the same time. No one would force him to do anything he didn't want to do.

So one morning, after a frustrating day of what he thought were unforgivable disappointments at school, he headed to the park instead of to class, and that week he started a new daily routine. He would sit on a park bench, either reading a dog-eared science fiction novel or holding a conversation with himself, his body jumping with its own electric charge. And then, when he felt it was safe to go home, he headed back to his bedroom where, when Jane returned from work, she would find him as if he had just recently come back from school

One morning, after being gone long enough for Jane and Ed to have left for work, he found upon arriving home that Jane, to his dismay, had returned from work early.

"Luke, what are you doing here?" she asked.

"Oh no." He just stood in the living room tapping his foot, his face looking floorward in an exaggerated pout.

"Luke—"

"What?!"

"Why are you yelling at me?" she asked, a concerned look on her face.

"I don't know!"

This was not an out-of-the-ordinary response for Luke. Articulation was always a fierce struggle.

"What are you doing home?"

"I'm not going back there anymore! I don't want to be with those people! They're *disabled!*"

"Luke," she said slowly, "Did you just walk out of school?"

"Hmm." He shook his head slightly as if trying to keep it screwed in place. "I don't know what to say," he snorted.

"Just answer my question, please!"

"I can't," he replied.

"Why not?"

"Because I didn't *go* to school!"

Jane stared at her beautiful, troubled son with trepidation.

"Where did you go?"

"I went to Tompkins Square Park to hang out with the *homeless* people!"

"*Luke!*" she said with dismay.

"You heard me," Luke replied truculently. "I'm not going back to that odoriferous school," he said, advertising his superiority to those—like his classmates—who might just say "stinking" or worse.

"Luke!" Jane said slowly and deliberately. "Now listen to me. This is nonsense. You cannot hang out with the homeless. . . . Do you hear me? . . . Do you understand? . . . You don't know what you're doing!" His intransigence brought a rawness to her voice. "It's not safe! You've got to finish school! It's just one more year!"

"I don't care! I'd rather be homeless!" he said, not seeming to realize that being homeless meant more than being unkempt and idle, but *without a home* as well. Which he wasn't.

"Luke, I'm not giving you a choice in the matter! As long as you're living in my house, you've got to finish school! *Do you understand me?*"

"I don't care!"

He was shouting now, his frustration making him shake in fury.

Jane slowly walked over to him.

"Please, Luke, you're frightening me," she said, taking his arm, "You need to be in school now." She spoke calmly, trying to guide him to the door.

"I'm not going!"

He stalked past her toward where the bedrooms were. Jane followed. She reached for his hand.

"No, Luke—"

"Don't touch me!"

He physically sputtered, struggling to resist her increasingly determined grasp. Then he let loose with a rough shove that threw her off balance. She let out a soft whip of a cry as she fell onto her bed, which was not far beyond the entrance to the sleeping alcove that she and Ed used for a bedroom.

"Luke!" she cried.

He stopped. He had the look of someone who had just been slapped in the face and had awakened to his senses.

"Oh no," he moaned.

"Luke!" She still lie on the bed, not sure if it was safe to get up. She spoke to him gently, but with an urgency. "Luke . . . I need you to go. I need you to go back to school." He didn't move. He just stood there shaking his head. "This is no good, Luke. This can't go on anymore. It's no longer workable. I need you to go back to school. When you get back there, I want you to go to Mr. Cafferty. I want you to tell him" she said, her heart pounding in her chest, "that he has to find you a place to live."

"Oh no." Luke's head was lowered, and he shook it from side to side, his hand in his hair melodramatically.

"Luke, I lived with a father who was violent and a husband who was—you saw with your own eyes. I can't live with a son who is. I can't put up with that anymore. Please, go to Mr. Cafferty and tell him that."

"No. No. I won't do that again. I promise! I'm serious!"

"I know you won't," she said sadly. "I know you didn't mean to. But you remember how frightened you were when your father would punch me? Well, I can't live with that kind of fear. I'm sorry, Luke. I love you, but this won't do. You haven't even *spoken* to Ed for the last six months and now you're hanging out in Tompkins Square Park! I just don't know how to help you anymore! You need people who can. Go to Mr. Cafferty. Please."

When Ed picked up the department phone, it was Jane on the other end. He couldn't make out her words.

In time, Jane was able to paper over the hole in the family by converting Luke's room into a darkroom. Up until then, she had, in conjunction with classes she was taking at the 92nd Street Y, set up and packed away her dark room equipment in the kitchen each time she used it, a laborious endeavor, but one worth its while: it allowed her to lose herself in the immediacy of vision and craft, in the hands-on magic of pulling gold from the submerged blacks, whites and infinity of grays. But one day, several weeks after Luke had been thrust into an unwanted, if inevitable, flight from the nest, Jane started to claim his boy's-blue-painted room by taking down his Star Trek posters and dinosaur models and replacing them with montages of images she'd discovered in art books and magazines and from her own emerging catalogue of work. She left the framed photo, the one of Luke standing in front of the statue of Abraham Lincoln at the Lincoln Memorial, where it was on his dresser drawer, the way office workers dot their desks with family mementos. Before they had used a small inheritance from Ed's grandmother to renovate the apartment, Jane's bedroom had consisted of a bunk bed and a dresser in a pass-through section of a doorless railroad apartment, and as a child she had always shared a room with her sister, so she began to see this darkroom as the very first room of her own. Even so, she kept the walls blue, allowing it to stand in for Luke: a sky of filial love.

She threw herself into her photographic work with her usual passionate intensity, all the more so now that she was bereft of her baby boy. In her darkroom she missed no one, not Luke, not Ed, certainly not the people at the office, but outside the room it took a while before she would stop hearing the echo of Luke's absence, before her mind would stop filling the silence with the sounds she *expected* to hear of a restless, isolated teenager moving around his room behind closed doors or the galumphing across the apartment to the refrigerator, the sound of his whisperings as he unsuccessfully tried to repress his urges to voice his internal dialogues and fantasies. She found herself looking forward to the weekly family therapy sessions with Luke and Ed that were mediated by Mr. Cafferty, Luke's school social worker, where, with great doe-eyed earnestness, Luke strived to make his way back into the good graces of his mother and to own a relationship with Ed by calling him his stepdad. At first, Mr. Cafferty had arranged for Luke to stay at a Catholic home for runaways—the kind of place Jane could have made use of if it had existed the year she ran away from home. Luke stayed there until Mr. Cafferty finally found an opening for him in an apartment program with a site on a block with sleepy warehouses in a corner of the Upper East Side. These circumstances seemed like a banishment to him, and he spent much fruitless energy trying to crawl back into the Eden he perceived in his former bedroom, his tiny fortress against the real world that he had defended with his arsenal of ray gun noises. But that was like trying to crawl back into a playhouse that he had outgrown. Being Luke, he had to struggle against the obvious for months before he would realize how much his life had permanently changed.

Once Luke realized there was no going back, he fought his new "parents"—his apartment counselors—tooth and nail and made his resentment clear to his old ones that they had abandoned him to drill sergeants. This turn of events, unsettling Jane, obliquely mirrored her own traumatic break from home, when, as a teenage runaway, she had passionately thrown herself headfirst into the sex-and-drugs maelstrom of the sixties as her way to numb the bruises of family and the terrors of rootlessness. She was a much tougher cookie than she knew Luke would ever be, and she felt her separation from him more violently than she ever allowed herself to feel at the death of her mother or from the abandonment by her brother. She could still recall how it felt when Ray had threatened to place her in a foster home twenty years earlier. She suspected Luke must be feeling something similar in his own very distinctive way. And it made her furious to have to identify with her brother even tangentially.

All of this familial combustion began affecting her interactions with Ed, and when she needed him most, she found herself at odds with him way too often, as if he was the person most accessible to pummel, to flail out against. Before her life could completely fall to pieces, however, she and Ed contacted Suzanne, a psychotherapist, and they started couples counseling. Jane very quickly felt listened to and protected and over the course of several months she allowed herself to uncork a part of herself that had been bottled up since her mother had died, and Suzanne's soft, measured voice would tap her desire for a mother's love like a snake charmer slowly drawing its sleepy subject from its coil. She started to feel a sibling rivalry with Ed for Suzanne's approval and found it, consequently, unbearable when Suzanne would side with Ed's point of view on a particular conflict. It reminded her of being the neglected youngest child in the troubled Cantore family, and finally during one visit, she put her foot down. She was no longer willing to share the teat with Ed. They needed to get their therapy separately.

She had earlier taken color theory courses at Cooper Union and then a photography appreciation course at the Y before she'd eventually signed up for a darkroom class under the tutelage of Nicu, a young, earthy Romanian instructor. She thrived in the company of her enthusiastic classmates and appreciated the attention that Nicu, hovering over her work, would pay it—East Village cityscapes, abstracted graffiti, portraits of people she met in Washington Square Park and of friends posed in draping fabric—scattered as it was across the worktable for all, but especially Nicu, to examine and comment on. She could tell that he was impressed with what she was doing and she started to feel like she had been accorded the status of first among equals, with her classmates always eager for her feedback. Nicu enjoyed the creative energy she added to the class, and often, at class's end after cleaning up, they found themselves sharing a cigarette together like friends.

"You have a strong aesthetic sense," he told her one day. "Very tactile, yes? Only in one case do I question it. Your male nude," he said, "Why do you feminize him with those flowers on his lap?"

She thought about his comment and asked him if he was familiar with Caravaggio's painting of Dionysus. He said he was. He suggested they chat over coffee somewhere, and they found a Hamburger Heaven to relax in.

"I think it is a beautiful painting," he said, stirring his coffee casually, his head askance, "but it makes me . . . uncomfortable. I think that's Caravaggio's intention. To make me uncomfortable." He laughed. "To make *us* uncomfortable. Male and female juxtaposed in one person. Even East and West meeting in one person—he's almost Oriental, Dionysus. We are meant to see him and his otherness with an intense enough clarity so that we can acknowledge our own sensuality but be . . . appalled by it as well."

"I think," Jane said, leaning forward intently, "that he's beautiful and Caravaggio wants to give you pure pleasure, to dazzle you. He's the god of intoxication, for God's sake. He's an invitation to indulge."

"For a homosexual, perhaps. *I* would not look at him and say 'Can I buy you a drink?' I would move on. And who is this nude of yours? He's not gay? Some gay friend?"

Jane laughed as she blushed.

"No! That's my husband!"

"And he didn't feel uncomfortable posing nude for you? With flowers?"

"No. We were having fun."

"Fun?" Nicu's dark eyes crinkled with a dry amusement. "Well, I think if I was going to model nude for a woman, I would not appreciate her decorating me with roses, even though your roses do echo the tones of his flesh. *Clay. Mud. Wood.* I think *rougher* textures would be just as attention-grabbing in their own way. That's how I would want you to shoot me—dripping with clumps of wet mud!"

She looked forward to these conversations. Nicu was smart and entertaining, and he clearly liked her talent, her skill, and more. It was the kind of banter she had enjoyed with Ed before they'd slept together and with Steve after they'd stopped. Stimulating, flattering and easy.

She had re-registered for Nicu's class the following semester and as her second workshop with him was nearing its last days, Nicu started preparing for an exhibition of student work. Consequently, Jane was away from home each night, going to the Y to help set everything up. One evening she came home around 10:30: much later than usual.

"We've got to talk," Jane announced from the bedroom doorway. Ed got out of bed to welcome her with a kiss; her response felt tentative, almost passive.

"I think I'm falling in love," she confessed quietly.

There was no response.

"I think I'm falling in love with Nicu," she continued. "And I don't know how to stop myself."

"What?" Ed said. He was at a total loss, helpless to respond.

"I needed to tell you this because I don't want to ruin our marriage and I'm afraid I'm going to."

"Don't," was all Ed could think to say.

Jane sank in her chair. She felt like she needed a lifeline, but was left instead to struggle on her own to get to shore. Her demeanor suggested she didn't think she could make it.

Ed continued, "Look, if I'm not what you *want* . . . if you need something I don't have within me to *give* . . . then just tell me and do what you have to do. I don't want anyone to stay with me against their will. . . . . But if that's not the case," he said, "it's simple. Don't do this."

"Don't you understand?" she replied. "I need your help!"

Ed felt totally inadequate to the occasion. He had no idea what she wanted. So he stood up and walked over to her and extended his hand, the one branded with the gold serrated wedding band. She tepidly placed her own small hand in his large one; she let it rest there, supported. He gently pulled her to her feet and slowly enveloped her with his long arms. She buried herself in his chest and held onto him tightly.

"Does this help?" Ed asked.

Jane looked up. It was Ed in her arms. Not Nicu. He was present and warm and his fatigue wore itself sexily around the eyes and she could sense the sweet smell of his body that was familiar to her. She realized she didn't *know* Nicu, he was an attractive stranger to her, and though she knew she could easily let herself get all wrapped up in him, enjoy the astringency of bracing new sex, she knew what it was about and it wasn't love. Once that would've been OK.

"Yes. It helps. Thank you," she said softly. "I'm sorry."

Ed felt strong and capable, standing there with his woman in his arms, at the same time as he experienced inside himself a sort of despair.

* * *

A few years went by. Jane continued to delve into her creative unconscious, leaning over her notebook at the kitchen table
or immersed in the chemical fumes of her own private darkroom
(no longer made to feel welcome by Nicu in his class at the Y).
She continued, as well, earning the higher income attainable by
working in huge corporate law firms, and was invigorated by the
ability to pay off debts and cover the costs of Dr. Mariassi and
Suzanne. She felt productive, more self-sufficient and empowered
by making positive changes in her life, and she decided to use
some of that energy to address her lifelong weight problem. She
enrolled in support programs and attended them religiously,
discussed the issues that were triggered by her change in eating
habits with Suzanne and watched as, over years, she slowly shed
some of the excess from her body. It took the kind of determination that she'd otherwise managed to muster somehow, against all
odds, in the course of her bruising scrap with life, odds that others
would easily be felled by. She was still the same person as the
little girl who, before she could even write her name, was intent
on becoming a writer and had readied herself by scribbling in the
rent receipt books her mother bought her from the five-and-dime
below the el on White Plains Road. The willfulness came naturally to her. It was the acceptance of limitations, her own and those
imposed by others, that caused her problems.

She attacked her weight problem with a mercilessness she felt
was vital to her staying on track. She shed those alcoholic friends
who encouraged her to indulge in her own vices, and said goodbye to the pot she had used to face each day with a smile because it
also made her binge eat. And when Tracy left Steve and he soon
added a crack cocaine habit to his riot of vices, losing his Queens
apartment to end up squatting in an abandoned East Village tenement, Jane no longer opened the door to him. The last time he
rang her front door bell she held her finger over the buzzer,
unable to press it, seized by a fear as terrifying to her as if a large

chocolate cake had been placed in front of her. When she heard the slap of the downstairs door, she ran to the front window and watched Steve, in scotch-taped glasses and in the company of what looked to be a black transvestite in a Tina Turner wig, walk haplessly down the stoop stairs. She walked back to the kitchen and took out a Vantage Menthol, flicking the ashes self-consciously into the black plastic ashtray, trying to put Steve and the cigarette butt out in one move.

Each pound cast off felt like part of the slow excavation of an essential self, the Jane buried beneath the ruins of a disastrous childhood. She walked lighter now, pulling energy from the ground rather than being wed to it, giving her both the strength of less burdened legs and a sense of being loosened from that pull of gravity both oppressive and familiar. She had to learn how to hold onto the Earth beneath her feet, how to accept feeling smaller in a world of heavy-trodding men, a faun among raptors, some well-behaved, some not. She stood tall in her shoes, feeling strength in her purposefulness. She was on a roll, reinventing herself psychologically, redefining herself, and she could not help but redefine who she was with Ed as well.

When she looked at him she didn't see him going through any similar transformation. He was still the same basically sweet, plodding guy, content to get by on office work while playing at being an actor. She loved performances he'd given on the various downtown stages he'd mostly worked on, she admired his talent, but she was growing impatient with his acceptance of his lot in life, of the little recognition, professionally or financially, he had earned. His cautious personality, once an anchor to her volatile emotionality, was seeming like more dead weight to shed. This wasn't right for her anymore. She didn't know what was, but she allowed this vestige of her old heavier self—her husband—to be the one remaining obstacle to finding out what she really needed for herself.

Until now, all her life had been either about taking care of others or at least living with them. For as long as she could remember, she was either watching over, first, Virginia, and then Luke, or in the process of moving on from them. Never had she had the moment, except for the brief time between running away at fifteen and getting pregnant, to take care of her own needs first. From the various operatic Cantore households through the East Village pads she'd crashed, the bleary months with other runaways in Woodstock, the home for unwed mothers, and the Scarsdale foster home, to her two marriages in the same tenement apartment, she couldn't recall living even as much as a weekend completely on her own. Was it OK for her to forego that experience just because at one time, as a single mother, she'd needed a partner *as well as* a lover in her life? She wasn't sure, but she was more and more convinced that she didn't have that same need anymore. She wasn't the same person. Or, at least, at thirty-eight years old, no longer wanted to be.

After mulling it over for several weeks, both with Suzanne and by herself, she took the slow, unsteady walk along the gangplank. She'd waited until she and Ed had finished seeing a movie at the newly-triplexed theatre on East Eighth Street and were watching the credits roll as the audience members dribbled out, to tell Ed she needed to talk to him about something important, and casually, even sweetly, with no bitterness, she told him she wanted him to start looking for another place to live and she explained why. Ed sat numbly in the now-empty theatre, surrounded by a sea of plush beige seats which muted Jane's soft, steady voice as she told him what seemed to be a prepared recitation of a short story, a story about people other than Jane and Ed judging from the studied calmness of her demeanor.

It's not that Ed had never been in this position with her before. In the first year of their live-in romance, she had told him, in sterner terms, that she didn't want him around anymore. That year had been passionate and difficult for them both and Jane tossed to and fro, dealing with the ways she needed Ed and the ways he disappointed her. They had argued so often that almost ten years later, here, as they watched uniformed teenagers comb the theatre for empty drums of popcorn, Ed could no longer remember which particular offense of his had motivated Jane to ask him to leave back then. To her surprise, he had said OK. It wasn't until he told her that he'd asked an actor he knew who lived on Fifth Street if he could crash there until he found a place of his own, that Jane, shocked and impressed with Ed's apparent independence, became uncertain about her decision and apologetically asked him to stay.

Ed sat and slowly breathed in his dejection. Self-preservation kept him from fighting it out with her; he was not willing to show her his resentment at being bandied back and forth. But he also knew the sad, confusing fact that he still loved her, and he could see how much thought she'd put into presenting her case to him. It surprised him that this wasn't apparently coming from pique on Jane's part. She didn't hate him. She just didn't want him anymore. He told her he needed to think about it, but by the time they'd walked quietly, peacefully, back to their apartment, he told her he was going to need some time to find a place to live. Jane was relieved that Ed was taking it so well.

"You don't have to rush," she said, taking his hand. "You know it's not that I don't love you or anything."

"No," he said quietly. "I don't know that. I guess that's good to hear, but I don't know *what* it means right now." She was looking at him tenderly, a pained look in her beautiful, searching, dark eyes, a look that managed, in spite of everything, to touch him. "I love you, too," he admitted. "But if this is what you want, I guess I won't stand in your way."

"It is," she said quietly.

Within a month, Ed had managed to find a studio apartment in the commercial heart of the West Village on West Eighth Street, next door to the 8th Street Playhouse, an apartment he couldn't quite afford but thought it the best he could find. With the help of Luke and a friend from his day job, he transported the few things he needed, some donated by Jane. His Spartan new apartment had a futon mattress on the floor, a blue-painted chest of drawers, a hanging plant they'd bought at an upstate roadside stand with a coiffure of innumerable small red buds, a large movie poster taped to a wall, a portable radio-cassette player and a telephone. They didn't tell Ed's parents of the change; when Muriel would call, Jane would tell her that Ed would call her back and she would then leave a message on Ed's machine to call his mother.

They both embarked on their lonely adventure with a mixture of sadness and anticipation, their lives freshened by the newness of their daily routines, by the possibilities inherent as newly-hatched singles. Both of them threw themselves into their artwork in their spare time, Jane contemplatively in her darkroom or at her desk, Ed obsessively re-working monologues for auditions and acting class. At night, they slept with their longing along with, in Jane's case, the sound of her neighbor's occasional whimpering late into the night and, in Ed's, the sound of his neighbors rocking their bedsprings until their dive into silence. And they spoke to each other by phone several times a week, an occurrence which increased instead of decreasing, until by the third month they were dating—each other—like friends who fuck, which they did on his futon.

One day, five months into their separation, Jane received a phone call from Ed during the work week. He'd had to walk out of jury duty, he said; he was in the grips of some kind of virulent stomach bug.

"Can I come over?" he asked. He sounded uncharacteristically frail on the phone. Jane said yes.

When he arrived, he went into their sleeping alcove and collapsed on the bed. Jane sat by his side and lightly rubbed his back. She felt his long lower back rise and fall with his breath; his sock-clad feet hung over the edge of the bed as they always had. She felt tenderly towards him and happy to be in his company. She didn't like seeing him in pain, she realized, and then it occurred to her that she didn't like causing him any either. Perhaps she had shed too much from her life, she thought.

He stayed over that night, then went back to his place the next day.

He didn't call the next few days, assuming things were as usual, but they weren't as usual for Jane. She felt bereft, as if experiencing rejection; he wasn't asking her if he could return to her. She called him in a few days to see how he was feeling; they talked in intimate voices, casually, lightly.

A week before Thanksgiving, when Jane spent a weekend at his place, she asked Ed to move back home. He stared at her without comment for a while.

"I can't do this again," he said. "Next time you ask me to leave, it will be for good."

She accepted his terms and within the next month—the sixth month away—he was back home.

It was during the spring of 1991 when Jane was surprised to receive a UPS delivery from her radiologist. She had recently gone for her first mammogram, but she had never gotten a postal delivery from a radiologist before. Usually it was her doctor who she heard from, via telephone, saying everything looked OK.

She opened the large flat envelope. Inside were her X-rays and two pieces of white stationery. She was confused at first, because the letter was not addressed to her but to Dr. Fleischman. It was a typed letter written by the radiologist describing what she saw in the photos in medical terminology. The words "of special concern" were, not, however, medical terminology. They started the last paragraph and referred to markings in the lower right side of one of the X-rays, and suggested it be brought up with the patient.

She pulled out the X-rays in trepidation and held one of them to the light. The gray, milky landscape before her said nothing to her. She looked over to the right side of the film. Here there was a massy conglomeration of little circles that seemed to ooze towards her breasts. *What was this?* What did it mean?

She got on the phone and called Dr. Fleischman's office. She spoke to the doctor's receptionist, telling her the story, not successfully suppressing the panic in her voice—not really wanting to. She was promised that Dr. Fleischman would call back.

By the time he had returned her call, Ed was home. He preferred to err on the side of caution—since Jane was having trouble doing that—and had reminded Jane that they didn't know the significance—or even if there was any—to this medical report. Dr. Fleischman was also confused. Sending the patient their mammogram report was clearly a mistake, and he said he would call the radiologist's office in the morning to complain and he would call back as soon as he had seen the report. There was nothing for Jane and Ed to do but wait.

The next day, Jane got the call from Dr. Fleischman. He said the radiologist couldn't decipher the markings on the X-ray, and so he could not comment on them. The wisest thing to do, he said, was to schedule an appointment with a breast specialist at Beth Israel and get everything straightened out. He gave Jane the number for a Dr. Sharon Aptheker. "She's brilliant," he said. "She'll be able to help."

They both took off from their respective jobs; it was a hospital holiday for them. It was a bright, sunny day and the large room in which they met Dr. Aptheker was flooded with bright fluorescent light. After she had done her examination of both the photos and Jane's breasts, she called Ed in and brought them both over to the X-rays slapped to the brilliant white of the X-ray viewer.

"What is all this?" Jane said immediately, pointing to the swirls that had concerned her.

"Oh, that? That's nothing. That's normal breast tissue. You'd see that on all mammograms. No. That's not the concern. This is."

She pointed down towards the corner of the film, where there seemed to be a white scratch on the film's surface.

"This is not organic matter. This straight white line over here. Nothing in nature comes this straight."

"That's inside me?" Jane asked, her brow all furrowed. "I thought it was a blemish on the X-ray."

"No," Dr. Aptheker said calmly. "It seems to be an object inside your breast. If you look at this edge of it over here, it looks almost like the eye of a needle. You can feel it a little bit with your finger, buried deep inside the breast. Is there any reason you could think of that you might have something like a sewing needle lodged in the underside of your breast?"

Jane barely shook her head, but she seemed to be indicating that "no" was the answer. She felt concerned by the stares of Dr. Aptheker and Ed.

"When it first entered your body, it's conceivable that it could've traveled to your heart. You can consider yourself lucky that it didn't," the doctor continued. "That's not a danger now, but I would not *ever* take an MRI if I were you. It could tear the needle right out of your body."

It wasn't just the fact of the needle's existence that bothered Jane: it was also her complete ignorance of it. How could someone forget the experience of a needle being inserted into one's breasts? She wished she could believe that space aliens had something to do with it rather than something that implicated her sanity.

Ed and Jane returned to their apartment with few words between them, still dazed by the turn of events. Jane went into their bedroom alcove and lay down on their bed, Ed following to sit on its edge. They both sat still for a while, waiting for an annunciation of some kind to arrive via the cool rays of northern light from their bedroom window. Ed listened to the whisper of Jane's steady breathing, decipherable under the neighborhood's distant roar. Without warning, Jane broke the silence.

"When I was around ten or eleven," she volunteered, speaking to Ed as if to herself, "I started to develop breasts. I was early for my age. I guess because I was overweight. My mother had been dead for a couple of years and we were in the care of my father." She paused. "One day, my Aunt Connie mentioned to my father that I needed to start wearing a bra. It drove him crazy. He carried on, shouting that I was too young, that I was a 'good girl' and the fact that I had breasts enraged him. I remember looking at them in the mirror while in my undershirt and hating them, wishing they would just disappear. I was afraid he would get mad at me." Jane stopped as if that was the end of her story.

"So what happened?" Ed said.

"Nothing. I don't know. I don't remember. He wouldn't let me wear a bra and I didn't, until we were taken away from him."

"You think this has to do with the needle?"

"It's all I can think of," she answered, pitifully. "Maybe I thought I could *puncture* them. Like balloons. Do eleven-year-old girls think like that?"

There were no eleven-year-old girls around to ask. Just a sewing needle, lodged inside her, it being its own frayed thread, rising and falling with her breath.

By the mid-1990's, the East Village had become so gentrified it was barely worth complaining about; it was now part of the neighborhood's character. It had lost its local dollar movie theatre where the community met every week at double features, but it eventually, after a period of cinematic famine, was replaced with a feast of multiplexes. The local pharmacist, the fruit and vegetable stand, the egg store, the fabric store, the gay disco called The Saint, and possibly the world's only Ukrainian-Italian restaurant all gave way to chain stores and sidewalk cafes and more NYU classrooms. The open drug-dealing market which had been tolerated by the police for years when half of the neighborhood was heavily Puerto Rican and the other half Eastern European—and all of it sprinkled with what the police would consider degenerates—had been hustled from block to block until finally, real estate pressures being what they were—not to mention a public exposé of local police corruption in the newspapers—the dealers on the street were now history. The prostitutes no longer had free reign on East 12th Street and the large homeless population which camped out in Tompkins Square Park had been outsourced, all to be replaced by more and more young attorneys, brokers and college students.

By now, none of the elderly Ukrainian, Polish or Italian tenants were still living in Jane and Ed's building, and even the aspiring punk rock singers and actors were becoming scarce, due variously to AIDs, ambition-fatigue, the siren song of their middle-class upbringing and the steep rise in rents. The building had been sold by the original Ukrainian landlords, who had let the building amass over a hundred building code violations sometime back in the seventies before Ed had moved in and they'd then done the work to remove them so that they could sell it at a nice eighties profit to an Indian landlord who understood the financial promise of the neighborhood. As each tenant moved or died off, he would totally gut each apartment and rebuild it with shoddy, more modern fixtures, enabling him to charge a substantially higher rent of the NYU and Cooper Union students who tended to share the apartments with roommates for a few years and then leave once their parents were no longer supporting them. Consequently, Jane and Ed's tiny tenement apartment was beginning to feel under siege.

"Things were so much better when all of Second Avenue was dug up for the Second Avenue subway and no one wanted to live here!" Jane used to vent. "Now all the old-timers are being pushed out by all this yuppie scum!"

The problem, of course, was not that there were no longer gun battles outside the front window or homeless squatting in the vestibule. Nor was it that Jane had been in the same tenement since 1969 when she'd lived there with Luke and Tony years before Ed had joined the family in '79. Nor was it just the bathtub in the kitchen, or the small water closet near the air shaft nor the narrow high-ceilinged apartment. And it was not just being in your forties and living in a walk-up. No, there were other reasons their East Village life was becoming more and more problematic and why Jane and Ed needed to get out.

It was also Lina.

Lina had moved into the apartment next door within a year or two after Ed had arrived, replacing sweet old Mr. Yevchenko who had gone to live with his daughter in New Jersey. She was one of two young Polish immigrants who at first shared the apartment: Lina the seemingly demure, pretty one and Suzy the one with dark punked-up hair and heavy black eyeliner who dressed like a mod London prostitute ten years behind the times. To everyone's surprise, Suzy turned out to be the well-adjusted one: sociable and with her feet firmly on the ground. And she found out soon enough that she and Lina were incompatible as apartment mates. "This was just a mistake," she said vaguely to Ed, who saw her leaving one day, lugging her luggage down the creaky tenement stairs.

It was Jane and Ed's misfortune to share a slightly buckling wall with Lina that ran along the length of both apartments, as well as a fire escape. This brought them greater proximity than they wanted to the sound of her loud squabbling with tenants with whom she shared an alleyway from her kitchen window, to the parties she held late into the night during the week, and, most seriously, to her attempts to bring an end to her seemingly fraught life by leaving the gas burners on on a semi-regular basis, necessitating the police walking across Jane and Ed's bed in their tiny cocoon of a bedroom to get access to Lina via the fire escape. Over the years, they overheard way too many things while trying to have family meals or quiet cozy nights in bed, including loud complaints to some guy in the apartment about hating to have to walk the streets, and cries of help when different men beat her, only to tell Ed on one such occasion to mind his own business when he asked from outside her apartment door if she was alright. On another occasion, when their decaying light fixture in the kitchen caused a small electrical fire and Jane shouted for help, she could hear Lina's quiet, measured footsteps, back and forth along the length of the apartment, making it clear that she couldn't give a damn. The only person connected to the building who Lina befriended, in a manner of speaking, was the elderly Ukrainian landlord whose lap she crawled onto when, at the tenants' meeting held to complain about her behavior, she started to cry.

"Everybody hates me!" she sobbed onto Mr. Lenkovich's shoulder as he blushed and stammered and tried to calm her down.

"Don't worry, don't worry, dear, you have nothing to worry about!" he said, while the other tenants watched in a state of stupefaction.

So it had almost been a relief when, suddenly, she seemed to have disappeared and strangers were seen coming and going from her apartment as if they lived there. There were times when this seemed fairly inconsequential and people ignored it. There were times, like when, early one Sunday morning, an already-stewed elderly gentleman offered Ed a shot of vodka on his way into Lina's apartment, introducing himself as Lina's father in the few words he knew in English, that the situation was amusingly pathetic. But it was troubling when Ed didn't know who the man was who was beating his wife while their baby wailed in her arms, or when people caught two young Italian men who were living there breaking into other apartments, or when some guys in the wee hours of a weeknight were partying on the fire escape and when told that people were trying to sleep, replied "Mind your own fucking business!" This time complaints were more effective, and when the new landlord, who was highly motivated to rid the building of old tenants so he could renovate and jack up rents, threatened Lina with eviction, Lina just as suddenly returned, apparently intent on keeping her lease.

But the year that Lina got pregnant by a guy who one day beat her on the head with a telephone before walking out on her was the year Jane and Ed started to feel like Lina's problems were now theirs. Lina, possibly because of her chronic smoking, found herself with the responsibility of tending to a fragile baby boy born a month early, and within a few days of it felt like she'd had enough. Ed and Jane could hear her screaming at it, threatening to throw it out the window, causing Jane to revisit the various violent traumas that had been visited on her and her siblings and the months in foster care when she feared for her baby's wellbeing. Meanwhile Ed found himself in the position that he imagined Jane's extended family must have been in when he used to wonder *why hadn't anyone stepped in to stop this*. So Ed, in anguish, called Child Welfare and made a complaint, hating getting intimately involved in anyone else's life, but determined to keep their lives and their apartment from becoming a window onto unending wretchedness and abuse.

For the next month they were not spared that. In between visits by Child Welfare counselors and the parenting classes Lina was forced to attend, Jane could hear her slapping her infant in frustration when he wouldn't stop crying. She and the other neighbors would see him with bruises when Lina's aunt would walk him outside in his carriage when Lina was working at a nearby restaurant. Poor little Nicholas, as he was called, was visiting Jane in her dreams where she'd be struggling to take him from Lina's arms only to have the night goblin policemen take *her* away in handcuffs, Lina shouting "See what she did to my baby!" Eventually Lina came to realize who it was that was continuously contacting the authorities and the cold war threatened to go nuclear.

And then one day Lina and Nicholas were gone, just like that, not a sound of baby or mother for a few days, and gossip spread through the building until Jane and Ed were visited by the officers and detectives they'd been interviewed by when they'd first started making complaints. Lina had taken her son to the hospital, they were told, because, as she put it, "He just stopped breathing." The doctors, however, saw indications that Nicholas' breathing didn't just stop on its own.

"There is a possibility," one Officer Collins said as officiously as possible, "that this case might go to court. I don't know how Ms. Zodzinska will plead at this point. If we needed either of you to testify, would you be willing?"

"I guess so," Ed replied.

"Yes," Jane said timidly.

The thought actually horrified them, but they felt little for Lina who had put them through a trauma of their own, and much for Lina's poor, helpless baby. They had all been helpless babies once, even Lina. But her inability to put her baby's needs above her own, her inability to even face the neediness of others with anything resembling empathy, made her dangerous and even hateful. Ed used to say that for years Jane had been stuck at the age of fifteen, the age she was when she ran away from home, and that explained her intense rapport with teenagers as well as its other manifestations in her personality. He hadn't said that in a while, and even she knew that she no longer identified with teens in quite the same way. She guessed she had at least the maturity of someone in her twenties by now. But Lina was stuck somewhere near the terrible twos, and that was monstrous in an adult and worse in a parent: a petite, feminine Frankenstein's monster. Jane was grateful that by some twist of fate (and perhaps it was just a slight twist), she had not become a Lina: that she had not been consumed by the cold emptiness of her low-lying fury but had somehow, against all odds, nurtured that ember inside her—the call to love and be loved—and kept it burning, if sometimes on a low flame. Lina gave her the shivers.

Lina didn't go to court. She accepted a three year sentence at Riker's Island. In the meantime, relatives of hers sublet her apartment to whomever they could find, until, after a while, a tall, quiet young Indian man, who claimed he was a friend of Lina's, stayed put. Rajiv, the landlord, told Ed and Jane that his hands were legally tied and he could not evict Lina while she was imprisoned. That made clear to Ed and Jane that they had three years to get out. Sharing such close quarters with Lina again—not to mention her unwholesome pack of friends and lovers—would be out of the question. Who knew what she would be like after three years at Rikers, probably blaming her predicament on her neighbors' nosiness rather than on the fact that she had laid a pillow on her son's face to get him to stop crying.

There ended up being another reason why Ed and Jane needed to move, though, as well.

After Rajiv bought the building from the Lenkovich family, he started to implement his gentrification plans by hiring a contractor as soon as he had his first apartment vacancy under his tenure. Lloyd, who'd worked for Rajiv before on his other renovation projects, offered him a good price for a workforce consisting of himself and a few young Mexican apprentices. Expansive in build and personality, he was a big bull of a man with a wide-open-friendly face and the demeanor of someone who'd never met a person he couldn't talk to. He loved to engage in enthusiastic discussion about all manner of things, practical and academic, and he ended up staying in the building twenty-four hours a day, mostly getting his night's rest in a sleeping bag in the vacated apartment that he was working on. He could've gone home to his wife and child in Harlem, but by and large he seemed to prefer the bohemian atmosphere of the East Village tenement he worked on, to which he assumed a proprietary relationship. Eventually, the turnaround of apartments was constant enough so that Lloyd was hardly away. People saw him as one of the building's residents, or as a friendly concierge who oversaw everything.

Ed and Jane had both, together and individually, spent time on the front step shooting the breeze with Lloyd during the warmer months of the year, as had most people in the building. They could hear Lloyd's deep, resonant voice any time of the day either from the hallway, the alleyway, through the floors when renovating above or below them, or through the front windows when he was lounging on the stoop. They had gotten used to seeing him throughout the building, in and out of apartments, even leaving them in the early morning, and eventually word spread that he was sleeping with the redhead, Dana, on the fourth floor, among others. Ed saw him leaving Perry's apartment on the second floor one early morning with both of them saying goodbye to each other in a way that suggested Perry was infatuated with him. Ultimately, the common wisdom was that Lloyd was happily providing services not contracted for by Rajiv. The younger new immigrants to the East Village were having an adventure, while he was finding it an amenable and invigorating watering hole. Just one more perk of the bohemian lifestyle, and the building hummed with the activity of revolving-door tenants, musical-chairs renovation and a decidedly no-strings camaraderie.

By 1994, Jane had returned to Hunter College, the school she'd attended for a few semesters back in the '70s before she found it too difficult to support Luke and herself and go to school at the same time. She'd now gone back to pursue a degree in psychology, and eventually found herself, to her surprise and not a small amount of pride, to be on the research track in brain development, and she put much of her creative endeavors aside in order to accomplish this. By the time the spring semester of 1995 had ended, Jane had gone back to working as a temp on the evening shift at her old law firm to help make ends meet. She would be driven home at midnight by the firm's car service and, more often than not, spend some time with Lloyd on the stoop before heading upstairs to her and Ed's apartment.

Since Ed worked the day shift at his firm, he would be getting ready for bed right around the time of these conversations. He would hear Lloyd's and Jane's voices floating up through the front window, Lloyd's hearty basso profundo dancing with Jane's velvet soprano. He couldn't make out words, just moods: little, occasional whirlwinds of enthusiasm punctuating the quiet patter. It annoyed him that Jane was frittering away the limited time that she could spend with him before he had to turn in for the night, but these chats didn't usually go on for long, and that, he reasoned, was the price you pay for being in love with an independent-spirited woman, determined to follow the dictates of her own mind.

One evening, he was feeling particularly annoyed, because it was going on for a longer time than usual. Not only would he not get to see Jane, but she and Lloyd would be keeping him up as they were breezily serenading the neighborhood right beneath his and Jane's third-floor bedroom window. He was running behind his schedule in the process of building a bigger and bigger grudge when he noticed that he no longer could hear their voices out the window. He had just finished putting away the iron he'd been using on the next day's shirt when he heard the apartment door open slowly. He went about his business without looking at the door, deciding that if Jane didn't feel a need to pay him any attention he wouldn't waste any on her either, and he continued his nighttime ablutions with that attitude to guide him.

Jane sat on the vintage love seat that they kept in their narrow living room space, watching Ed busily going to and fro. She was unusually quiet, and finally Ed noticed that she sat pale and weary-looking, with an extra weight to her bearing.

"Ed," she said softly.

"What?" was his indifferent reply.

"Something—" Ed noticed her hand shaking as it hovered over her mouth. "Something just happened. . . ."

Ed watched impassively as Jane continued.

"I was sitting on the stoop, talking to Lloyd. Just innocent, friendly stuff," she continued. "The weather, if it was a tough day, things from our pasts. . . . Things like that. And I forget what led up to it, but at one point I said, 'You must know everything that goes on in this building,' and he says 'A lot but not everything,' and I said something like—oh, I don't know . . ." her fingers imitated a spooling motion as if to get her memory into play . . . "I think I told him he could probably tell me some juicy gossip, like which tenants were getting it on with each other, it being like a big dorm here lately, and he laughed and then asked me if I ever cheated on you."

Ed was less impassive now.

"And I said '*No!*' I was like, I didn't expect that. I said 'Of course not!' and he said 'You never even thought about it?' and all I could think of was to laugh. . . ." Ed could imagine her face blushing deeply and wondered if that would've been noticeable to Lloyd from the dim lamp light outside the front door, supplemented by the light that cascaded lightly out from the hallway.

"And he said something like he thought, for example, that he and I had a special relationship."

Your husband doesn't get you, does he? is what Lloyd also said. *You know what I'm saying.*

"And I didn't know what to say," Jane said, looking to Ed for understanding. "So I said that I thought we had a special *friendship*. And he said 'I think you know there's something else going on here.' And then I stood up and said it was getting late and I better say goodnight and I went into the hallway and he came after me, asking me to stay a little longer and I said I couldn't and then when I got to our floor he took my hand and held it for a while and he was making me nervous, so I said 'Ed is waiting . . .' and he started to walk upstairs but . . . he wasn't letting go of my hand! And I got so scared, and I said 'Lloyd, please!' and my hand was hurting because I tried to pull it away and his grip . . ."

Jane was shaking now. Ed crouched next to her as if to draw her into his embrace.

"And I said, 'Lloyd, you're hurting me, you're hurting my hand' and so he let go and I got away." Ed reached into his back pocket for his pack of Kleenex and drew one out for her to wipe the few tears away with. "What am I going to do, Ed? What am I going to do?" The building replied for Ed with a muffled, sleepy silence as if they were talking in someone else's dream. "He's here every day when I am and when most people are away at work. I feel so *unsafe* here."

Ed had put his arm around her, but, although troubled by Jane's muted pallor, he was not moved by her distress as much as his gesture indicated. He had no trouble imagining her downstairs with Lloyd, her eyes animated, her laugh inviting, her nostrils flared; he knew she was capable of sending signals she was not aware of and that it was confusing to guys, as it had been confusing to him fifteen years ago; it was like lowering your body into cool, clear water on a hot summer's day; it was delicious, and the response it elicited in you opened *her* up even further, and many men, even husbands of good friends, loved their moments alone with Jane, believing they had a "special understanding." That was part of *Ed's* "special understanding:" that the other guys could think they had one, but not in the way they thought. Ed knew that Jane was still to some extent Daddy's girl, and he knew what Daddy had taught her, how stimulating a man's attention could be, and how scary sometimes, too.

And also, Ed thought of friendly, affable Lloyd, who had something similar in *his* nature, his own kind of seductiveness, conscious or not. After all, Ed had felt that Lloyd was *his* friend, too: jovial, comradely, *hey man, what's up*, but really it turned out Lloyd thought of him as some kind of patsy, or at the very least as an inadequate spouse, not quite as "special" to his own wife as Lloyd was.

Ed was angered by Lloyd's presumption, but he was especially annoyed at Jane. If she hadn't signaled to Lloyd *and* him that she felt no urgency to see Ed when she got home, this would not have happened. Jane would not now feel violated, Lloyd would not have made assumptions, and Ed would not have to *handle* this in some way.

"Don't worry about it," Ed said, holding the same hand that Lloyd had held so tightly. "I'll take care of it."

"How?" Jane asked nervously. "What are you going to do?"

"I'll talk to him."

"What are you going to say?"

"I'm going to tell him to leave you alone." There was not much else he felt he could do. Though Ed was over six feet, Lloyd was, too, and two to three times his girth, a guy who pounded floors and walls all day and who would have no fear of any physical threat from Ed. In fact, to Ed's distaste, the only ace he held in his hand was the unstated race card.

Ed heard Lloyd's heavy tread coming down the stairway.

"I'll be right back," he said to Jane.

"I love you," Jane said pathetically.

"I know," he said. "I'll be right back."

"Lloyd," Ed said from the staircase as he followed Lloyd down to the second floor, "can I speak to you a second?"

"Sure," Lloyd replied, as if he had no expectations of what the conversation could be about. "You're up late. What's on your mind?" he said with a friendly smile.

"Jane just told me what happened," Ed started, trying to squelch the slight tremor in his voice.

"I'm not sure what you mean."

"I think you do!" His eyes locked on Lloyd's but Lloyd accepted his glare like an easy fly-ball catch in center field.

"No, I'm afraid—"

"You grabbed her hand and wouldn't let her go, after you asked her if she ever cheats on me!" Ed bit the words out furiously.

"I think there's been some kind of misunderstanding . . ." Lloyd said with an expression that suggested sympathetic concern.

"Well, I don't! My wife is not a liar! Nor is she stupid!"

"Well, if she misunderstood anything I said, I'll apologize to her next time I see her. . . ."

"*No!* Don't talk to her at all! From now on, stay away from her! If I find out you so much as talk to her, I will be contacting Rajiv *and* the *police*. Do you understand?" Ed didn't let his discomfort over being stuck in this classic American racial dynamic get in his way; he knew he was using the typical cop's suspicion of blacks as a substitute for muscle.

"Whatever you say," Lloyd responded, shaking his head sadly, not conceding any ground.

Ed went back to his apartment, acting out the loving concern for Jane that he hoped masked his anger at her. It did, but in a way that made her feel insecure anyway.

It was now clear to both Ed and Jane that this incident, the constant plaster dust from eternal renovation and the impending return of Lina was squeezing the feeling of "home" *out* of their home. In contrast to the days when the building's tenants were a united community on rent strike, now—with most of those residents gone or leaving—each tenant was an island unto him or herself, or—as it now felt to Ed and Jane—a leaky row boat on an unsteady sea.

It was the morning after Ed and Jane had heard that they were accepted into the housing development they'd applied for and they were celebrating with an impromptu display of affection under the bed linens. Driving relentlessly into the future, forty-five year old Ed shifted into higher gear only to swerve into his first collision with his sacroiliac joint just before reaching his desired destination. His subsequent anguished, graceless contortions were, for a moment, the stuff of farce for Jane, who had a high appreciation for physical comedy, but mirth started to morph into anxiety as she watched Ed's face flush in time to his body's sudden spasms. "Shit!" he whispered between clenched teeth. He carefully got out of bed to discover that he was OK when moving cautiously, but when he relaxed he could expect to be visited by stabbing needles of pain.

He consequently made an appointment to see an osteopath who managed to squeeze him into his schedule that day and who, on examination, made it very clear that Ed was going to have to avoid heavy lifting for a few weeks' time. This was not fortuitous timing, Ed knew, but since they had a month's time within which to prepare for moving, he assumed he could do most of the packing in the last couple of weeks.

This infuriated Jane, who always experienced exaggerated anxiety around anything that resembled a departure. She approached the move as if, if everything wasn't taken care of right away, her father might show up, find her preparing to escape, and forcefully confine her. This kind of lesson had been hard-wired into her, so that through most of her adult life, leaving for vacation, leaving the *neighborhood* in the early years of their relationship, and—during certain periods of depression—even leaving her apartment, brought out her fight-or-flight instincts. That being the case, even though she had her own serious back problems, she started on her own to pack up the apartment in large cardboard boxes, fuming at—or about—Ed all the while. She knew he was unhappy at having to move—having to leave behind these artsy digs for a bland, middle-class apartment complex—and so she viewed his injury as an act of willful obstruction. She had to get out and he had to make that impossible, and she acted as if she would never be able to forgive him for this. Her fury became large, consuming her—when Ed looked at her he saw a thick wall of fissionable hatred facing him—and she pummeled him with her words for most of the month, even when he finally joined her in her labors.

By the time they had made their move, said goodbye to their home of fifteen-years-and-upwards from their front stoop under Lloyd's surveillance, Ed, too, wasn't sure that he was capable of forgiving *Jane*. No matter how warm their exchanges might be, how playful or affectionate, Ed could now feel himself submerging his love, confining it and locking it up in some puny chamber deep inside, denying himself access. He would no longer allow himself to feel vulnerable around her. After these years of ups and downs, arguments and rapprochements, exhilarations and crises, Ed now related to her as if he had finally met the part of Jane that her friends had warned about. She *could* destroy him. With steady emotional pummeling. And when, in the months after the move, they'd made love, it was more violent than it ever had been before, which *she* experienced as a deepening in their passion, but which he could barely feel at all. His own body was insensate wood.

One day in January, a year and a half later, Ed and Jane were sharing a moment of now-rare concord driving Rocket, their eleven-year-old hand-me-down Camry, up the wavy, hilly highway of Route 17 across the southern Catskills. They were on the four hour drive to Binghamton, New York, on a bright, wintry Monday afternoon so that Jane could interview the next morning for the graduate program in neurobiology at the state university there. Ed had taken off from work to drive and accompany her, and his having volunteered to do so made Jane see him differently than she had come to see him since they'd moved to Manhattan's west side.

Jane experienced Rocket's zooming highway speed away from the New York metropolitan area as liberating, even empowering, and Ed's accompanying her as more empowering still: perhaps the stands she'd been taking to jar Ed from his complacent lifestyle were bearing fruit. This was a marked change for Ed considering that, only recently, their mutual disaffection and seeming disinterest in each other's state of affairs, their accumulation of grievances and Jane's general sense of restlessness had convinced her that the only positive direction their marriage could take was towards divorce. Which, one day, she had clearly and sternly announced to him. He, consequently, picked himself up and moved into the living room to sleep on the futon mattress that was still awaiting a sofa's wooden frame after more than a year of their living in that apartment.

"You've said that once too often," was his reply.

He hadn't moved out—she knew neither of them could have afforded to, although a more impetuous person would not have let that stop him; he'd merely moved to the other side of their one-bedroom apartment which overlooked a small park from the sixth floor. For weeks, the apartment had been filled with the unmistakable frostiness of roommates who could just barely tolerate each other.

When she'd graduated with honors from Hunter College— she, the first of her family to finish high school—she'd felt a sense of accomplishment that had managed to evade her efforts in poetry and photography. She'd been inspired by her teachers there, and encouraged most especially by Lisette, a young Puerto Rican professor who'd also had to leave much behind to attain success. Lisette had counseled Jane never to let a man get in the way of her achievements, just as *she* hadn't when she'd left her unsupportive husband, taking her year-old daughter with her so that she could successfully realize her academic dreams as well as attain an academic's salary. Lisette had met Ed at a departmental luncheon honoring the graduates and had liked him, but she'd casually teased him for being "one of those underachievers," as she'd put it, when he'd told her of his being an actor with a day job, and that term nettled Ed; it was a while before Jane, who thought Ed overreacted, realized that perhaps Ed *could* be seen that way. Perhaps all of her artist friends could. She found herself shifting perspective, considering the possibility that perhaps she was developing a higher seriousness of purpose than her friends who had dedicated their lives to a kind of perpetually poverty-stricken child's play. She could do more than merely express herself; she could *accomplish* something that could change people's lives. Ed's uphill attempt at producing aesthetic product while hobbling by on service industry wages seemed a sign of a profound immaturity to her.

"I was a clearly labeled package," Ed had defended himself. "You knew from the beginning that I was an actor. I never indicated to you that I was just 'trying this out for a while.'"

"No, you didn't," Jane agreed. "But some of us grow."

Jane was aware after she'd said that that she'd insulted Ed and she couldn't help feeling a twang of sympathy for him. She had never in her life, after all, been as close to anyone else. If he now seemed petulant and withholding by half, he could still tickle her, charm her, and even excite her in his better moments. And she knew he loved her, and he had loved her for all of these seventeen years. It's just that all of these qualities seemed diminished in her eyes. Diminished by fatigue and the festering emotional sores of ongoing arguments, by age's heightened intolerance of discomforts as well as its lessened propensity for carnal yearning. In some way it was as if the East Village had defined them as a couple, and moving away from it had robbed them of that definition. They were no longer a variation of new bohemians, but merely two separate individuals sharing a common space and a history of affection for each other.

Ed, driving Rocket, did not see a liberating rush of possibilities. He was not trying to indicate a new attitude about the evolution of their relationship. He was just up for an adventure, even if it was only the automotive kind. He needed a break from the current routine, and driving to somewhere new served him just fine. He was enjoying being focused on the present: the steering of the car, the play with speed limits, the community of drivers on the road, perhaps the inherent danger that's ever-present in hurtling along a long stretch of paved road, a danger absent in a sedentary office. That, and the sense of consequences: that if you put yourself out there in the world, that anything could happen; it was a pretend crap shoot. He needed a sense of acceleration. And in that sense, perhaps, Jane's assessment of his situation was right.

Jane had made it clear that her chances of being accepted to Binghamton were slim, but that she wanted to make a go of it. She knew she'd have a spot waiting for her at Hunter if she wanted, but Lisette had encouraged her to try for the best, and Binghamton's reputation in the field was stellar, their neurobiology department better financially supported than Hunter's was. So Ed saw this trip as both an excursion and as a way to spend at least *some* potentially pleasant time with Jane, who would probably be less of a bitch to him than she *had* been because he was helping her out. He loved Jane's company, normally, and he loved mattering to her, but he did not see much of a future to their marriage: her temper only hardened him, and his distancing only angered her further. Mentally, he was on his way out; his love for her seemed more and more at the expense of his self-respect. This lent the trip a nihilistic devil-may-care aspect: it was as if he was taking a two day trip with his ex, cavalierly unconcerned with the norms of convention.

The highway rose up to meet the city, which only became visible as they reached a plateau of highway intersections. A dun-colored mass of industrial infrastructure sat before them, cushioned between low-lying grayish hills and capped with a milky sky. The Front Street exit left them alongside the narrow, blackish Chenango River which they crossed on an equally char-colored bridge. Suddenly, their sparkly white Holiday Inn loomed, surrounded by rundown nineteenth-century factory buildings a stone's throw from Binghamton's miniscule downtown. Inside, the hotel was carpeted with the sound of Muzak, occasionally interrupted by the chimes of elevator "dings" as the doors opened and closed. Once in their room, they threw their small traveling bags on the folding luggage rack and quickly acclimated themselves to their friendly, sterile, temporary home. Irrespective of the TV's glossy advertising menu reminding them of the accessibility of adult films, Ed claimed his own double bed by falling back down on it. She couldn't have him back just because she was being appreciatively sweet to him today.

The next morning, Ed drove Jane to the campus, all 1960s space-age architecture sitting on a vast, empty plain under eternally cloudy skies. He walked her to the Psychology Building and when they found the Graduate School Office, Ed wished her luck and rambled around the campus for a while before heading out to a local mall—one of the many that were laid out towards the horizon—for a bite of lunch.

Over the course of the day, Jane was introduced to the various professors and their departments, some emphasizing research projects, others cognitive therapy training. Hank McDonnell was the mild-mannered, warm neurobiologist who liked working in a rural environment; Diana Goodwin was somewhat more officious and talked about how she had to have a merciless approach to get what she needed in the department; Sidney Bloom, the head of the cognitive therapy division, talked about the small professional theatre he was running in his off-hours when Jane mentioned her husband's experience on the stage. After a lunch break, Jane met with Ted Rudnicki, an imposing man in his forties who looked like he did his lab research between mountain climbing and smoking pot. He was charismatic, assertive and very interested in her background as a writer. Jane repeated what she had told the others about the various research projects she had assisted on as an undergraduate, and while doing so, she felt his steady gaze from behind his wire-rimmed glasses.

"I'm very tough to work for," he said after listening to her and taking a pause to reflect. "I'm not even sure it's good for me to take on another graduate student. I've had some casualties. I've been accused of being difficult. But I could use someone who writes well, and science writing is a major teaching responsibility for our grad students."

Jane instinctively enjoyed handling the challenge of his virile personality, and she was in full flower as she smiled and said with a laugh that she got along well with people others found difficult. *After all*, she thought confidently, *I was born to it . . . Daddy, Virginia, Tony, Steve, Luke, all those lawyers, my crazy friends, even Ed in his lesser way. I can handle "difficult,"* she thought grandiosely.

"How did the day go?" Ed asked her when he'd returned to pick her up.

She filled him in on her impressions and added: "It's tough to get in here. It's very competitive, so I don't think it's likely. There was this one guy who didn't think he wanted to take on anyone new, but he liked the fact I was a writer. He's had some bad experiences with grad students, so it probably won't happen. Ed, I really have to thank you. You've been so supportive on this trip. I'm glad you came up with me. I hope you weren't too bored."

"No, I liked the change of pace," he said, not quite acknowledging the warmth of her gratitude. "It was like a little vacation, a drive in the country. No problem."

They found Rocket and lifted off the barren planet, heading towards the highway home.

* * *

Three months later, Jane came home to find a large manila envelope from the University of Binghamton in the mailbox. She stood there in the building lobby just holding it in her hand, wide-eyed and jangly, her nerve endings crying "Tilt." Why in the world would they be sending her a big envelope—unless . . .

When Ed came home, Jane didn't say anything right away. Ed was now back to sleeping in the bedroom, and things had a pleasant, if tenuous, air about them. Ed's going to Binghamton with her had softened Jane's aloofness a bit; Jane was acclimating herself to the life they had been living in New York and her eventual return to Hunter for graduate school, and that change in expectations made Ed seem more acceptable to her. She wasn't feeling that his dead weight was dragging down her aspirations as much as she had before. She waited until Ed was changing from his work clothes to quietly inform him.

"I've been accepted to Binghamton."

"What?" Ed said. "That's wild!"

"As Dr. Rudnicki's student. To help in his research. I really can't believe it! Isn't this great? Our whole life could change! I've got to call them in a few days and let them know if I accept the offer."

Ed stared at Jane. Jane had presented her applications to grad schools outside the city as a lark, as a way to gauge her worth in the eyes of the academics in her field, as a learning experience, not as an actual consideration. But Ed sensed that that was no longer the case.

"Are you seriously considering it?"

"I'd be a fool not to! Do you know how prestigious their department is? They get so much more funding than the department at Hunter does. My degree would be worth so much more. . . ."

"Jane," Ed said, the sensation of a deep gully yawning beneath his feet rising up to meet him, "we need to talk. . . ."

"Not now!" Jane implored impatiently. "*Not now.* Let me just enjoy this for a little bit. *Please!*" He knew that glare and decided to step out of its range of vision. Maybe this wasn't the best time to discuss this total change in the direction of their lives. Maybe he just should have congratulated her and waited for the right moment. He wanted to think of himself as a supportive kind of guy, but he was feeling his anger rising slowly. Once more, Jane was in the driver's seat and Ed felt like he had been assigned to the back of the car, to be whipped around in whatever direction she would take him. And he was finding this less and less charming.

Jane, on the other hand, felt that everything was falling into place. She felt certain now that she had a destiny, even a calling, and a serious chance at a place at the table in the world of mature adulthood. To be accepted into Binghamton at the age of forty-five was a singular achievement. This, she realized, was where her long, difficult path had always been heading. Her life experience was going to inform her work in a way that would not be possible for someone in their twenties, it would give the story of her success a special meaning; it would no longer be her handicap. She had done the work and, through her own abilities, she was moving on. She thought of Lisette's advice and was determined not to let anything get in her way. She knew Ed, in the past, to have always gotten behind her eventually, and she assumed the importance of all this would become clear and inevitable to him in time.

Over the next few days, the dynamic never changed. For Jane, the bright spring daylight that flooded their living room each morning underlined her own rebirth, while to Ed it merely seemed discordant. Each time Jane enthused to someone about the possibilities of Binghamton in Ed's hearing, it made him more nervous. She seemed to be suggesting to people how "we" could pull it together, without once bringing the other half of the "we" into the equation.

Finally, after one of those overheard conversations, Ed confronted her.

"Before you go on about this anymore, we have to talk," he said.

Jane turned to look at him. She looked at the man she had spent the last seventeen years with and remembered all those qualities that had allowed her to feel comfortable living with one person for so long, something she'd not believed she would ever be capable of at one point in her life, maybe not even desirable. Since then, Ed had become essential to her and now, hearing the muffled drumbeat rising in her chest, she tried to resist her body's call to war. She would need to keep her past and future in some state of accord, and wringing Ed by the neck for not intuiting the rightness of this opportunity, for not seeing the blessing for what it was—and for not recognizing her part in bringing it about— would not, she knew, get the best results.

"What?" she said with the kind of patience which suggested the opposite lurked nearby.

"We have not discussed *once* where I fit into this."

"Well, I figure I would go up for the summer to work in Rudnicki's lab, and you could join me in the fall. We'd find a place that would be good for the two of us. . . ."

"Jane, you don't even know if I want to move to Binghamton at all!—What would I *do* there?"

"Do I have to know that now?!" She was beginning to lose it. "*Something!* We would see! We can't decide that in three days' time. . . . Why are you doing this? Can't you just be supportive for now? I would be for you!"

Ed was not accepting this.

"I would've at least *talked* to you about it beforehand! We are a *couple* after all! And you are talking about a major disruption of our lives!"

"Oh, I just can't believe you!" Jane's voice rose as she stood up from her seat, combusting in anger, her eyes aimed at annihilating him. "You can't even allow me *this!* I've just had the biggest success of my life so far and you can't allow me to feel good about it for three whole fucking days!"

"You should feel *great* about it, but you shouldn't *act* on it without including me in on the decision-making. You're changing my life for me and I might have something to say about it!"

"You *went* with me for the interviews!" she cried. "Why are you waiting until now to tell me you have doubts about doing this?!"

"You said you had no chance of getting accepted. I went along so that you could have the experience, and because I wanted to fucking . . . take . . . a trip! I needed to break up . . . the *doldrums* I was in! I was sleeping in the living room, if you remember, because you told me you wanted a divorce!"

"But you haven't been sleeping in the living room for months! I thought that was behind us!"

"Have I ever said to you *once* that I wanted to move with you to Binghamton? I'm still not sure where our marriage is going or if it's going anywhere at all and you want me to move to a city where I wouldn't know anyone but you and don't know where or how I could get employment? I mean, the area is entirely *depressed!*"

"This is what I mean! I can't believe you would wait till *now* to bring up these issues! Why didn't you bring them up before?"

"We *have* talked about our problems. We tried that stupid couples counseling just last year and that didn't work. He waited for the last scheduled session to discuss how you contribute to our problems because he didn't think you could handle it before you saw he was on your side as well. And you didn't handle it. You haven't taken anything he said about your rage into consideration, including now. No one can talk to you until you say so? Forget that!"

"I've had enough," Jane fumed. "This conversation is over!"

"If you want me to be part of this scenario of yours, we're going to have to have this discussion before you accept the position!"

"I won't let you ruin this for me! Get out of here, you son of a bitch! Leave me alone!"

Ed stormed out and Jane slammed the bedroom door behind him. He could hear her sobs on the other side and there was no pleasure for him in that. The sound of her crying never ceased to lacerate. He went into the blasphemously sunlit living room and sat on their futon mattress that was still on the floor, making him feel like a sulking child during playtime. He tried to let the brightness numb him, as he felt the marriage continue to unravel, further and further.

Jane was determined and angry, and empowered by her acceptance. Sometimes she could imagine a new life for herself *without* Ed, but when she thought of the practical considerations, the math didn't work. She would need their car, for starters, and surely it would be helpful to have some other income while she lived on a stipend and a student loan. But mostly, they had been together for so long, and when they weren't thorns in each other's sides, they were each other's bulwarks. At least, she knew that he was hers. And she wasn't naïve enough to think that this forty-five-year-old woman wouldn't need emotional support starting graduate school, competing with twenty- and thirty-somethings whose bodies could probably withstand more punishment than hers. And someone would have to devote attention to Luke when needed, and it might be too difficult for her from two hundred miles away.

Both of them were loathe to end it all, but each felt that the commitment to each other was demanding too much of themselves. Jane felt she had come too far in her studies to stop now. So, later that night, she strode over to the living room where he was glumly watching Garry Shandling smiling through clenched jaws for half an hour, and stood towering over him, her arms crossed.

"Can you turn off the TV for a second?" she asked, her nostrils flaring unflirtatiously.

"For more than a second," Ed replied, and killed it with a well-aimed zap of the remote. "Sit down," he said.

She didn't.

"I need to know," she announced, "are you with me or not?"

"If 'with you' means am I ready to drop everything and move to Binghamton because you've bullied me into it—"

She clicked her tongue disparagingly and rolled her eyes.

"—then no, I am not with you. If you mean am I ready to discuss a way to see if this can work out, then maybe. If you want to take the risk of going up there alone and see if our marriage can improve long distance, then maybe I could see my way to making that kind of change eventually. I might be willing to travel up there on some weekends and maybe you could come here, but it cannot work the way things are going. You cannot treat me this way anymore, bandying me about depending on your mood. If you think I am just an obstacle in your way, then I will get out of it, but if I am part of what you want for your life, then you have to take me into consideration. You've got to slow down and look around and see where I am before making a decision that affects me."

Jane's stance softened. She was impressed with his considered response, and besides, maybe she could see a way to get all the things she truly needed through negotiation.

"You know what I'm like," she pleaded softly. "You always tease me for saying I *need* something when I want it. But I don't *feel* it that way, Ed! I feel like I've *got* to have this! I don't want to live in the city all my life, and I don't want to live in debt forever. I *need* to make the most of myself. No one cares about my poetry and I've got to do something that's important to me. All my life I thought I was lucky just to have survived my family. But I've finally gotten to the point of my life where I don't feel I'm entitled to have the world take care of me because I'm an artist or because I've been fucked over. I've got to work hard—to *contribute*—to get rewarded. And I can do it now. And it's unbelievable! I *didn't* think this would happen—getting accepted to Binghamton—but the fact that it has *means* something. It means I'm pursuing something that's attainable."

"Sit down," Ed said again. She slowly shifted around to get down on the futon with him. "I understand that. And I'm really impressed. But we've been a family for over fifteen years. If you want to remain one, it's not just about you or me, it's got to be about us. And 'us' was not considered here. I cannot upend my life this way after these last few years where you've been furious at me all the time while only now letting me know what's going on with you. I will not do that to myself. There's a price to pay in a relationship for mistreating it."

"Oh, come on!" Jane interrupted with an impatient whine. "What? It's all about me? I'm so terrible?"

"It's been a tough few years. And after years of you being furious at me, I'm frankly fucking pissed at *you*. I will not bend over backward for you anymore."

"You never—"

"If you want to do this so badly, then you're going to have to take the chance that we can mend. And then maybe I'll *want* to move. I don't know. If it's a risk you want to take, I'll help you. I'll try to work with you. But I won't go any further than that. I've been your disciple—your camp follower—for years now— don't laugh—you've taken me many places on your whims—"

"You enjoyed them, didn't you?" Jane laughed.

"Sometimes. Plenty of times. But not lately. You can't assume I'm in the same frame of mind as you are. There are *two* heads involved here."

"Oh Jeez!"

"Sorry. That's the deal. That's where I am with all this."

Jane's heart sank a notch. On top of trying to manage working in the lab of a difficult professor, and immersing herself in graduate studies *and* teaching classes (which Binghamton had their grad students do from the first day), Ed was demanding that she work on preserving her marriage. The one thing she had hoped to count on, to prop her up against her academic insecurities—those of a Bronx-raised, working class, high school dropout whose family advice had been, "You're smart! You could be a secretary or something!"—now needed propping up itself.

She knew, however, that the marriage could fall apart whatever her choice, so she decided to err on the side of ambition. The next day—a Monday—she called Dr. Rudnicki to accept the position. And she told Ed that she would take up his offer, if that was the only way possible to go ahead with her plans, and they would live two hundred miles apart for her first year away and then, if things went more smoothly between them, Ed might transition upstate. One half of her said *I'll just have to be nice to him all the time and he'll come around to changing his mind*; the other half replied *Goddammit*.

They drove up several times in June to scout apartments in the area, or more specifically, homes to rent, since there were few apartment buildings of any kind except in Johnson City where a lot of undergrads lived. Jane thought that wouldn't be a good environment for her. What she really wanted was a nice country house not too far from school, with a bucolic enough atmosphere to be both comforting and conducive to studying while also, hopefully, enticing to Ed. Ada Stanhope, the Century 21 realtor in Vestal's Starr Mall—Vestal being the town in which the campus was actually located—sent her to look at a house in Greene to the northeast of the city. Jane loved Greene, but the house was an empty, carpeted box right on the main road, nothing nearby except for the farmer landlord who had had it built for his late mother-in-law. Jane sadly inspected the blank apartment for sockets, listened to the crescendoing whoosh of the cars as they passed and realized that this particular country home was more nakedly depressing than bucolic. Of course, the price had been right, but if she was going to be depressed, she'd be better off surrounded by people.

"What you really want to do," said Ada, later that day, "is try out the town of Owego. It's around fifteen miles straight west on 17; it's a lovely little town. Picture perfect, adorable little stores. We don't cover that far over, but maybe you can find something. Ask around."

Owego was even further than Greene by a little bit but in the opposite direction. Jane wasn't sure she should travel that far, but decided they should give it a try. Within minutes of exiting Rte. 17 at Owego's first exit, they found themselves surrounded by the Susquehanna River on their left and a picture-perfect display of Victorian homes on their right. They turned off Front Street and made their way to Main.

"Stop the car!" Jane shouted. "Look! An 'Apartment to Let!' Let me take down the number. Look at that house! Isn't it beautiful?"

It was, in fact, an expansive, three-story rambling affair on a street straight out of Disneyland's Small Town U.S.A. The block had large weeping willows and the building with the available apartment was next to the town library which was itself adjacent to the Methodist Church. Jane felt that, far from spooky like the house in Greene, this would be a really comforting locale, a home and neighborhood that could actually mother you with its domestic energy, whispering through the breeze that all was well as you stared overwhelmed at your piles of papers and textbooks in your large, lonely, floor-creaking apartment, trying to evade the grip of your doubts.

That night, Jane called the landlady, who lived in the nearby town of Appalachin, from their hotel room in Binghamton and they drove back to Owego the next day to view the apartment. It was on the second floor of the slightly musty old mansion, one of four apartments in the building, a two-bedroom, spacious, high-ceilinged country flat with new faux-19th century wallpaper plastered throughout. The car ride to the SUNY campus was less than a half hour away, which was no more time than it usually took to commute to work from one part of Manhattan to another, so Jane went for it.

The rest of the month was spent buying furniture and appliances, putting up shades and setting up accounts. The month was filled with the excitement of creating a new life and the tension of getting a lot done before the beginning of Jane's scheduled appearance at the campus neurobiolology lab. Looming over all this was the challenge of having to stand on her own two feet, alone in a strange town with no acquaintances other than those new ones she would make at school, most of whom would be a generation younger than her. Even Professor Rudnicki was probably younger than her. She felt both brave and horribly foolish, poised between potential triumph and humiliation, and by the end of June, she found herself, against her better judgment, relieving the pressure by being impatient with Ed's inadequacies: a nail poorly hammered, the wrong purchase on a shopping assignment, and even his failure to be in tune with her tempo—she was ready when he was not, he was ready when she wasn't—until she found herself making the classic complaint: "I have to do everything around here!" and she was sorry. She didn't want to lose her cool, but at the same time she genuinely felt she *was* doing everything: after all, *she* was trying to move their lives forward, while he was being the drag on the line—*you can do this if you want but you can't take me with you*. She was frightened and unsupported except in the most tepid of ways—*you're on your own, kid, best of luck*—and she was furiously disappointed. The night before Ed was going to head back to New York by bus, they had a loud, angry argument at the Vestal Outback, during which she made her disappointment clear.

"I thought," she confessed with anguish, "that if you really loved me, you would eventually offer to support me, maybe go back to school for a more lucrative career, have a child with me that I could stay home and take care of. I even tried to get pregnant to force the issue, telling you that business about being infertile from an infection I got from this guy I slept with. . . ."

"Which was true, as we found out later," Ed forcefully pointed out.

"I wanted you to *want* this for us. For me! For *you!* But you didn't. You didn't mind just getting by so that you could pursue *your* dreams. You never got past your narcissism enough to think about *our* dreams, what would be good for *us*."

"Why would I think you weren't doing the same? I always supported your poetry writing, I discouraged you from working fulltime because I knew it was too oppressive for you—"

She rode over his words with "Well, I'm the one thinking of the two of us now. I'm the one who's working so we can have a house in the country and a comfortable income. And the least you could do is help me and stop punishing me."

"*I'm* punishing *you!*"

"Yeah, the way you always do. By withdrawing from me. By nursing your grudges against me. I'm this horrible temperamental monster or something. You knew the way I was from the beginning! It's too late to say it's not acceptable, to opt out right in the middle of things. You know me better than anyone. After all these years, you know I'm not going to change. I just can't, no matter how much I want to."

"Well, maybe I can!" he said.

Jane looked in extremis, fighting for her life.

"*Why can't you just forgive me?!*" The words came out like an ejaculation, her face red with fury. It was all that was left to say, not a plea, but rather a heartfelt accusation. *You have no mercy.*

Ed ran out of fight, so he replied in silence. Suddenly they could hear the other Outback customers around them trying to eat their salads as if on some planet free of Eds and Janes. The waitress placed the grilled mahi mahi and the seared salmon in front of them and they tried to eat dinner like it wasn't the end of the world, but just the end of the weekend. The restaurant seemed dark, like a nightclub with the spotlight on their table and with everyone watching them play their silverware sonata during their dinner from hell.

And so began their new life apart. Jane spent time in the lab getting accustomed to working with the white rats, whose care she was now in charge of, and to working with Rudnicki and his two Russian assistants, Ivan and Yelena, a husband and wife who had been scientists in the Soviet Union and were now working in the States in lesser positions. Rudnicki's secretary, Debi, and Ivan were the friendliest to Jane, Rudnicki being both casual and distant in a manner suggesting he didn't want to get too close to the hired help, and Yelena looking at Jane warily, as if she was some sort of competition, whether for standing in the lab or with Ivan, Jane wasn't sure. To her surprise, she loved being with the rats the most, even though she had to be careful of being scratched; they were her charges, her babies, and she spoke to them the way she did the canary she'd brought up to Owego from the city or the way she did with her plants. They would bustle around their crowded cages, pink noses poking through the grill, squeaking for loving attention at the sound of her entrance. She made it her priority to treat them as well as possible during their short, hopefully useful, lives.

Ed, in the meantime, found the arrangement uncomfortably easy. He was almost alarmed at how effortlessly he could get used to a regimen without her. Certainly he missed her, but since they spoke by phone almost every night, and spent weekends together (he took the bus one weekend, she drove down the next), it was more like they were dating than either married or totally unattached, and in some ways it was the best of both worlds. He answered only to himself and by the time they saw each other, they could remain on good behavior for a longer period of time. Their days together remained bumpy, tentative and insecure, but it wasn't always contentious. The resentments could be tapped easily—and were—but after the dinner at Outback's, they managed to keep from getting hurtful.

The summer went moderately smoothly: a little too much country heat in Jane's southern-exposed apartment, some virginal exploration of a radically different home base, the country racket of crickets and freight trains, the whole house creaking when one of the other tenants was in the hallway, taking the car to do the laundry, mapping out Binghamton's gigantic malls, walking three blocks to Owego's town center to stare at the monument to the soldiers who died preserving the Union. Jane wanted Ed to get a sense of how easy living in the country would be, without the hard-edges of an overly-muscular steel and concrete metropolis.

Ed did get a sense of it, but he also got a sense of a life that would revolve totally around Jane to begin with, and for that to work out, Ed had to be convinced that Jane's powerful needs didn't pulverize him, smother the life out of him, subsume him: in other words, make him an extension of her. And he wasn't convinced yet.

They were forced to change their patterns as the summer came to an end and Jane's graduate student responsibilities increased. In addition to her course load, she was now teaching a science lab writing class to undergrad Psych majors. After the Labor Day weekend, she informed Ed that she could no longer drive down to the city every other week. They'd only be able to see each other when he visited her, which he kept at every other week, to keep his sanity. Jane was really disappointed. Even though she had gotten to meet the other new grad students and befriended many of them, her weekends out in Owego felt lonely. She had so much schoolwork to do that she couldn't commit to socializing. If Ed was over, he would keep himself busy while she worked, much like their routine in the city when she was at Hunter, but he would still be around, his presence lending a humming normalcy to the environment. Days were getting shorter and colder and her large high-ceilinged apartment seemed cavernous and shadowy without him; the intense quiet—broken only by the rolling thunder of freight trains passing through town—only exacerbated the deep rumbling in her heart. She felt an almost gothic melancholy: a foreboding that perhaps she would soon have no one to share both her apartment *and* her heart with.

As autumn closed in on her, she started finding strange messages on her answering machine when she arrived home late from school. What with studying in the library, cleaning up the lab, sometimes conferring with lab students, she'd only have time to grab Chicken McNuggets from the McDonalds off the highway exit for dinner. She'd carry her meal up the dusty carpeted stairs of her dilapidated apartment mansion to find a red light calling out for her attention. She'd anticipate Ed's voice only to hear during playback the rambling rural twang of a stranger, the metallic copy of his voice poisoning her bedroom with bizarre threats.

"I'll kill you, you goddamn motherfucker, as soon as I get out of this joint. I know where you live, you shit, and you can bet your ass I'll find you and put a bullet through your ugly skull. You thought you could set me up, man, but you ain't heard the last of me. And you can tell that bitch I'm going to fuck her up good."

After a while, seeing the red light on the phone no longer suggested Ed's comforting banter to her: it created dread. She started imagining a hard-wired ex-convict hiding in the darkness of the hallway, waiting inside to jump her after having walked through the always-unlocked front door. Finally, Ed convinced her to contact the local sheriff who advised her to change her phone number. She did so, but it underlined how vulnerable she felt living alone. *Ed had to get over his resentments*, she thought, *it's no good like this.* The week that she had to deal with all this, she found it hard to concentrate on schoolwork and was afraid if she fell behind so early in the term, she'd never catch up. She'd feel totally fine during the day—a well-liked member of the Psych Department community—but at night she'd hear the hum of anxiety course through the telephone wires along the quiet of Owego's Main Street, and now she wished she hadn't chosen Owego's bucolic isolation over the cluttered student neighborhoods closer to school.

She was most comfortable when in the lab. Ivan and Yelena, after all, were close to her in age, and also had considerable life experience behind them, including watching a teenage son growing up American; and then, of course, there was the splenetic affection of her white pink-eyed subjects who greeted her each day, hungry for her touch. She felt confident handling them and this spilled over into her relationships with her lab students when she showed them how to delicately, but firmly, control their test subjects. She loved mentoring young people, as she always had, and these Psych majors generally warmed to her, especially since she took her job teaching their two credit class seriously: she had total faith in her ability to help them become good science writers. But in the classrooms where *she* was the student, she felt a bit more agnostic, ten-to-twenty years older than her classmates. And in Statistics, she fretted over holding everyone else back; she was so much slower in picking it up—it was a lot more difficult than the Statistics she'd taken as an undergrad. To be safe, she decided to hire a tutor from among one of the others who excelled in the class.

To her surprise, it was in her cognitive therapy class, which was a required class for the Psych grad students even if it was not going to be their major field of study, that she made her biggest social breakthrough. One day, Professor Bloom asked the class for a volunteer to enact the role of a therapy patient. After a moment of quiet paper rustling throughout the auditorium, Jane raised her hand. Professor Bloom welcomed Jane stage center and explained that he was going to give an example of the way a therapist would interact with a client. Sitting under the proverbial spotlight, the first person Jane thought of was Luke, and when Professor Bloom asked Jane how he could help her, she instinctively took on Luke's demeanor, her body slumping, her head down, refusing to willingly interact. She became moody and unresponsive, moved her head in exaggerated bounces as Luke might if cogitating a probing question, sometimes responding with a surly return like "Why do you want to know?" And somehow, in playing Luke, she found that she could access something of herself, as if she could allow all of the misery and fury she usually tried to sculpt into sociability to just *be*, and it was as safe in Luke's persona as it was in her therapy sessions with Suzanne—even safer, because it was a "performance" that no one would suspect as revealing anything other than a talent. Perhaps watching Ed's work on stage all these years, even watching him rehearse at home, had prepared her for this moment as well. She'd never had a desire to act, but right now she was enjoying it, bringing her very own fiery glare to Luke's disorder. The class was electrified, even frightened. Was this Jane they hardly knew having some kind of breakdown? Even Professor

Bloom was thrown—thrown, and yet thrilled, because it really challenged him to use his skills. It was a riveting class, and when Jane broke character at the end and smiled in relief that she had succeeded at this absurd game in front of so many people without making a fool of herself, the class laughed in delight—and relief as well. Classmates gathered around her at the close of the lecture-demonstration like autograph hounds.

She was proud of what she was trying to accomplish, but as autumn's cowl wrapped itself around the year, she more and more had to work at squirreling away the fear that things could fall apart. She was having an increasingly difficult time with the workload and was spending more time on her students' papers than she could afford to: it was taking her from her own studies. Luckily, Ed was understanding about that when he visited, but then this pattern underlined her fear that her studies were taking her away from him as well. By the time he left on Sunday night to catch the New York-bound bus from Ithaca—their quality time together being as limited as it was—she was not ready to let him go. *Stay another day*, became her refrain, and Ed would invariably respond that he couldn't take off from work. There would be the tension of disappointment and then the affectionate embrace—with shadows of subtext—and then Ed would be out the door, walking down Main Street to the town center on his own, getting on the nighttime Shortline bus, sitting with strangers in the dark, free and alone, like a pebble falling down a well all the way to the city.

One weeknight in October, he came home from the gym to see a message was waiting for him on his answering machine. When he played it back, there was the lush sound of an orchestra, and a woman sang in a thick, mournful sigh, *Ev'ry time we say goodbye, I die a little / Ev'ry time we say goodbye, I wonder why a little / Why the gods above me, who must be in the know / Think so little of me, they allow you to go.* Ed knew who the sweet, tender stalker was who sent this his way. It felt loving and crazy and he felt strangely shaken by it. He played it again. It was beautiful, a fantastic song, but he wished it wasn't on his answering machine.

"I got your message," he told Jane when he called her up. "It threw me at first. Is that Doris Day?"

"No, honey, it's Ella Fitzgerald. Every time I play that song I think of you and it makes me cry. I wanted you to hear it so much, so I decided to just leave it there for you when you got home. Do you like it?"

"I love it," he said softly, sadly. "Are you OK?"

"I wish you were here. I wish you could find a job on campus. If IBM hadn't closed their Binghamton office I bet you could've worked there. They're hiring at the Seven-Eleven in Owego. *You* could do that, Ed!"

"I'm not going to work at the Seven-Eleven, Jane. We'll work things out over time. We need time, that's all. We've got to let things work for a while. We've got to even see if you want to stay there for more than a year."

"I miss you. I need you."

"I miss you, too."

When the conversation ended, both of them experienced the emotional fatigue that results from an immovable rock being wooed by an irresistible force. They were being slowly wrenched from each other; the different paths they were adhering to seemed desolate and gray to each of them at the moment.

In Binghamton, autumn's chill seeped into your skull and burrowed itself inside you; and for Jane it permeated the competitive atmosphere of grad school as well. People were friendly and helpful, but all pre-occupied with the assigned work and their own ambitions, and except perhaps for Ivan, there was no one to help Jane cut through that chill. Rudnicki kept a moody reserve that would intermittently break when she least expected it, and then his amiable demeanor would turn aloof again, leaving Jane to pretend she wasn't hungering for his approval. Debi would toss a sarcastic remark about him to Jane from her desk right outside his office and Jane would let Debi's sarcasm serve as a momentary bit of warmth, but Jane didn't have an inner voice of her own to cheer herself on; she was driven instead by the lonely, unconvincing urgings of a little girl talking herself out of a panic. Sometimes this would be enough to get her through a day of frisky rat scratches and head-banging statistical analysis, through the challenging stimulation of the academic discourse she was afraid she might not be able to contribute to adequately, through the research in the library that was piling up, but increasingly she felt her confidence run dry, and she had to run on determination alone. And that's when the loneliness of the vast valley outside, along the dark, cold Susquehanna, would make its presence felt.

When Ed came up the next time, she felt so soothed by their domestic tranquility, by the closeness of him, the omnipresence of his body mass nearby, his open appreciation for her attentiveness to her students, that she found his leaving unbearable. She volunteered to drive him to Binghamton so he could get the bus there just to spend the extra half hour with him, time she knew she needed to spend on her class work. But once they arrived at the station, she had trouble letting him go, and she cried when he said goodbye. She felt that she couldn't deal with the loneliness any longer; some old deprivation was raising its head with a silent roar, robbing her of the will to persevere. But then somehow she rallied. The order of things demanded that Ed return to his job in the city, and so she knuckled down and put all of her attention to her school work.

Even in moderate winter weather, Binghamton's sharp, windy blasts were like assaults; the main thing was to get indoors, go from place to place and not dawdle. As the semester moved on, her workload demanded the same thing: so many tasks to accomplish, so many claims on her attention; her mind, too, only had destinations with no time for the roads leading to them. She was certain now that she'd made a mistake living so far from campus. She spent each night driving toward the pitch black of Route 17 spilling westward for almost half an hour, time that could always have been used more valuably. She'd pull in at McDonald's for the same old Chicken McNuggets and then eat them at the kitchen table with a textbook, index cards and a yellow highlighter for dinner settings. Before she fell asleep in exhaustion, either she or Ed would have phoned each other to small-talk goodnight, and then she'd be out until her alarm woke her to morning darkness and the whipping sound of the cold.

The beginning of the holiday season was approaching, and Jane didn't see how she could afford to go downstate for Thanksgiving. She really wanted to see Ed and Luke and her cousins, where they had gone for the last several turkey dinners, and this swelled her longing for the embrace of the familiar. As much as she loved Owego and its quaint small-town atmosphere, she felt homesick for the people who knew her well. When Ed visited in the middle of November, she got him to commit to staying upstate with her for the upcoming holiday. He would bring Luke, and the three of them would have their own small family celebration.

After making these arrangements, she again drove Ed to the Binghamton bus station on Sunday night, but this time when they got there she really couldn't let him go.

"Please, Ed, just stay one day. One more day."

"What am I going to do while you're at school? It doesn't make any sense. I'll be with you for four days in a couple of weeks. It's just a couple of weeks."

"Please . . . !" She held his hands tightly. The light of the bus station reflected on tears welling up in her eyes.

Ed couldn't look at them. He felt he was being wrestled to the ground by the intensity of her emotions.

"I've got to go," he said tenderly, but firmly. "I'll miss the bus," and he broke free of her and exited the car.

As he passed in front of Rocket, he turned towards Jane. She had rolled down the window.

"Ed!" she cried. He could only see the shape of her face in the darkness, but he heard what sounded like sobs.

"Ed, please, I need you!" She was choking out the sobs in the darkness. Ed went over to the door and leaned in.

"I love you. I've got to go now. I've got to make this bus. Please don't do this, Jane."

From within the black well of the open window, he heard her words struggling through her tears.

"I can't do this without you."

Ed felt himself dying inside.

"I can't do this, Jane," he said. "We can discuss this tomorrow. I'm not going to do this now. It's not fair." A steady cascade of sobs filled the silence. "Look, I've got to go. Go home and get some sleep and we'll talk tomorrow. *I love you.* You're doing great! Just don't give up! I've got to go now," and he ripped himself away from her, listening to her sobbing falling behind him into the deep pit of the musty old Toyota in the near-deserted parking lot.

Jane just sat in the car after Ed had disappeared into the bus terminal, letting her sobs slowly peter out. She took a tissue from the small box in the glove compartment and blew her nose violently as if it was her final wail. She sat there in the dark, catching her breath. She didn't know what had come over her: it was like something way down inside her, deep in her gut, had cried out for help. Why? Were things that bad? She felt sadly ridiculous. She was a mystery to herself sometimes. She felt a fatalism that overrode her concern that she was going to end up pushing Ed away from her forever. The fatalism of fatigue. She turned on the ignition and started to make her way out of the lot. The powerful lights of Ed's bus veered into the rearview mirror, momentarily blinding her. It occurred to her that if she stopped the car in the driveway, she could make a gigantic scene, preventing the bus from leaving, performing her own act of civil disobedience akin to lying down in front of a bus carrying GIs to some front. But she didn't. She turned to the right and the bus's lights disappeared from view as it took Ed off in the opposite direction.

The emptiness of her apartment was almost like another person, its presence so all-encompassing. She opened the texts piled on her desk in the back room, with different colored post-its sprouting from them like effulgent fall foliage ready to drop, but she found it hard to concentrate, the country silence being so deafeningly loud behind the brittle hum of the refrigerator, making the quiet of her apartment starker and closer. She mentally shoved back against the distraction and read through the texts almost brutally, desecrating the text with thick yellow washes of her marker. When she'd pushed back her bedtime as much as she could muster, she slowly closed up shop and went through her nocturnal rituals without thought, until she had closed down for the night.

The next day was as gray and icy as usual: she had to walk downstairs with a pot of hot water with which to de-ice the driver's door and then turn on the car's defroster and run back upstairs to finish getting ready. It was good seeing the familiar faces once she got in out of the chill after trekking from the campus parking lot, and no one treated her like they had noticed anything wrong with her, no hint of her panic or self-hatred. The end of the semester was approaching and there was that sense of fraternity and excitement that comes with surviving the crucible and some of that was shared with Jane. Teachers were interested in her responses, classmates double-checked her notes, and Jennifer gave her the explanation for a question on the last statistics exam which had stumped her. Her little white furry friends didn't treat this day any differently than any other, and they beckoned frantically for her attention with their little pink noses poking through the wires of their cages. Ivan seemed unusually quiet, probably some contretemps with Yelena, Jane thought. Late in the afternoon Jane stopped in Rudnicki's office and was small-talking with Debi when Rudnicki, in his usual no-nonsense stride, broke up the party and said, "Let's talk," without stopping on his way to his inner office. Jane gave a feeble wave to Debi and walked confidently in after him.

Rudnicki walked to his desk and swiveled around to face Jane, leaning his butt against the desk top, supporting himself on his hands spread behind him—his customary position. He motioned Jane to close the door behind her, which she did.

"Look," he began, tossing his graying mane behind him with an assertive flick of his head, "I told you I'm a tough taskmaster. You know that about me. Now, I admit, I'm not having any problems with your lab work, and I know how well you're doing teaching the lab writing course, which was one of the reasons I took you. But to be blunt, you're doing B work in Statistics and that's not good enough for me. If you can't have a 4.0 index, it's not going to work. I have to think of the reputation of my project and the department, and my graduate assistants have to ace A's in everything or it makes me look bad. It's a poor reflection on my judgment if I use below-par grad students on my research. So I'm going to have to end this arrangement at the end of the semester. I suggest you look for another placement."

Jane stood palely across the room with the dim gray that passed for daylight in Binghamton peeking through the blinds behind Rudnicki, leaving his features in shadow. Normally, their conversations consisted of a certain amount of banter, especially on her part; she would try to make herself comfortable through conviviality, which he seemed to respond to. But she knew she was in for an upbraiding of some sort at "tough taskmaster" and she masochistically accepted it. At other times, she might have responded with "Ted, I'm getting A's in all my other classes," but his manner would've had to be less brusque for that kind of interaction. Plus she herself thought the B was unacceptable, and though her tutor thought her progress was fine and she knew that some others in the department wouldn't get all A's either, she was Rudnicki's only graduate student now, and only what he thought mattered. He was one of the most brilliant men in his field, and having his name on her résumé would take her places in the specialized neurobiology field. But he was now telling her that *she* might bring *his* reputation down. It was as it had all been prophesied at birth: it was a miracle that someone of her background, a one-time high school dropout, had made it this far, but now she realized, no, miracles were absent in this lifetime, this had been a fluke, a crack in the world's order. All of her family would be shaking their heads, tsk-tsking her, if they could materialize from the crowded Bronx kitchen of the past. *What were you thinking? You never listened! That's how you get into trouble.* Jane didn't even have to think this consciously; it was all inscribed into the marrow of her bones, in the prematurely arthritic, battered bones she had marshaled with willpower—and the great urgent desire to scrawl her name large onto the world—to get herself here.

In the last few weeks she had been walking around with this deep sense of dread, a sense that was slowly growing inside her, centimeter by centimeter, draining the future from her. Last night she had to let Ed fly loose from her desperate grip, and now all she had worked for, all she had risked for, she let slip away passively.

She stood in front of Rudnicki without a comment, wasted by the blow. She barely noticed him now, as he headed to the door.

"I have a meeting with Dorsky, so I've got to get going. I'm sorry it didn't work out," he said, though he sounded neither sorry nor relieved, just perfunctory. He left her alone with the door open. Debi's room was quiet, she'd probably gone for the day. Jane didn't know where she belonged quite yet, until little by little, in vague, cloudy glimmers, she did.

She found her way to the lab. Yelena's voice was unspooling in the background in that high Slavic pitch. It sounded two hundred miles away. It sounded like she had never heard it before, like she had never even met a person who had that particular voice. It was no more familiar than the squeak of any particular white rat around her: it was just part of the anonymous chorus of people she didn't belong with or hadn't met, who populate this waking world. She put on her heavy gray coat and pulled her fleece cap hard down over her head and carried her heavy shoulder bag and textbooks out to the parking lot.

Rocket was her only friend, and it waited for her, happy that she finally realized that it was *just you and me, baby*. It beckoned across the campus lawn. *We're going home*, it blinked with its metallic gloss. Jane hurried before even Rocket could turn on her, become distant and anonymous, just another car in a sprawl of them parked in endless formation, before it, too, no longer belonged to her, like this campus, like her marriage. She made it in time. The car still claimed her. The worn, boxy interior of the car was familiar, and as comfortable to her as a grandfather's lap. *Let's take you home*, Rocket said. *OK*, Jane thought, eyes blank and mind receptive, hungry for Rocket's cosseting. The ignition responded with an effortless, if noisy, purr, and the grounds of the campus started to move beneath them, rolling them off the premises.

Jane was driving in an automatic state, as if Rocket was in charge. Binghamton, Route 17, the other cars—all of them fell over the cliff of history; in her mind she was only where she was going, no longer where she was. She sped with a numb, yet almost ecstatic, determination. She was going to get there and get there soon. She thought she heard a voice like her own beckoning for her attention, but Rocket was in control. There was no looking back. There was no Ed. There was no Luke. There was just her flat on Main Street, up the dusty stairs, where "home" was in the bathroom cabinet, in two big orange vials, and Rocket knew the way.

She pulled up and parked in front of the Victorian structure and took her bag, but left the textbooks in the front seat. The street did not exist for her, only the steps in front of her, the porch, the creaking stairs, the door to her apartment. She closed the door behind her, hung up her coat in the closet, and looked around at the modest, yet cavernous, apartment. She walked to the back room, which she used as her study, and where she kept her books.

There she found the volume of Steve's poems that had been published last year. Steve had died five years back, having contracted AIDS; his car-crashing through life finally found its last wall to hit and it hit him back hard. Jane and Ed had been at the memorial for him in the East Village when the book came out. The final poem read was the generally-acknowledged masterpiece written a few years after his having married Tracy. It was a love poem to Jane, a poem Jane and Ed had seen years ago, a poem so beautifully written that they both had been able to see it as a masterpiece without having to consider the awkward confession at its heart.

Jane picked up the volume and took it with her to the bathroom after filling a glass with water from the kitchen faucet. She placed the book on the top of the toilet tank along with the glass and then took out the two prescription vials. She opened the first vial and poured a mixture of white and vanilla-colored tablets into the palm of her hand. She cupped them into her mouth and drank from the glass of water.

She had a hard time swallowing.

She must be patient.

She takes them quickly, three at a time, opens the other vial with poisonous green capsules and they go down as well. There must be a couple of hundred pills before her and all the time in the world. She gobbles them down, happily obliterating her sense of starvation. Then she picks up the book, sits on the closed toilet seat, and finds the poem called *Jane Cantore*.

Much later, Jane will find herself sitting across a sunny meeting room from Henry, a mild-mannered man perhaps ten years older than she is. He will be sitting in a gray cardigan and casual khaki slacks, an undistinguished face in glasses, his hair receding far to the back of his head. He will be talking about his wife's suicide and the depression it left him in. His eyes will crinkle as he recalls how he lightly stroked a kitchen knife across his wrist to play-act her actions, to try to understand how she could do that, and then he saw the white line that the knife left as an instruction to *cut here*, and he did. He will say that he still really doesn't know why she did it, but he can't help presuming it was because of him, that he failed her in some profound way. As Henry takes the time to awkwardly pull a handkerchief from his pants pocket, Jane will think: *He could be Ed or he could be Luke. I could have caused them so much pain that they might not have been able to bear it, or if they did, they might walk through life one of the walking wounded. They wouldn't have been as good at that as I was. They're not as tough as I am; they didn't have the training.* The chance to respond to Henry will go around the room and when it's Jane's turn, she will only say "It wasn't because of you, Henry," and for a moment Jane will not be able to find any other words. Then Jane will thank Henry for reminding her of the people who love her and who she had almost let down, and a catch in her throat will unbalance her, robbing her momentarily of her equanimity.

Later that day, Ed will drive up to Four Winds from the city. Jane will take him for a short walk around the manicured grounds and hold his hand while they talk. She will ask him if he remembers her always telling him that she had a secret, and he will nod, looking at her quizzically.

"I don't want it anymore," she'll tell him.

She'll recount how profoundly affected she actually had been by her sister's suicide, but not in the way he might imagine. It wasn't grief or despair, but rather education. She learned from Virginia that *it could be done.* That if she ever finally decided she wanted to check out, if the calamity of being Jane was too overwhelming, suicide was doable. And that all those Percodans and codeines she had hoarded over the years were not just for occasional recreational abuse, as she had told him when they'd lived their East Village lives, but for preparation, should it ever come down to it.

"Now it's over," she'll say. "I don't want them anymore." She'll look Ed in the eye, wanting to ask for his forgiveness, but she'll feel that would be an unfair burden on him. She'll promise him she won't do anything like this to him again and silently hope that she hadn't ruined everything for them already. "No more secrets, Egg," she'll say, and lean her head against his shoulder.

She won't, however, tell him how she'd carried Steve's book of poems into the bathroom with her the night she tried to self-destruct. And she won't tell him what she won't know herself: the festering secret that her very own body—at least for now—is keeping from *her*.

V

THE BETRAYAL

After the patient (for she *is* a patient even though there will be no attempt here to cure her) is delivered to our safeguarding, wheeled in with all of those distended teardrops of plastic that hang from a demented maypole on the back of her chair; and after, with great pomp and ceremony, she is led to the hospital bed where all watch as if from the stands of the U.S. Open as she climbs it like God's largest toddler would before cautiously rolling her delicate bloated mass deep into its embrace; and after she is tucked, plugged, patted and tagged like the most precious of farm animals, she finds the moment to grab her hovering husband by the hand.

It is her first day back here after her abortive attempt to go home turned into a nightmare. She had experienced being seven stories high over Manhattan as she might've atop Everest addressing the Creation, breathless and without recourse to serenity, horrified at the absence hovering over everything. She'd scurried desperately from room to room of their one bedroom apartment trying to find where the pockets of air were hidden, none of the prepared medical equipment doing the job adequately enough, until she'd collapsed heavily on their bed, her exhausted husband doing the same after tagging along behind her like a faithful puppy. Back at sea level now, she is rested for the moment, but still weary.

They are alone now—except for us, of course, high up in the section the French call *paradis*, in seats we never have to pay for (very good seats though, no matter the price). We are used to the sound of emptiness that buffers our presence from those we are prepared to bear witness to as they dismantle—usually slowly, certainly surely—all they love from this life before their corporeal vehicle crushes the breath out of them. Or whatever.

They are alone and they are staring into each other's eyes, sucking in the sight of each other's smeary, earnest face, closer to each other than they've ever felt, more penetrating than any lovemaking. (Well, you can tell that's what they believe.) Sweet-eyed, near-bald, bold beauty, whose dark irises we can see from even here as tender bullets, knows this is the one chance she gets and she should take it.

"I want you to know," she says, a breath above a whisper, "I'm sorry for every time I ever hurt you. Can you forgive me, Egg?" (She calls him Egg, I'm sure of it. Like breakfast.)

Her tall, willowy-from-sleeplessness, significant other, hiccups a shock of air.

"Of course!" and then he adds, "I'm sorry for every time I hurt *you*. Can you forgive *me*?" Contrary to what you may think, he is saying, *you were no more trouble than I've been.* They both know it's his gift.

She smiles wanly, touched. Her lips imitate the shape of yes.

He pulls the large pink padded chair to face her bed and sits staring at her, presuming to rob us of *our* function, but he is mortal so he will tire of it. She lets her eyelids float slowly down, down, then they reach once again for the shore, then submerge again, all the while accompanied by the oh-so-gentle roar of oxygen that sounds to her as if transmitted directly to the brain. From the window a dull, rectangular slab of morning light announces, without enthusiasm, the arrival of a new day. On the opposite wall, near the doorway, a golden Christ is crucified in almost obscene miniature. He seems uncommunicative, an object shiny and hard and demanding, a stern Lilliputian nun who has no power this morning in this cancer care facility in this corner of the Bronx in this second year of the new millennium to save His new ward from her trepidation of being abandoned by the world one last time. She keeps Him out of her sight as she does the meaningless black TV screen which lowers over her like a security camera and upon which nothing can hold her interest. She no longer craves diversion. She craves us.

The husband has been gone for a while; she had urged him home to sleep; she wants him to sustain himself; she needs him whole. There had been no night for them, up through the hours in a Manhattan emergency room where doctors finally told her they would have to tap her lungs daily, an invasive procedure, if she wanted to treat her symptoms. She had resigned herself to this, to peaceful succumbing, to acceptance of being tended to—cradled—here by professionals and family and friends . . . and by whichever of *us* would meet her challenge to break ranks and mother her—perhaps in the Renaissance manner, very Italian, very genteel and celestial as would become us.

Or, on the other hand, as re-imagined by Steven Spielberg. Whichever.

Late morning light has swept the room, dusting it with limpid vividness. A stocky, handsome man in his fifties stands in the doorway, hair brightly lit by age, shoulders bowed by the weight of fattened muscle, by years of physical labor, by the Bronx, by hard knocks, by a volatile tenderness. He waits a few revolutions of the Earth before he quietly sits beside our sinking lady of eternal hungering.

Time moves gently, but soon enough, before the Bronx has moved too much further eastward, she exhibits a polite delight at seeing her visitor. She sings his name softly, greeting the morning with it.

"Ray. Ray. You're here."

"Yeah. Ed called me. Hey, it didn't work out at home, it's OK. This is a good place. Everybody says so. And, you know, I'm nearby, Janie."

They smile tentatively, as if they're not sure what to say next. This Ray stares down at his hands, one large fist inside another, shifting his seat as if to find the right spot to anchor in and, if there is none, to be ready to bolt.

"You were mad at me in the hospital," he says.

"I was?" With her right hand, she rubs the back of her head, feeling her black head whiskers, re-appearing too late to matter. "I don't remember."

"Yeah, you were."

"You're my big brother," she looks at him, happy as a lap cat. "My good-looking older brother."

"Oh, stop," he says.

"You know, being your sister was the only ace I had way back on 217th Street. Girls were only friendly to me because of you. Boys, too. They all tolerated the fat baby sister because they wanted to hang out with you."

"Hey, they all liked you. They were just stupid kids."

"Maybe. Jimmy Sadecki used to write me letters in the summer and it made Ginny angry cause he didn't write to her. She said there must be something wrong with him."

"I forgot Jimmy Sadecki. Yeah. Nice guy."

Two ghosts have been evoked, and thus Ray and his pale baby sister, two large peas in a pod, ponder those dead or lost to them. Perhaps one in an unmarked grave, perhaps the other retired with family, tending some garden, paying his taxes, or maybe a bitter divorcee nursing his morning gin and tonic, or a gay prosperous rancher with a trace of a Bronx accent—who knows?—but not, at this moment at least, thinking of them, and when he does, it's a rare occasion.

The Bronx keeps moving. Ray looks down again.

"It's been too long."

His Janie doesn't reply. *My big handsome brother is now talking to me*, she's thinking. Her gaze rests calmly on his downcast visage.

"It's not like I didn't think about you," he goes on. "I just didn't want to argue no more. We always argued. We were always fightin' each other. I don't even know why. About all sorts of crap. As if we didn't have enough to deal with."

"I know."

"And you know what's funny? I came to think you were right. You know, about Reagan. I mean, he left us the biggest deficit ever. I came to think he wasn't so great. So what was that all about? Why did we argue about dumb things like that? That's no reason not to have a sister." Ray looks down to discreetly rub his eyes with his finger as if it were to clear away a speck of dust. *My big macho brother*, she thinks. The morphine helps her enough to forget that she is the patient and she feels pity for her stolid Ray, all that bulk, all that Italian-American poise unsuccessfully masking the bruises that don't heal ever. *Poor Ray, he's going to have to be the family survivor.*

"Well, now that I actually have some money," his sister confides, "I actually don't want to give it away to taxes. I guess you can say I'm kind of a Republican in a way." She gives him the lie in a spirit of friendship.

We watch them re-acquaint, she perched on high, he almost beseeching by her side, granting her a dignity her illness has done its best to sunder. Little chuckles, little sighs, superficial memories propel them past the landmines of ancient grievances never to be deactivated; the sweet banter must substitute for forgiveness as they re-solder their tarnished bond, the silver of it highlit by the creeping sunlight.

Later, when her husband returns and her brother takes his leave, she will say, "Ray and I had a nice conversation today," her voice spraying lightly like chimes.

Figures move, trade places, fidget and oblige. Our Lady, grounded, is the sun to their planetary movement. Occasionally she'll rise, dragging gravity along with her on her way to the bathroom or to sit in the armchair for a change of perspective, all the attendant activity around her following. She is getting used to breath again, not having to struggle for it since being re-admitted, getting cool kisses of oxygen every day. She talks to hubby, sleeps, makes and takes phone calls, fades in and out of effortless oblivion, wonders how she got here. This wasn't how it was supposed to work. But everyone is nice, the smart black woman doctor with her shiny gold spectacles and delicate hands, the soft fleshy West Indian aides, the brassy Italian day nurse whose presence taps the voices that have embedded themselves in Jane via the coarse fertile soil of the Bronx Cantores from whom she comes.

At night, after her Ed leaves and the flurry of visitors has stopped, it is as if she is alone in a Best Western far away from home, everything clean and everything wrong, the humming world outside not hers, the sterile silence indoors not hers either. The Jamaican attendants seem louder as if they don't know the meaning of night, and help is slower in coming. Someone is posted at the door to watch out for her, and when she's not blandishing Jane with *darlin's*, she moves her slyness outside to chat with the girls. Jane drifts in and out of sleep, wakened by occasional cackles. She'll have to speak to someone in the morning, she says to the just-dormant panic. The sly-faced one responds slowly to her calls and promises her Ativan for her anxiety. It seems to take a lifetime to arrive.

She is happy to see the dawn press against the drawn shades. The oxygen kisses her good morning just as her husband will sometime before noon. The shift changes and the young light softens the rested faces of those who attend to her and her medical hardware. The morning routine is a nuisance, but it feels as replenishing as it does embarrassing, being wiped so delicately, if intrusively, by strangers. Ray will arrive soon, as he will every day, carrying a New York Post in case she wants to read something, which she will casually browse through to make her brother feel valuable, flicking the pages but no longer interested in printed words, no matter how much pleasure they may have given her before.

By the time Ed arrives, Jane already has new visitors: she is surrounded by a growing coterie of her girlfriends, some on chairs, some standing by the window, all here to start to tender the closing stitches of their friendship.

One friend has come all the way from Madison, Wisconsin to see her. Her voice tickles and her jack-in-the-box energy inevitably lightens the self-consciously somber mood of the others, all trying not to acknowledge the obvious: their friend is dying. None of them give famous last words, but rather assurances they'll be back soon, never marking an end to the continuum that is quite clearly ending. They are in awe of death and it endows Jane with the power of a priestess (always the first on her block, she will lead the way). She is their trendsetter as they approach fifty.

Jane holds the oxygen tubing in her hands, playing with it as she talks, her pinkies splayed as if lifting cocktail glasses. She is warmed by the attention and the morphine both, coaxed into a pleasant self-containment and the politest of self-centerednesses. She conducts her visitors as if they were an attentive ensemble: delicately, maternally, with her humor tempered and her almost brutal vividness now comparatively genteel.

"I worry about Ed," she says ethereally. "He needs someone to take care of him."

Ed wilts slightly in the unwanted attention.

"I'm fine. I have what I need *here*," clearly meaning her. He unwittingly denies her the chance to trade roles with him, if even for this one grateful minute.

"Maybe I can clean your apartment or something," says her long-distance visitor. "I want to help in some way! I've traveled all this way just to see you guys. Let me do something. I can take care of 'your Ed' at least that way!"

"Are you sure?" the husband asks. "I hate to—"

"Yeah! Let me. I can come by tomorrow morning first thing."

Jane watches longingly as they make plans about the world outside, the world to which they will all return.

"I'm feeling sleepy." She wants her guests to start to leave so her husband can return his attention to the here and now of *her*.

She feels lucky today to have him and jealous at the thought of lending him to some future lucky person. She wants the waning stalk of a man, her weathered, slightly bowed, once-tender love, near to the touch. She wants his beseeching gaze to herself.

She's kissed by fairies as they waft out of the room. A tall woman enters as they leave and gives this Ed a hearty sisterly hug. She greets Jane with a charged enthusiasm as if to bring her back to life.

"Hi, Jill," Jane says wanly. "I have to rest now." She wants to pull Ed close, so his touch will anchor her as she falls back into the gossamer netting of semi-consciousness. Instead, she listens from afar as he and his sister engage in quiet conversation.

She is slowly gaining *our* perspective.

After the daylight has given way to the isolated flames of low fluorescence, and the husband has kissed her forehead and fled, the black magic of evening saturates her with dread. Nurses enter from the blinding hallway, their conspiratorial shadows following them as they fuss with Jane's machinery. She drifts in and out of the diminishing world inside and the now-diminished one without and, in searching for the safe haven beneath her eyelids, she trips on waves of breath that escape in soothing little moans.

A small figure appears and stands tentatively at the doorway, watching Jane, listening to her. She turns as if to find someone in the hallway she might recognize, but eventually returns to let her gaze keep guard over Jane's figure floating in sleep. Finally, she walks across the room to the one large chair, neatly folds her jacket and sits down. She leans forward, searching for signs of wakefulness through which she could gently intrude, to let Jane know she is not forgotten.

"Hi, sweetie," she coos when Jane's eyelids do one of their periodic slow, heavy levitations. She waits awhile for Jane's mind to wander in and out of focus. When her drugged visage floats in her direction, she ventures in whispers "Hi. . . . It's me. . . .

Sandi."

"Ohhhh!" Jane exhales. She grabs at consciousness like a drowning woman reaching for a life raft, with earnestness and grievous effort. *Saved!* Someone to rescue her from this shrinking, smothering world.

"Oh, Sandi! I'm so glad you're here!" Before her eyelids can pull her down the ocean depths, she seems to remember something. "How did you find me?"

"It wasn't hard," Sandi replies comfortingly. "I found you alright."

"It didn't work out," Jane sings out forlornly, letting the note escape before continuing "and I had to come back here, but . . . I don't know . . . it doesn't seem right somehow. When Ed leaves," her eyes are wandering away from her friend's bright face to find some dusky imaginary corner that she can place where she will, "when he leaves this place changes. It's like they wait for the families to leave and then they show their true nature."

"Oh, honey, are they mistreating you?"

"Oh, worse!" Jane intones. "They don't care! They only care about the living! They treat the dying like . . . phenomena to study or . . . like a machine that needs tending or something! We tried to do home hospice, but I couldn't breathe and I couldn't get into the hospital bed Ed got me. I couldn't get the equipment to work right. We actually went to the emergency room at St. Vincent's by ambulance but I didn't want to stay there. I need someone to figure something out. Poor Ed can't do it by himself."

"I can talk to Ed," Sandi says, "maybe we can come up with something. . . ."

"I think the apartment was too dusty! All those books! I need to get rid of those books. Then I bet, if the place is all cleaned up, I can go back home. Do you think you and Les could help Ed? Then I could go home again!"

Sandi strokes Jane's wrist, leaning forward from her chair as if over a narrow precipice, the dusk-lit room some shaded glen in a mountain jungle, the silence loud with a hushed menace. She whispers to Jane, as if to avoid detection.

"I don't think I could do anything before this coming Thursday. Is that alright? We could put your books in storage or something and we can clean up all the dust and then you can be in Manhattan near all your friends. This is so far away. Two fares! And I would visit you more often."

Jane is relieved. She asks Sandi to help her get more comfortable on the bed and once her pillows have been fluffed appropriately, they fall back into a pleasant patter of high, breathy, sometimes tremulous notes until Jane closes the conversation by lowering her eyelids. Sandi stands and places her hand high on her chest to quell some feelings fluttering there, then reaches out in what resembles a benediction to rest her palm on Jane's broad forehead. She stands awhile, imagining her breathing is feeding Jane's, the flesh of her palm transmitting something from her heart.

And who am I to second-guess?

Jane has an active night. In between occasional roundelays of gentle moans, she burbles with maddened conversation, working the netherworld hard, organizing her approach to an easier expiration. She's approaching her demise like she has a life ahead of her, with all her options open, and in her slightly addled condition, she's busy mapping detours from the inevitable. As Ray and then other family members and friends slowly stream in on this Sunday morning, Jane has made her way halfway home, part here awake in this medical establishment and part high over Manhattan, watching over the waning world from her balcony view. She greets everyone from her high perch on the hospital bed with a medicated grace.

It's crowded, with not enough chairs for everyone to sit on and the conversation runs across the room like a game of ping pong, one person relaying with her tragic royal highness at a time, with occasional splintering chatter. There is sweetness, there is conviviality, there is the hesitancy of dread, all alternating with each other, only to be interrupted by a respectful silence when the phone rings. Jane lifts her arms high like a child wanting to be lifted towards the phone which Ray hands to her while delicately attending to the unwieldy cord.

"Hello?" she says, cradling the receiver to her ear while twirling its cord compulsively with her free hand. ". . . I'm OK! I've got lots of visitors. Bobby and Donna and Rosie, Ray, your parents, Vivian . . . When are you coming? I haven't seen you in such a long time! . . . You were? I don't remember. I thought it was a couple of days ago. Who's that in the background? . . . Ed, Sandi was here last night and she said she and Les could come over on Thursday and help you put all of our books in storage . . . Hold on, I'm not finished! I was thinking that if the books were gone it wouldn't be dusty and we could try having me at home again! . . . I know, but I'm thinking now that maybe it was the books and the dust and if they helped you pack the books and bookcases and clean up . . . What? What's the problem? . . . I know you're tired, that's why they'll help you. . . . You can get a *new* hospital bed. You can order it from somewhere. Maybe you can find one online!" Suddenly something occurs to her. "Ed, don't you want me home?" A look of anguish shoots out from her dark brown baby doll eyes. "*Please*, Ed!" And then, as her husband's slow, insistent baritone is translated into reedy caresses from a telephone receiver, she seems to plummet from soaring entreaty to rock-bottom conviction. "I can't believe you don't want me anymore."

Ray starts to lean towards Jane's bed and Rosie calls her name in admonishment. Jane has been clutching at the telephone cord and now she pulls it close to her chest.

"Oh my God! Oh my God!" She sits up, jolted by what appears to be insidious revelation.

"What's the matter?" says a small, elderly woman seated on the club chair, speaking to no one in particular.

"*Are you having an affair with Jeannie?!* Oh my God! That's why she wanted to help you clean! She's always been after you!" she cries. "I knew it! . . ."

The guests roil in commotion, crying out to her. "Not Ed!" "Jane, don't be silly!" "You have to calm down!"

"Why don't you love me anymore?" she wails. "Then why don't you want me home? . . . I can't believe you! I can't believe you! Oh my God! What's going to happen to me! You don't even care! . . . You don't care."

She hangs up the phone and crumples into rolling soft sobs, her body quivering, her face puffed into folds as she tries to hide it behind her small pale hands, now freed of the phone by her brother. The women are gathered around her, trying to pull her back to shore with hugs, with cooing, with pocket tissues.

"Ed loves you very much!" cries the fragile elderly woman, her voice cracking with emotion.

"What's going on?" says her baffled husband.

"Jane thinks Ed's having an affair," she says, blowing her nose.

"Ed? *Our* Ed? How is that possible? I don't believe it!"

"Of course he's not!" she says with exasperation.

The throng envelops Our Lady, courtiers, suppliants, pressing their claims of reality. They remind her of her husband's trustworthiness, his love, his determination to do everything possible to look out for her interests, of the despairing effects of opiates on perception. She hears them but seems to hear her suspicions just as loudly and she has the look of those abandoned by their divine faculties, off-kilter, thrown from the world of Bronxes and such and landing where there's no voice to guide her.

I've seen this before and I'll see it again. Nothing to be done. Nothing that *should* be done if *truth* be told.

In between the contradance of clenching pain with the liquid weight of sedation, between the labored excursions to the restroom and the daily attention of a variety of uniformed attendants wiping, pulling, stripping, calibrating, the week is now about Jane's fight against her expulsion, her struggle to clamber back home. That very afternoon, her friend Jeannie has returned in distress within an hour of Jane's accusations, to plead and reason away Jane's sense of injury, only to receive an unconvincing acceptance from her seriously compromised old friend. Jeannie will hang around like a chastened lady-in-waiting while others come and go, distressed to find Jane buffeted by what seems to all like extraneous drama. Ed arrives and firmly takes her hand to sadly admonish her for even assuming he could betray her. But there is a gulf that can't be bridged, and at most, Jane will intermittently resign herself to the betrayal, because she loves those that have disappointed her so sorely and doesn't want to feel further from them than she already does. She will, meanwhile, twist and turn, plot and ponder all week on how to regain her seemingly lost footing in her husband's heart and get back home.

She buttonholes her visitors to draft them to her cause, her friends and counselors from her cancer support group who make the trek, her East Village pals from twenty years back or more (some of whom she hasn't seen in a very long time) all of them confused and sympathetic (though none convinced of Ed's infidelity). She learns pretty quickly that the family won't help, most of them empathizing with her husband's predicament, each wondering how they would manage once this responsibility was visited, God forbid, on them. They envision her husband totally consumed by her proposed re-entry to their apartment, death all around him as he struggles to care for her from among the living; they see him age more and more each day, the stress lines digging permanently into his thin, haggard face. She needs to be among professionals, they reason. But her friends—in actual fact much *like* her husband—think that she who is dying should be granted all that can be granted that she asks for—and would much rather visit her at home, a comfortable, unintimidating environment only a short commute for each of them. Her cancer care counselor, Miriam, a sturdy oak of a woman with a maternal voice agrees to Jane's supplications to show Ed the error of his ways and, on the phone, Jane pleads with a Suzanne to help her. "She's going to arbitrate a meeting with Ed and me next Monday," Jane tells another friend, Marcie, who hustles over after work every other day, a busy little beaver, being her one friend who lives a short distance away from here. Marcie bustles around trying to look after Jane like she would a ward, and she's taken a neutral position on this issue since she sees both Ed and Jane each time she visits. She proffers ideas she hopes would make choosing sides unnecessary.

"I want to go home," Jane says one day to Dr. Shepherd. She has had her husband escort her and her coterie of medical equipment around the room to the chair in front of the window facing the London Biscuits Baking Company factory. She is getting heavier and weaker, but she still has enough strength to sit regally in her chair, even if buffered by medications to keep her floating aloft in place. She talks softly, but firmly, still able to maneuver through the fog of morphine to make her case with poise. She likes Dr. Shepherd and her studious, considered demeanor, her diminutive build honed to an efficient sharpness, her gold-wired spectacles—that contrast nicely with her mahogany skin tone—a miniature head lamp that brings the only hint of a heavenly glow to the room, the dull gold crucified body of Christ on the wall notwithstanding. "Maybe you can help me convince my husband to take me home."

"I thought, Mrs. Cantore . . ." all medical personnel continuing to mistake the maiden name she uses for her married name ". . . that you found your apartment unworkable for you. Do you remember that? I'm surprised that you want to try that whole . . . rigamarole . . . again."

"Well," Jane elucidates patiently, "I have friends who will help Ed clean up the apartment. We have a lot of books, you see, and I was thinking that they've attracted a lot of dust and that was the cause of the problem. If *you* think it's doable, I'm hoping Ed will see that it is, too. Right now he doesn't want me near him for some reason. . . ."

"Jane," Ed says wearily.

"I know I'm a lot of bother, but I should really be at home. With my things. With my plants. Where my husband sleeps. We can arrange that again, can't we?"

Dr. Shepherd looks down at her hands folded in front of her and takes a minute to respond.

"Well, we certainly can take the steps to make all the arrangements for hospice care one more time," she says with a sigh. "I have concerns about the workability and whether your theory about the dust is, in fact, the problem. With the amount of *ascites* accumulating in your lungs, even anxiety would be enough to exacerbate your fear of not catching your breath.

"This is what I think: I'm going on vacation for a week and I'm not comfortable with you making this change while I'm away, when I'm not able to ascertain your medical condition. Let's see what's going on when I get back and if still looks feasible, we can start everything rolling then. I think that's the best way to go, don't you agree?"

"Oh," Jane says, her hopes slightly deflated. "But you're saying we can do it when you get back? Ed, is that OK with you?"

"We have to see," Ed says. He's sitting further back in the room, on the edge of her hospital bed. And he's not giving an inch.

"Ed!"

He shakes his head, despairing. She doesn't notice how much of a struggle it is for him to hold the world up for her. Perhaps he's afraid he will collapse under the weight of infinite crises. To Jane, he is a boulder, and she has always used him to hold her up; she cannot see him any other way. *He can handle this. He's just refusing to. He's already throwing her away.*

"Give me some time," he pleads. "I'm still recovering from the night we spent at the Emergency Room. I can't think straight when I'm this tired."

Jane etches a path along the top of her cheekbones with two fingers of each hand as she smears tears away from sopping eyelids.

"I thought my husband would love me to the end," she says, muffled by her attempts to check her quiet sobs.

Dr. Shepherd reaches out to place her tiny hand on Jane's knee, inflated with fluid.

"I think your husband loves you very much. Let me talk to him for a moment outside and then I'll give him back to you. Then he can help you back to bed if you like."

"I don't want his help," Jane says, almost to herself, as she flattens her hospital gown where Dr. Shepherd creased it.

Jane sits alone, downcast, her head leaning slightly to the side as if looking down a steep mountain at the life she used to live below, a life where people now go about their business without her. She is oblivious to the fact that Dr. Shepherd is telling her husband that by the time she returns from vacation, she believes Jane's condition will have resolved the issue for itself. But to Jane's Ed, this is irrelevant. Because the pain he's causing his wife is now, but, even so, he doesn't want to lie to her to make her feel better. He doesn't want to make a promise he won't keep, and so to protect himself from the sin of deceit, he surrenders to the vanity of pride.

Later that day, Miriam says to Ed, "I respect whatever decision you make. But I wonder will you be able to live with it?"

"Yes!" he says unequivocally, passionately.

Up here, we believe him implicitly. We believe he *will* live with it until the day he dies, with or without someone to look over his eventually helpless self.

He walks back into the room after Dr. Shepherd leaves and asks Jane if she wants to go back to bed. Despite her vow of independence, she takes his proffered hand and lets him put his long skinny arm around her ample undelineated waist, and they walk to the bed, her head held high in wounded indignation.

VI

GETAWAY

For the ten years or so after the bus has carried me from Woodstock, my life is primarily poor and urban. My friends become my mainstays, the route by which I can try to escape the struggle of being me; they become our family—Luke's and mine—and my life is never lonely even if it's never quite working out, either.

During most of those years Jeannie lives down the hall from me and we become close friends, back and forth in each other's apartment all the time, laughing, conniving, enthusing, she the thin pixie to my wounded Wonder Woman. We nurse each other through our various devastating crushes and her mad imaginative energy exhilarates Luke who loves pulling her into his fourth dimension. She loves to write poetry and tells me I've got to see what's happening at the scene in the St. Marks Church, where poets like Allen Ginsberg are major presences and soon we're collaborating over a Smith-Corona, smoking cigarettes and joints and basically disturbing poor Mr. Yevchenko with our shrieks of inspiration. I find I also love to write, just like I knew I would as a child when I'd scribble in rent receipt books I'd make my mother buy me at Woolworth's. And then with Jeannie's friend, Meryl, a punk musician, so beautiful and brainy, we perform at the Church's open poetry readings as The Juicy Cunts, making our own irreverent feminist statements. Sometimes, I get jealous of Jeannie and Meryl's closeness, I love them both so much. I think they're smarter and cleverer than I am, they've both been to college. My passions are always so huge and people sometimes run away from them. But for ten years, at least, we are an anarchic team, even when we share our lives with men.

Marcie is one of the many people I get to know at the daycare center, which eventually provides me with a paycheck after I crack open a textbook on bookkeeping. Together at work almost every day—until I leave to try to catch up on my aborted education—and with her Kathleen one of Luke's best friends, we single mothers hold onto each other for dear life, husbanding each other's tiny families as needed, giving each other both welcome and unwelcome feedback on our symbiotic households. We can't imagine ever being less close than we are now, and we can't imagine the marriages and friends and moves that will prove us mistaken.

So for this part of my journey, my bus is crowded with scrappy poets and idealistic parents, and except for Hunter College and summer getaways with some of the daycare crowd to Fire Island or upstate, I am content to keep my routes south of Fourteenth Street.

But two of my good friends, Ellen and Karl, ten years older than me, are intent on taking me further afield and they bring Luke and me up to their remodeled one-room schoolhouse for a few summers. Karl always drives—it's his prerogative: he's a take-charge guy—while their girls, Jackie and Rachel, play-act as noisy, pesky old lady tourists with Luke, as an angry bus driver, mock-disciplining them; Ellen and I typically banter from front seat to back about the daycare center where we both work. I can't remember the car anymore. I'm sure it's boxy and sensible and bought used because Karl and Ellen wouldn't have it any other way. They're very sensible people and that's both soothing and oppressive to my impulsive "bad girl" nature. There was not a sensible moment in my upbringing, so, at the best of times, I relish the regularity of my honorary little Jewish family, and at the worst, I plot rebellion. I love going up to their schoolhouse with them: I love preparing our meals from local produce; I love the casual walks up and down the steep hills that I can take by myself or in someone's company; I love working with Ellen on her garden. But I come to hate being in the car. Once there, we are in Karl's control. It's like a prison. We must do exactly as he says. On the trip up, if Ellen and I tell him we need to make a rest stop, he refuses because he wants to make good time.

"You know we've really been doing very well so far, and I think if we're just a little patient, we can get there in time to get our shopping done in town and still get in a swim. Just another hour. What do you say?"

Ellen never argues with Karl. So it's up to me to stand up for myself.

"Karl, I really have to go. . . ."

"You know, I'm really not sure if there's a good place to stop and I don't want to get off the route. . . ."

"There's a gas station," I say.

"Oh, you don't want to go there. I can't stop now. Let's just hold it in and we'll be there soon enough."

It ends up taking me *several* hours to detox from the pent-up fury I feel but am not comfortable enough to express. I'm a guest at someone's summer home; he's not my husband. Ellen looks straight ahead into the distance and I sit back angry at them both and their patriarchal relationship. Since my father was taken away when I was eleven, no one could treat me like a child and get away with it. Not Virginia. Not Uncle Al. Not Ray. And certainly not Tony. But I had no leverage with Karl. If I didn't go upstate with them, he'd be disappointed—because he likes me ("Oh, you're really something!" would be his delighted reaction to my spiritedness) —but it wouldn't be a problem for him. Luke and I, however, need a place to get away to for a little bit each summer, to have our non-city experience together before he goes away to his camp for kids with "special needs." I realize I must do what I can to control my temper. So clean country air or no clean country air, I smoke a lot of cigarettes on these trips, concentrating my contempt into the flick of my ashes and as cool an expression as I can muster. Dave Cassidy—my late great teacher, my champion, that great mass of mischief— used to tell me, when we poets used to hang at his and Lynn's apartment after a reading, that my angry glares were like Sicilian daggers, but Karl, maybe because he was a social worker, merely found my anger "interesting." In any case, at the end of the day, way after my anger had subsided, Karl would still be his level-headed self, having taken care of everything that needed being taken care of, and I would allow the sound of his even-tempered voice to give the day its closure.

The first few years that I went with Ed to the schoolhouse for the week or two before Ellen and Karl were going to use it, we rented cars. We never had very much money, so the first year we chose the cheapest of the rental chains and we got this really cute lollipop-red compact. We never did that again because Ed kept getting stiff necks from bending over to see adequately through the windshield, but it looked spanking new and it expressed something different—more me, and hopefully more us—than any other car I'd been in. That Ed sometimes had trouble starting it didn't bother me, because eventually it would flip and it would be fine for a day or so, but it was driving Ed crazy.

Ed, like Karl, was also comparatively even-tempered, but much more accommodating than Karl was. Our first vacation was a great time to fall in love with each other all over again. Once your life becomes a routine, you never spend time with each other like you had in the beginning, so that's what vacations are for. That first vacation was about rediscovering what we enjoyed about each other, having fun together, and having fun somewhere in each other's vicinity: feeling the joy of someone's presence for days at a time. Laughing a lot, playing badminton badly without a net, reading while lying on Karl's hammock, driving to the East Sidney Dam Recreation Area for a splash in the lake with unevenly sunburned farm families, buying fruit and vegetables from a roadside stand . . . up in the country, Ed and I hardly ever argued.

We had a nice rhythm together: he slept late while I coveted my morning solitude, observing all the birds with my bird-watching guidebook or sketching the plants in Ellen's garden, maybe jotting down some lines for a poem in my journal; and after I fell asleep in his arms each night, he'd get up and read his collected plays of Shakespeare or do whatever he does when he communes with the close country darkness. We'd both get up in the middle of the night and walk out in the frost to pee under the soaring black dome of stars (and occasionally accompany each other with a flashlight to the outhouse in the back). We did this pretty much for the next twenty years. But with different cars.

In those first years, driving at night was tricky. Even with the brights on, Ed would be peering intensely ahead: the darkness always seemed to be swallowing us up more quickly than the light could illuminate, so we were often passed on the road by a burst of blinding lights from behind. You couldn't always tell which light in the distance was actually on the road and which was off it. We ended up using the car almost every night to see whatever junky movie was at the drive-in, even sitting there in a thick fog one time, waiting for occasional images from the Disney double feature to float up from the mists; in later years we'd rack up the miles to see every movie in Oneonta and to eat at Brook's Family Barbecue. We lived high off the hog compared to Ellen and Karl. And every night, we'd crawl up County Road 3A in the pitch black, twisting around corners, our engine echoing loudly past the homes, until we'd figure out the hole in the darkness which served as our driveway and sink into the all-encompassing shadow of the schoolhouse's unlit front yard. Ed would hold the flashlight for me as I struggled to undo the locks and then, success! —and the door would swing open with a rough squeak. We'd find the string for the light and pull it—pop! —and get a good gander at all the dead flies on and around the fly strips over the kitchen table.

Each day's—and each night's—variation of a routine was a balm, and every part of us relaxed. The heat of the summer sun was only occasionally intense in these secluded dales, just enough to bathe the schoolhouse in comforting warmth, and the loud stillness of the night gave everything a calm focus. I found a country self, a self I really liked, unlike any sense of self I felt in the bruising pace of the city.

We'd take long drives around the area at least once each year, visit the pastured horses from a stable down the road, discover villages like Butternut of only a few picturesque homes, and in the first few years we always took a break to visit Luke at sleepaway camp around a hundred miles east across the Hudson River. These were painful times for Luke and me: he always pined to come home to where he could be relieved of having to try out new activities every day and socialize with those dreaded others—and most especially where he wouldn't have to deal with the mosquitoes which he hated so—and I was pained by the guilt of separation from my tall, reedy "baby" boy, no longer a baby to anyone but me. These visits weren't much better for Ed either, since Luke clearly wanted to keep me to himself and resented Ed's intrusion into our relationship; he wouldn't look Ed in the face for the whole time we were there, even if they were actually conversing (reluctantly on Luke's part).

During the drives back and forth across the Catskills on these visits—the winding descent east and ascent west—we'd stop at Woodstock for lunch on the way down, and Rudy's Big Indian on the way up. Rudy's was a chic, large restaurant run by some Buddhist group a few miles north of Big Indian, New York, situated all by itself on the opposite side of the highway when heading west. Every time we'd gone there, we'd dined out on the terrace with great open vistas below us. That first summer with Ed, having felt carefree and privileged while dining among the beautiful people, Ed slipped into a Cary Grant imitation, sticking to it even as we neared our little red compact in the parking lot when we were leaving. He was now my tall, skinny, debonair man about town—in very short hiking shorts, a t-shirt and blue sneakers—and the incongruity of the two images, lubricated by Ed's playfulness, tickled me no end. I love when Ed (or anyone for that matter) makes me laugh, and he could've had me at that moment in the backseat if he wanted to—but instead he chose to struggle with the ignition. He fussed over and cajoled the engine in Cary Grant's personality, until the car was finally seduced, and we started to mount the steep driveway that led to Route 28. As we crossed the eastbound lane to head west, the car stalled smack in the middle of the road. "Cary" started cursing in great agitation and I laughed in hysterics at Ed's off-handed gutsiness, willing to fake an Alfred Hitchcock scene just for my amusement while oncoming cars sped east in our direction until, just as the approaching car started to slow, the ignition caught and we sped out of the way.

"What are you laughing at?!" Ed exclaimed heatedly.

His continuing the "drama" just made me laugh louder.

"That wasn't funny!" he continued. "We could've been killed! I'm shitting in my pants and you're just sitting there enjoying yourself—!"

"I thought you were acting!" I said. "I thought you were in control the whole time!"

"*No!* I was *not!*"

Ed's Cary Grant-like exasperation set me off on another wave of sweetly painful cataclysms. Ed started to smile, amused that he had the ability to decimate me like this.

"But you were cursing in a Cary Grant accent!" I managed to say.

Now Ed started laughing with me.

"No, I wasn't! 'Cary Grant' died when the ignition did."

That little red car was a piece of shit, but its little stunt was a gift: a quick hit of beaming love. I *was* disappointed that Ed didn't have that wild and crazy personality I'd endowed him with in that moment, but his own personality always kept at least some of Cary's residue for me.

* * *

I needed to get my own hands on the wheel and one summer I asked Ed to let me drive on the country road near the schoolhouse. This time we were sharing the year-round use of an old copper-colored Dodge with Jill, Ed's sister, who kept it most of the time except for when we wanted to vacation; it was a hand-me-down from Ed's parents, a shoddy, boxy contraption that neither of us was fond of. Ed drove me in the Dodge to some fairly flat terrain where there was almost never any car traffic, pulled the car to the side of the road and stepped out of the driver's seat, abdicating the throne with grace. I walked around the front of the car with excitement and trepidation, and sat in the driver's seat as if I was sampling it for comfort. I adjusted the car seat to fit my body's dimensions, adjusted the nearby mirrors under Ed's instruction, and guided him as he adjusted the one by the passenger seat to my specifications.

"OK, now turn on the ignition," Ed said when I had finished setting up house.

The gentle whir of the ignition gave me an almost sexual nervousness and I held onto the steering wheel, letting myself enjoy the blankness for a moment. Then I grabbed the automatic shift gear, eager to get going, and manipulated it clumsily into drive.

"I know there are no cars here, but get in the habit of checking for cars before you move," Ed said, and I turned around, hoping I would actually see one, validating that this isn't just child's play, but part of the real driving world. The branches of the trees above fluttered calmly, effortlessly, over the edge of the road; there were no fast-approaching cars to break the silence.

"Now put your foot on the gas pedal gently," Ed said, and the ground slowly slid beneath us as I aimed the car toward the center of the road. I felt like an overgrown child, exhilarated by the next level of responsibility entrusted to me.

It was easy and yet awesome, too. It took no effort for me to move this giant piece of machinery down a paved road and, I also knew, it would take little effort to run it into a tree or a ditch. Ed would throw little tips my way: "Stay on the right of an unmarked road," "Slow down when you're approaching a curve and then accelerate into it," all the ones, you could tell, he had received when he learned to drive, because it sounded like he was repeating them verbatim. At first my turns were wide and a little reckless, and my stops were short, but with a few more useful "little tips," I had these problems conquered. I felt so happy, taken care of, and eager; I knew I was turning another corner in my life. Someday soon I would be my own driver. I'd be able to get where I wanted to go without depending on others to get me there. I could go places no one else wanted to visit and head home when home was calling. I'd no longer be limited to my own weighted ambling, but would be able to experience the lightness of speed. I could experience the world voraciously if I had the mind to. And most importantly, driving would give me license to experience myself as a functional citizen of the world, not a victim, not a runaway, and finally, not a child.

Since we were only upstate a couple of weeks a year, it took me a few summers of practicing with Ed before I would apply for a license. The summer Les and Sandi came up for a week with two-year-old Parker, and Jackie, now fifteen and devoted to me like a much younger, enamored sister, in tow to help baby-sit, was the summer I tackled State Route 7. Les and Sandi were such slow-pokes on the road—I found it very frustrating driving behind them. Brave Jackie, who chose to drive with us and sit in our backseat behind this novice, was totally in my corner on this issue, her rough sandpaper laugh encouraging my bad girl hunger for speed. Other than to make me giggle, her prompting was to no avail. Ed thought driving at speed limit was, after all, not a bad idea for a student driver, even if that meant annoying all the locals who unnerved me by sitting on my tail before they passed. I can still remember when Route 7 felt scary to me—this was a road for adults, not thirty-three-year-old kids behind the wheel like me—and a car clipping towards me at sixty miles an hour in the oncoming lane had the potential to kill me, but I kept my attention on the slithering rural pavement before me and we made our way east to Afton.

In Afton, there were a few stores that you drove up to rather than park in front of. I had been so proud of my first day driving out of town and I was relieved I wasn't going to ruin it by making an attempt to park at this early stage. All I had to do was pull up to the sidewalk where there was a little wooden post as if waiting for me to tie my horse to it. I was coasting to a halt and somehow my foot placement must have gotten confused because when I thought I was braking, I accelerated instead, and the car jumped the sidewalk to pop the wooden post on the kisser. I jumped up in my seat with a shout of surprise, and luckily we were only moving at around two miles an hour. I pounded the brake sharply within seconds, though we probably wouldn't have gone through the store window anyway, and we all had a chance to deflate in our seats before Jackie and I broke out in fits of laughter. Ed wasn't as amused, but I had this vision of Lucy Ricardo doing something similar, and the part of me that identified with her mischievous attraction to trouble actually made my little accident seem like a comic badge of honor. Eventually, Ed lightened up and I could see the worm of a smile crawl into his dour expression.

The next summer I graduated from "car school." We did some brush-up practicing in Oneonta, and then I went to the local Bureau of Motor Vehicles to sign up for a test. The tester was a very nice man in his fifties, who spoke to me very gently, very patiently. I drove slowly, remembered to use both hand and mechanical signals, and did perfectly. We drove on the residential streets one block north of Main, in front of beautiful Victorian homes, with no other cars on the road. I was asked to park on a block that had only one car parked on it (his?) with a whole empty block behind it to reverse into. It was so easy, I was exhilarated. Ed had taken the test three times when he took it as a teenager in Brooklyn, all because of the parking. I felt so smart for having taken the test upstate. In any case, I aced it on the first try and a few days later I went for my license. In anticipation of all this, I had gotten my hair cut by Gino in the city before we'd left for upstate, and I put on a little bit of makeup (which I seldom bother with) and took what Ed always called my best photo for my first driver's license. Ed kept it after it expired so he could show people his 34-year-old movie star wife in her red raincoat, peering straight into the camera with this penetrating gaze elicited by a clerk who was chatting away when she snapped the picture.

Now when waking up in the country and hearing the house wrens, the blue jays, the robins all start their scattershot opening notes of what would end up being a major morning symphony, I would rise with quiet stealth from our bed, leaving Ed solidly undisturbed in heavy sleep, throw a sweatshirt on over sweatpants and, camera in hand, surreptitiously drive the car out of the valley of our front lawn up to the road and cruise around the roiling hills that surrounded us, looking for picturesque farmhouses to photograph in black and white. The early morning light spread calmly, evenly across the large surrounding valleys, lending the images a quiet mysticism, a Zen stillness, and I felt a creative bliss with each framing and focusing of the image. After an hour or two of this contemplative driving, I'd idle home to the schoolhouse where Ed would be puttering around the kitchen, preparing his cereal. Beautiful mornings in a marriage, with the Tri-County radio station serenading us in its scratchy voice with its amateurish mix of local chamber of commerce promos, top pop favorites and the occasional telephone call-ins spreading domesticity even out to the nearby stoop, where we'd gather with our cereal bowls and listen to the birds now in full choral swell.

I'd always loved using the car to trace the surface of the countryside with our wheels, and Ed and I could get pleasure just from riding, riding over and under and around the fertile contours of the land, finding surprises around each curve, discovering new roads and new connections to old roads. Now either one of us could take the wheel and there was satisfaction in discovering ourselves in relation to the landscape—*this is where we are*—in a way you cannot get from standing still, and there was pleasure as well in the climax of finding our way home from previously undiscovered countries—this is where we connected with places that had really always been all around us. Riding and roving, making those connections and being soothed by the roundness of roundabout: it was a massage of the brain.

That year was the first time that, when we ended the vacation, *I* would start the drive back through the Catskills. I remember the exhilarating terror of the fierce curves pulling out of Oneonta, pushing further up the mountain range and then zooming down its subsequent meandering descent through the beautiful cascading countryside near Meridale. I swerved erratically until Ed suggested I focus up ahead to catch the road where it slips from sight, letting my hands on the steering wheel follow, and this is how I completed my first drive home to our sea-level metropolis: my eyes glued to the road ahead.

The following summer I had more occasions to practice driving, but during the trip we took the second week of our vacation that year I only did a little of it. Our plan was to first visit Les and Sandi at their rented cabin in Vermont, then head to Acadia National Park in Maine and, finally, back to the Poconos in Pennsylvania where Luke was at camp. We had driven the Dodge up again that year and it was acting eccentrically, to our exasperation. During the week we spent at the schoolhouse, the main problem had been that, for no reason at all, the horn would erupt into an unending blast—when we weren't anywhere near the car. A couple of times it happened in the middle of the night, echoing across the valley, shouting through the frost out to the far reaches of the visible Milky Way above. We figured it must have something to do with moisture, but there was little we could do to prevent it from assaulting the universe at whim. The only way we figured out how to silence it when that happened was to undo some of the wiring under the hood and then re-attach it when we wanted to use the car again. We didn't know what we were doing. We brought it into a mechanic in the town of Sidney, but he could neither get it to perform for him nor figure out what the problem might be, on top of which he seemed quietly hostile, not one fond of strangers in town. We were dutifully intimidated, and continued to hope for the best, but Ed's view of the Dodge was permanently damaged. He now called it "shit-colored" among other invectives when referring to it; I kept urging him to stop, sure that it was best to treat it lovingly—I prefer to make friends with the animate and inanimate world around me—but Ed held to his eye-for-an-eye point of view and did his share of "horn-honking" back at the Dodge.

For several days the car behaved, and so when we set off for Vermont, we weren't worrying about it. Ed had mapped out a route which was mostly off-highway. We estimated that the drive, with stopping, shouldn't take us longer than five hours.

Ed had only driven around thirty miles on Route 7 as it twisted along the Susquehanna when, having driven a couple of miles past the last town, we started to notice that the car was losing speed ever so slightly—enough so that we didn't realize what was happening until, as the road made an almost unnoticeable ascent, the car slowed to a halt. Once Ed turned off the car, the ignition no longer responded to the key's entreaties. We stood stock still in the middle of Route 7 on a bright and sunny day, no one any-where around. Ed had me sit in the driver's seat with the car in neutral as he pushed the car over to the side of the road. We had passed a gas station a mile or two back, so Ed decided to walk back there to make a phone call to AAA to get emergency road service. I sat alone in the car, watching Ed slowly shrink to the size of an ant in the rearview mirror before he disappeared behind a turn in the road. I got out of the car and leaned against the hood. Happily, it wasn't one of those sweltering days, and I spent most of the hour alone, staring at the countryside and listening to the portable radio we were bringing to the bungalow we would be renting in Bar Harbor. I felt vulnerable sitting out there all by myself for so long: what would I do if Ed didn't come back? I know that thought passed through my mind, but I knew to answer it with the certainty that, of course Ed would be back—as surely as the sun was shining and the road was quiet. A car stopped once to ask if I needed help, but I told them my husband went back to call AAA, so we would be OK. Mostly I let the tinny sound of whatever music the Oneonta rock station had to offer—inevitably including the perennial "Stairway to Heaven"—shout out to the countryside in its trebly voice while studying the vastness of the hilly, forested landscape in the distance. In moments like these, stillness was its own adventure.

I took advantage of this sunny interlude in the twittering countryside to let my heart dictate the beginnings of a lyric to me, to try to catch the extremity of this enforced stillness in words and I remember writing them down on the New York State map over the Finger Lakes section where we would not be going. Somewhere in our bags, I knew, was the daily journal that I'd kept since before I knew Ed, where, among other things, I jotted down poems, letting the words describing the day transmogrify into other words falling from some bountiful nowhere to the blank page. But I didn't want to rummage through our bags right then, so I allowed Rand McNally to be my page. I do so love building with words; I'm happy to build anywhere, even, as in this case, to impose my landscape on upstate New York's, much as it imposes its on me.

Eventually, Ed's ant-sized figure re-appeared on the horizon, bobbing up and down as it approached in its infinitesimal speed, until soon enough, his lanky gait and dark crop of hair made him distinctly recognizable. He looked tired, resigned, peeved, his mouth curved in a cynical pout, his eyes emitting a kind of New York City irony. Within moments, a weather-beaten pick-up truck appeared from the opposite direction, made a U-turn and backed up to hitch our pile of junk to its rear. We got in the truck and drove to a nearby town a few miles south of Route 7, where the mechanic pulled into a repair shop to tinker with the car. He seemed to have some success, because we soon heard the timid roar of the car's engine when he turned on the ignition.

"Well, the car seems all right now," the mechanic exclaimed, but he had no insight as to what the problem could be.

Ed stared blankly, blinking his eyes, then shook his head at me to say "Here we go again." We used the pay phone to let Les and Sandi know we were running late, and headed on our way.

It would be pretty tense driving this way all the way to Vermont, wondering if the engine's music might stop. But we didn't have to, because as we entered the tiny metropolis of Amsterdam, New York, by crossing over a crowded bridge, the car collapsed while stopped at a red light on a five lane road. Ed made continued efforts to start the car while traffic behind us at first honked and then slowly fanned out into neighboring lanes. Finally, Ed turned on the caution lights and, in short time, a good Samaritan contacted a nearby mechanic for us who located a short in the security system Muriel and Herb had had installed, which he temporarily disconnected.

We thanked him profusely, greatly relieved. Because he had an answer, we had more confidence that the problem was actually solved. I called Les and Sandi and told them of the new delays, and we started along the yellow brick road, uphill out of Amsterdam on residential streets that petered out onto another county road heading to the Vermont border.

In Vermont, we had no view whatsoever. The thick forest formed tunnels of trees around us, and we were swallowed up by shadowy darkness. By the time we emerged from them, the sun was setting. We finally reached the bungalow colony where Les and Sandi were staying after ten hours on the road. We stayed a couple of days, played with the kids (Parker now had a baby brother), swam in the nearby lake, and watched their marriage almost disintegrate, before we moved on to Maine.

The drive there was long and beautiful: black, stony hills pocketed with an abundance of glassy blue lakes, and then curving, rocky shoreline sprinkled with quaint, whitewashed towns that glistened and glowed in the summer sunshine. We pulled into our slightly shabby cottage park outside Bar Harbor before sunset. If the landscape felt expansive, our cottage didn't, and the claustrophobia it engendered probably contributed to the testiness that developed between us. When we were with Les and Sandi, we felt like a model of a loving relationship in comparison, but perhaps we took some of their gender war with us. In any case, Ed was not as romantic as I would've wished at first, and then I was so bristly, it just pushed him further away. Somehow we were joyous and loving exploring the mountains and shores of Acadia National Park, but by the time we squeezed into the confines of our cottage, we were as stony as the landscape. I was so fucking disappointed, I didn't think I'd ever get the glower off my face, and then we'd get out of the car and the landscape would embrace us with its winding glory in a way that we couldn't get from each other alone. If we'd slept under the stars, I think we'd have found our way into each others arms. We kissed and hugged on the mountain trails and, climbing over reefs, we took pictures and held hands, we covered ourselves in each other's clothed embrace—and hated each other once we closed the screen door behind us each night. On top of that, the car horn started going off in the middle of the night again, and again we spent time at a service station and were back to getting mystified responses, this time in a thick Down East accent. By the time we said goodbye to the slap of ocean on reef and to the rainbow-colored biology lessons which blanketed the boulders, we were tired of each other, knowing we had a two day ride ahead to get to Luke's camp in the Poconos.

Ed was really cold to me on the trip west to the Pennsylvania border and, perversely I started warming up to him. When I'm pissed at him there's the comfort of knowing he's around even if he is less than I want of him, but when he glares in my direction, I'm like the baby of the Cantore family with no one to play with. Anyway, we were off to see Luke and that reminded me of how deeply I loved, and how rich I felt for feeling it, and I just spread that richness around Ed as well. I just wish he wasn't so hard to thaw sometimes. Luke was even moodier than Ed when we saw him; he always was when I visited him at camp: he wanted me to know how miserable he was away from me. From counselors we heard how he surprised everyone by abandoning his introversion to play a rock star in the talent show. All this complimenting his abilities as an actor created the only bond he would allow between him and Ed that day, otherwise not even looking in Ed's direction. Here I was, flush with love for being near my baby boy, while still the frustrated owner of two surly males and a cantankerous car. It felt sad that my love couldn't make everything right, but I have to admit that my son's pining and adoration was a flattering kind of sadness. Both guys warmed up to me in a competitive manner, and I carried my burden feeling loved, but wishing I could feel that way more often without the drama.

Two years later I was looking forward to sharing the driving with Ed on an ambitious California excursion, but in L.A., Hertz gave us this giant wedding cake of a car as an automatic upgrade, a white Lincoln Continental, and I felt like I was driving Moby Dick. I hated it. With every advance or reverse of the car, I felt the potential destruction it could cause in its wake as it ripped through the automotive clutter of L.A.'s streets and highways. I made Ed do all the driving in L.A. after I had a panic attack trying to parallel park the damn thing in Venice Beach.

We were stuck with Luke on that vacation. He was 19 years old and surly, and at the last minute he told us he had walked out of the summer Special Ed program we had arranged for him which we'd hoped would keep him from totally isolating all summer. The thought of him alone in the apartment for the nine days we would be away was unacceptable. Luke could take care of his physical needs but he could too easily get lost in the hyperactive world in his head, which he preferred to dealing with people in the real world outside it. I love my son. I'm a good mother, and I know what he needs, and he needs structure desperately. So Ed and I decided we should take him along. I was angry at Luke for so determinedly going in the opposite direction than he needed to be heading, for being the obstinate teenager he was, and maybe as well for being autistic twenty-four/seven, if truth be told. And now he was going to be on vacation with us unwillingly. What a lot of fun that promised to be.

On top of that, we'd be staying with various relatives of Ed's for half the time we'd be in California, people I'd never met before. I hate meeting new people, I'm so much more aware of my size around them and what they might be thinking about it— as if other people weren't overweight as well. I feel so New York, so Italian, I take up space with my hands, my exuberance is like my vehemence, I make a strong statement—like Chinese red or Italian boot black—and some people are beige people. (Ed hates beige.) And I guess I imagined Ed's California clan as being very beige people, sensible Jews, comfortable and suburban. Well, they were suburban and of the Jewish persuasion, but otherwise I was completely off-mark.

Still, there we were, stuck with Luke, Ed's vast and unfamiliar California cousins, and Moby Dick on the freeway. Moby had to go. Ed called Hertz and they promised we could trade it in for a full size vehicle as soon as one was available. None were available at the moment. So we were stuck in L.A. with the super-featured Lincoln, everything push-button, which was not yet the norm in 1987. It was an intimidating power machine, emblematic of the large corporate conspiracy that created a need for luxury cars with mahogany paneling. One day the car almost killed Luke. He wanted to stay in it when Ed needed to run into a supermarket to get something, but after a while it started to get too hot. It never occurred to us that someone wouldn't be able to get out of a locked car if they were in one, but in the new corporate conspiracy model, the car had to be *on* for any of the features (like doors or windows) to work. Luke pounded on the window for my attention since I was waiting on the street. I was mad at Ed for taking so long and I kept running over to Luke to calm him down and then over to where I could see the supermarket exit. When I finally saw Ed with his plastic bag of purchases, I started shouting. "Luke is stuck in the car! He's frying in there! Hurry!" Ed started to walk towards the traffic light which was the equivalent of a short New York City block away. "Where are you going?! Just cross the street! It's an emergency!" Ed was flustered—the two-way traffic on Lambershim Boulevard was fairly intense, so he stood there awhile as I yelled at him until he saw his one opening and he ran across the street to free Luke from the suffocating jaws of Moby—just in time for one of those L.A. motorcycle cops you always hear about to roar up to our car and—in his tight pants and shiny helmet—humiliate a New Yorker for bringing his lawlessness to this fascist state. I would've had no trouble shouting at a New York cop, but this Clint Eastwood guy acted like he could quietly kill you with no remorse and—even worse—no neighborhood accent. Ed stewed uncomfortably, handing out his driver's license, and I couldn't help laughing as Ed pathetically glared at me, as if to say *This is all your fault!* The cop enjoyed Ed's squirming and let him off the hook with a warning: "You're not in New York anymore. We have laws here."

Not the same ones we did. Ed's mother's cousin, Hinky, whose house we stayed in while in L.A., never met a closed door that she respected, and twice in three days, without knocking, walked in on Ed and me in the bedroom we were using. "Don't mind me," she'd say, "I'm just looking for something," while we'd try unsuccessfully to look nonchalant under the covers. I wanted to kill her, but I'm pretty sure L.A. would've had a law about that as well. She was loud, overweight, demanding and, as Ed pointed out, very warm and affectionate, especially to Ed, and she had her eye on everything and everybody in her household. And for that weekend, that included me. We told her of some plans we had to go to Venice Beach and relax by the ocean. She went ahead and planned a family get-together for the same day. "Ed!" I kind of whined, "she doesn't pay attention to what *we* want!" Ed felt like a captive being pulled apart by wild horses—she was family offering

us hospitality, I was his wife who'd never seen California before—and he decided we'd do both. We went to the beach early
and then returned for the family get-together. A houseful of
cousins—strangers to me—were sitting around waiting for us
when we arrived late, tracking in sand. Hinky didn't know who
she was dealing with, trying to manipulate *me*. "Just a little bit
longer," I'd said to Ed when he suggested it was time to leave the
beach, and of course one thing led to another while we watched
the surf pound the shore under a temperate sky. Hinky had to
restrain herself from screaming bloody murder—I'm sure she had
shown no restraints before we arrived—while everyone else
waited docilely in the living room for the shouted orders from the
kitchen. "Where were you? People've been waiting for an hour!"
she expostulated, but then Ed said sweetly, "I'm sorry, we lost
track of the time. Hi everyone, sorry to keep you waiting." Ed's
charm seemed to work magic on his family on both coasts and that
was certainly the case on the west one. We then "meeted and
greeted" for the rest of the afternoon, Ed, of course, knowing his
cousins, if not their kids and spouses, and Luke and I not knowing
anyone, but at least some of them—including Hinky's lovely
henpecked husband, Pete—went out of their way to make us feel
comfortable. One cousin's teenage daughter thought my New
York accent was as funny as her mother's and would imitate in
gross exaggeration certain words I'd say, and giggle. I *did* have a
few words I could've said to her in a *really nice* New York accent,
but I "cooled my jets" to use an expression Luke favored. That
afternoon, I felt the way Luke must have in that fucking white
Lincoln, pawing at the windows. Ed said the smog had improved
tremendously since he'd been there twenty years before with his
family, but some of his relatives made up for that in my opinion,
and I was looking forward to our trips to California's national
parks, just the three of us. Luke was still being horrible around us
but he was fine when in the company of Pete, who was giving him
special attention, and so I was mistakenly hopeful that Luke would
mellow as a result.

Before we left L.A., Ed drove the wedding cake to LAX where he traded it in for a slightly more modest olive-colored Mercury Sable, so that I could comfortably assist in the driving. I was sad to leave Pete, as were we all, and I managed to leave Hinky politely and without incident, not to mention without the affection that Ed and Luke seemed to feel for her. Their private garage's door beeped a warning to all oncoming traffic that we were backing up from the depths of their basement level parking spot into the dangerous daylight of L.A.'s traffic arteries, and soon we were zooming away from that metropolis of fuel combustion, past chocolate brown hills and sandy-colored lemon groves and we found ourselves some thoroughfare tranquility north of Bakersfield.

After a couple of hours of rural driving, we squeezed onto the narrow, winding, tunnel-like road to Kings Canyon National Park. It was like driving into Emerald City, except that instead of emeralds, it was constructed of majestic rock, rock that in its grayish-brown somehow managed to include all the colors of the spectrum in it as the lazy late afternoon sun washed over the canyon of road. The drive slowed to 35 miles per hour and what, on a map, would look like we had reached our destination, was actually another forty minute drive. It was a long, beautiful tease, waiting for a destination that, it seemed, would never arrive. And then it did. We pulled up in the darkness to a jam-packed camping area in the center of which was a modest lodge with a lunch counter in its lobby. We had sandwiches and chips for dinner and then found our way to the adjacent rooms on the second floor, one for Luke and one for Ed and me.

The next day we rose into the hills, slowly walking the trail, Luke hanging by my side, sulking whenever Ed joined us. We walked up rocky inclines curving up to the sunny blue skies, Ed growing more petulant at both having his communion with nature and me marred by hostility from Luke and at my focusing my energies on making this vacation a meaningful experience for my covetous boy, and the tension between us all made our scenic climb a somewhat compromised epiphany. Finally, the stone highway along the edge of the hill moved into a dark green glade that beckoned with the rushing sound of water. We encountered hikers with heavy backpacks climbing stone steps leading to a natural bridge across a lush, soothing waterfall. It wasn't even the halfway point of their journey, but we made it the climax of ours and found a place to sit and listen to the flow of the falls and the occasional ricochet of stray voices. We found there our moment of family repose.

After days of tension between the guys, Ed and I finally had a blowout one night, just as we reached the Red Roof Inn in a town outside of Yosemite National Park. We sat in the car shouting at each other with Luke watching on, before Ed, in a huff, finally escaped from the car to get the keys to our rooms. I felt that we were so loud that it was embarrassing, even though I doubt anyone heard us past the closed car windows. But they could have if they'd just walked by. Luke had a detrimental power over us, his hostility to Ed in particular undermining me. I was in California to *live,* to discover and grow, but Luke was determined to resist any and all changes that came with growing—with life—and so far, our explorations together of California's emphatic landscapes were more, for him, about holding onto me than anything else. This was the opposite of the romantic vacation Ed and I had planned and I found myself angry at *Ed* for not trying hard enough to turn things around, to transcend Luke's antagonism, for not just magically winning the day and releasing me from this conflict between husband and son, between being overwhelmed by the expansiveness of Western vistas and subsumed by the regressive forces pulling us back to those East Village tenement walls. Instead of supplying release, this particular car adventure was supplying combustion.

Although Yosemite was hot and crowded, I was determined to "give" Luke California, make this a special memory for him, feed him enough spectacular scenery so that he might experience what life could be like at its most glorious, give him motivation to try to improve himself and prepare for more such possible adventures. It's hard for a mother to give up on these kinds of dreams: that she could have the most high-functioning autistic child the world has ever seen. For years, I enjoyed his haywire verbal associations as an example of untapped genius, and so did many of our creative friends. Then it got less amusing as he morphed into a truculent six-foot teenager who might insult your guests for an evening's entertainment, never leave his room other than to indulge in the safely chaotic images on a movie screen, or hang out with the homeless instead of going to school. I was still hoping to turn this accidental vacation for three into a special experience. But I'm not sure how much Luke took in of the panoramas around him; his focus seemed to be more on the increasingly narrow physical space between his body and mine, on his seeming desire to become an actual part of me. Ed, in contrast, grew listless, bored with the heat and the park's commercialism, and allowed me almost too willingly to hike separately with Luke which I thought would be more relaxing. My previous images of Yosemite had been majestic ones influenced by the stark black-and-white of photographs by Ansel Adams and the like, but during that dry August, it was a barren, relentless backdrop to our festering family drama. By bringing Luke with us, we had taken much of the anxieties and resentments that we needed the vacation from along with us. I was so angry I could cry, but I chose to let the anger be at Ed rather than let it fray that intimate cord that binds me to my son.

The drive down the Sierras the next day zigzagged across an infinite golden landscape, and the joy it afforded us—that is, Ed and me—softened the anger between us. We pulled over for a couple of scenic turn-offs, walked out of the car and breathed in the vast openness like a meditation. We took in the embrace of the view as if we were receiving it from each other, standing side by side. Luke stood away, staring at the ground, thinking, thinking, rolling over his thoughts the way he has to, in deep silent conversation with himself. Somehow I had gotten myself across the country—and that was *something*—and life was powerful for this moment. Then we continued west on our trek to Ed's cousin Liz in Marin County.

After highwaying around the perimeter of San Francisco, we crossed a bridge to San Rafael and soon found ourselves on a winding road leading out of town into the hills. As per Liz's instructions, we turned left where we hit a tiny shopping mall with a health food store and quickly another left onto a dead-end road that had a sign with an arrow bent at a sharp 90 degree angle saying "10 miles per hour." This was the steepest road we had driven on so far and it was terrifying, not because of any sheer drops along the side of the road (the homes were where the drops would be) but because the steep grade made us feel that as soon as we'd stop the car, we'd roll right back down if Ed so much as lifted his foot off the brake. We managed to bypass Liz's home, almost hidden—as it was—hanging over the side of the cliff, but with her help (she popped out of her house at the sound of the car rattling the calm of her sleepy community) we backed up at the right angle so as to be able to park.

Liz was a kind of hippie sexpot, with untamable long curly hair, and a tiny curveball of a body. She was warm, animated and intimate, and she insinuated herself between Ed and me each night to cuddle up and talk the night away. I didn't know how to react to her pansexual vibes, and her flaunting of her disdain for taboos in general didn't make me feel as at home as one might imagine— there were still a few taboos I thought worth preserving. She had already told us about an affair she had had with another second cousin in Seattle, so I found myself watching her warily.

She had a really sweet, twelve-year-old daughter that lived with her, named Delby, who had the red-haired Celtic features of her father, a coke addict Liz had left when she had gotten clean of her own habit seven years earlier. "Everyone" in Marin had done coke, been in twelve-step programs and become healers, according to Liz, and she was no different.

"I'm learning Reiki, it's so amazing. It opened me up in ways that were overwhelming. I had had so many painful blockages, my chi could hardly flow at all. My family *so* fucked me up, you don't know, Ed, you just don't know."

Since Hinky was Liz's mother, I would almost buy it, but I pretty quickly mistrusted Liz, who, I felt, could easily find ways to blame Hinky for the powerful needs which entitled her to do whatever she wanted. I hadn't been immune to that way of thinking myself, but I never would've articulated it as a justification for anything, because I wouldn't have believed myself for a second. No, when I was like that, my preference was to function like a sleepwalker or a drunk, either ignorant or remorseful in the morning. I knew I had no justifications for some things I did, like when I slept with my friend Rita's husband in the years before I knew Ed. I thought it unsettling that Liz knew what she was doing when she was doing something she shouldn't, and felt she deserved to be able to. It gave her a boldness that was slippery, not like my blustering kind.

But Liz and Delby were gentle and matter-of-fact with Luke, and that—and the fact that they had a peaceful, tiled backyard that overlooked the mountains where Luke would quietly sit and read when not conversing with the much younger Delby—made Luke relaxed, even logy. Luke didn't like too much stimulation, and what with meeting hordes of Ed's family and having to be with both Ed and me while hiking on mountain trails, not to mention the tension between the three of us, this was probably the first time Luke got what he needed from the vacation. Delby's talking to him like he was just an older cousin from New York and not like someone she had to talk slowly and loudly to, like most people did with him, presented him with a social situation he felt he could settle into like a comfortable groove. So Luke didn't hang at my side the way he had earlier, and, if Liz had not pushed my buttons, that might have afforded Ed and me a bit of the vacation we had originally hoped for.

Liz didn't like to drive that much (though, of course, she did drive on a regular basis), and she wasn't even fond of being *in* cars. She sat in the back seat with Luke and Delby and gave Ed directions when she took us out to Point Reyes Beach. She insisted that Ed drive at speed limit as if driving above it at all was something crazy New Yorkers did, though our experience on California's roads told us otherwise. Her mother had lived in L.A. for thirty-five years without learning to drive, so I imagine Liz picked up that heightened sense of danger on the roads from her. You could see her jaw tense up when she'd tell her beloved cousin that he needed to *slooowww dowwwn* and Ed would apologize. The roads wound all around the varied terrain: here hot, golden, dry valleys, there dense woods shrouded in mist, and sometimes rocky hills where the cliffs led down to a distant, crashing Pacific. Finally, at the end of gray-green pastures that sloped down to the shores, passing isolated pairs of black cows and a frisky goat or two who would stop and stare as if posing for pictures and then move on to the business of grass-munching, we came to a small parking lot at Point Reyes Beach. It was August, mid-day, midweek, and there were only a couple of cars. It was not what New Yorkers would call beach weather: the sky was layered with cloud like a thick gauze, and the breeze was sharp and wet. I carried a thin woven blanket to place on the sand, but I wrapped it around me like a peasant skirt to help keep me warm. We walked down a path between two stark hills headed towards the beach and upon turning round a bend found ourselves confronted by the unexpected. In the distance, high on a hill of sand that climbed up toward a rocky promontory was the lithe naked figure of a bald man whose body was caked in white powder, straddling a wooden chair while large, silvery, feathered wings draped his shoulders. Way below him, ahead of us on the path, was a woman in a floor-length fox fur coat and a lavender silk scarf wrapped around her head like a headband, snapping away on her camera, shouting out directions to her unearthly subject. Neither of them acknowledged the three adults and two teens who passed by. Luke was distressed. "Just ignore them," Ed said and Luke shook his head, constantly outraged at the human species' constant breaking of its own rules, rules Luke cherished as guideposts. We turned the corner and the beach opened up before us, and we were Lilliputians among sprawling reefs in a sandy hideaway, the ocean and the wind enveloping us in a gentle roar.

We succumbed to its call and wrapped the wind around us by rushing into its arms. Delby ran ahead to skirt the shore and Ed allowed himself to be seduced by the towering black rocks, clambering over them in his Converse All-Stars. Luke tentatively followed Ed's path, but would only go so far until he sat on a ledge and shimmied down like an overgrown child. Ed was reliving some childhood urge and used his long legs to conquer the uneven, treacherous surface. Delby tore herself away from her shell collecting to clamber up effortlessly after Ed, practically weightless as she was, while Liz and I watched from below as we shouted in alarm, our words fighting with the shout of the surf. Ed waved that he was OK and stood high above as if he'd conquered Everest, marking the peak with his wide stance. Then Delby stood next to him, her hair whipping around her, his little elfin friend. There was something thrilling about Ed's deftness and long-legged agility, and I ached at not being able to overcome the burdens of my weight and join him: I could never be so surefooted with gravity favoring me as it did. I felt earthbound, like the rock itself, and both wistful about my damned eternal limitations and aroused by my husband's mastery at scaling. Liz probably felt similarly about Delby's fearlessness; they were our proxies, our emissaries, the photo-negative of our fears, and they gave us courage we were hard-pressed to experience. We certainly had both been reckless in our lives, and should have been brave enough to allow our loved ones the freedom to clamber away from us even if it meant the possible risk of harm. But it was easier said than done.

"Delby, I want you down now!" Liz shouted, but Delby shouted back "I'm OK!" and Ed shouted "She's fine!" and so we had no choice but to protect them with our vigilance. To our relief—and disappointment? —they managed to maintain their agility as they ran down the side of the rock, riding gravity's pull like surfers on a great big black beautiful wave.

Ed rode *California* like a wave, easily landing wherever the altitude took him, but he did so without Luke and me, who navigated the west coast like hikers on some breathtaking earthquake faultline. It was a dramatic landscape with a deceptively mellow vibe lent it by its easygoing climate and sleeveless decorum, and the mixture of harsh extremes and lilting sunlight felt untrustworthy, like Liz and her laid-back grip on people or like Ed's cousin Tamara's husband, a relentlessly friendly artist who, when we met him and Tamara for dinner in San Francisco, would not let me talk to anyone but him. Underneath the warm breeze of people's affections lay something that slowly and sweetly pressed the air out of your lungs with an unacknowledged urgency. Ed seemed happy to bid his breath adieu, soaring high on his cousins' attentions. But I found it unnerving and, insofar as Ed and his family were oblivious to that fact, I felt very much alone. I was glad to have added the west coast to my résumé, but I would've felt more at home in, maybe, I don't know—*Guatemala? Corsica? St. Petersburg?* —someplace where, if people were going to murder you, you'd expect it. Someplace where they wouldn't award you with a wedding-cake-car to pummel through a five lane freeway. Someplace cops didn't pretend they were a superior race, but instead were comfortable in their own corruption. Someplace like New York. I was sad to go home, hoping to have discovered the glory of the legendary golden state, only to discover that I was not a golden person. I'm a tomato red, like putanesca.

Ed had no relatives in New Mexico, so our various trips there were free of complication—other than the complication of marriage. We visited that moonscaped state three times over four years, and we always left New Mexico with "complications" unraveled, smoothed out by the thin air, the pink rock, the Old Testament weather and by our mutual enthusiasm for the unworldly experience of being there. If aliens ever landed in Roswell, it might not have been for exploration: it could have been for a homecoming.

For our first trip there we were based out of Santa Fe in a motel across the street from a long strip of shopping malls. But once past that scenic blot, New Mexico revealed itself as a collection of hallucinations. One road took us to a small downtown area of old Mexican streets now adorned with the quaint monied charms of art galleries and antique furniture stores re-selling the hacienda. Other roads led up mountains past abandoned Catholic missions, their windows like emptied eye sockets that continued to view the barren, desolate foldings encircling them; or to still-occupied pueblos, with their prayer sites like clay staging areas in the middle of flat settlements, vulnerable to all the gods at once. One of those roads led past large tracts of woods brutally charred, showcased behind fences marked with U.S. Department of Defense warnings, this being only a prelude to other kinds of ruins—the Indian kind, cliff dwelling civilizations charred only by the sun which had dried out their ancient Manhattans with their stony apartment complexes naked to the elements. Taking that road deeper into the mountains, we ourselves were naked to the elements: entering the surreal suburban landscape of Los Alamos—home to the atomic bomb—we were pelted by a sudden hailstorm, a late spring temperature inversion that left us helpless for half an hour, overwhelmed by a deluge of ice crystals, and then, with a harsh burst of sunshine, all of that suddenly gone like it had never happened.

We drove north to Taos where we got a chance to view Georgia O'Keefe's paintings in a gallery, her large simple flowers like the expansive landscape, exotic, primitive, VIBRANT, intensely delineated. We drove north to the Rio Grande Gorge Bridge, not to cross it, but to brave our vertigo and peer below into the abyss of river. I was emboldened by my Nikon to bend over the railing to capture the composition calling out to me, causing Ed to reel in panic behind me and turn away after I ignored his desperate imprecations not to bend over too far. I felt grounded by my artistic vision and by my greater body mass, while he, on his God-given stilts, was overwhelmed by the dizzying spatial pull. He couldn't watch: his mind completed the scenario of me plummeting into nothingness and he losing me to the powerful grip of gravity.

"You're such a sissy," I teased him when I followed him off the bridge's platform to our waiting rental car.

We drove back toward Santa Fe, turning off the road to visit the hot springs of Ojo Caliente, where Ed *would* lose me. After pulling up onto a dirt plaza past a ramshackle dusty hotel where we purchased tickets, we bade each other farewell to enter facilities where we'd be led by guides of our own gender. Two short and beautiful Indian young women showed me where to leave my clothes and led me to the showers where I tried to avoid the self-consciousness over my body that I've always carried with me. The women seemed to be used to all sorts of bodies and were very matter of fact: bodies were their job. They wrapped me in a larger white towel and led me to a dimly lit room of wooden bed plat-forms. At the end of the room was an enclosed pool surrounded by desert rocks and lit by an invisible skylight, simulating an outdoors environment. Immersed in the dark green steamy waters were various women: ranch wives, hippies and local business-women adding to the warmth with small talk. I sat on the edge and slid in and was soon reclining against the edge, saturated with the friendliness of heat, letting the voices of women echo around me like a coven of bell-like cooing that played with the shifting light like a memory before it was one. Periodically, women would slowly leave and a couple of new ones enter, until finally I reached my saturation point. When I left the glassed-in pool area, one of the Indian women surrounded me in the dark with white linen that covered me to the floor and she led me to a bed where she wrapped me lovingly like an enchilada, and my body felt like a highway of sensations pulsing through me; I was lit up by an hallucinatory intensity the likes of which I had never experienced, not at least without those Timothy Leary chemistry sets. I fell in love with my Indian and managed not to stifle any of the pleasure of being every ounce of me—not an everyday occurrence, I assure you. When Ed and I met afterwards in the late daylight of the arid reservation outside, we felt weightless, buoyed, as if we'd been emptied out and left all new, and now, as if we'd been tripping and had taken our own separate journeys, we re-awoke to each other's presence and let the world seep in peacefully.

We drove back to Santa Fe that night, the road slowly sloping down from the top of the world, the big fat white moon floating in the blackness over the peaks hovering around us, an occasional white or red light in the hills signaling life. The scene was like a vast photo-negative, and I'll never forget it, I said to myself, not ever. And I haven't. Later in the week, I'd take many snapshots of Ed's long legs clambering over the Puye cliff dwellings, and I used my infrared lens and black and white film to capture the Santa Fe National Forest, positioning myself for what I hoped would be immaculate compositions of flowing landscape violated by the clean lines of fences, trying to capture the liberating tension of textural contrasts—a soothing meditation for me—with Ed indulging me, standing by the car watching as I paced each shooting area until I found the point zero for each exposure. But that photo of the road down from Ojo Caliente stays in my head, the only place it was ever developed, engraved in memory: the serenity of the night stillness always at my disposal.

I need to keep that.

We got Rocket in 1992 from Muriel and Herb, Ed's parents. They were ready to move on to a new car and they offered us their six-year-old Camry. Now we could take as many trips as we wanted, when we wanted, not have to schlep on subways and commuter trains when visiting family outside of Manhattan. I had just re-contacted my cousins after years of therapy and I decided I needed family of my own in some shape or form, and now we had the means to visit them in the outer environs of Westchester, as well as Ed's family scattered around Brooklyn. We'd keep the car through Christmas and then store it until spring.

Luke was the one who christened it Rocket. The name was definitely more fantasy than reality, Rocket being a sedate, square gray affair that trembled at each stoplight. Muriel and Herb had always seen their cars in very practical lights and made no attempt to find accurate reflections of their tastes and personalities during car purchases—and in that way actually found one. I had told Ed I would never, ever buy a gray car, but a gray car was what was being offered, so I claimed Rocket as my own by accessorizing: pine scent hanging from the rearview mirror, a box of tissues in the glove compartment and a postcard of a Frida Kahlo painting taped onto the sun visor.

Because of alternate-side-of-the-street parking, one or the other of us was driving Rocket several times a week, circling the neighborhood for parking spots when it wasn't in storage, and Rocket came to fit us like an old worn winter coat. Little by little it needed patching up: new glass for the driver's mirror, a paint job to cover East Village vandalism, a cover for the trunk lock to keep the neighborhood junkies from getting their hands in there, a new left taillight to replace the one stolen overnight and then returned the next day sitting next to the car on the sidewalk (even though the car was now parked on a totally different block!)—the usual New York City wear and tear.

We went through similar wear and tear. The summer Rocket took us to Mt. Washington in New Hampshire, my arthritic left knee finally gave way while I tried to walk down the relentless hiking trail. I had to send Ed ahead to get help as I sat on the gravel road, frightened and in pain, watching the dense New England forest be slowly snuffed out as the evening light died around me. On the drive north we had zoomed like we were releasing ourselves from the city, flying into the sexiness of new places: once, in fact, when I was in the driver's seat, I couldn't resist the sight of Ed's long legs in his hiking shorts, and stroked the inside of his thigh with my right hand until I found myself compelled to unzip his fly and drive ambidextrously, Rocket with one hand and Ed with the other. Ed came way before Mt. Washington did, even before we found ourselves behind a parade of New Hampshire Hell's Angels all bearing "Live Free or Die" on their license plates, on their way to staking their claim to New Hampshire's sky-high teat. Ed had to drive up the mountain, the only way being a two lane dirt road with no guard rails and no shoulder that wound its way precipitously around tight corners. He later would say that was the scariest road he'd ever driven on and was grateful he hadn't steered us into the abyss. But driving home, it was as if we had crawled out of one. Ed drove the whole way back: I was a broken rag doll covered with mosquito bites, weighted down in depression. For three months I could only walk with difficulty until I finally got my day in the shop. This knee here, well, it didn't come with the original package any more than did Rocket's new left tail light.

And then, only a year later, Ed had his knee operated on for a torn meniscus, and what with this and that, we've both had to get more and more accustomed to the clinks and clanks of worn hardware: knees, shoulders, sacroiliac joints, hips, timer belts, axels, brakes, rusted tailpipes. We've all reached middle age together.

We made the most of Rocket, wearing her out very slowly on special excursions and family visits. Ed always drove when we visited family—it made us feel more like a family that way, each of us in our respective roles—and it was with Rocket that he finally mastered the Saw Mill Drive and Route 9A at night, those winding lanes with oncoming headlights piercing the median guardrails like a light show at a heavy metal rock concert while you're striving to find the curve beneath your wheels. With Rocket we explored Skyline Drive in Shenandoah National Park and met the quiet parade of deer at dusk that surround you in a dream-like haze as you glide by them at 10 miles per hour in a matching floating parade. We did the Connecticut I-95 relay twice a year to visit my friend Catlin at her farmhouse, a relentless straight stretch of speeding, enraged drivers, which would suddenly deposit us in Catlin's bucolic little town by the Long Island Sound. We wore down the roads around the schoolhouse each summer for a week or two and once a year barreled through the rutted, muddy, backwoods roads that led to the mountain getaway that Sandi and Les eventually purchased—in fact, often down *several* muddy roads since we, time after time, would take the wrong turn-off and barrel through to God-knows-where before we'd wise up, putting Rocket through too much wear and tear for such an old soul. Except for perennial tailpipe problems, she usually pulled through, though. (Until she didn't.) She was a sport.

A few months ago, when we drove our brand new Volkswagen Passat to the bed-and-breakfast in Cold Springs, the snowfall cast a thin layer of vanilla icing across the local roads, and traffic crawled cautiously, while we, with our automatic traction control system, gripped the road and scoffed at the other travelers driving like toddlers on training wheels! But back when Ed drove me to the University of Connecticut for a grad school interview in old Rocket, the drive across the thick, icy glaze of driving snow on the Interstate was like a tightrope walk: a slight wrong move and free fall.

The drive to S.U.N.Y. Binghamton for my interview *there* was so exciting to me. Ed had surprised me by volunteering to chauffeur me. He had been sleeping in the living room since I'd told him I wanted a divorce and so I was thrown by his supportive generosity. He had shrugged his shoulders and tossed it off as a good reason to take off from work.

"I could use a little adventure," he said in explanation. I assumed he was being modest about his generosity, and this newly adventurous guy was much more to my liking than the mid-life crisis one he was becoming.

The first half of the drive was the same one we always took to get to the schoolhouse each summer. It was familiar enough to be comforting and uninteresting. But then, instead of turning off at the tiny Catskill village of Roscoe, we stayed on Route 17 and the trip went widescreen, each vista a discovery, an exploration into the future, and, in fact, it became a very beautiful stretch of road, even in the faded colors of winter. This part of 17 was a rolling panorama of forest, now transparent with the bare branches of those trees that had let go of their leaves. Right smack in the middle of this bare-bones Eden, an industrial park belched smoke steadily into the fresh country air like a malignant dragon daring an American Don Quixote to challenge it to a duel. Once this dirty country secret faded out of view of the rearview mirror, the road gently ascended to meet the higher elevation of Binghamton.

And then, a day later, we ran the highway rapids back down to New York and that could've been the end of my Binghamton adventure. Yet, somehow, I had managed to force open a window there, allowing serendipitous light to break through when I met Ted Rudnicki, one of the Biopsychology professors. He was excited by my writing background and I could hear the clockwork whirring during our meeting as he played with various configurations of possibilities. In support of my observation, a few months later I received a large white envelope in the mail bearing my acceptance to the Biopsychology graduate program.

Those should've been among the most exciting moments of my life—I, who had only had a high school equivalency diploma and whose college matriculation had been interrupted for over ten years raising Luke while Ed and I tried to make ends meet—but instead, it was undercut by Ed's not agreeing to accompany me in my temporary move upstate. He had believed my assurances that my acceptance was unlikely but that applying anyway would be a good experience for me, and considering the distance that had recently grown between us, he couldn't commit to leaving his— admittedly meaningless—job and moving to an area where he didn't know anyone other than his sometimes contemptuous wife. (That had been me.)

I had moved into a world of ambitious, active people, and Ed was not that. He was content with barely making a living and doodling in the acting world. At one point, being able to even maintain a job had been a great achievement for me, and I had been entirely at home in a world of artists who were hidden in the nooks and crannies of the workaday world. But I was now past that point, and, unhappy with the meager impact my poetry was having on the universe of writers, I hungered to make my mark. I also decided I wouldn't mind having real money for once in my life, having property and savings and all those other assets people Ed grew up with could take for granted (and which he had left behind for art and romance). This could be a journey worth taking where I could look back in pride at my Herculean accomplishment of moving from someone heading fast towards an early grave to someone who could, one day, even be "venerable." Now it's true I could've pursued that career while remaining in the city— Hunter would've accepted me to their graduate program—but Binghamton had more prestige, and besides, I saw the journey as one that could lead me away from our wearying, granite metropolis towards a tranquil, comfortably-furnished—maybe even *distinguished*—country home. So I accepted the invite from Binghamton. I was going to force this change on my life and on everyone in it.

Now, when I think back to those months driving Rocket from school to apartment, back and forth along the Susquehanna on those always humid, sometimes gray, days, I'm reminded of how lonely my independence felt. I was aggressively pursuing my future while feeling unmoored from my past. Neither Ed nor Luke nor any of my friends or relatives were anywhere around. I eventually made the beginnings of student and faculty friendships but that took a little while. And even then, so much of those days was about me, Rocket, and Calvin—the canary I had brought up with me from the city. Calvin and I lived in a beautiful second-floor apartment in the quaint town of Owego, half an hour west along the river from school, in a grand, rickety white Victorian building. I loved it—it reminded me of the goal I had set for myself of living comfortably in the country—but it also demanded I spend more time on the road than I could genuinely afford. All that time driving I could've been studying or grading my lab students' papers, and the drive back to Owego each night—especially as winter lowered its cold, clammy grip onto neighboring Broome and Tioga counties—was more and more filled with a gloomy anxiety.

Ed and I originally vowed to visit each other every week, each of us taking turns making the four hour trek. I'd barrel home down the highways in Rocket, no longer interested in the scenery or the drive, just in getting to the destination, and the commute became hellish heading to the city and wearying heading back upstate. As schoolwork began to pile up, I felt the pressure of spending all this time wearing down the roads was going to defeat me. So Ed and I started to see each other only every other week, when he would, after work, ride a Trailways bus from the Port Authority terminal up to Binghamton every other Friday night. I'd work late at school and then pick him up around 9:30. I'd sit in the car waiting for the behemoth and its klieg lights to wind its way to the lonely, glaringly-lit bus depot, parked with all the other family members and students waiting to pick someone up. When I'd see Ed's tall, thin figure emerge from the station, I'd stand outside the car and wave. I was so happy to see him, so hungry for his love, his affection, his confidence in me, it was like I was welcoming a soldier home from the war every other Friday night. And this was the only way home could come to me, since I was now untethered from it, so many miles away.

But when Ed was gone again, all the way down what felt like the steep descent to Manhattan, I had to struggle by myself with the long, solitary, cold nights of Owego. I thrived when immersed in the daylight activities and interpersonal connections at school: the intellectual challenges, the social exchanges with my younger classmates, the earnestness of both my undergrads and my baby lab rats, and the droll company of Ivan and Yelena, the couple who ran the lab for Rudnicki. But night wrapped itself around me in a tight grip, and I'd drive Rocket into the highway blackness each night away from the small industrial city to my quiet apartment in the dark, sleepy town where there'd be just Calvin and me—and not Ed, whose presence had warmed me for almost twenty years and whose absence now made me feel somewhat buried alive. And to accentuate that feeling, Rocket started wearing down, sporadically having electrical shorts which added a layer of panic to my life. Everything here revolved around Rocket's ability to get me places. When I would leave Rocket in the local garage, the mechanic let me use one of his old cars for the day, asking me for a fifty dollar deposit. I'd feel like a beggar driving around the Southern Tier in a hand-me-down. I tried to concentrate on my rosy future and not dwell on the obstacles that I had to overcome, one of which was the miles of road between me and everything else.

I no longer remember the drive home from campus the day Rudnicki told me my B in statistics would lower the reputation of his team and he therefore had to let me go. All I know is what Ed said I later told him, that it wasn't me driving the car but this other Jane who took over, this willful creature whose lead foot was forged in some dark, cavernous foundry, a monster of determination who brooked no interference. I was her captive; I let her break the sound barrier to get Rocket and me home, let us be temptation for an accident aching to happen. All I could think about, according to Ed, was the end point, waiting for me in that outsized, dusty Victorian mausoleum I had tried to make my home.

Days were excised from my memory by all the pills I swallowed that afternoon. This is what I do remember: Ed and me speaking long distance to Suzanne, my long-time New York City therapist, during which she urged us to contact a couple of Westchester-based psychiatric hospitals. Everyone was treating me like I could just blow out the window in a strong breeze; they spoke to me fastidiously, tenderly, firmly. They were talking to the child in me, the little girl who just now, forty years later, was responding to my father hurling a shoe at my back or punching me in the nose in the front seat of the Oldsmobile, the little girl who this time almost succeeded in jumping out of the passenger seat while the car was still in motion. *No, stay in the car*, everyone was patiently telling me, *you must stay in the car*, and having fucked up as much as I had, first by attempting suicide, then by failing at it, I was now in a childlike state, dutifully doing whatever was suggested.

Ed had phoned his boss saying he had a family emergency to deal with, and at the end of being upstate with me for a week and a half, he drove me to school to pick up my things and speak to the department heads about what I was doing: Dean McDowell told me I was welcome to come back for the spring semester and he'd find a place for me in *his* lab. Rudnicki had taken a sudden leave of absence, since this was not the first time something like this had happened to a grad student of his. And then, the next day, Ed and I packed some suitcases of mine into the car, placed Calvin's cage in the back seat draped under a cotton cloth, and once again we took the three hour descent to the Hudson Valley. This time I was an adolescent being driven to boarding school; I was nervous, humbled, and yet anxious to begin, to get away from the clammy pity I received from everyone, most especially from my poor, shaken husband, stumbling over his long limbs trying to take care of me. I would miss Calvin, though, and was cheered by his eventual trilling during the long drive downstate; perhaps, in time *I* could be trilling, Ed could be trilling, even Rocket would trill once again, rather than sputter as it had been doing more and more. As we had all been doing.

I wouldn't see Luke for a while, though. Not until my stay at Four Winds was over and we could attempt to pretend this had never happened.

Two months later, I was back in Binghamton for the second

semester, a few pounds heavier and a great deal more self-conscious. The new plan had me teaching a required course to freshman undergrads and going to therapy each week, and nothing was feeling quite right. I felt tyrannized by the indifferent freshmen with their merciless hormonal rampages barely suppressing their amusement at the fat middle-aged lady they saw me as. And each time I visited my therapist, whose office was at his farmhouse, he kept asking me why I had come back, letting me know that at this fragile moment I needed the stability of my marriage more than I needed a graduate degree from Binghamton. I had come back because I didn't know what else I could do for myself and I needed to do something or I'd just feel despondent, waiting for my life to get started again. In the meantime, I'd apply to Hunter College to see if I could continue my graduate studies in the city next fall.

I had two homes now, but at neither of them did I *feel* home. I knew that I was unlikely to stay upstate for very long, so now my Owego apartment felt provisional; everything I had done to make it feel like home now had an expiration date on it, as if mentally, I had packed everything up and marked them for the movers. And yet our apartment in the city now felt like Ed's. He had taped onto the refrigerator a sheet of yellow ruled paper with the rules of engagement we'd negotiated in a few couples sessions at Four Winds, rules like say "I" instead of "you" as often as possible. Ed was better at rules than I was, and the apartment started to feel like it didn't belong to me, like it was old in a new way, like it had been transported to the southern hemisphere and all the sunlight was hitting it from the wrong direction. I realized that I had never fully left Four Winds psychologically. Home was a vast estate with gentle hills and quiet promenades, filled with people like me who understood how much struggle there was every day in trying to seem like you belonged somewhere, and where someone else was now doing at least some of the struggling with you—the therapists, the professionals—and we could bathe in the warmth we lavished on each other, which was so much easier than lavishing it on ourselves. At Four Winds we were all on the same page, and it felt sad that people like Ed, we knew, would never understand us no matter how much we asked for their attention. Home was in a large room with bay windows and many chairs and sofas, and I was not ever going to be going back there any more than I would ever go back to 217th Street in the Bronx where my mother would be standing at the front door calling me in from the rain. No, now I would have to find equilibrium *never* being home, and I was finding it tricky.

And then it got trickier. Each morning, when I dressed for work, I would put on one of my new skirts in the snugger styles which were becoming stylish. I had decided I wasn't so fat that I couldn't look respectable in them, even having gained some weight, and anyway, the looser mid-length styles that flattered me most were impossible to find. And now, only a few weeks into the semester, I was starting to have trouble closing the waistband. I was so frustrated, not being aware of having overindulged in any way that might have caused this. I swore at my body and at the curse that had been placed on it by my genes, and felt humiliated that the fat teacher was getting fatter.

It started to become increasingly clear that my waist was growing at way too fast a rate. My abdomen seemed to be slowly filling with air, pushing out at the world, crying for attention. It got it. When my mother had gotten sick, she had, at first, mistaken her increased girth as weight gain, which she tried to deal with by futilely replacing her meals with cans of chocolate Metracal. I had thought, three years earlier when I'd passed the age that she'd been when she'd died, that I was home-free, that I had been pardoned of what had been a life-long early death sentence. But now, as I watched my expanding belly, I was more and more confirmed in my belief that I had been mistaken. So, late one Sunday, overwhelmed by the panic that I'd been trying to suppress for most of that week, I called Ed on the phone and told him I needed him to come up and take me home.

It was already eight in the evening, and I knew it would take a while for him to rent a car and drive halfway across the state. He told me not to worry, that he'd be there as fast as he could, and *then* I worried, seeing him in my mind's eye speeding on empty blackened highways, the brights not illuminating the road's curves fast enough, the darkness swallowing him up, the same darkness that was enveloping me here, where I was sitting up late in this quiet, quiet town, the only lit window on Main Street, where nothing was happening outside my belly.

He arrived at two in the morning. I was still up; I could hear his footsteps squeaking up the hall stairway. I sat over the kitchen table, my large black textbook opened flat in front of me, as if my life in academia wasn't over. He knocked on the door. I opened it. I was delivered. He put his long arms around me and pulled me to him where I could rest.

We were going to be together again for a while.

There was a snowstorm the next day, leaving a foot of blinding whiteness over everything. On top of that, Ed had checked for messages back in Manhattan and found out that his father was going in for an emergency bypass in Florida. I was glad for the snow, because now it was not just me that would keep him from his father's side. He was just not meant to be there. He was meant to be with me. In the afternoon, we joined the neighbors outside digging out cars, and with borrowed shovels we carved out a path through which we could maneuver our now-white-caked Rocket free from the curbside when ready to depart. The next day, we packed up Calvin and anything else we could comfortably manage in a repeat performance of my November departure, and joined the trail of cars with thick slabs of snow roofing as they precariously worked the highway.

We've slowly etched the grooves of a new route into our consciousness over the last three years, a route that we've taken so often it's like a visit to family. We bump up against the congested traffic going uptown on West Street until we are released onto the

Henry Hudson overlooking the Upper West Side; after five miles of whipping along the river, we burrow beneath the streets of Washington Heights to scramble onto the Cross Bronx Expressway with its stressed coupling and uncoupling of connecting highways that wrangle the Bronx into submission. After navigating the lanes that appear and disappear and clot in traffic-ridden mergers, right before we would end up leaving the Bronx entirely we instead take the 7C exit to Pelham Parkway West, and cruise the leafy boulevard for a couple of traffic lights before we turn left on Eastchester with its grubby industrial warehouses, and continue until the monied corporate structures of Albert Einstein Medical Center rise before us. Ed would take me up the driveway loop to the main entrance and I'd sit in the lobby until he'd find a parking spot, and then up to 10 West, where everyone knows me (but I wish they didn't) —my new undesired home away from home, where everything is clean, friendly and depressing. The staff loves us there because they know so many of us will be dying shortly and even more because some of us will not, and we patients play the game of musical chairs, hoping we will be one of the winners. I don't know if it's more depressing when the beds are all taken or when many are empty, the emptiness suggesting both the possibility that not many are sick today or that not many have survived. I take my determined stance to live, but the 75% chance I've been given of living at least five years is encouraging only if you can ignore—as you would a river through a bridge's grating—the view of the 25% chance of not.

Sometimes after an overnight stay for chemo, Ed would drive me to Fort Tryon Park for the last bit of nature and scenery I could manage before I'd be too sick to leave the apartment for a week. I'd feel like Humpty Dumpty, huge and fragile, and Ed would treat me with a delicate concern that I'd know would make me cry in pity for him if I didn't have to concentrate so hard on living in the present, where each detail needed my mind's eye to grasp it in a vise-like grip—*where had I seen sunlight and trees and families before? have I ever visited this planet?* During chemo is when I start to prematurely age, the poison in my veins zapping the cancer cells and the rest of me in small but steady gradations. Who would believe this bald, pale, fat lady had ever been too much of a hellion for anyone to look after, someone unwillingly consigned to a foster home after getting pregnant as a runaway? During bouts of chemo, that fifteen-year-old girl now looked reckless to me, oblivious to all the pitfalls around her. I would've been one of those elderly neighbors who would counsel her to calm down, savor the sunshine and the trees, find family, make a comfortable nest for herself, invulnerable to the destructive winds that visit us so often. Because now I was *aware* of how afraid I was, and how easily you could lose all those things you take for granted. Even things like daylight. So I now would bathe in it, sprawled awkwardly along a stretch of ground overlooking the Palisades, regally high up and lucky, but not a lucky filled with joy, but rather one of gratitude. *Take advantage of this moment!* And hold onto whoever will offer their hand. Today it was Ed. Over the next week, and then every third one for three months, in addition to him it would be whatever friends—some longtime, some who'd returned from where they'd moved on to—who could watch over me as I dissolved in a miasma of weakness and nausea. And this was the case for each successive re-occurrence of the disease, and is even more true now, except now it also includes women from the various Caribbean islands who live in the Bronx and are paid to watch over me and the others here who need attention.

All these routines had finally made the car a regular part of our lives, like suburbanites who do highway commutes. Rocket was looking shoddier and shoddier, but still managed to get us to Einstein when needed, to Gilda's Club meetings on Wednesday nights, even to Luke on emergencies. One steamy summer night in Washington Heights, on a narrow, ramshackle street one block long and suspended on steel girders over a dirty urban cliff, I had to sit in the car while Ed climbed the five flights of stairs to Luke, who had been placed by his apartment program—on short notice—in an apartment without phone or window screens or dishes, his new furniture left packed in boxes. Luke has gone through many emergencies, coincidently enough, these same years that I've had cancer, and Rocket has usually taken Ed to all the various apartment programs and hospital wards since, typically, I haven't been well enough to deal with all this.

During the good times—during remissions, or even on the third week of my three-week chemo cycles—Rocket would take us back upstate or to Cape Cod where friends lent us their homes off-season. I still associate highway speed and country roads with the happiest of times, even while hobbled by the war raging around my immune system. I need my peace more than ever, my time to contemplate the life all around me: the seagulls and the house wrens, the surf grass and the wildflowers, the gloxinia on our apartment balcony. We take long excursions so that I can spend more and more time in nature, surrounded by life, noting its particularities and articulating them carefully in charcoal and pastel, quietly, purposefully, each stroke of the crayon a contemplation, an affirmation, a *capture*. This is one of the ways I nurture the life around me—with my attention. And the natural world responds so much less complexly than would the people in my life should I devote such attention to them, who no longer *need* my nurturance in any significant way except as a moment's reprieve from life's stresses, *one* of which would be how to deal with what is happening to *me*, this person who takes up time in their day and who has grown roots of her own in their respective gardens. They dote over me in the same way that I dote over hummingbirds and sunflowers. How can I help to keep the people I love alive, every one of them, other than to nurture myself in the same doting way? So I try to. And Rocket is one of my facilitators.

Sometimes, though, it's a long, uphill slog up a road which you hope'll peak where a future will again be visible on the horizon. In the meantime, what damage the cancer hasn't inflicted, some of the medical care has, including an early botch-up that unnecessarily left me minus one of my kidneys, a condition which

I knew—in my recuperative period of fury—would eventually, at least, be compensated for monetarily. During my first period of treatment, which ravaged me much more than the disease had yet had a chance to do, each new debilitating symptom incited my determination to make up for this hell with some wonderful indulgence once I recovered: Ed and I would go places that we never could've afforded to before but would now be able to with the help of my malpractice attorney. Then, after four months of chemo tests showed no signs of cancer, I started the arduous haul to get back some semblance of a healthy life: watching what I ate, taking long fast walks and regular swims at my old gym, taking meditation and art classes at Gilda's Club, even eventually doing some volunteer work in a children's hospital and fantasizing re-applying to graduate school in the city. And around the time that I now had a cap of dark tight curls—permed by way of tamoxifen—I felt it was time to make a commitment to a future I could believe in, and I told Ed I wanted to plan a trip to Italy. I knew Ed would never have had the courage to take that leap of faith without me pushing him. He was no more certain of my health (though he talked a good game) than he was of my forth-coming malpractice reimbursement, and I knew I would have to convince him that we would definitely be able to pay back any debt incurred. The bottom line was: he could not deny me. Somehow it seemed to make him more amenable to the idea if we added Rome to my plans to see Florence and Venice, and, if that's what it took to drag this Fellini fan along, I was all for it.

It was meant to be a celebration of one whole year in remis-sion, surrounded by the glories of the robust human forms from the Italian Renaissance, the verdant hills of Tuscany, the beautiful slapstick sounds of the Italian language—my joy at being alive italicized by a vacation. The weeks before the trip were tingly for the both of us, neither having crossed the ocean before—actually we'd never taken a step off North America. I get anxiety when I prepare to leave home, and this was no exception. There is always that slight dread, the sense of danger at escaping home—*there will be hell to pay*—that ancient gut feeling instilled in me by Daddy. But sometimes I persevere and fly my coop. This time the dread weighed me down more than usual with a vague physical memory that I couldn't quite place but which kept signaling to me that something was wrong. I noticed that my skirt was a little tighter than usual and my appetite irregular. Would I never be free of the fear of this fucking cancer? Would I spend the rest of my life hearing its echo in every one of life's propositions? *What if—? What if—?* This was *foolishness*, this was anxiety plain and simple. We were going to leave home, travel high above the planet and soft-land safely on the other side of the world where people converse freely in my grandparents' mother tongue, where they know nothing of Albert Einstein Medical Center or the Cross Bronx Expressway, where Brooklyn Bridge is a chewing gum, where the hard sidewalks of New York are a fantasy made up by Columbus. I didn't want this to be torn away from me by either my parents or my sister reaching out from their graves and holding me hostage to the dismal, narrow fate of the Cantores, who, outside of my father's army service in Burma, never did or saw anything of the world outside the New York metropolitan area, trapped by the disfiguring curse of no possibilities.

So I kept my anxieties to myself, channeling them into the usual pre-vacation irritations that Ed was familiar with, and which he tolerated with a very slow simmer. I started carping that I hoped he would be independent enough in Italy to allow me to go off on my own when I needed to—perhaps to sit and sketch faces or street scenes or images from paintings.

"You can do what you want," he said, dismissively, but as an afterthought added, "but I guess I did think this would be kind of romantic: the two of us in Italy."

"I'm just saying . . ." I responded.

"Do what you want." He sounded slightly petulant, which annoyed me—as everything was doing that day. Then he seemed to remember he was talking to someone recuperating from cancer, because he said, "I'll be OK" in a reassuring tone of voice. But I didn't feel assured of anything.

We landed outside Venice in the hazy white of morning, from where we took a waterbus filled with boisterous Italian boys who slapped each other on the head and parried insults to the approving laughter of other Italians on board. The insistent sun heated up the cabin's windows and, combined with the frenetic boys, made me happy to be Italian, like I was being welcomed home to the sunnier parallel universe I had always longed for as a girl. Ed and I looked at each other, flabbergasted by the anarchic energy around us, and laughed at the youthful clown shows, our laughter made easier by a night on the plane without sleep.

Except, perhaps, for the Venetians, who took their city for granted, the streets, we found, were filled with people who looked foolishly happy. We pulled our luggage up and down over the small stone bridges and around dizzying labyrinthine corners until we found our *albergo* on a quiet *calle* over a small canal. I pulled my way up the *albergo's* stairs and settled happily onto our bed, listening to the sound of Venice rising through our window, the echo of voices and footsteps underlined by the absence of engines. A city without cars! It felt prelapsarian.

Venice surprised me. I was most looking forward to our trip to Florence, but Venice was a city of neighborhoods, and I love neighborhoods, the way when you walk a street you can feel it open up to you in a way you never can driving through. It seems more personal, more human, life-size—but not larger: you are not overpowered by it, but rather entreated by it. *Look here*, say the shop windows, *wander in here*, whisper the churches, *look around here*, beckon the tiny stone bridges. We did all of these things on our way to view the art galleries and cathedrals where the heroic images of the painted figure overwhelm you with longing, the searching, twisting, swirling of bodies drenched in liquid pigment have much more life in them than we do, and so we borrow from them and feel more alive even as our feet feel more and more exhausted. Ed and I wandered the museums at our separate speeds, parting and re-connecting over and over, and that turned out to be as much distance as I needed, until we had to leave for Rome and I was furious at him for robbing me of more time to float up and down the occasionally stinky, celestial canals, sleepily in gondolas or humming along the Grand Canal by *vaporetto*.

The long train ride to Rome was marked by my coming down with a cold, which did nothing to protect Ed from my combustible frame of mind. The fucker was going to have plenty of time to see Rome in his lifetime—probably with some beautiful Italian girl who'd fall in love with him like I did (though someone much thinner and younger)—but, from the way the earth pulled on me heavily, I sensed that I might never see Venice again and I had fallen in love with it and was more than willing to cheat on Ed and continue my affair with this most seductive of cities, a city with which I felt the most intimate communion. Because the people spoke the language that my parents used for whispered, urgent gossip, the voices that echoed through the narrow old streets seemed to confide Venice's ancient secrets to me subliminally, and I felt I belonged in a way Ed couldn't, nor could all those German, English and Chinese tourists. Venice made me finally Italian in a way that seemed really flattering—*bella*—and not like a bellicose, clueless *goombah*. It slyly included me in—and now I was leaving it forever, I thought, for the cold dying days of the twentieth century.

From a city without cars, we arrived smack in the middle of a city overwhelmed with traffic, tourists, business people and the homeless barreling through the pollution of criss-crossed boulevards and alleys. I was terrified to even cross the street—me, a New Yorker!—and nursed my resentment at Ed, who struggled in a state of denial to make everything work out cheerfully and efficiently. We stayed in the Hotel Columbus, a big modern hotel catering to Americans, surrounded by the sounds of construction. The friendly blonde woman at the desk, who spoke British-accented English and around five other languages on the phone, made up for my hostility by clearly finding Ed attractive. Worse, he seemed to relish it, and that wasn't going to help him one bit with me.

But sick and unhappy as I was—weak, congested, achy and isolated by my festering body of secrets—we felt the power of the mysteries of the ancient city beneath the impatient metropolis. We were ejected from our own lives' time frames and placed in some continuum of eternity that was jolting, as if face-to-face with the truth of mankind's DNA. Nothing was dead in Rome—nor in Florence or Venice for that matter—the presence of the dead was more vivid than the swarms of Nike-clad, camera-toting tourists who wandered the rings of the Coliseum, crawled over the ruins of the Forum, or stood face-to-face with the classical statuary looted by—and exhibited in—the Vatican. We overheard a young tour guide recite Antony's and Brutus' speeches from Shake-speare's *Julius Caesar* as we sat in the remains of the Forum's plaza, and we imagined ourselves bearing witness. We are not here just to spawn and decay, I realized, but here to share the stage, to contribute our selves to the world that meets us, and my world was Caesar's, too. And I have to admit being amused by Ed's awed assault of the Coliseum, the man in my life now boy-like, walking among gladiators.

Florence was overcast most of the time, and by this time *Ed was getting colder to me*. I ignored him, besotted as I was with the idealized human forms that endlessly filled the museums and churches. They were as far from our bodies as the gods were, but they made me horny anyway, even for the Ed whose presence I felt enslaved by, what with the heavy weight of our real, flawed, sometimes irritating relationship to pull at us, and whose warm, imperfect body could not compare with the eternally youthful, glistening ones in marble which inspired this lust but could not satisfy it. In the Duomo in Siena, I found a chapel to the Madonna which tapped another hunger, and I sat alone before her milky figure in the dark alcove and let her gentle gaze cradle me: I'd found the perfect mother, not one that could abandon you or disappoint you, not one who could decompose, but one whose love was impermeable, like glossy stone. She didn't break into a loud squealing laugh or worry about her weight or play with your hair or cry when your father hit her. Her maternal expression was constant, and you could fill your belly with peace and serenity and consequently walk lighter through the day.

As we left the church, we were caught in a downpour and, soaked to the skin, we climbed the cobblestone streets to the bus stop. When we got back to our *pensione*, I entreated Ed's body with my touch and his body warmed to me, but Ed did not, and he turned away from me when he was finished and I wished *I* was marble rather than this needy flesh and bone and this angry heart.

We returned to Venice a year later. Just Venice this time. I knew I wasn't going to be as active. The re-occurrence meant that, even after renewed treatment, things weren't going to get better for long. But I thought, what could be more relaxing, more healing, than a stay in that carless city that moved at a gondola's pace, with its indolent Italian temperament. I had to convince Ed. He was afraid to be too far from a hospital. *Medical insurance*, I told him. *Traveler's Insurance.*

"I'd rest a lot," I told him. "We could get an apartment with a lot of atmosphere so I wouldn't mind just staying in bed if I need-ed to."

And that's what we did. Ed found an apartment online in a *palazzetto* overlooking a canal that included a bedroom with a gauzy canopy bed and portraits of some Venetian aristocrat's illustrious ancestors. A balcony in the back faced the clotheslines of the other apartments on the dead-end block. I could sit under the breakfast table umbrella and listen to the housewives chatter in Italian across the courtyard, or when they disappeared indoors, to the sound of the Italian-dubbed reruns of "ER" that wafted over me through their open windows.

The first few days, we strolled around in the hot September sun, just walking through neighborhoods. *People lived here.* It was not just a touristy ghost town. People led their lucky lives in the most ridiculous city on the planet, a city that could not logically exist, may not exist much longer, but does exist, palpably, in the present—with the stubbornness of stone and mortar and sulfurous salt water. Ed finally succumbed to gelato, having resisted it out of a misplaced loyalty to American ice cream. And I succumbed to Ed's ministrations, letting him look after me, letting us have our belated *affectionate* romantic stay in this urban tribute to Venus that we knew for sure this time would be our last chance at one.

The first Friday we made our one long excursion. We took a *vaporetto* to the train station and bought tickets for Verona. The train originated there in Venice and so we had many seats to choose from. Each row had two seats facing two others. An elderly woman eventually sat in the window seat opposite us and a young, thin guy around twenty, his hair in the carefree, shiny, stray spikes fashionable in Europe, lounged in the one opposite Ed. His friends were forced to stand, as the train had filled up by now, and so he grabbed one of them and pulled him down onto his lap. For most of the ride he kept his friends in stitches, imitating a flirtatious woman in his high falsetto, and being extravagantly gestural in his flighty impersonation, squeezing and tickling— even kissing—his lap partner. I envied his lack of self-consciousness: his body was an elastic play-thing—alive, electric, festive, physically intimate with an unbridled sexuality and yet not sexual at the same time—literally shameless. Some of the young men were crying with laughter and the other passengers were enjoying the clowning as well. Ed looked flabbergasted, as if propped in the front row of a circus he had not paid to see, and I loved it all, wishing I could see my body as a vehicle for slapstick, light as a feather, almost inconsequential. At one station, a long line of German-speaking teenagers walked down the aisle, many of them making clear their disdain for the buffoonery, which served to goad our court jester into higher gear, satirizing their studious dignity, while they, in turn, scoffed coolly among themselves. The Germans were sophisticated and attractive, and the Italian was as playful as a puppet, and I, sitting heavy and weak and aged prematurely by a kind of *biological* warfare, ruefully saw their international rivalry as energy which, needing to be husbanded, was being unnecessarily frittered away.

We strolled slowly through the upscale streets of downtown Verona, past the Roman amphitheatre, the pricy shops, the Piazza delle Erbe mobbed with tourists, until we found ourselves overlooking the river that wound its meandering way through the city. I needed to rest and regain my strength, so I sat on a bench and Ed sat on the long stone wall overlooking the tranquil scene. Across the way sat beige villas laid out decorously over the steep, undulating hills. Everything about Verona spoke of serenity, gentility and commerce. It was hard to imagine hard times or struggle. The rushing river whispered eternity, the constant flow from here to somewhere else, no suggestion of emptying out or evaporating into barrenness. No, it spoke instead of fertility and growth and I contemplated it wistfully like a tourist who will be returning to a harsher country.

My energy resurrected, we found our way to this church I had read about in our Lonely Planets book, off the beaten path. A long, dark, medieval cathedral, it had on its walls uncanny ceramic renderings of figures from the New Testament, still alive in the likenesses of 13th century Italians. They were less ennobled than they were specific: John the Baptist had gristle on his chin, Mary Magdalene's red curls were intractable, the Virgin's grief was recent, and way up above, Jesus' thin frame, viewed from far below his bare feet, suggested the seediness of poverty and the pitilessness of death. These people were less biblical than they were ordinary Veronese citizens who never really died, whose pale white porcelain skin still glistened with sweat and tears, though coolly contained by art. I loved them, they were all the contradictions of life's corporeal corruption and art's ephemeral permanence—something almost ungraspable preserved for eternity, kind of what you intuited life was supposed to be until you were abused of that premise.

The train ride back to Venice was crowded, and Ed had to convince people to get up from the seats we had reservations for. I was feeling my own loss of permanence more strongly now, having seriously fatigued myself, and I felt that my insides were expanding to the point of mild nausea, while the world outside my body pushed back relentlessly.

"Tomorrow I'm going to rest," I said to Ed, my hand in his as we chugged eastward across Italy's thigh.

From the *vaporetto* that left the train station heading towards the Rialto, Venice looked inky black, like a town closed down. Occasional caverns of bright light would flicker from the buildings along the Grand Canal, otherwise seemingly turned down for the night, and elegant jet setters could be seen descending their noisy narrow hallways. Ed and I stood along the edge of the boat as if we were witness to Venice's vices, its gambling dens, perhaps, or some form of midnight saturnalia, and it seemed like something faintly sad and sexual whispering in our ears, like an echo of an old desire still ricocheting across the universe. Ed stood behind me, his towering body pressed to mine, his arms around me. I leaned back on his chest and felt lucky as the dark breeze kissed our faces. The bridge at the Rialto was festooned with carnations of white lights, a respite from the eerie beauty, a happy ending to the day's travels. Soon I'd be home in my *palazzetto*.

I mostly slept the next day while Ed combed the streets of Venice for birthday presents. I was going to be 48 years old on Sunday, which was a day away, and we both knew there were not going to be many more birthdays ahead for me. I felt Ed's absence all that day. Whenever I'd awaken from behind the canopy bed's gauzy drapes, all I could hear came from outside the window: the steady roll of footsteps on stone, the sporadic toss of a voice above the throng's soft roar, the lonely, echoing call of the gondoliers—

Aoi!— as they rounded the bend of the canal. The apartment itself was dead still. I comforted myself knowing Ed was stressing himself out for my sake, worrying over each purchase, trying to second guess my taste. He would be striding up and down bridges and stone steps, pushing through crowds while I lay inert, closed off from the breathing, moving city, pulled down, down, in surrender to my disease. I let go of my loneliness, left Ed to the energetic world, and succumbed to the cozy comfort of obliviousness.

That night I persuaded Ed to show me his presents before my actual birthday began in the morning. He took out a small Venetian jewelry box. Inside it were earrings of a translucent purple stone and a delicately beaded necklace. They were beautiful gifts of pure denial, gifts that I would have few occasions to wear, but wear them I would, bald or not, fat or not. I would not be denied these gewgaws by which Ed could imagine me beautiful again.

Then Ed brought in a tall object, a small tree perhaps, wrapped in green and silver paper. I tore it open to find a face in my hands, a giant gold-painted feather from whose surface a face rose as if from a mold. It was a woman's face, peaceful, beatific, it's hollowed eyes staring soothingly out to me.

"Take a picture," I said. I climbed onto the bed and drew the gauze curtains, then peeked out from behind my golden mask, no longer the invalid now, rather, the mysterious courtesan. I allowed the face to become my own, so that it was now I who was the pacifier and not the pacified, I who could spread grace around me to all corners of the globe, not the anxiety my sickly demeanor usually managed to communicate. I wanted to bear the face of genteel beauty to the world and not this mask of death I knew greeted it.

When I awoke on my birthday, the feather lady stared enigmatically out at me from across the room, balancing against the wall on the delicate mahogany dresser. The pale light through the windows bleached the master bedroom. And I knew I wasn't going to get better. There was a small torque of pain in my gut, steady and dull, slowly tightening its grip. I told Ed we had to cut the vacation short by a week and go home.

We had to wait a day, until Monday, for Ed to make all the necessary arrangements. He ran around San Marco from phone booth to phone booth, waiting his turn to call airlines, the landlady, medical insurance, my doctor in New York, all the time surrounded in his franticness by frolicking crowds of tourists. That night I had him take me to a *trattoria* around the corner from the Piazza San Marco, overlooking the Grand Canal, so we could say goodbye to Venice. We sat surrounded by elegant diners, all chairs facing the water so we could catch the sunset over the medieval towers. In the main piazza, the little bands competed with faux gypsy serenades, and as Ed and I, on our way home, walked over a stone bridge, a gondolier below us belted out "Amore," cutting through the kitsch to some sad beautiful echo inside us all, so that we and three other couples stood motionless on the stone walkway above him, arranged as if we had been placed there by some old Hollywood hack, replicating a scene we'd all seen so many times before even if we'd never actually seen it. I held Ed's hands tightly in mine, and he played his role brilliantly and bent down to kiss me. Why did that moment have to end?

Why do any of them have to?

The next morning, Ed lugged both our suitcases down the two floors of the *palazzetto* and we were preparing to make our way through the large wooden front door when we bumped into one of the British couples who also had an apartment there. They were older than we were, in their sixties was my guess, and the woman had lost her brittle, haughty manner evident when we had first bumped into them. They both looked either like they were fucking a lot after a long hiatus or had just discovered gelato, their faces rejuvenated and glowing.

"Oh, are you departing so soon?" asked the woman, one hand in her husband's grasp, the other pushing back the stray wisps of her golden honey hair. "Have a lovely trip home," she said warmly, confident, perhaps, that she was going to have many more years—even into her dotage—when she could regale her great grandchildren with delicately censored memories of her visit here. She, like most everyone else, I remember thinking, was going to make it to 2001 and beyond; only I was going to have to actually take the odyssey.

We thanked her and wished them both well and headed out the palace door. We created a gentle ruckus with our luggage wheels loudly kissing the cobblestones, then turned several corners and crossed a bridge to wait for the water taxi we had ordered to pick us up at the appointed spot—across the canal from our bedroom windows. Ed was starting to fret when the taxi was twenty minutes late and a great shadow slowly crept over the city. Just as raindrops the size of flowers started to land in casual little bull's-eyes, a short man ran in our direction from across the walkbridge.

"Signore—Mr. Edward!" he said, as the sky started to pelt us. "This way, this way, they told you wrong, this way!"

All hell broke loose and in moments we were drenched as the three of us hurriedly rolled the luggage back over the bridge in the direction of the Rialto. It was hard for me to go very fast and Ed had his available arm around my waist to support me. I was halfway between panic and exhilaration, fear of both getting sicker than I already was and of missing our flight, and thrilled by the chaos of the adventure, by the surprises life still had in store for me. We arrived at the motorboat and the driver helped me step down as it rocked in the turbulence and led us to the seats down behind him in a small open cabin. Ed and I sighed in relief as we caught our breath and the taxi driver revved up the engine, leading us out to the Grand Canal. As we headed towards the open bay, pure slivers of lightening dramatized the postcard view of the city before us. It was God's little gift of drama where none was needed, and if we had somehow blithely forgotten the sense of urgency our early trip home signified, some higher power was here to remind us that, even amidst the serene architecture of the

City of Love, you can be suddenly sucker-punched by the loud clap of danger.

VII

The Expulsion

A week has gone by; there is a current of only tentative intimacy running between our no-longer-young marrieds, humming at extremely low volume. Ray comes each morning with the Post and sits by the bed to watch over Our Lady and engage in gentle, light-spirited conversation. The elderly couple show up a few times, the woman with dyed honey-colored hair sitting bird-like in the huge pink plastic chair, watching over the patient from a distance, ready to call the nurse at a moment's notice if need be while her husband rambles around the facility to keep himself from getting bored. Ed arrives around noon each day to take over, wrapping Jane up in his attention even as she alternates between a soft dependency and a cool reserve with him.

One day, a woman with extremely short hair comes by and leads Jane in a meditation after a short amiable chat. She holds one of Jane's hands in hers and reaches over the bed to hold one of Ed's, whose other hand completes the makeshift circle. She asks Jane to close her eyes, to breathe easily, and in a voiced whisper directs Jane's attention to whatever tensions exist from burdened toe to troubled head, one slow and easy step at a time.

"And now feel your body, very slowly, very easily, rise from the bed, floating gently above it, and now it's rising some more, like a feather lifted by a steady, comforting breeze, and you can see yourself floating all the way up into the clouds, and it looks like Heaven, and you are bathed in a warm, lovely white light. And you look into its source and you surrender all your gravity to it, this powerful, clean, serene, white light."

And then, in quiet, all three just breathe slowly, those standing watching over the patient as if they are breathing into her, feeding her with their attention, while the honey-haired lady sits nearby and decides it's time to take out the book she's been reading so as to not let her own fierce attention interrupt all that peaceful breathing.

"And now, very slowly, I want you to comfortably let yourself float down, very slowly, until you meet your body here on the bed, nestled in the security of gravity's pull, holding your husband's hand and mine, a very smooth and gentle landing. And when you're ready, you can open your eyes. Just take as long as you need, because we'll still be here."

"Thank you," Jane says softly when she finally opens her eyes, returning to them here in this daylit hospital room. Now they can hear the thread of nurses' voices unspooling down the hallway, the barely audible thrum of traffic carpeting the Cross Bronx Expressway, all suddenly returning as if back from a trip. They can hear the sharp crack of a page turning from the direction of the large pink chair.

"You can do this with her as often as you like when she's starting to feel panicky. She was always very responsive to meditation in the workshop. I think it will help."

"How are you, babe?" Ed asks.

Her eyes light up in recollection of where she's been, what she's seen.

"It was beautiful. I was really in Heaven! And I can't believe—*Steve* was there! I saw Steve!"

Ed looks surprised, maybe disappointed.

"Oh yeah? And what about Dave? Did you see Dave there, too?"

"Naaah," she replies with a smirk. "If I did, he would've probably tried to cop some pills. But I was so glad to see Steve!"

She seems more with Steve at present than Ed, happy, inflated perhaps by the infusion of breath Ed and her priestess have lent her, buoyed equally by her visit to Heaven and, no doubt, by morphine derivatives. She spends time with Steve where *he* lives now, not having to be in a hospital room for the moment. Ed is lonely, exiled to the company of earthlings he's not married to.

There are three faces to Jane.

At night, when she is alone or with hospital aides, her eyes are watchful, taking measure of all inside and out, a controlled fear measuring the lift of the ocean inside her as it rises above her chest AND keeping guard against the wickedness of the honey-voiced and sly-faced Portia who sits outside her door gossiping with colleagues when not checking in on Jane. Each breath becomes more precious and she concentrates on keeping it easy, keeping it easy, keeping that delicate flow, as if, if she doesn't breathe consciously, she won't breathe at all.

Then there is the way she looks when morning comes and visitors trickle in. Her face widens slightly in imitation of pleasure: a mask, overlaying the fear, with which to greet and soothe those that love her and express her gratitude, until it takes too much of her energy and she asks them to leave so she can recharge with a little dose of oblivion.

And then there is the imploring look she has for her husband that says "Where have you been?" or "Why won't you rescue me?" or "Don't you love me anymore?" or sometimes it just says "I'm dying, Ed! I can't do this without you! Don't make me go alone!"

"They want to remove my wedding ring!" she says to him one day. "My fingers are getting fatter—see?—and the ring, it's starting to hurt, but I don't want them to remove it, Ed. It's my wedding ring! You've got to think of something!"

But he can't.

"It's just a ring, honey. We don't want it to cut into you. It should be a bond, not a torture. You can take it off and I'll hold onto it for you."

"You'll just give it to Jeannie!" she cries, to Ed's apparent despair. "I don't want to ever give it up!"

"Don't be ridiculous," he pleads.

But ridiculous loses its meaning when the world has become a stranger and life is about plastic-tubed lifelines and a small room far from home where Jesus' crucifixion serves as wall decoration and no one lives with you but there are endless visitations and your agnostic husband and sister-in-law lead you in sweet, increasingly-less-clumsy guided meditations.

"You feel your body rising. . . ."

"You are as light as air. . . ."

"There are clouds all around you. . . ."

And at these times her face approximates a sleepy ecstasy as she practices a death mask.

A week of effortful breathing and the slowly tightening torque of pain combines with the rising tide of meds to leave our patient cast on the battered shore of her bed, weakened and more fragile.

This day, her husband arrives early accompanied by an elegant woman dressed more formally than most of Jane's visitors, morning make-up still fresh, clothes still pressed. As Ray gets up to cede the room to the two of them, the woman goes over to the side of Jane's bed to bend over.

"Oh, Suzanne! I'm so glad you've come," Jane says in a voice shorn of its usual clarion ring.

"Hi, Jane. I'm glad to be able to help, and to get a chance to see you," this Suzanne says in a soft, even voice. "How are you coping today?"

"I'm on extra pain medication today. I had a lot of trouble last night," Jane says groggily. "I want to go home. Maybe you can help me get home now. Ed might listen to you."

"Well, Jane, I'm going to arbitrate as you both talk it out. But first I want you to have this." From her purse she pulls out a long delicate chain that slinks down to its full length hanging from her fingers. "It's for your wedding ring. I know you don't want to lose it, and this way you can wear it around your neck and not cause circulation problems for your fingers."

Jane is overjoyed while Ed, bright-eyed, looks on with secret jealousy at simple ingenuity in action.

Suzanne stands between the two of them, Ed having positioned himself at the foot of the bed, lending Suzanne primacy of place next to Jane and unconsciously re-creating the bed as a playing field upon which the opponents will contend. There is shadow over them this morning, little light has pushed its way through the windows at the far end of the room, only a pale brush of opalescence, a soft illumination as if from a dappled stream that runs above them. Today Jane has a gentle monotone, a breathy short run of words to make her case, and then she rests. Her case is simple and clean, no need to mobilize much energy to make it, which today is a good thing. Then Ed's voice falls like stones into a pond, first the earnest pitch and then the sullen plunge, a longer case being made insofar as it's a justification. Jane looks sadly across the bed as if bruised by each stone as it falls.

Suzanne takes a moment before turning Jane's way. She says that before she came she was prepared to persuade Ed to make a second attempt to bring Jane home and find ways to make it work, but now that she sees her, she's afraid they might be too far down the road for that. The move might be too much for Jane's system to handle.

"You look more fragile than you sounded on the phone last week," she says. "To be truthful, Jane, I suspect the case is moot. That's what I'm thinking."

Jane looks resigned and weary, and Suzanne reaches out to hold her hand.

"I'm sorry," she says.

"It's hard," Jane says. "This is the hardest thing I've ever had to do."

"I know," Suzanne says.

"When I first moved into this room, I used to resent having to look at that crucifix on the wall. I hate the Church and all its patriarchy and I didn't want it around me. But lately, I haven't minded it, it kind of comforts me sometimes. Do you think God will help me, Suzanne? It's so hard sometimes, I don't know if I can do this."

"Yes, I think He will," Suzanne says, her face folded in shadows by her hair as she bends slightly over Jane.

Ed stands away, mortified and unconvinced. It was always he who helped Jane up until now. He feels despondent at the thought that the only help Jane could get would have to come from a crucifix on a wall. He threatens Jesus in his thoughts, "You better ante up!"

Suzanne leaves to return to her practice, telling Jane to phone her if she wants to talk. Ed moves over to where Suzanne had stood to grab Jane's hand and reconnect after a week of intermittent discord.

"I love you, Jane," he says. "I'm so glad Suzanne brought you a chain for your ring. Let me get a nurse to help you remove it from your finger, OK?"

Jane's gaze swivels up to meet Ed's visage towering way up high.

"Thank you, honey," she says, and as he walks away, her face still angled toward where the ceiling meets the opposite wall, she seems to notice something. She seems to notice us.

Her eyes focus and, for a moment, she freezes in recognition. What are you doing here? Are you here for me? Are you an angel? I've never noticed you before! Your wings! . . . I never would've guessed. So beautiful! So *fierce!* Is that so you can zoom right down to save me? You're almost scary, empty, like no one's there. You're an angel, not a person, so maybe there *is* no one there. Is that why you're so perfect? Is that why your beauty makes me shiver?

And when she answers in the negative, her gaze has already unlocked from us up here to find us in that sanctum where we are as she always hoped we'd be. Doting. A maternal kiss of breath. A cream puff for the soul. Her newly born child, this time without flaws, old enough now to lift her in his arms, smother her in sweet baby kisses, pay her back in spades for all that love.

She has been in this room two weeks. At the door stands a tall, haggard young man. He doesn't fit his clothes, he doesn't fit this room. He is a walking misfit. His dark hair is long and combed flat down the sides of his head, his hair at uneven lengths. He is halfway in this material world and half evaporating, disappearing in his cavernous clothing, his pants tied with a cloth strap. He looks the way Jesus did when he returned from the desert, wasted from a forty-day contest with the Devil, Jesus with Scotch tape wrapped tightly around the frames of his glasses. Ed stands behind him, his hand on Jesus' shoulder.

"Go ahead," he says.

Jane is a large, white, pasty doll under the covers with many plastic spider webs attaching her to machinery. Her face is impaled by tubes reaching up her nostrils. Jesus looks uneasy seeing her like this. He stands awkwardly, halfway between the large pink chair and her bed, as if he wonders what the protocol is.

"Take off your jacket," Ed says, and he removes it from Jesus' shoulders.

Jane's eyes have followed the two men in and she smiles with her eyes, her mouth still pursed for weeping.

"Hi, Mom," says Jesus. He looks down at the floor, not at his mother, wishing for invisibility in a six-foot-two-inch frame. He doesn't ever achieve it.

"Hi, honey," she says. "I'm so glad to see you."

"Luke has to be back by four o'clock," Ed says. He puts his arm around Luke's shoulder, gathering him up and placing him at the bedside. Jane lifts her hand and her son grabs it, holds it warmly. He is her boy again.

"How are you, Mom?"

Jane continues to smile passively, stuck in the moment, dumfounded by the reality. He is here, thirty years here, present in the flesh and owner of a future she can't begin to fathom. She doesn't dare to. She's been fed just enough Ativan to get her through this moment.

"I sleep a lot," was all she could think to say. "Look at you! You're my boy!" she says, squeezing his hand.

"I'm not a boy now, Mom," he says sadly, his eyes praying, praying that he still was.

Ed walks over and puts his arm around Luke's shoulders. He speaks softly, as if confiding, but he is including his wife in the conversation.

"She may sleep a lot of the day, but you'll be helping her even just with your presence."

Luke nods his head.

"And I thought it would be good for you to get to see her one last time."

"Of course," Luke says, his facial features seeming to imitate a sense of gravitas.

"And if you feel the need to talk to someone, if you're over-whelmed or something about all this, they have a social worker here for that purpose. Someone who people can talk to about their problems."

"I *know* what a social worker is," Luke says, never budging from his morose stance.

"So let me bring the chair over next to the bed for you and you can hold her hand and talk to her if you want."

Luke accepts the offer and is easily shoveled into the chair and, wraithlike as he is, he bends forward—still holding his mother's hand—to make his presence known as his mother slips in and out of focus.

Throughout the day, visitors trickle in and out, old friends, new friends, the nurses circumambulating about. It is a steady, lazy flow. A few hours later, when Ed returns from a short food break, he walks in on the tall woman on one side of Jane's bed and Luke standing on the other, both holding Jane's clenched hands. The sister-in-law is firmly and clearly orchestrating a levitation of our Lady's spirit into the heavens, *let yourself go*, *let yourself go*, not taking no for an answer.

"Look into the light, Mom," Luke says earnestly, repeating the mantra new to him. "Look into the light!"

Deep in night's recesses, when the harsh hall lights carve narrow crevices near the doorway, angels and husbands and gods and sons seem very far away. Jane is hanging off the edge of the world with only a sly-faced nurse's aide to half-heartedly hold her to this planet. The pain in her gut takes full advantage of her isolation to tear her with its butcher's blades and no one seems to notice.

"Look at you! Why are you crying, darlin'?" asks the aide seductively when she finally arrives at her bedside. She stands in shadow, her face obscured, only her voice fully present in its cutting sheen. "What do you need? Something for pain?"

Jane lets the tears drench her cheeks as she nods her head.

"Where does everybody go?" she pleads, her whisper choked by delicate sobs.

The aide starts to leave the room to call in the nurse. "What do you mean, where does everybody go? You know I'm right here, darlin', right outside this door."

"No! You're not!" Jane shakes her head, her eyes shut closed in protest. "You're lying!" she exhales to the now emptied room.

Once morning comes, it brings in morning staff, showered, clean, fresh-eyed day folk, richer in warmth if more sparing in personality than the ward's night creatures. Visitors and phoners are concerned by Jane's complaints and Ed and Marcie discuss having people stay overnight with Jane, Ed deciding to hire a private aide as well. There must be no shortage of friendly faces responsive to Jane's needs during these, her final weeks on Earth.

That afternoon, Ed speaks to the head day nurse about the change and why, and her granite blonde Bronxness alternates with a respect for tall—possibly Italian—husbands as she argues with Jane's assessment of the night staff, and then concedes to his inconvenient persistence with the proviso that anyone he hires must be on their short list of acceptable helpers, people familiar with the ward's routines. When that night comes, Ed will stay over, and the following night, when Marcie is scheduled to stay, Ed will greet the new hire with a signed check. On that same appointed night, Marcie will bring in a wide-ruled notebook and draw up a schedule for the coming nights, different names falling into place over time, and a journal will be started, to inform each caretaker of what occurred on the previous watch. And Jane, she sleeps better this afternoon, knowing she will have company in the dark woods of night.

Over time, though, those dark woods make greater claims to the landscape of Jane's day. In the middle of the night she wakens to fears that she is dying; in the daytime she realizes her bad dream is an oppressively solid reality, and we watch Jane squirm under its weight. She keeps disengaging her oxygen tubing and re-inserting it, testing which position is better, how to better place it so that it will direct its cool flow where she can partake of it fully, but no, there's never enough. She starts to pull off her hospital gown as if even that feeble cotton wrapping is sitting heavily on her, only to have Ray or Marcie or whatever nurse's aide notices gently admonish her and tenderly retie the gown's strings around her neck.

"No, no," she tells Marcie late one morning, "No, I have to get out of here. Can you get my clothes for me?"

"Well, Jane—"

"*Please!* They're in that closet behind you. We have to figure out how to get out of this place. *You will help me, won't you?*"

And Marcie stands humbly by, hands clasped in front of her in shame, unable to help, only able to disappoint her friend in the most nurturing of tones she can muster.

"Do you want to go for a walk? We can stroll down the hall-way in that lazyboy if you like," referring to a large leather chair on wheels that sits in the room's corner.

And that's how Jane attempts her escape, slowly rolling

around the hallway, her slow penetration of the air around her suggesting breeze, suggesting breath, until eventually these suggestions begin to dissipate under the concreteness of her overwhelmed body. She feels like a ton, she and this heavy chair, slowly, slowly inching across the hospital floor, and now the slowness is exhausting her and it all ends with a simple, "I'm tired."

Marcie wheels her back and then monitors her as she clambers onto the hospital bed like a rock climber hoisting herself over a ledge. She wearily shifts herself around until she's seated high enough on the bed and then sinks into the mattress as Marcie plugs her wires back in the wall sockets.

Jane is staring ahead of her as if absorbed by the momentary flutter of my wings that accompanies any fidget.

"Marcie—" Jane says.

"Yes, hon."

"Am I going to die in two days?!" she asks as if she's just heard a rumor to that effect. She sounds equally concerned and hopeful.

Fat chance.

"I don't know, honey," Marcie says, feeling hopelessly ineffectual.

"Are you bored?"

It's Jane, but she isn't talking to me. She's feeling sorry for her guest who has been sitting with her for the last few hours, watching her roll in and out of sleep, an older, thin friend with infinite patience, someone who has found the key (or proper medication) for walking through the world without jostling it.

"No, I'm not bored. Sometimes I read the paper when you sleep. I also like to watch you and I imagine I'm sketching your facial features."

"I look old," Jane says. She looks fairly bald, very overweight, pasty as white clay as well. She still has enough vanity to feel rueful about where disease has taken her physical features, even if she's abandoned any attempt to disguise it.

"Did you know you have beautiful ears?"

"I do?" Jane giggles. She would blush if she had the blood to spare.

"They're small and close to your head. You always had a beautiful head, and hair to envy."

"Oh, Ellen." Our Jane wets around the eyelids, her face makes an aborted attempt to crumble, but it's as if it's unable to counter its puffiness. Then she is instantly wiped clean of sorrow and asks Ellen, like a wondrous child, when does she think she will die.

"I want my love to go on!" she says wistfully to Ellen, and then she turns to us to make sure, whoever we are up here, that we've heard.

"April," Ellen answers Jane's original question. Does Jane remember that it's mid-April now? As for Ellen, she does not concern herself with polite conventions. A question deserves an answer.

Jane lets her head rest to the side.

"April in Paris . . . she sings softly, "da da da da dah . . ."

The song evaporates into nothingness. This is as close to Paris as Jane gets.

"*The way you* . . ." she starts up again, as if she's grasping at clouds of song floating by, but this one seems like it will get away.

"*The way you* . . ." she continues, not letting the forgotten words interrupt the flow of the melody. She tries once again.

"*The way you* . . ." and now the blanks *are* the words and her head sways as if they're being sung. "*Oh no, you can't take that away from me.*"

And then she seems to realize that perhaps they *can*—in fact, we will—and she discards the song like a bad luck penny.

"*Que será, será* . . ." is her melodic reply. She reaches prettily, yet wanly, for the note. It seems all the songs are leading her in the wrong direction: the melodies may thrive on breath, but the lyrics keep reminding her of what is lost, what is over, they reek of finality, and she suddenly abandons her impromptu concert, shaking the endeavor off. And then Jane surprises her friend by saying, as if to someone outside the room, "I'm not going to sing in the basement!" And then, very simply, almost as a matter-of-fact explanation to a child, adds in singsong, "And *ev*-ery-*one* is *dead*." She lets herself sink back into the pillows, stepping away from the limelight. She shakes her head wearily when she turns to Ellen and says, "You need a lot of patience."

Later, the nurse's aide comes by to wash Jane. She will bide no nonsense and gently insists that Jane go with her to the bathroom. Jane rallies the will to sidle to the edge of the bed, slowly lowers herself and trudges obediently, if uncertainly, after her.

Gravity is taking more and more of a toll, it pulls Jane down like a lazy, grasping lover who she must fight to resist and this demanded concentration makes her stupid, like she must re-negotiate the mechanics of human activities. She holds onto the bed railing when dismounting and tries to balance her weight before moving, as if she's a large vessel filled to overflowing, careful not to spill. She must keep the awkward hospital gown and plastic tubing untangled so that no movement can be spontaneous and each one resembles a formal ritual: close the flap, uncatch the tube, move it to the right side, no, the left, as it falls from the port inserted below her throat. She must be watched vigilantly to guard against her tipping, even in the bathroom. She is stripped of her privacy, if not of the isolation that comes of going where everyone goes it alone. Her body is merely a wall between her and the living, less and less who she is, merely a way others can see her, this body that sullenly greets the world, from her face to her barely-veiled buttocks. That is how she is recognized—through her flesh—but it's all just a heavy garment for winter to her, a strange, cumbersome object.

Today, her body is too awesome, she cannot grasp the whole of it, she can't bend easily enough to meet it, and after she steers it widely to the commode, she, for the first time, gives up trying to manage the details. She is approaching helplessness and it's inevitable tidal pull to where she must depend on others for the most basic of needs. She manages to rise from the seat and make it to the opposite wall, her gown hanging from her like a scarf, leaving her bare and large to the world. She calls to Ed in the tiniest of voices.

"Egg, can you help me?"

She is staring at the tile wall at hand, as if it's a window that she can look out of.

"Can you wipe me? I need help."

She is asking for the ultimate love request. But her husband fails her. He stands there, wide-eyed, broken, aghast and ashamed. For a moment, his wife loses her humanness and appears to him like livestock and he is sickened.

"I—" he stammers.

"I can't reach," she says in that same distant voice. "It's alright. Just wipe me. OK? I need to go back to bed."

"I'll be right back," he says, and leaves her there, leaning against the tile wall as he runs to the nurse's station for help.

When he goes back to her room, he stays away from the bathroom, letting the attendant tend to Jane's needs. When Jane carefully treads into sight, she is merely focusing, in her vacant way, on navigation, not apparently cognizant of having been let down in any way. She merely needed her ass wiped, and it was, and now she needs to be in bed, and both needs are of a kind. Elemental. Her husband, however, seems humbled. He spends the rest of the day vaguely trying to look invisible, no matter how hands-on he remains for the rest of the day. He has seen human helplessness writ large—in adult size—and it seems to appall him. That's the difference between him and us: we are not compelled to look away. We see human wretchedness whole. It does nothing to diminish our own alabaster beauty.

* * *

The bathroom journey has gotten laborious for Jane. Tonight, the hired attendant, leading her back to the bed, plays lifeguard, her arm around Jane's waist as Jane strains for breath, each step demanding more lung power than she can muster. Daisy tries to discreetly push her patient from behind as she struggles to crawl onto the bed, and when she finally succeeds at flopping herself down, wracked from her struggle with the rising sea in her lungs, she is holding on to the tortured white sheet for life.

Marcie has run around to the other side of the bed from Daisy, the new aide, and gently strokes her friend's soft, stubby head.

"Is this it?" Jane asks, eyes as wide as overcoat buttons. She is no longer panting for breath, but mentally she's still experiencing the sky pressing down on her from horizon to horizon, zipperless, no escape. It's as if she's in shock.

"I need help. I need some help. Dear," she addresses Daisy— she can't remember her name, "can you get the nurses' attention? I need something. I need something to put me out of my misery!"

"OK," Daisy says calmly. She doesn't hurry. She walks out the door like it's a job she's totally familiar with, done many, many times. She knows the routine and she does it.

Marcie tries to preoccupy Jane until the nurse arrives and who, just like that, administers with a blessed little sting a sip of mother's love into her fleshy arm. Jane looks calmer just to see the hypodermic arrive in the room and soon she allows herself to drink of the cool stream of tubed oxygen for sustenance.

"You know," she says to Marcie, "it would be nice to sit on the sofa. Do you think you could help me?"

"What sofa? There's the lazyboy. . . . Are you sure you want to move now after all you've just been through?"

"I could just sit on the sofa. I wouldn't have to do a lot. The sofa in the living room. I could look at the begonia and you could water it for me."

She seems to have forgotten her request to be moved there. Perhaps she *is* there.

"Where's Ed?" she asks. She tries to recall what could possibly have happened to him. "He should be home soon, I guess. He'll bring me potatoes. I'd like some potatoes."

Marcie tries to take part in this alternative-world conversation.

"He'll bring what?"

"Some nice red potatoes. And then I'll wash them under cold water. You like potatoes? My mother makes potato pie. It's made with potato and eggs. It's so good. She makes it for all the holidays. Everyone likes my mother." Jane stops mid-thought to confide, "She's dying, you know. The Big C. It's too bad. Everyone will miss her. I'm tired now."

Marcie watches the waves of sleep wash gently over Jane until the tide has pulled her out once again. When she wakens many hours later, as early light peeks discreetly through the blinds, only Daisy is still around. After Daisy has attended to her needs, once with a bedpan and once with a request for pain medication, Jane again asks for Ed.

"He'll be in later, Mrs. Cantore."

"I haven't seen him in three whole days! He doesn't love me anymore!"

"Oh no. He was here just yesterday. You've just forgotten."

"He was? That doesn't seem right. I want him to remember something. I have to tell him all the time and he can't forget, but he does. Can you remind him?"

"What, dear?"

"I want to be cremated. I've told him three times. I don't think he pays attention. Maybe you could bring it up when you see him sometime."

"You know what? I'll write it in this blue notebook over here that he's left for messages. I'm sure he'll see it."

"That's a good idea," Jane says.

The orderlies are rolling breakfast wagons through the halls and a young Hispanic attendant brings Jane a plastic cup of orange juice to roll around in her mouth.

"Can you do me a favor?" Jane asks, cup held gingerly in both hands, pinkies splayed as if to keep her afloat. "I don't know where my brother Ray is. He's usually here every morning. I hope nothing's wrong! Could you dial him for me? Please?"

She has forgotten that her brother told her he had a doctor's appointment.

"Well . . ." says the attendant, uncertainly.

"Just ask him when he's coming."

"Do you know his number?"

Jane sits up straight, raiding her brain for information.

"I know there's a blue notebook somewhere. Maybe it's in there."

The attendant carries the book over to Jane.

"There are some numbers here," she tells Jane, "but only one *man's* name. Is your brother named Ed?"

"No. Ray! Ray! Look up Ray."

"Sorry, ma'am. Only Ed."

Jane is getting flustered, her eyes dart in tiny fidgets back and forth, piercing through the chaos of ensuing panic.

"Call them all! Someone will know! He's been here every day! I can't lose him *again*!"

The aide leaves a message on one person's machine. That person will be able to hear Jane in the background shouting "Oh my God! Where's Ray! Where's everybody?" sounding like bedlam before the nurses manage to give her a shot of Ativan.

Jane sheds more and more of her past and increasingly is limited to the all-encompassing present. She responds to her physical urges with an immediacy that takes no heed of experience. Once again she insists that she needs to go to the bathroom and rejecting the offer of a commode, asks hubby for his help. A very young nurse's aide, new to Jane, has been sitting with the two of them; she speaks sweetly and calmly like a young novitiate, and Jane and her Ed have warmed to her. Now the aide and Ed meticulously detach and motorize all the relevant machinery until Jane is ready to disembark on her long journey across the room.

Jane and the young sister disappear into the vast echoing bathroom and Ed stands vacantly beside the door until the two women finally shuffle into view again. With each of her escorts holding one of her arms, Jane prepares to mount the bed, much like a gymnast would, by grabbing the partially lowered metal railing and hoisting herself up. She starts to rise onto her knee, but she misjudges the effort needed and loses her balance, slowly sailing back into the large space between her escorts. Ed and the aide spring forward to grab her by her shoulders, but Jane is massive now, her body striving to become one with the universe, and unable to keep her aloft, they can only cut her fall by sinking along with her to the floor.

There is a shout, there is panic and surprise, everyone is frightened but no one hurt, except Jane's pride as she sits, captured by gravity, magnetized to the floor, way too heavy for Ed or the sister to pull her up without seemingly pulling her apart.

"Oh no, oh no." Jane's hands try to guard her from calamity, shaking and stirring the air before her as if this was baby's first fall.

"I'll get help," says the sister and she scurries to her feet and out the door.

"Oh no," Jane whimpers, "how come everybody else gets to get skinny with cancer and I just get fatter and fatter? It's not fair!"

Ed, dumbfounded and shaken, can only put his arm around her. Everything happened so quickly. You could lose someone entirely this way, they could simply slip from your grasp in one careless second, and you'd be standing there, the caretaker, with your charge whisked from your arms all at once.

Suddenly chaos strikes. Sister and other nurses run into the room, followed by Joan, the day nurse, her black rectangular glasses and stridently blonde hair at one with her harsh shouting as she berates the young nurse's aide for allowing this to happen. Is this drama necessary or all for Ed's show? He isn't sure, but he hugs Jane more tightly as it dawns on her that this might be an emergency in addition to a humiliation.

Ed and the sister try to explain the suddenness of the fall, but Joan insists on pummeling the aide harshly while apologizing to "Mr. Cantore" for Sister's ineptness, all the while making a spectacle of her attempts to fix the situation.

"Now, carefully!" she admonishes another aide who tries, with Joan, to grab Jane from fore and aft, but without success. "Get Robert and Dixon in here immediately!" she shouts as Jane covers her face in her hands, not wanting to even be *seen* by this Robert and this Dixon. Shortly, two muscular orderlies in green uniform marshal their way over to Jane, and with Joan's military instruction, manage to heave Jane up off the floor like so much freight. She stands leaning on the edge of the bed with both hands, trying to get her bearings before sundry aides and hubby all support her, hands to her back, as she crawls up in time to Joan's brisk commands. The fuss continues as nurses grab sheets and wires and disentangle all while Jane tries to maneuver into a comfortable position.

"There you go!" the day nurse's voice slaps the air perfunctorily, mission accomplished, before she switches modes to comfort "Mr. Cantore." "She'll be OK now, but I'll speak to Dr. Shepherd about giving your wife a catheter so that she'll no longer need to make these treacherous journeys to the toilet." And then, in a louder talking-to-stupid voice, says to Jane: "Calm down, Mrs. Cantore. Everything is fine. No, the oxygen tubing goes around your ears, like this," and she reaches out to Jane, an officious mother tying a bonnet tightly to baby.

When the scene quiets down and the crowd has dispersed and Jane, Ed and the attendant are alone in the room, Jane tells Ed she wants to go home.

"I don't like that woman. Except for the morning shift, like you, Jasmine," she says to the young aide, "the staff is horrible."

"You like that Sylvia and Bethany, remember?" Ed says pathetically, desperate to throw a positive light on the situation.

"I want to go home," she repeats.

"This is really a nice place," says Jasmine meekly to Ed. "It's just this ward. I hate to work in it. It's the only one. I'm only here this morning because they were short and I needed some overtime. The other wards are wonderful, very respectful and quiet."

"Why is that?" Ed asks, shocked to hear it from staff.

"I don't know. Politics. The head nurse picks all the people on the ward, and here they all look out for each other rather than the patient. It's too bad, because it's really a great place. Most patients and families love it here."

Jane is almost nodding off when Dr. Shepherd appears, not an apparition, but a placeholder from the everyday world, a sober, reasonable universe that runs as expected. She takes Jane's hand and grasps it.

"I heard you had an accident."

"I lost my balance," Jane says breathlessly.

"I've given orders for them to place a catheter in you so that you don't have to leave the bed. And there's a bedpan you can use. But we don't want you to fall, OK? You shouldn't have to worry about that."

Jane looks forlorn.

"I want to go back to Einstein. The nurses love me there."

"They love you here as well."

"No, they don't! They're not nice at all."

"I'm sorry you feel that way. I'll talk to them about it, but you know what? I'm thinking perhaps your morphine level is too high and it's making you confused. I'm going to lower it a little and see if that helps in any way. OK?"

"I don't know," is Jane's response. "I want to go home."

Sometimes we all want to go home. Isn't that strange? Even up here in the ether, we sometimes get overtaken by a need for gravity, for dirt, for the undertow of sweet corporeal sadness, for the weight of the elements' abuse, all the trappings of home. We want to reverse the direction we are all going or all have gone, further and further from our humanness. We hunger for the immediacy of finiteness, of mortality. Even if almost every moment on Earth was an abomination—the greatest physical suffering—holocausts of cruelty and deprivation—we can still get at least one moment's pang of nostalgia—those telltale signs of addiction—for that apricot nectar, that mother's smile, those baby's fingers, sunlight on dappled water, that ecstasy arising from skin, enough so that a little voice whispers urgently, "I want to live!"

Jane, even with a catheter, still wants to walk across the room to the bathroom. All her visitors try to restrain her from pulling out her wires, from attempting to dismount from on high, to spare her the dangers of falling. But she still has the urge to walk, to use her feet, to go somewhere, anywhere, instead of allowing herself to flow towards the inevitability of nowhere.

That night she grabs her husband's belt and tries to undo it.

"Let's make love!" she says giggling, her face flush with joy.

"What?!" Her husband is surprised by her boldness.

"Egg Yolk! Don't you want to have fun?" She unstraps his belt and starts to undo his fly. Ed's hands jump up to fend off his wife's attack, but now he slowly lowers them in bemused acquiescence. They are alone in her room, the door is closed. And as Jane pulls at his open pants, the door flies open as a nurse strides in to check on Jane's medications.

"Oh, don't mind me!" she laughs. Jane laughs, too, as Ed hustles to re-dress, his face a flower of redness.

"Can we go home now?" asks Jane, flush with her newfound discovery of pleasure. "I'm feeling so much better. Can we?"

Her face is all lit up in anticipation of his answer.

This isn't the body she wants anymore. This one is useless. There's no more room in it for her. A woman's body is often visited by others, but then they leave at one point or another. But this guest is squeezing out the hostess, making a shambles of her domicile. This body will no longer serve.

"Sweetie,"—she forgets her niece's name—"can you get Charles for me? Where's Charles?" Her voice is mottled with sleep, a sound from the subterranean part of her consciousness. "Charles can help. He'll help."

Her niece, a woman in her thirties, with black mermaid hair always floating a half second behind her, hovers over Jane in the night. Daisy, the hired aide, is dozing on the big pink chair in the corner.

"Who's Charles, Aunt Jane?" She strokes the side of Jane's head.

"He knows all about these things," Jane rambles on. "He's not afraid. I need him now. He's on that phone. If you pick it up, he'll be there. You'll see.

"Oh—!" She grabs her niece's hand. "Oh! My mother could help me! Why didn't I think of that? Ed will be so happy! He's never met her, you know. You're not my mother, are you? You could be related."

"I *am* related, Aunt Jane. It's me, Chryssie."

"Oh yes. I remember now. You're Ray's baby. I guess it's my turn to be his mother? When is Ray coming? Did he find Charles?"

Chryssie listens through the night to all the names Jane can invoke between shots of Ativan administered to calm her. Names of people Chryssie never met, names she can't decipher, a desperate, pious incantation of names. Every hour, then every half hour, there are injections for pain or anxiety, injections of fleeting value, apparently gifts from only minor saints. And when she runs out of saints, all there is left is escape, and Chryssie finds herself talking Jane down from her labored attempts to scale the bed's side railings.

"I think they'd better call a doctor," Chryssie confides to Daisy when Daisy's eventually joined her by her side.

"Oh, these nurses know what they're doing," Daisy says matter-of-factly. "This is the struggle. I've seen it many times."

Chryssie seethes at Daisy's nonchalance.

"Perhaps she wouldn't *have* to struggle if they increased back her medication," she whispers urgently.

When Jane starts pulling out her oxygen tubes, Chryssie decides that's her cue, and she asks Daisy to watch Jane as she goes out in the hall to beg the nurses to reach the doctor on A.M. call. In the stillness of the hospital night, I can hear her arguing in the distance, her more emphatic words tolling like the little heaving of a sob down the empty hallway.

She is fighting for her life as if, if not now, never. She reaches up from the bottom of her well, moans with the effort and tugs out the oxygen tubes as if they're blocking her breathing instead of aiding it. She tosses the tubes aside and grunts as she grabs a side railing with which to pull herself to the bed's edge, the boundaries of her world. Chryssie runs to catch the plastic tubing and return them to her aunt as Jane now tugs at the strips of the hospital gown. That, too, must go. All must go, must get out of her, off of her, there must be no obstacle between her and wherever home is.

The nurses call the chaplain. Maybe he can help. Chryssie is exhausted. It's her dying aunt who's seemingly inexhaustible.

As all of the women intermittently fuss about her, cooing, injecting, re-tying and admonishing, a young man in a sports jacket and white clerical collar quietly parts the waters, and the women slide away as if they are the tides rushing out. He's a thin man with slightly hunched shoulders, shoulders that are used to bearing a lot each night. But it's a job he likes—rock star of grace: sometimes in the quiet of the night, in-between bouts of reading soft-covered books or of quiet meditation or an occasional snooze, he sings his song and the applause he gets is in the form of glazed-over eyes and surrender. To him it's a peck on the cheek, one of the hundreds by which he nourishes himself.

He sits with Jane; he knows Jesus is watching over her and so he needn't hover in worry, and that calms her down. She is happy to see a priest, even if she is uncertain that he is anything other than some other mother's son. That is enough. He's a nice man, he's not asking anything of her—not asking her to die easily, for example. If she needs to struggle, that's just fine with him. He talks like the ocean, he is the promise that the escape of breath can be like floating, not the drowning that she fears. She lies back, letting the chaplain merge in her mind with Luke urging her to go into the light, good boys both. She loves them and remembers to love everyone else, too, and then she sleeps.

She sleeps for two whole hours and then she jolts herself awake, clutches at her hospital gown and tries to rip it off as if to make room for breath. She stares up at me in horror. "Murderer!" she screams in silence. Her chest rises to meet me, but never enough. She tries again and again until she falls back to bed, swaddling herself in moans.

There'll be no carpet of sunlight unrolled today; the world is under an expansive awning and, starting as always with Ray, a collection of glistening, collapsed umbrellas accumulates over and around the chairs and the window. A steady hush, courtesy of the interface of rain and outside traffic, seals the room tightly. Jane is in deep sleep, but not a peaceful one. She groans steadily through the day, working arduously somewhere where neither Ray, nor later Ed, nor Jill nor the others who trickle in and out of the room can witness. The visitors hobnob quietly or read newspapers when on their own. They might as well be under a tent, sequestering their energy, keeping secrets from prying angels as they tread softly, huddling and unhuddling throughout the day. Eventually Jane's groans are loud enough for Ed to call a nurse. Can anything be done to ease his darling's struggle? Jane wakes up to receive an injection of Ativan.

"Are you in a lot of pain?" Ed asks solicitously.

"No," she says, spacily. Her eyes timidly scan back and forth as if trying to recall what she has lost.

"Am I supposed to stay in bed or should I get up?" she asks.

Apparently that question is not quite resolved for her. Late that night, after Sandi has arrived to watch over her and has put away her travel gear, Jane, wild-eyed, again plots great escapes, keeping Sandi on her toes. She struggles incoherently, mumbling explanations that have a logic beyond Sandi's grasp, as she tries to leave the confines of her bed. At one point she convinces Sandi that she needs to get up to use the commode, and Sandi, not knowing the latest protocol, finds herself re-living Ed's experience as Jane is unable to get back on the bed.

"I need help!" Jane pleads. "I need help! Someone, please! How am I going to do this?" Flustered, pale, humiliated yet again. She wants to be back in bed before anyone can see her, helplessly weak and fat, her bulk exposed for all to see and roll their eyes over. Where is the dignity in dying that everyone else manages to earn? She is the bald-headed clown of a three-ring-circus drawing painful belly laughs from multitudes in some hospital skit, and when the male aids arrive to hoist her once again, in trying to balance her fear of drowning in the roiling sea inside her with her dread of unfamiliar men shoving at her haunches, she cries out, over and over again, building steadily to a state of panic.

"Ma'am, you've got to calm down! Now!" one of the male aides shouts. She is petrified and, quiet now, she starts to tremble, where once, perhaps, her pre-afflicted self might have raged in holy terror.

"You shouldn't talk to her that way!" Sandi's thin high voice attempts to reach his volume. "You're scaring her!"

Jane trembles, ensconced in her throne of mussed bed linen, hyperventilating until, as she accepts a morphine/Ativan injection, she whimpers that she needs to go home.

"I'm here, honey," says Sandi, putting her arm around Jane's shaking shoulders. "I'll look out for you."

"The nurses at night . . ." Jane says breathlessly, ". . . I don't know where they come from. Where do they *come* from? The night nurses? . . ."

They come from night's darkness, from stark shadows and

abrasive hall lights, from distant, unknown, wearying big city lives, pulled from the population of hard-knock skeptics. They've seen it all, they've watched you and yours die a thousand deaths, they've cleaned the piss and shit of people all their lives, they love you from behind hardened faces and jaundiced eyes, but they do love you. Just not as much as the soft-lit day ones who've shared their beds the night before with sound, sleeping husbands to warm them.

Anyway, it's not the nurses who scare her. It's that world underwater which is trying to drag her down, whose tentacles she tries to evade with each breath until they come so close to her, so close that she can feel their shadow like short hairs brushing against the back of her neck. And she wakens with a start to this sterile hospital room where West Indian patois drifts through the doorway and the lights have been smothered out and the whole hospital underwater and the nurses have shark eyes and Ed has left her to fend on her own. The feet of winged trespassers who skulk around the edges of the night dangle from the ceiling and she needs help now, now before they strike, and she cries out and the sharks put in their heads and the feet continue to dangle, unperturbed, and she cries as loud as she can until Sandi's there beside her, Sandi who doesn't see that she, too, is floating underwater, the fool, thinking she's in New York somewhere, and how can she explain, until finally she can hear Sandi's voice, "I'm here, Jane. I'm right here."

"Am I dying?" Jane asks, her eyes focused on our hanging male feet.

"I don't know, honey," says Sandi, hovering over her charge, her back to us.

Jane turns to face Sandi. "I can't do this," she says. "It's so hard. It's really hard work! I just can't do it *quick!*"

"I know, honey," Sandi says. "I know."

She strokes Jane's face over and over, not realizing she's making it harder for Jane with each stroke, harder to let go of her addiction to the tactile world.

* * *

Each day, a round robin of visitors comes by to give the benediction of friendship, of family, and, if nothing else, to bear
witness. Ray is there every morning, as always, to denote the
commencement of yet one more cruel visit by the soft-washed
sun. And Ed, most every day and occasionally at night, remains
the pillar of her day, her steady angel of good intentions and little
power, but whose deep-eyed, angular features are imprinted on
her consciousness like a second self, an impression as familiar as
her own in the mirror. Ray and Ed and all the others gather the
fragments of Jane's waning days and they coalesce into little scars
they can carry for a lifetime.

One Jackie, a woman near thirty, with a strong theatrical
presence but a tentative demeanor, stands troubled outside the
closed door of Jane's room one evening as, inside, aides change
the bed linens with Jane on them, the television turned on loudly
to smother Jane's terrified screams. *Is this really necessary? Should
she be butting in? Is she letting her old friend down after a lifetime's bond?*
Whether it is a justified action or not, she is a helpless witness to
her friend's torture.

Almost every visitor will at some point have Jane beg them to
take her home, watch her strip off her hospital gown or tear off
the tape that holds the IV to the port that has been inserted above
her collar bone, or attempt to straddle the bed's railings as if it
was a monkey bar. They will remember her cries for help that can
only be subdued by shots of morphine or Haldol or Ativan or all
three, and will recall when their soothing words seemed to help,
and especially when they didn't.

This evening it is Jackie who attends to her, finds the nurse
when Jane's pain intensifies, holds Jane's hand to give her courage, tickles her with her wry sense of humor and warm familiarity. And then, some time in the middle of the night, it will no
longer matter if Jackie had dozed in Jane's arms when she was
three years old or had treated Jane like a favorite aunt all her life;

nothing, nothing will matter to Jane other than the urgent need to escape, to run away—except that this time she wants to run away *to* "home," wherever that place is where she no longer has to struggle, to fight full-fisted those that would weigh her down, close her off, imprison her in pain.

"I want to go home! I want to go home! Jackie, help me!"

"But Jane," Jackie coos, "you're too weak to go home now." She holds onto the tubing that Jane is trying to pull from her nostrils, gently re-inserting them. "You need these to help you breathe. And these tubes here carry the meds that relieve your pain."

Jane continues to pull any string she can find, something to unravel *this fucking mess, maybe these strings around the sleeves*, all, *all* must go. Jackie starts to laugh at Jane's feistiness while trying to calm her.

"Oh my God, don't take off your clothes!" she giggles, too late as Jane liberates her flesh from the closeting of fabric, even while still pinioned by the heavy grasp of disease, morphine and the fully-reclined hospital bed.

"No! Listen, Jane!" Jackie restrains Jane by holding her shoulders. "You're too weak to leave right now. You'll fall and break something. You don't want to do that."

"Why don't you mind your own business!" Jane snaps at this irrelevant busybody, whoever she is. She is panting heavily and flailing at the bed railing, patting it down to find the release lever, but the panic has fatigued her and she sinks back into the sleepy mire.

A few hours later, she rises from the deep enough to whisper, "Hi, Jackie," when Jackie offers up her visage for Jane's recognition. She address her with a sad tenderness and soon she will agree to a bathing by the day attendant along with the rough passage that accompanies any shifting of her increasingly corpulent self.

Each day the same struggle. Must go home. Need to go home.

Pulls at wires and tears at clothes and then a heavy collapse into sleep. Her husband bends like a sapling in a windstorm. One day he confides to Dr. Shepherd that he feels like a villain having to deny her "home" so many times each day. She tells him all dying people want to go home.

"It means more than just home," she explains. "We think they mean the place where they no longer need to struggle. Home like in mother's care. A resting place. Maybe even death. It's the struggle that's so hard."

"Mother's care," Ed repeats. "She didn't have much of that in her life. Her mother died young."

"It seems," Dr. Shepherd responds, "that those who lived in the most fear when they were young, experience the most fear at the end."

Ed's face darkens. "That's not fair," he says, biting off the words in bitterness.

"No, it's not," the doctor agrees.

"Honey," Jane tells him later that day, "I need you to pack up my things. I need to go home." She tries to raise herself. "Look in the closet." She reaches for her oxygen tubing, but Ed comes over to gently dissuade her.

"No, no," he says as he tries to lightly peel her fingers from the plastic. She gives in easily this one time.

"Why don't you love me any more?" she asks in quizzical despair.

And then, in a few moment's time, she's managed to prop herself up on her elbows.

"I can't do this anymore!" she cries. "It's not happening! I have pain in my vulva, it won't come out, the baby won't come out," she starts to whimper.

No rest for the weary. Jane is climbing mountains in her sleep, struggling for breath with harsh abbreviated intakes. She needs more air than her lungs now seem to have room for. It sounds like breathing on just the upper reserves of lung. But there is nothing to do but attempt the ascent.

When she's awake, her eyes are wide and opaque as if she needs to draw breath in through them as well. She barely focuses on those that mill around her body, there is only the waves inside to notice, lapping higher and higher in her chest, threatening to crest over her esophagus. It will take all her concentration to keep her burdensome mass afloat. If she sleeps she will drown, but if she drowns she'll rest. Her face expresses a sadness beyond sorrow, a bottomless dull grief at the recognition that Jesus could smother her with a pillow like she was an unwanted child. A soft, satiny pillow of air, the whole sky stuffed down her throat. She thought He loved her more than that.

Her body still in earthbound minutes, still bearing heavily on bed and fabric, moistening it with warm damp kisses of sweat, needs attention.

"How are you, Jane?" asks the nurse's aide on one of her visits.

"I need a bath," Jane says.

And she sets in motion a carousel of chaos. It is determined that four people will be needed, two nurses and Ed and Jill to move Jane around to help the nurses reach her various body parts while, in the meantime, changing the sheets. As they roll Jane's haunches over to the side, she grabs the bed's railing for life as if she's going to be tossed overboard, her face a mask of terror, the waves inside her threatening to rise up the wall of her throat.

"Help!" Her voice is a faraway whisper, emanating from the other side of a bounding storm.

Ed and Jill simultaneously reach across the bed railings to soothe her with their touch. They coo solicitously while towards the aft of the storm-tossed vessel the nurse's aides snap out orders to each other for maximum efficiency while in these treacherous waters. The more they bustle, the greater the ruckus and they unintentionally exacerbate the sense of crisis for Jane, verifying for her that all on board are helpless to save her from the abuses of the psychotic sea we swim in.

And finally, also like a storm, this business of bathing and lin-en-changing passes. For a few moments, Jane leans against a bank of pillows, letting the waters subside and then rise and fall in calming little laps against the shore. Ed and Jill are drafted to help her sit up more comfortably.

"Are you OK, honey?"

Jane nods almost imperceptibly, glazed over, indulging in the luxury of not having to struggle for the moment—Ed is near, the sheets are clean, her body is fresh with the bracing coolness of the washing: this is all. This is the all of it, this day. This is the life. Her right hand floats up to her face as she pulls in a slow drag of cigarette from the air between her two raised fingers before she realizes that a smoke couldn't be the right thing to have just now, and then she slowly mimes the purposeful stubbing of it out with a gentle, twisting of her wrist over the bed sheet. She looks at Ed and then at Jill as they quietly speak to her and each other and she is able to, for the time being, be soothed enough by the familiarity of their voices to leave them behind closed eyelids, knowing they are in a good safe place.

There is a visitor in the room. It has been wheeled in and now stands away from the bed, a tentacled presence, waiting to be called to service to invade and extract, a clean modular suction machine. It is quiet, but ready, impervious to Jane's strenuously asthmatic heaving.

Throughout the night she mimes the struggle to escape, grasping at the bed railing or pulling at her gown, restlessly wavering between smothering sleep and panicky wakefulness, neither of them a full mercy from the other. Jill awakens from the cot set up nearby in the shadowed evening of the room. She goes to the bedside and listens to Jane's wheezing and decides to call for the nurse.

"That's what we call labored breathing," one of them tells her.

"When it becomes congested, we can suction her, but until then, it's not worth the discomfort it will cause her."

Jane overhears voices and asks if she can go now.

"Where do you want to go?" Jill asks.

Jane looks forlorn. Jill is not her friend; she's her jailor.

Jane shakes her head.

"I don't remember," she says.

Her rasping breath is slow and arduous, like digging through a mountain with a spoon, steady, steady, grating, without apparent end.

Hours go by. Sometimes her lungs seem to find an easier path through which to breathe, and then back to the heavy lifting. Personnel does its daily roundelay—nurses, family from Jill to Ray to Ed. A new day intrudes.

It is the middle of the afternoon and Ed sits bedside. Jane's breathing is thick as if a seal of skin is closing across her esophagus and she's now trying to tear through it by clearing her throat. The attempt sounds to Ed like she is being throttled.

Jane shoots up in bed, her eyes wide, her face burning pink.

"Help!" she cries in a strangled whisper. "Help!"

"I'll get help! I'll get help!" Ed says with urgency. He runs out into the hallway to dragoon someone from the nursing staff. When they return, she is still sitting up but not as high, like a wooden doll in semi-recline, seeming both alert and numb. The nurses wheel the tentacled machine towards the bed and one of them places the tentacle to Jane's lips.

"Now, you have to open your mouth a little," she says, and manages to glide the plastic tubing between Jane's teeth and insert it down the well of her throat as far as she can. Jane gurgles out choked little screams: she is being attacked from all sides as the tube sucks up ejaculations of mucusy fluid. She is helpless and traumatized, and all Ed can do to help is hold her tiny hand tightly in his big fist, as if he could squeeze comfort into her.

"They're just trying to clear your passageway," Ed says softly, hoping he can make a difference. "So you can breathe a bit easier."

No doubt he is questioning the efficacy of his actions: how do you help someone who's drowning to breathe easier? How do you stop this from happening over and over again until you cannot even pretend to help but must witness your wife's torture like a bystander. "They're just trying to help," he says, feeling like no help at all.

Jane is finished being suctioned for now and sinks back onto her pillow, and as she sinks into sleep, Ed listens to her soft, rhythmic, distant wail, the cry of a child forlorn. His child.

For another twenty-four hours, Jane rasps and moans and gurgles. She flails weakly at the bed railings and tugs at her hospital gown, the gown being the stronger of the two. Sometimes streams of unintelligible words rush out of her, incoherent arguments, the last demands she makes on the world made inaudible by morphine and Ativan and the heavy weight of breath. Marcie, Ray, Jill and Ed all witness, all attend, all grasp at understanding how they can help. I also witness, as you can see. I witness her struggle. I witness their love. I witness the variety of all their fears. I witness the mechanics of a terminal care facility, the webs of plastic tubing, the quiet workday bustle of this spic-and-span repository for the dying. I witness the Earth turn, spiraling from Now, with all these players always stuck inside it. And crushed in its relentless vise is Jane, squirming futilely.

Her gargled breathing is Ed's cue, this Wednesday spring morning, to ask the nurses to determine if Jane needs to be suctioned again, a process that has become less and less successful as Jane, even in medicated sleep, resists the intrusion of the plastic tubing down her throat. Dr. Shepherd comes by instead to examine her patient's condition.

Ed watches her gently trace her stethoscope around his wife's sternum, listening quietly. She removes the scope from around her ears and uses her fingertips to gently sketch a small circle on Jane's chest, trying to ease her patient's congestion as gently as if she was drawing circles on the surface of a pool of water.

"I wouldn't suction her right now," she says to Ed. "I'm concerned that she may be being suctioned too often because of the family's concerns over her discomfort, but you must remember that the suctioning can be equally disturbing to her. It's a very invasive process. So if anyone's concerned, I suggest they ask the nurses to listen to her breathing as you just did and let them determine if the suction is needed or not."

Ed stares wide-eyed before him, wondering how he can save Jane from the panic she experiences when the struggle to breathe intensifies. He understands the limited recourses available.

"I need to ask you something," he says quietly. There is an uncomfortable pause before he continues.

"Is there some way . . . this process can be accelerated? It's so difficult to listen to her suffering like this. Maybe if the medication was increased . . ."

"I personally don't believe that Jane is suffering right now as much as you are," Dr. Shepherd replies studiedly, purposefully, gently. "I believe the medication level she is at has already rendered her mostly unconscious."

"But yesterday she asked for help as if she was terrified."

"That's very difficult for family to witness, but I don't think it's possible for her to be as conscious as she might seem at those moments. It's as if she's talking or crying in her sleep. Of course, I can't tell you that for sure, since no one ever comes back to tell us what they're experiencing at this point, but the medication levels we're giving your wife are already doing the job of hastening the end. The same meds that block her consciousness slow down everything else, including her ability to clear her passageways. I believe she is simply going through the normal process of dying and we cannot deny her that."

Ed stares pensively past the doctor. Perhaps he's trying to weed out the meaning of words when she says "cannot." Does she really mean "cannot" or is she using the word as in "should not?" He's not sure. He seems to sadly accept it as the former as he slowly nods his head in indication of understanding and resignation.

"How much longer do you think she has?" he asks.

"I can't say," is her reply. "But I do believe that she is at the stage where the end is imminent."

"Do you mean today or tomorrow?"

"I'm sorry," she says, touching his shoulder, "there's no way to know."

Ed turns to look across the room where Jane is lying, massive, unconscious, a faltering breathing machine, a groaning, undulating sea of helpless woman. Her slightly grayish pallor suddenly seems to obstruct him from seeing Jane the way he usually does when he unwittingly superimposes the face of the woman he's known for over twenty years over the morphing face of this dying one. All these faces . . . the same woman . . . a lifetime of feelings and associations. His mind finally erases the traces of ensuing death from his view of her; she is Jane again, and he pulls up a chair beside her after Dr. Shepherd leaves—urging him to take a break—to sit vigil instead.

"I'm going now." It is Ed, whispering into Jane's ear with Jackie at his side. She will relieve him of his deathwatch duties this evening. For the last five hours Jane has not been heard from, outside of the guttural wheezing as she tries to lift her breath and send it aloft. Ed will keep his support group appointment tonight. Perhaps there he will be buttressed should he break down in tears over how his efforts to save Jane from suffering sometimes caused it instead, that his desire to save her was always futile and counterproductive and wrong-headed. Or perhaps, bent over in stress, he will merely report today's facts numbly and receive credit for bearing up through it all. In any case, he sees no major changes this afternoon. Jane has not responded greatly to continued suction when the nurses have deemed it appropriate, and he expects this to go on. "I'll be back tomorrow morning, hon. Jackie is here to help you." What else should he say? They say hearing is the last of the senses to go. "I love you," he says. What will it hurt to say even if that is no longer meaningful to her, blotto as she appears to be.

Ed leaves the room to Jackie. Jackie sits for a while, studying her charge, who has deteriorated much since her last visit: her face is absorbing the color of clay, and her breathing thick and rough as a rope. Jackie is surprised how serene Jane's features look, almost as though she has transcended the struggle her body is going through. She sits over Jane's bed as if over a cradle, losing her self for a bit in a reverie. How beautiful to watch a face in repose, absolutely free of the anxieties of desiring, of craving, of living. Jackie plays with the thought that Jane has achieved some kind of Buddha-hood, a passive, round, stone-like imperviousness, if you don't count the bubbling gurgle pushing from her throat.

She stands up and walks to her bag to extract the latest issue of *Vanity Fair*. She sits near the window and, the fading dusty blue of day easing behind her, she looks at the clock. Twenty minutes have past since Ed left. Time now to settle in for what looks like a peaceful night.

And then with a giant retch, Jane shoots up in bed, a long difficult wheeze trailing slowly behind her. Her eyes are wide with the shock of knowledge and her mouth opens wide, aimed high in my direction. She pleads just one moment of intervention, one lifetime's worth of benediction, one second of celestial beauty's sustenance, her mouth stretching wide enough to swallow the universe, all of God's angels included, all that beauty mulch for her ravenous appetite, as large as a newborn's wail, and from deep in the hole of her maw, she spits up the juice of a burst little valentine, the one that had secretly been planted when no one was looking.

"Jane! Jane!" Jackie shouts. "Oh my God! Nurse!" She runs to the doorway. "Oh my God! Oh my God! We need help!!" She runs to Jane's side to grab her hand. But she's terrified by the greed of the giant serpent's mouth Jane is offering, and by the blood that trickles in little spurts, and she runs back out to the hallway. "We need help!!"

When the nurses hurriedly arrive, they can see immediately that Jane is gone, she has left the building that was her corporeal home. She has fallen back onto the pillows, her neck arched back, her mouth frozen wide open, her face a grayish-green as if cast onto some rocky shore, dragged from ocean depths.

"It's over now," says one.

"Mm hmm," says the other, moving Jane's head into a position less grotesque, as if she found her final moment resting on a deep, fluffy pillow.

Jane no longer looks at me in either desperation or accusation. She is now oblivious to my charms. Just as I ready myself to end my assignment, to prepare to welcome her to our fold, Jane no longer looks as if she cares whether she gets the help of angels or not—perhaps for the first time in her life. She has seen the worst there is to see—her features tell us—and we might as well save our ministrations for one who cares.

Jackie stands in the corner of the room as hospital staff come and go, finishing up their odds and ends. She breathes heavily, trying to calm herself down. *No*, she tells the head nurse, *Jane's husband left less than half an hour before Jane died*. She thought it was almost as if Jane *wanted* Ed gone, that she would never be able to leave if Ed was still around, she wouldn't have been able to say goodbye. The thought touches Jackie and she starts to weep, huddled in the corner. Her own father had died just this past year, just like that, without being sick, without a moment's hesitation, as if leaving had been as easy as turning on the TV, and here Jane, her lifelong friend, had struggled to stay among the living and then struggled harder to break her ties to them. Jackie now felt this knotted connection to Jane like an anchor being pulled to the ocean floor, like she would go with Jane if the anchor's rope ran out, and she pulls her tears into the hallway where she sees Marcie approaching.

Marcie reaches her just as the head nurse does, who informs

Jackie that Jane's husband has been phoned, but they had to leave a message since he hadn't picked up. They will need to move Mrs. Cantore from the room as soon as possible, she says, but Jackie and Marcie, who now understands what has transpired, urges the nurse to wait so Ed can see Jane before all traces of her are gone.

"I don't think he went straight home," Jackie says.

"Well, we can't wait forever," the nurse replies. "We'll give him an hour."

An hour later, Sandi has arrived and the three women hover over Jane when not conversing out in the hallway, guarding her jealously from the staff as if she might be spirited away. The room phone finally rings briskly and Marcie runs over, past the clay-like Jane slipping only slightly from her pose of high grotesquerie, to see if it is Ed. It is, and he will be there as soon as traffic allows.

When he arrives, it is two hours since Jane's expired and the nursing staff is grateful that they can soon get on with their business. Marcie, Jackie and Sandi escort him in. He stands before her, surprised by how beautiful she looks, because, indeed, in these two hours, gravity has pulled her mouth down to a more relaxed position, and with her head rolling slightly to her left, so has the corner of her mouth been pulled over into an almost crooked smile. He has not seen her in such repose for weeks.

"She's smiling," he says, and Jane's friends also notice her smile for the first time, as if it has slid into place on Ed's arrival. They ask him if he would like to be left alone.

"Yes," he says, and they close the door behind them on their way out, leaving Ed alone with his now jade-colored beauty, his lifeless life partner, cast cold on the bed with a blissfully remote expression, her smile actually oblivious to her surroundings.

Ed talks to her softly, more for his own sake than hers, letting this cool totem stand in for the Jane he cannot imagine not existing, the Jane always present in his concerns. He talks to her hesitantly, his words seeming half foolish, like an actor addressing an empty auditorium and hearing his words echo. He tells her how sorry he is that he missed her passing, that he hopes she will forgive him for having left when perhaps she needed him. He calls her his beautiful baby and he will miss her forever. He stares at her pathetically for several minutes and then he does something that surprises us.

He crawls onto the bed and squeezes into the space next to her. He lets his head rest next to hers, his arm across the pillow frames her in a semicircle. He closes his eyes the way he has for most of the nights for the past twenty years or more, feeling the proximity of the desired other, the lover every lover worships as they sleep beside each other. He samples that feeling one last time, knowing it is over for them. He touches her cold, greenish cheek with his lips and is surprised by how sweet it feels to him, not revolting at all, like kissing ice cream, and then he sadly steps out of her bed.

He walks to the door and tells the nurses they can come in now.

He walks back by Jane's far side and holds her hand as the nurse's enter; he will accompany her for as long as he can.

"Oh my," says the first of the two nurses, "look at her, she looks just like an angel!"

"Isn't that something?" says the other, and they methodically go about their business. The first nurse unclasps the chain around Jane's neck from which her wedding ring hangs and hands it over to Ed who lets the chain crumple into his palms. The nurses undo her hospital gown, doing her the favor no one would do when she was in the midst of her struggle. And when they are through with their ablutions, they, together, in one swoop, lift the sheet over Jane's body, and when Ed sees Jane not give even one iota of resistance to being enclosed, to becoming faceless, he knows his wife is truly no longer, she is somewhere else, she is nowhere, she is with us, and the sheet rises to meet her in the white.

www.ingramcontent.com/pod-product-compliance
Lightning Source LLC
Chambersburg PA
CBHW020909200626
46814CB00001BA/257